ANNA FRC

By

Kenneth James

LLYFRAU
CAMBRIA

Front Cover photo credit: Roger Vaughan Personal Collection
Cover Design: Carolyn Davies

CHAPTERS

One

The evening meal being over, and the diners having adjourned to the lounge and reading rooms, the Black Lion Hotel had been transformed from a frenzied workforce to a host of relaxed and sedate guests. Down below in the basement kitchen the flagstone floor is drying out after being well scrubbed. Most of the serving staff have gone home, but as always the middle-aged, live-in cook and the headwaiter, who also acts as catering manager, remained relaxed at the long preparation table sipping wine.

The hotel, built at the lower end of a sloping road, meant the kitchen gave access to the street through the utility yard. As it was a warm night, plus the large stove still burning its remnants, the door to the yard was left half open, letting in the distant raucous singing of revellers in the Kings Head up the road. Outside a full moon hung brilliantly in a sparkling August sky casting an assortment of shadows on the streets of Hay-on-Wye.

The well-fed cook shifted uncomfortably in her chair and sniffed at her glass showing displeasure. 'I think there's a funny taste on this wine, Dan,' said Esther, still dressed in her whites.'

'It's free, Esther, be grateful for that,' answered the elegant waiter, a man in his early forties and proud of his position. 'All I can taste is the left-over cuts of the lamb joint.'

'Well, I suppose it helps quench my thirst.'

'I must say the new boy did a good job of cleaning that floor.'

'Yes, but her upstairs will soon be counting the cost of the soap he used.'

'She cannot have it both ways. She asked for a high standard of hygiene, now she has it.'

'Any complaints about the food tonight, Dan?'

'No, in fact there were a few, "Give my compliments to the chef," remarks.'

'Why do I have to drag the good points from you?'

'Why do you need them? If there are no complaints, that is a compliment in itself.'

They sipped their wine and helped themselves to some spare buns, and remained quiet for awhile. As always the conversation quickly dried up, for the nature of the routine work left little new to talk about. Suddenly, Esther stiffened when a noise could be heard from the yard. She turned her eyes to Dan and then at the open back door.

'There's someone out there,' she whispered.'

Dan turned to the door and placed his glass on the table. Then he put his forefinger to his mouth as a gesture to say nothing. Quietly he rose from his chair, picked up the fire-iron rod and approached the yard door. A resounding clang of dustbin lids caused Esther to jump to her feet, stifling a scream with her hand

'Saints preserve us!' she cried.

Peering into the darkness of the yard with the rod aloft in his hand, Dan called. 'Who's there?'

From a scattering of bin lids and wooden boxes came a weak and pleading voice. 'Help me. Esther, are you there? Please let me in.'

Dan called out, 'Esther, come quickly. There's someone collapsed on the floor.'

Esther ran to where Dan stood over a crumpled body. She knelt down and pulled the loose clothing from around the girl's face. Esther gasped. 'I don't believe it, it's Agnes. Dan, give me a hand to get her inside.'

'Agnes?' said Dan, shocked. 'Here? Good God what does she want coming back? '

'Never mind what she wants, give me a hand. '

As they struggled to get her in, the girl moaned from pain and held her swollen abdomen, tears streaming down her young face. Indoors they quickly realized the dire situation of the pregnant nineteen-year-old.

'Get some water on the boil, Dan, and fetch Nellie. Then make yourself scarce, this is woman's work,' she said, rolling up the sleeves of her white blouse.

Dan stared momentarily at the girl not believing the sudden unfolding of the situation. 'Right away, Esther,' he said. 'I'll stoke up, and get a bowl and the big kettle on the stove and then I'll get

6

Nellie,' the normally cool waiter flustered. When he'd done that, he hurried through the yard out to the street and up the road, dusting his waiter's suit as he ran.

No time to organize any proper delivery accommodation, Esther got some clean blankets from the nearby storeroom and spread it on the floor, rolled one up as a pillow and then helped Agnes to lay on her back, placing the make-shift pillow under her head.

It took only minutes for Dan and Nellie to return. Dan went to check the fire and the warming kettle, leaving Nellie and Esther to assist with the delivery. He got some logs from the yard and threw a few in the stove.

'The water will be ready soon. I'll leave you to it. I'll be in the storeroom if you need me.'

Agnes was calling out in pain, pushing and sobbing, her head swinging to the left and right, her hands groping the floor for some kind of hold. Soon the baby was born and unceremoniously smacked. The child gave out a loud healthy cry to the relief of the make-do midwives. Agnes gasped a huge sigh as Nellie wiped the beads of perspiration from the mother's flushed face. This was not the time for asking questions, casting blame or being indignant to the worn out young woman.

She had disappeared from the hotel over a year ago, and to return in such a shameful manner would indicate she had been left abandoned and friendless. The ignominy of such a situation would mean general condemnation. So the women accepted the present scene with compassion, and relieved at their personal achievement of natal success. Nellie lifted the newcomer up into her arms, smiled and called to the mother.

'Agnes,' she said. 'You have a baby girl.' Then she placed the infant in her mother's arms.

Agnes, too weak to appreciate the birth, her eyes swollen, her cheeks hot and prematurely aged, could not smile but was at peace with the child and greatly heartened for the safety of her baby. The pregnancy was over, but even then she knew it was the beginning of a time that would need courage and determination to see her child through an arduous life.

'What are you going to name her?' asked Nellie.

Agnes looked up with misty eyes and thought for a time. Weakly, she said, 'I shall call her Anna,' Yes, Anna after my dead grandmother.'

Esther could not hold herself. 'Who is he?' she asked. 'The father, tell me!'

'I shall tell Anna who her father is when she is old enough. Nobody else need know.'

'But you must have some means of support.'

'Please let me stay here until I get stronger. I'll leave as soon as I am able.'

'We know you ran away with a man, Agnes. Tell us who he is. What have you been doing this past year?'

'I fell in love with him, but when I told him of the baby, he never came back to me. I waited and waited but he never came back. Something must have happened to him. He loves me I know he loves me.'

Nellie looked at Esther and shook her head. Then she held Agnes's hand. 'You'll have to face it, my love. You won't see him again.'

'How have you managed, Agnes?' asked Esther.

'When he didn't return I took a job labouring wherever I could. I'm sorry, but I'll say no more, or make blame. I must look after my baby now. That's all that matters,' she whimpered.

The two women looked at each other with resignation and let the girl rest, the newcomer to the world lying on her breast. Agnes closed her eyes and drifted into a semi-conscious state, exhausted but her mind uncontrollably reliving the past year. A year that saw her reach the height of love and security, only to fall into an abyss of lost hope: Pictures were coming and fading of the cordial, handsome stranger who came to the small town and impressed her with his charm and generosity; his tender ways and stories of his time in the Dowlais Steelworks. She could see him, tall and strapping, his gentle arm around her waist.

He was a foreman of engine fitters, he'd told her, who had been ordered to Brecon as a temporary advisor to the railway. Though born in Hay, he worked in Dowlais since moving from his

8

hometown five years ago. A good job, he said, in Dowlais with good money, money enough to put her up at a flat above the ironmonger shop in Brecon.

Those two short weeks he stayed with her were the happiest days of her lonely life. Then he came to see her once a month after his employer had called him back, still full of love, still caring and tender towards her. She had always known her impecunious upbringing had made her timorous and reserved. But Tegwyn understood her and cherished her, promising marriage and a new home in his town.

When she told him of her pregnancy he was overjoyed. But then the monthly visits stopped and suddenly she was alone. No longer could she afford the rent. She was evicted—'Tegwyn!' she suddenly cried out. 'Tegwyn!' Exhausted, she fell into a deep sleep.

Esther glanced at Nellie and whispered. 'I don't know a Tegwyn? '

'Nor me.'

The door to the upstairs burst open and the owner of the hotel came in, a severe woman with staring black eyes and an intolerant expression on her long face. 'What's going on down here?' she snapped.

Esther slowly stood up from the feverish girl. 'It's Agnes. She's just given birth to a baby girl.'

The woman's mouth dropped open and she held her heart. 'Get her out of here,' she ordered. 'This is a respectable hotel and I want no shame or scandal laid at my door.'

'She's got nowhere to go, Mrs. Humphries.'

'She found somewhere to go when she left me without a scullery maid.'

'She hated the job. She's young and wanted better.'

'I took the waif in when she was wandering the streets. I gave her a roof over her head and good food in her belly. I gave her a job when nobody else would have her.'

'And measly pay,' said Nellie. You had your pound of flesh out of a desperate orphan.'

'You mind your own business. I didn't invite you here, so take you leave now.'

'Excuse me Mrs. Humphries,' said Dan, as he pushed past her in the doorway.

'What have you got to do with this, Dan?'

'A little Christian compassion, that`s all'

'I want her out of here.'

'Then I suggest you pick her up and throw her out. Or, you could get the police to take her away.'

Mrs. Humphries thought of the embarrassing scenario with police and nosy neighbours, reluctantly she relented and barked, 'She can stay for two weeks and no longer. She can sleep in the storeroom in the box bed. I do not want to see her anywhere near the guests.' She turned and went.

'I don't know what we are going to do with her when she's fit and well.'

Dan's sad face expressed the inevitable. 'If no one wants her, there's only one place that will take her.'

'Oh Dan, she can't go to the workhouse.'

If there is no place for her to go, where else?'

The kindly cook and butler managed to convince the hotel owner to allow Agnes a month of free board and lodgings, but could not persuade her to let the young mother remain any longer. At the end of the month they packed her a generous bag of food and gave her what money they could afford, and then she left poring gratitude and tears on her benefactors.

Two

Eighteen years later, Dowlais 1897. A young man with a serious expression on his greasy angular face and dressed in working clothes, went into the subdued lighting of the crowded public house known as the Rolling Mill. The room had many workmen supping their ale and blowing smoke from their churchwardens and briars. When he entered many of the customers stopped talking and gave him a sympathetic nod. He had made his way to the pub at the lower end of Horse Street after finishing work. The street was typical of the hilly town and the parallel streets that sloped up from the High Street to the busy shopping area of Union Street.

The man was in a sombre mood and thirsting for a mug of beer. Everyone looked at him and offered grunts of condolences; he nodded gratefully as he breasted his thickset frame up to the bar. He called to the barman.

'A pint, Dick please, I'm dying of thirst.'

The bearded stout barman said nothing as he reached for the glass and placed it under the tap of the barrel. As the froth reached the top of the glass, the young man licked his dry lips.

'Just finished, John bach?' asked the barman.

'Aye, Dick. Twelve hours of noise and heat, sweat and toil.'

'You haven't been in for a few nights.'

'I had things to do and people to see.'

'Aye, it was sad news. Sorry to hear about your Dada.'

'Aye, aye, mumbled the crowd,' and they returned to their drinking and conversations

John straightened his five-foot six-inch figure and drank half his pint greedily, the froth giving him a white moustache, and then he banged his glass on the counter. 'I told him I could have got him a job in the Goat Mill, but no. His horses were more important to him than his own health.'

'He was the best hostler down the colliery.' An old man called from his bench by the wall. 'He loved them and they loved him.'

John turned around and leaned back on the bar. 'Aye, but they couldn't pull him out when the prop gave way and brought the dam roof on top of him. He should have come with me to the steelworks. I hear tell that treacherous hole needed maintenance for months.' He turned back to the bar and finished his pint. 'Another, Dick, if you please.'

Just then a girl emerged from the door at the side of the bar, her long black dress covered with a long white apron, her haughty expression commanding respect from the drinking customers. John's eyes widened as she sprightly went behind the bar as though she owned the place. Her hazel eyes glanced at him. He stared back, but she shook her wavy black hair that touched her slight shoulders and gave him a cold look. She picked up a large jug from a low shelf behind the bar and began to retrace her steps. 'Missus wants a jug,' she said curtly, then disappeared back through the door.

John combed his mousy hair with spread fingers and looked at Dick, surprised. 'Where did that beauty come from?'

Dick smiled, 'From the kitchen.'

'I mean from what part of the universe?'

'I know what you mean. She marched in here this morning saying she's desperate for a job and board. Was prepared to scrub, serve behind the bar and even clean the spittoons for a couple of pennies as long as I gave her bed and board.'

'And the wife agreed?'

'The wife took a liking to her. I find her a bit too proud for her own good. A girl who's prepared to do all those chores has no right to be high-and-mighty.'

'She staying long?'

'I don't know, I told her to go down the drift if she's prepared to work hard.'

'Are you mad?'

'Sorry John I forgot about your Dad. Anyway, from what I can understand she's looking for someone, so the wife tells me. Who? Don't ask. I'm not allowed to be so forward.'

'What's her name?'

'When we asked her she said, just call me Ann, that will suffice.'

12

'Fill my glass, Dick. I'll say one thing, she's the type that can send a man's mind spinning.'

'How many rails you rolled out today?'

'I don't count them I leave that to the overseer. All I know is that there are orders coming in from all over the world and business is booming. They're building railways all over the place, give us a little of the profits, I say.'

The girl emerged again. 'Missus says I've got to lock the doors.'

'Well lock them, then,' snarled Dick; this lot don't mind being locked in.'

She ventured out into the street to feel the clean air, but there wasn't any. The breeze brought an acrid atmosphere from the smoking stacks that towered over the steelworks; smoke that pervaded the town stealing the freshness of the night. Just over the High Street wall came the rumbling of the coggin mill, the rolling mill and the goat mill. They were heavy, ponderous steel mills that rolled out the rails which fed the world's railroads.

This was Dowlais, a boomtown built on a hillside; a tangle of streets and alleys bustling with energy and hard work, busy shops and cafes, chapels and pubs, benefit societies organized by the workers, such as the Oddfellows.

The town was surrounded by industry, not only by the iron and steel works, but quarries, pits and coal patches. It created thousands of jobs for locals and immigrants. The coal stacks could be seen for miles around and tapered into the grey night clouds, silhouetted by a strange eerie glow upon the hillside. Rising from the smouldering mountain were snaking flames and billowing fumes. It was the red-blood glow of the festering tip of slag, dross and lava that stretched along the terrain for half a mile.

The girl stood there transfixed for some moments, her eyes turning colour in the reflection. It was so surreal it made her feel uncomfortable. A shiver spread through her body and she hurriedly made a quick return inside, locking the door behind her. Her shocked expression did not go unnoticed in the room. She looked around at the drinkers, but they were so familiar with the outside conditions they had long become oblivious to the unnatural phenomenon.

'What's the matter, girl?' demanded a drinker. 'Have you seen a ghost?'

'The mountain, it must be on fire. It's glowing like Hell itself.'

The crowd broke out in laughter.

'How long have you been in Dowlais? asked John.

'Why? What's that got to do with you?'

'I wager you arrived today. You've just seen the results of the steelworks labour force. That's the slagheap mountain. Getting bigger every year, it is, and who knows when it will stop growing. '

'Aye,' said another. 'If you're ever feeling cold, just take a stroll towards the burning tip and you'll soon warm up.'

'I'll give you better advice than that,' said John, as the ale relaxed him. 'If you're ever wanting to be warmed up, just come to me, my lovely.'

Laughter broke out as the girl's face turned crimson. Annoyed, she returned to her duties in the rear of the premises.

John was pensive for a moment; thinking of the funeral a few days ago and the loss of his father. He remembered the time when he'd been in high spirits before his grandmother died: Those times when his family and parents were together and happy. He could still see her ashen face; one of the last victims to be taken by cholera years earlier. And his mother, weak and overworked from looking after and tending the eight children she had given birth to, she spent her last three breaths in his father's arms.

There was a void which some of his siblings could not bear; they had enough and moved away to rural areas to avoid the pollution and dangers of unsanitary conditions. And now after the death of his father, John and his oldest sister were the only two of his family left in Dowlais. He thought of the girl he had just made fun of. He would not have liked any of his sisters to be treated in such derogatory manner. He suddenly felt ashamed and regretful.

'What's going on in the back room tonight, Dick?' he asked casting his thoughts aside.

A meeting of one of the benefit clubs, the Druids I think.'

A short, elderly man brushing up to the bar nudged John's elbow, his flat cap low over his burnt eyes and thin scarred face. He used to be a puddler in the steelworks guiding white hot pig-iron through the sand bed in the casting house. But a stray piece of dross caused a sudden splash, and that was the end of his job.

'Will you have a drink with me John?'

John looked down and grinned, knowingly. 'Spent you last penny, have you, Evan?'

'Aye, you know me too well, John Hughes. But I'll pay you back one day.

'When will that be, Evan? When Crawshay is allowed into Heaven?'

'I'll get work one day, even if it means cleaning the boots of the Masters.'

'Dick, give Evan a drink on me. I'd give him my week's pay rather than let him stoop that low.'

'Conditions are greatly improved since my father's time,' snapped Dick as he handed Evan his pint. 'You were one of the finest puddlers in the casting house. The trouble with you was you gave too much to the iron masters and not enough care to yourself.'

'You can't be a good puddler standing back from the pig iron,' said Evan. 'The splash was unexpected.—thank you, John. One day I'll...'

'Forget it, Evan. Can you find your way back to the bench?'

'Aye, I've got enough sight to see me around.'

John turned back to the barman, 'Poor Evan. He looks more like fifty-five than forty.'

'You'll not catch me in the iron works nor will you see me down the drifts or mines.'

'You've never had ambition, anyway?'

'I did. My ambition was to be lazy, but the missus won't let me.'

John smiled wryly. 'Where's that girl gone, Dick? I'd like to apologize to her.'

'Don't waste your time. I've only known her a day, but one thing I've learnt, she's as hard as nails. When she finds the man she's looking for, they'd better call the Burial Board.'

'Will she be here tomorrow evening, do you think?'

'If she hasn't found her man, I'd say so.'

'Then I'll give her my apology tomorrow.' John finished the last dregs of his pint, banged the glass on the counter and stared at

15

himself in the mirror behind the bar for a moment. 'Goodnight, Dick, goodnight lads.'

There came a collective hail of goodnight as he left the premises.

Three

John's close friend, David Rees, was enjoying the Sunday pork lunch with his family, the dinner casting a savoury smell through the room. Around the table were his two sons Emlyn and David junior, the daughters Rebecca and Ruth, and the 65 year-old lodger, David's father-in-law, Karl Veldon.

Karl was getting his few rotten teeth into the pig's trotter, squelching and sucking, much to the disgust of thirteen-year-old Ruth. She looked at her sister Rebecca, three years her senior, twisting her lip, but Rebecca held back a giggle and shook her head. However, Ruth was having none of it.

'Do you have to make that noise, Mr Veldon?'

Mr Veldon lifted his watery eyes and grunted, but said nothing. Young Emlyn, maturing at ten years of age, began to suck loudly and sniff pretentiously on a potato.

'That' enough of that, Emlyn,' his father warned.

'It's very hot, Dad.'

'Your behind will be very hot with my strap if you carry on, boy. Are you ready for tomorrow?'

'Looking forward to it, I'll have my own money to do what I want.'

'You'll have your own money when I've taken the housekeeping out of it.'

'It will be my money, Dad.'

'And if I should have claimed the same over these past years you lot would have starved to death. Why do you think I work, for the benefit of the Masters? No. I work to keep you lot in food and clothes and a roof over your head. I want you to promise me something Emlyn, spend a little and save a little, that way you'll always have something in your pocket.'

'Leave me some to spend and save then Dad.'

'Do you work to keep Mr Veldon as well, Dad?' said Ruth.

'Never mind Mr Veldon, he's too old and ill to work. You make sure our lunch boxes are ready in the morning.'

The rather plump but pretty Ruth frowned. 'I wish I had a job.'

Her sister, slimmer from coal-drift hard work, looked at her with some sympathy, thinking how the drudgery of Ruth's day must be. It had been her chores two years ago before her father secured her a job up at the drift mine. It had been necessary, her father had told her. He being the only bread winner and having to feed all six of them.

To her surprise the coal drift was not too bad. It was hard work filling the drams but the achievement of earning money and holding her head up was satisfying. She had thought she'd be the only girl up there, but there were others as well as young boys. As long as the weather was dry everything was all right, but the winter was harsh and there were times when she longed for her fire at home.

'Be glad you're in the warmth of your own little home,' she advised her sister.

Emlyn looked up. 'Is it very cold up there?'

'I'll look after you,' said Rebecca. 'It can be quite dark deep in the drift. But it can be worse up on the surface when it's cold and wet. Ivor Pippins, who works on the washery, is always cold and wet. Keep clear of the washery if you can. They don't normally put ten-year-olds on the washery, so you should be all right. Just make sure you pack your feet well, or your toes will drop off.'

'He' won't be working in the washery. He'll be on the draft doors down the drift,' said his father.

'That sounds boring,' complained Emlyn.

'It's easy but dangerous. You'll be shown what to do by the gaffer. It's work to settle you in so don't complain. You'll soon be building your muscles.'

'Where do you eat your lunch?'

'Where you stop and when you're told. If you're lucky to be outside at the time you can shelter in one of the old railway wagons up on the patches. But don't rely on being outside too often. The overman expects high production all the time. You'll probably just be opening the doors for the drams to go through, or fetching and

18

carrying. But if you're given a pick or a shovel, take your time until your muscles get used to it.'

'I'm glad you work up there, Dad?' said Ruth. 'You can look after Emlyn better than Rebecca.'

'Rebecca won`t be there long.'

Rebecca gave a look of surprise to her father, though he didn't notice.

'I'll be at the coalface,' their father continued. 'But I dare say 'I'll see him often enough when I haul the drams up. You'll be my filler one day, Emlyn. But you'll have get those muscles as big as apples first.'

'Why is that, Dad?'

His father gave him a look of distain. 'Do you ever listen to what I tell you? Filling a dram is hard shovelling work. You need to fill them quickly. The more drams I can haul to the surface the more I get paid.'

'And I'm going to be stuck here with the old man and a young troublemaker,' moaned Ruth, concluding that everyone has a more exciting life than she.

'Time will pass, my lovely,' said her father. 'But be sure you'll not be working in any drift mine. Young David will be attending school as soon as Emlyn is earning enough for Rebecca to stay at home. I only wish your mother was here, God rest her soul.'

It was then Mr Veldon looked up and said in his breathless, weak, almost incoherent voice, 'I wish my daughter and I had never come to this cesspit of a place. She would still be alive now and I'd be in the old country.' He stared hard at young David. 'How old are you now, boy?'

'Six, Mr Veldon.'

'Six! Six years she's been gone and you took her place.'

'That's enough of that,' said the father. 'She was my wife. And we've looked after you ever since the funeral.' He stood up. 'And you've not had to pay so much as a farthing towards your keep!'

The old man began a bout of coughing. He threw the remains of his trotter on to his plate, struggled to his feet and walked towards the back door, his chest rattling and the cough uncontrollable. He disappeared into the back yard.

'Don't listen to the old man David' said the father, sitting down again. 'He's not well and he's lonely even though he has us for company. He's never settled in Wales. He longs for his own country, so he keeps saying.'

'Then why doesn't he go home?' asked Ruth.

'How many times have you asked that? You know very well, why. He's too weak and poor to go home and too stuck in his ways to appreciate his free board and lodge—right, Rebecca and Ruth clear the table, Emlyn, you make sure you have an early night tonight. Up at six and don't forget; we have a few miles to walk before we get to the drift.'

The boy looked at his eldest sister. 'Six? Will you give me a call, Rebecca?'

'Don't worry. I'll drag you out if you're still sleeping—Dad, you never mentioned I would be finishing work.'

'The drift is no place for a girl. I'm sorry I had to sacrifice you in the first place.'

'But I don't mind it up at the drift. Where will I get money from if I finish work?'

'Once we get on our feet, you'll have house-keeping money and you'll have your personal spending money.'

Rebecca wasn't convinced and began to sulk. 'I might as well get married and have my own house.'

'Believe you me, girl, you'll find it hard to get a house or a man.'

'What do you mean by that?'

'Men don't want the responsibility of wife and children these days. They just want a cheap woman, and you don't fit into that category. You'll not get married until the right man comes along.'

* * *

The sun rose over the coal tips bringing an eerie atmosphere as the monstrous shadows of chimneystacks grew and crawled over the rooftops of Dowlais. Between the structures the sun lifted the darkness from the streets bringing a welcome illumination. As it rose higher it spread its warmth across Dowlais to the villages of Penywern, Pant and Pengarnddu, diffusing through the windows and stirring the workers. They were to go to many different

20

occupations: to the furnaces of the steelworks, the dark tunnels and drams of the pits, drifts and the levels, to the washery, to the locomotives and to the glowing, grumbling mountain overlooking the valley.

Eventually, the sun stretched to the green pastures of the Twynau Hills where the sparkling Morlais Brook ran down to its first tunnel. It had many more subterranean passages to travel through before it would break into the open valley and join the river Taff to Cardiff.

People began to open their doors and mix with a dozen nationalities. Men touched their flat caps in salute to their neighbours. Women wore rough aprons from their chins down to their ankles, most of which were made from worn sacking; their hair tied up in buns or covered with scarves. Sleepy youngsters rubbed their tired eyes. They gathered and walked in silent crowds, except for the sound of boots and shoes stamping the ground. Briskly they walked as gentle mumbling began to rise among them, then the talking became louder. Some were swearing their lives away disappointed they left their homeland for such modest earnings. Others laughed aloud, while the majority chatted and hailed morning greetings.

Onto the Guest Keen ironworks walked the Spanish from their humble Alphonso Street. And so did the Welsh from Upper Row, Lower Row, Cross Street, Rees Street and all the other rows of terraced houses. Small houses overcrowded with families and lodgers. They had made the village their own and had come from the farms of Carmarthenshire, the valleys of Breconshire and Neath, Cardiff and the shores of Swansea and Aberavon; all came to the bustling town of Dowlais seeking prosperity in the prodigious industries of the boom town.

The Irish, the Poles, the English and Welsh filled the streets making their way to their place of work. Some took route past Guest's Stables where the horses were being prepared to pull drams and wagons of limestone. Others went further up to the Pengarnddu quarry situated on the hillside where men sledge-hammered limestone rocks into boulders and boulders into manageable sizes for easy loading into wagons, and the donkeys dragged them along the dirt path to the blast furnace plants.

Then there were those going north to Pantyscallog and on to the larger Morlais Castle quarry that overlooked the hazel wood and the Taf Fechan River. Soon the sound of dynamite would be exploding, sending shock waves through the trees bending the boughs and peppering the foliage. Another hundred or so made for the coal drifts up on the east side of town. And there were those making for the Goat Mill Road to the impressive, impenetrable steel mills built with huge rough blocks of hewn limestone chiselled out of boulders from the quarries.

The people, dwarfed by the huge foundries, workshops and the giant smoke stacks, began to diminish as they entered their work places. The steel workers and millwrights into the rumbling of the mills, the engineers and blacksmiths into the roaring of the engine house, the puddlers and blowers through metal doors of the blistering blast furnaces.

Onto the hills and tips the miners were disappearing into the holes of the drift mines, levels and patches, while others faded over the crests to the pits of Pant Y Waun and Fochriw. The hills crawled with cosmopolitan hordes to the sounds of bellowing and thundering, explosions and blasting, clanging and din of steel making. In the distance, the festering and smouldering lava tip grew to mountainous proportions.

David Rees, his lofty, sinewy figure, protected Rebecca and Emlyn as they were pushed along with the crowd down the Goat Mill Road. There they left most of the workers and made their way up a score of stone steps towards the huge red-brick engine house. Passing the engine house they travelled on, taking short cuts through the works.

Leaving the works' building in the distance, they eventually reached the coal levels and drifts where they stopped with a crowd of miners; again, there were men women and children ready to take up their jobs for the day. Standing akimbo at the entrance to the drift mine was a middle-aged man with a thick black moustache holding a pocket watch in his hand. He said nothing but noted every face that came to the drift mine. David was about to enter with

Rebecca and Emlyn when the man raised his hand and stopped them.

'This boy the newcomer?' he asked David,' eying up Emlyn.'

'Aye, this is my lad, eager and ready.'

'Take him to the number four doors and show him the ropes, and keep him out of sight; they're getting very fussy about working youngsters these days. '

'I'll do that.'

The man looked at Emlyn with a grave expression. 'And Boy, when you open those doors, you be sure you put your back up against the drift wall. If the dram should catch you, your father will be carrying you out in his arms.'

'Yes sir.'

'Right, off you go.'

The town had become quiet after the rush of the workers but the shops began to open in High Street, Union Street, North Street and all the little corner stores in the side streets. On the corner of Vaughan Street Michael McCarthy was hanging out the tin ware he had made in his shed at the bottom of his garden: Saucepans, kettles, frying pans, funnels, roasting trays and many other utensils that his deft hands could manufacture.

In the Rolling Mill pub, Dick was shouting up the stairs in vain to raise Anna, and though she lay awake in her bed she ignored the coarse voice of the landlord.

Dick trod heavily up the stairs and rapped on the door impatiently.

'Girl, I'm not paying you to be lazing in bed all day, get up or get out.'

'The missus is my boss,' she called back. 'I'm not one of your drift-mine girls.'

'You lazy merch, it's gone seven and there's clearing up to do.'

'I'm no stranger to early mornings, but that's all done and finished with.'

Dick raced back down the stairs and went into the kitchen. 'Bess, that girl has got to go.'

Bess, a full figure of a woman in her mid-forties, wiped her hands in a cloth and slapped it into the big bosh. She fingered her untidy grey hair to the back of her head and gave her husband an unfriendly glance. 'You treat her like a street girl. She tells me she's a scholar. What's more she gives me no cheek and works hard. I'll get her up, but leave her to me.'

'I'm telling you, woman, she's got to go.'

'When I say and not before.'

Bess went up the wooden stairs and stopped outside the small door that led to Anna's room. She knocked. 'Ann, my love.'—For it was Ann she had told Mrs Thomas was her name. 'We need to be up early for the clearing up and preparing the day.'

'I'm out of bed, Mrs Thomas, just give me time to wash my face and put my clothes on.'

All right, love. But don't be long, Dick's in his usual early morning mood.'

Anna gave a loud chuckle, 'That's men for you, always wanting the women to do the chores. He works hard tapping the barrels and pouring the pints.'

'Huh. You know a lot about men for your tender age.'

'I don't know them. I know of them! That's the difference.'

Bess shook her head, her uncombed hair falling over her brown eyes. Not understanding Anna's words she began to walk back down the stairs. 'I'll be in the kitchen. Clean the tables and sweep the floor in the bar and sitting room.'

'I will. I'd appreciate it if you do the spittoons and urinals.'

Bess tut-tutted to herself, 'I wouldn't have you clean those, my lovely. But don't tell Dick.

Four

John had one more rail to take through its moulding process before his twelve-hour shift finished. He, and the Rolling Mill crew, watched with tired eyes as the mobile overhead crane lifted the six-foot by sixteen-inch square, two and half-ton ingot, out of the soaking pit. Immediately the workers could feel the heat of the huge white-hot bar as the crane hauled it into the air and rumbled across its overhead rails transporting it to the mighty Rolling Mill.

This was a dangerous period of the shift, for the men were tired from a long day and their concentration needed to prevail to the last detail. The crane gently lowered the ingot onto the roller conveyor that fed it to the two giant steel rollers, each weighing 20 tons, and known as the Cogging Mill. The men affectionately called this mill the Mangle, for it did the same operation as a mangle, but squeezed white-hot steel through its rollers as easily as a domestic mangle would draw in a wet towel. As these huge wheels dragged the ingot through, groaning and sparking, it began flattening the steel, the massive rollers creating so much pressure on the ingot that the vibrations could be felt through the ground.

'Get ready to stop the conveyor rollers,' called John.

'Slowing down,' responded the crane controller.

The ingot came out the other end of the cog rollers thinner and longer. The massive top roller of the Mangle was lowered a little and the motion reversed. The same was done to the rollers of the conveyor, pushing the steel rail back through. This was done several times until the rail was 27 feet long and just 8 inches square.

'Right, Miguel, it's all yours.'

'Right, John, leave it to me. You get home to look after your seester now,' said the Spaniard.

John left the mill house and made his way to a side room where his personal belongs were. There, he took off his protective apron and put on his coat and made his way through the workshops and into the Goat Mill. He could see Miguel supervising the rail being

25

drawn into the Goat Mill where it would finish at the required length of 45 feet and in the perfect shape of a railroad rail. He waved to Miguel as he left, grateful his friend and colleague would cover the last ten minutes for him so that he could avoid the crush of the whole shift finishing. Out into the freshness of the evening air he took in a deep breath and sighed. Passing the hundreds of rails laid piled up on in the rail bank, he could hear the loud hissing of the hot saw cutting the rough edges of the newly formed rail Miguel was supervising. He smiled to himself, glad the shift was over. Another one for America, he thought, and he walked up the Goat Mill Road, tired but content. The sun had lost sight of Dowlais, leaving a dusky atmosphere as shadows began to creep down the hills and nearby banks and mounds of debris. He hardly noticed the train coming across the ridge bringing a load of slag and dross from the furnaces to the burning tip, nor did he turn when the ladle was overturned and the explosion of sparks filled the sky like a firework display.

He was thinking of his sister Elizabeth. She had not been in good health the past few days and he had tended to her each evening after work. He was hoping she would be feeling better when he reached home, for his vigilance at nights had been long and his day shifts fatiguing. He turned left down High Street when his old mate interrupted his thoughts. It was the short wiry Evan, his flat cap down over his eyes, his untidy loose trousers and worn coat making him look like a tramp.

'Hey John, boy. Just finished your shift, I see,' said Evan, slapping him on his arm.

John stopped. He always had a few minutes for the ex puddler. 'Aye, Evan.'

'I haven't seen you down at the Rolling Mill lately.'

'Liz hasn't been too well.'

'Aye, I heard she had the fever. How is she, boy?'

'Better than what she's been. I think she's improving.'

'I'll see you down at the Mill tonight, then?'

'I'm not promising that, Evan. Liz comes first.'

'Of course of course, it's just that I had a little job cleaning out the Cross Keys in Church Street. Just a temporary little job, but enough to buy you a drink, see boy.'

'Save your money, Evan. I don't need repayment.'

'I know that. But I like to look after my friends, you see.'

'You don't have to pay me to be your friend.'

'I know, I know. It's just that I'd like to show my gratitude.'

'Your good intentions are appreciated. I'm sorry Evan but I'll have to go.'

'I hope to see you later.'

'May be.'

As he crossed the road towards the Bush Hotel, where there was a two-horse stagecoach about to leave, a young lady was peering from the stagecoach window. Her dark hair and youthful looks reminded him of the new girl working in the pub. He stared for a moment and was rewarded by a faint smile. However, it was not the girl. His heart felt a little lighter knowing it was not the girl from his local. Why he felt that way he did not know. Perhaps it was because he'd not had the time to apologize to her, or perhaps it was because she came into his mind more than she should. He felt strongly about seeing her again. He surprised himself thinking about her so often. He turned his head to the children who began cheering and waving as the coachman cracked his whip and the coach moved off. He noticed a couple of familiar female faces at the bottom of Church Street watching it go. Ladies he had been tempted to befriend in the past, but his moral upbringing had given him a guilt complex about such fraternization. He had not known a woman so intimately. He turned away and could see further down the street where the landlord of the Carmarthen Arms was putting a couple of empty barrels out. Turning right into the uphill Horse Street he licked his lips as he passed the Rolling Mill public house, but straight home he must go. Then there was the Bute and the Forge and Hammer, another couple of places he could have a drink, but he remained resolute and walked by, his three-bedroom house being just a few doors up from the Forge and Hammer.

'Hello, Liz. I'm home,' he called, as he walked through narrow passage and entered the small living room. He was pleasantly surprised. 'Liz, I thought you'd be in bed.'

Liz turned around, her pale face giving a welcome but weak smile. Her delicate figure stood at a rectangular stone sink drying some dishes John had left that morning. 'I thought I'd wash these and make you something, but you're early.'

'Miguel covered the last few minutes for me. He told me to get home to you. Now don't you go making a meal. I'll sort my food out. You're feeling better, then?'

'I felt strong enough to get out of bed. I thought a few light chores might help me get my strength back. I've prepared some broth.'

'You sit down now. I'll sort things out. I hope you're going to have some broth the same time, it will help build you up.'

'I've already cut up some vegetables and there's a little meat left over. It's all in the pot if you could place it on the coals for me.'

'I should have thought of that, shouldn't I?'

'You've had a lot to do with your work and me bedridden. You can't think of everything.'

John poked at the burning coals in the fire basket and placed the saucepan on top. 'It looks good, Liz. Are you sure you're all right?'

'I'm fine. Much better now.'

He went to her and placed his hand on hear brow. He grinned at her. 'You do feel cooler now. And there's a slight pinkness coming in your cheek.'

'Really John, I am feeling stronger now.'

He held her shoulders and looked her in the eyes. 'I don't want to take advantage of your improvement, Liz, but do you think I could have an hour out tonight?'

'If you don't go I shall be annoyed. 'You've been very attentive this past week, you go out and have a drink. And thank you for being my brother.'

He grinned again. 'I had nothing to do with it.'

An hour later John had washed shaved and changed into his casual but neat and tidy attire. His black coat covered a light grey waistcoat, and his striped shirt was open at the top with a light grey silky-type scarf tied neatly around his neck. He entered the subdued gas lighting of the Rolling Mill pub; the shadows on the wall animated by the naked flames. In his jovial mood he pushed past his friends, evoking pleasantries from the crowded room as he tapped shoulders. He noticed there were several women in the pub, which he thought unusual, for the Rolling Mill was mainly a man's' pub, full of smoke and at times bad language. There were a few men standing at the bar supping their tankards who were strangers to the pub. John stood there and waited for Dick to finish serving one of them. Then the girl came in and glanced at John, placed her hands on her hips and waited.

'Well, are you drinking?' she asked him, curtly, her curly black hair hanging loose, her white blouse revealing a little of her shoulders.

' You serving?' he smiled.

'I'm not a model in a shop window.'

'I'll have a tankard, please.'

'Please? Polite, aren't you?'

'I don't want you thinking I'm as rude as I appeared the other night.'

She turned her back on him and filled the tankard from the barrel. When full she turned with a questionable look on her face. She placed the tankard on the counter.

'The other night?' What are you talking about?'

John sipped his drink, feeling awkward. She had obviously forgotten him and his bad manners. 'It doesn't matter.'

'If it doesn't matter you should not have mentioned it.'

'Sorry. Forget it.'

But the statement had aroused her curiosity. 'I don't remember you in here the other night.'

'It was about a week ago.'

'You couldn't have made much of an impression on me.'

'Obviously not. Maybe you're not an impressionable girl'

Anna gave him a haughty look and went to serve a waiting customer. Dick was busy too, but he called over to John over the hubbub of conversations 'How is your sister, John?'

'She's coming along fine. You're busy tonight.'

Dick, placing a pint on the bar, bent his head towards Anna and raised his eyebrows. 'Main attraction.'

John watched Anna moving around behind the bar, hardly able to take his eyes off her. He noticed she never smiled. She had a dour expression that rarely changed. She was efficient, spoke well, treated everyone with the same seriousness, occasionally snappy, but never smiled. He felt privileged when she finished serving and came back, leaning on the bar near him. She ignored him even though he remained glued to her features.

'Did you find your man?' he asked softly.

'What?' she asked, raising her voice, for the general chatter had become louder.

'Did you find the man you were looking for?'

She turned and gave him a quizzical look. Her hazel eyes brightened up. 'I remember you now. You're the man who had the wrong impression of me.'

'I'd had a couple of drinks and was in a mischievous mood.'

'Yes. Most men have unfortunate moods—why is Dickie boy asking about your sister.'

'You don't miss much.'

'A woman doesn't miss anything.'

'Woman? I'd say you were a young beauty about seventeen.'

She looked at him defiantly. 'Listen, I am twenty,' she lied. 'And don't you forget it.'

'Sorry. I meant it as a compliment. You can pay me back. How old do you think I am?'

'I don't care how old you are.'

'Well, I'm a couple of years older than you. That almost makes us the same age.'

'Does it matter?'

'He looked into her eyes and said softly, 'No Ann, it doesn't matter.'

'I thought I didn't miss anything, but I seem to be missing something here. What's the matter with your sister, anyway.'

'She hasn't been too well lately, had a bad bout of fever but she's over it now. I know it's none of my business, but when a girl like you says she's looking for a man…'

'Who says I'm looking for a man?'

'I think it was Dick, who mentioned it.'

'He got the wrong impression, too.'

Her voice was terse but melodic. He wasn't deterred. Her beauty and defiant eyes beguiled him. 'Well, are you?'

'As you said, it's none of your business. However, maybe you can help me. I'm looking for a man named Tegwyn Morgan.'

Dick suddenly started hammering with his mallet, tapping another barrel, cursing it for being so stubborn.

John turned to the noise unintentionally and thought for a moment, but had to admit he had never heard of Tegwyn Morgan.

`Is he a relative?`

'You don't need to know.'

'Oh. Sorry. Can't say he sounds familiar, anyway. But I can ask around.'

'That will do no good. I've been to every railroad depot and station in Merthyr, Brecon and Abergavenny. It's as though he never existed.'

John gave a puzzled expression. 'You've been travelling. Why around the railways.'

'Because that was his job.'

'Ah, well. I'm a steel roller. I wouldn't have come across a railroad man.'

'Ann, me darling.' called an impatient drinker. 'Is it only that end of the bar you'll be serving? Does a man have to die of thirst before your pretty legs will come to him.'

She sauntered four yards to where the Irishman was standing.

'Are your legs stiff from sitting down? What will you have, as if I don't know.'

'Well if you know, me darling, you don't need to ask.'

John smiled and called across to him, 'Give the girl a break, Paddy and mind your manners.'

'Ah, John, how is your sister now?'

'She's a lot better, Paddy.'

'Ah that's good news to be sure. Nice to see you out boy…thank you my lovely. That looks a fine brew indeed.'

Anna returned to the end of the bar to John. 'You can't help either. That's all I get from people, negative answers.'

'Was he on the line gang? Or did he drive a locomotive? What sort of work did he do?'

'My mother, God rest her soul, told me he was a foreman of engine fitters.'

'Ah, Ann, my love—sorry, that was too familiar. But I'm truly sorry to hear you mother has passed on.'

'It was some years ago. I'm over it now.'

'Nevertheless, I think you've been looking in the wrong places for Tegwyn Morgan.'

She straightened up. 'How can that be?'

'Engine fitters also work in the engine house at the steelworks. Big blast engines they are, and if he was a foreman I am sure he would be known.'

Anna's eyes widened with revelation. 'He was a steel worker?'

'It sounds quite plausible.'

'What do I have to do to see the authority at the engine house?'

'Whoa, steady on. They won't let a stranger in there. But it's Saturday tomorrow, my last shift for the week. I'll scrounge a little time off and take a trip up to the engine house. I'll make a few discreet enquiries and let you know.'

Anna was raising her hopes that she might finally meet the man she had been searching for. The past two years had taken her to many places in the vain hope she might find him. She looked at John, and for the first time he could see softness in her eyes.

'Will you be here tomorrow night.'

Reluctantly John could not say for sure. 'I don't know. I'll have to see how things are at home. But I have Monday off work. I could call for you. I might have news for you then.'

'No! Don't call here. I'll meet you somewhere.'

'Right. Do you know where the new Wimborne Institute is?'

'No, but I'll find it.'

'It's just up the High Street. It hasn't long been built. It's a red-brick building, you can't miss it. Go down Horse Street and turn left. It's a few hundred yards up the road. You'll have to cross the road. It's on the opposite side.'

'I haven't been further than the front door of the pub since I arrived.'

'Follow my directions and you'll be fine.'

She looked at him with a suspicion. 'All right, I'll have to trust you. I'll be there.'

'Half past nine all right?'

'Better make it 11. 30, I'll have my cleaning up to do from the night before.'

'Fine. 11.30 it is. I'll look forward to seeing you.' Then she was called to serve a customer again, but before she went John looked her in the eye. 'By the way, you don't have to worry, you can trust me.' She left, and John had a warm feeling inside of him.

As he supped his pint contentedly looking at himself in the mirror behind the bar, he saw, through the mist of tobacco smoke, a familiar figure approaching. There was no mistaking Evan coming up behind him, his flat cap low over his face as usual. Evan's five feet three inches just reached to John's nose, but in John's eyes he was much taller. Without looking round he called to Dick, 'Dick, two tankards if you please.'

'No you don't,' said Evan. 'This is my turn.'

'You're sounding happier than usual, Evan.'

I may have a regular job up at the Cross Keys.'

'That's good news, Evan. We'll celebrate your future.'

'Aye, I may have one now, but I never thought I ever would.'

Five

The townsfolk took advantage of the morning sun. The women searched for bargains in shop windows, their empty shopping bags hanging from tired arms. The newcomers in town were looking for work. Men, too old for work stood on street corners whilst children roamed the streets. It was an unusually warm September and everyone who could, wanted to be out and about. Not a breezy movement was perceived in the air, which gave the smoke from the surrounding tall chimney stacks freedom to go straight up and pollute the heavens.

John was standing at the bottom of Horse Street wondering if he should wait there for Anna. He thought better of it, his eagerness to be with her might not be reciprocated. He quickly realized she might prefer to walk alone to the meeting place. Looking down the busy High Street, animated with carts and noisy vendors, he could see the two-wheeled covered wagon of Jones-the-Peddler. His horse stood patiently in its shafts while he sold his diverse goods. John could see he was doing good trade for there were five women around the back of the cart peering in. The doors of The Boot pub were open, the landlord rolling out empty barrels. Outside sitting on a bench was a solitary male figure leaning forward, elbows resting on his knees. His black top hat was slightly tilted and he seemed to be deep in thought. There was no mistaking Joshua the Preacher who was, no doubt, thinking up his next public oration. Turning left, John was soon among the people, mostly women, walking up the High Street pavement. Passing the Bush Hotel he was about to cross the road when the clip clopping of a horse pulling a hansom cab checked his progress. He could see it was one of the steelworks dignitaries on his way to Merthyr, no doubt to a meeting of the mighty iron and coal masters, he concluded. He crossed the road and made his way to the new Wimborne Institute that was nearing completion; a building he was looking forward to enjoying, as the facilities were being installed for the benefit of the workers. At the double gabled red-brick building, he sat down on a bench outside and waited.

Anna came out of the Rolling Mill ten minutes later and followed the directions John had given her. Her brisk, busy walking style caused her long black skirt to swish and flow as she hurriedly made her way up High Street. Occasionally her jauntiness made it necessary to hold on to her small navy ribbon hat perched at the back of her head. John was standing looking out for her and soon caught sight of the beauty he admired so much. As she crossed the road he waved to her and she, looking for him, waved back in return. He welcomed her with a big smile as he bid her good morning. She gave no smile, but her flushed oval face had an expression of relief.

'You're here, then,' she acknowledged, a little breathless.

'Did you think I wouldn't keep my word?'

'I never trust the word of a man.' Her small hand pulled at the collar of her white blouse beneath her coat as though to leave some air down her front. 'Dick wasn't too eager letting me go. He's never satisfied with me.'

'Knowing Dick he probably has designs on you.'

'That's the reason I raced out.'

'You should have taken your time.'

'I can look after myself.' She turned and looked at the new building. 'So what's this supposed to be?'

'It's the new Wimborne Institute Social and Welfare Club, build specially for the workers.'

'Why is it called the Wimborne? That's a strange name for a club.'

'Lord and Lady Wimborne had it built. They are opening it officially in a few months.'

Anna looked impressed. 'Are you serious? A Lord and Lady actually coming to Dowlais?'

'Why not? Dowlais exports iron and steel around the world. The Grand Duke Constantine came to Dowlais, and the once owner of the ironworks was Sir John Guest; his wife, Lady Charlotte built the schools and even Lord Nelson came to Merthyr. We produce pig-iron and make rails for countries all around the world.'

36

'Don't go on, I'm impressed.'

'Do you want to sit down?'

'We can talk just as easily walking.'

'Whatever you say.'

'Well?' she asked as they walked on.

'You get down to business pretty quick, don't you?'

'The outcome of this meeting is very important to me.'

'I'd rather we find a bench and sit down.'

She stopped and affirmed. 'I do not want to sit down.'

They began to walk again in a leisurely manner up High Street.

'I don't quite know how to tell you this.'

Anna stopped abruptly; a startled expression stared hard at John. 'What is it? Tell me.'

He gently pulled her along by her arm. 'I went to the engine house and asked around. I know quite a number of the workers up there. Most of them didn't know who I was talking about, but there was one old man in his forties—he looked more like sixty. He knew of a Tegwyn Morgan who worked there many years ago.'

'Yes? And?'

John stopped and turned to her. He looked into Anna's expectant eyes. 'Ann, I'm afraid he died many years ago.'

Anna's eyes widened and stared straight through John. She was silent for some time, the two of them standing there whilst people walked past glancing at them, what appeared to be, a lovers tiff.

'I'm very sorry, Ann, I really am.'

She began to walk on again, John joining her. She said nothing to what seemed an age, but in fact it was just a hundred yards. He glanced at her prompting to say something; she did, quietly but in a deliberate manner.

'So that's why he never came back. Typical of my destiny to be disowned by both.'

'Disowned by both?'

'Disowned by death. He was my father. A father I never knew or met.'

John was shocked. Why didn't you tell me he was your father?'

'What difference would that have made? Whether he was a friend, acquaintance or my father, it would not bring him back.'

'I could…I could have been gentler breaking the news.'

'He's dead however the news is given.'

He sighed with a little frustration and appearing guilty for his course handling of the situation. 'We seem to have something in common,' he suddenly said.

'In what way?'

'I've lost my parents, too.'

'Yes, but you have family to lean on. I have none.'

'You can lean on me. I would be honoured.'

She gave a quiver of a smile in gratitude, but said nothing.

They walked in silence again, John ushering her around the corner into Market Street. Climbing the sloping road they made their way up past the police station and neared the Market Street gateway on their left, one of three entrances. The building was a huge indoor quadrangle built around a piece of land leaving a square of open ground in its middle to cater for those who didn't require indoor vending. John suggested going in, but Anna shook her head.

'I'm not in the mood for a market tour.'

'Sorry. Well, there's a teashop lower down Union Street, would you like a cup of tea and a bun, or something?' he said feeling awkward, for he had no finesse in such a situation.

'I don't want to go back to the Rolling Mill right now,' she said with a sombre tone. 'A cup of tea would be appreciated.'

At the teashop they found a table for two by the window. A pot of tea was served. Anna made no move; she was deep in thought as though pondering what next to do. John poured and filled the two cups.

'The sugar basin and milk are there for your preference.'

She said nothing but helped herself to both.

'Ann, I want to help you if I can. I've grown very fond of you and I don't like to see you all alone in the world.'

She looked up from her tea, her eyes impassive, her demeanour composed. 'Fond of me? That's a new one. Do you mean lust?'

'No! I'll admit I had difficulty sleeping last night, thinking of you and your predicament. When I was given the news of…Tegwyn Morgan's death I…I really was disappointed for you…but when

I…when I realized he was your father, I was…devastated,' he said, fumbling his speech.

She looked at him with some surprise. 'You needn't be. I had no feelings for him. I wanted to find him because he owed me a life. He owed me all the years I grew up struggling without him. He owed the pain I had when comforting my mother on her deathbed. Yes, he owed me.'

John sipped his tea and looked at her, but she did not return the admiration. She then drank her tea and they sat quietly for a time.

'I'll help you out whenever you need help.'

It was then she lifted her face to his. 'Can't you understand? I am not like your women who go down the mines, or those who clean out the pubs. Or take in washing. I'm demeaning myself in the Rolling Mill. I'm a scholar. I was brought up to belong to a better class. I only took the job until I could find my father. You? You, look after me? You're a kind man, John Hughes, but you do not have the wherewithal to look after me.'

'You must have had a lofty upbringing if I am unable to match it. Even if you found your father alive, he would only be a humble workman like myself.'

'I detect anger in your voice, but I want what's mine. If you laboured in the steelworks for years on little pay, but was promised a pension, and then it wasn't delivered on retirement day, wouldn't you feel cheated?'

'Where have you worked for years, Ann. Where did you get your education?'

Anna dropped her head. 'That's for me to know.'

'Was you father giving support to your mother then?'

'I never knew my father. I only know what my mother told me about him.'

'I see.'

'You do not see. My mother believed she would live in Merthyr one day. That was, until my father disappeared. She couldn't believe he deserted her so she came searching for him. She told me he'd promised her a good life in Merthyr. In desperation she came here, but instead of finding my father all she found was streets full of poverty, dirt and disease. She worked in filthy pubs earning her fare back to…home.'

'Dowlais is changing, Ann, changing for the better. There's plenty of work here, they're erecting new building all the time; libraries, modern schools, shops, cafes, a cinema, and there is culture like the Dowlais Silver Band, The Dowlais Choir and plays and concerts held in the Oddfellows Hall.'

'What's that got to do with a penniless, homeless orphan?' You can get that anywhere.'

They remained there for another twenty minutes, he unable to think of a comforting word and she looking lost and unforgiving.

John stretched out his hand and touched hers. 'Come on, drink your tea, we'll have a stroll around the place and get some air.'

They walked further on down Union Street in silence towards the main shopping area. It appeared many of the better-off folk were out and about, for there were couples strolling arm in arm, some with children, others with men friends, but it was mostly women dressed in long skirts and tight fitting tops emphasising their slim waistlines. Ornate hats, some flowery others with thick coloured ribbons hung down the backs. All were showing off the latest trend. But there were others, too. Their skirts were well worn and faded, shoes that needed repair, hair clipped up with pins and headscarves, carrying old shopping bags with nothing in them. A groom holding the reins of horses of a stationary landau had trouble with the impatient animals as they first took a step forward and then backward. There were a couple of street vendors shouting about their cheap goods.

John glanced at Anna. 'Just like any other town, Ann, isn't it?'

'Yes, but the people here are part of it, I'm not.'

And then a loud voice getting louder as they neared, overpowering all other street sounds. Someone shouting which took the thoughts of doom away from Anna's troubled mind.

'Is there someone drunk at this time of day?' she said with an sardonic tone.

John smiled as he caught sight of the source. 'It's Joshua.'

'Joshua?'

'The self-ordained saviour of the Dowlais sinners, there he is,' he said, pointing, 'on the third step of the Odd Fellows Hall, converting the atheists.'

Making their way to the crowded scene they stopped at a discreet place outside the drapers shop and listened to the dark-bearded preacher. The wide steps of the Odd Fellows Hall made an ideal platform for him. Anna smirked at his appearance. He was all in black with a frock coat covering his well-worn trousers, his lean tall frame lithe and animated, his well-worn top hat precariously perched on his head and eyes alight with excitement. His long face was flushed from adrenaline as he flayed his arms round. His head turned to the sky and with his rich bass voice boomed to the crowd to repent:

...'You busy yourselves wallowing in your own vanity. You seek only the pleasures of life and indulge in the ways of Satan. But I give you fair warning, the day will come when all will be judged, and all your finery and perfumes will not match the fragrance coming through the gates of Heaven,' he said, pointing to the sky. 'For Heaven requires only the highest qualities of man before you will be accepted. The most pure quality of life is True Love for your fellow beings and for your God. The cleanest is Chastity, the most honourable is Faith; faith in yourselves to have the strength and determination to follow your God; Sincerity that will give your fellow beings trust in you and an endorsement of the trust you have in God, and lastly, Devotion to the Almighty who will carry you through life. If you have just one of these qualities you are on your way to the next, if you have none, then dig deep into your soul for you are on the road to Hell. Though you may not understand the Lord, he understands you, and knows you. So trust the Almighty to see you through life and he will deliver. Prejudice is the instrument of evil. He that taketh not his cross and followeth after me, is not worthy of me, said the Lord...'

'Come on, I've heard enough of this nonsense,' urged Anna. 'The man is demented.'

'You're not convinced, I see,' said John, as they walked away.

'I have never have been since I was compelled to read from the Old Testament as well as the New Testament.'

'Made?'

'Never mind, you must have heard of Adam and Eve.'

'I was a regular in chapel when I was a youngster; Welsh Wesleyan, I am.

'Well then, you know Cane killed Abel which left only three people left on the earth. Then Cane was banished to the Land of Nod where he surprisingly found himself a wife. Where did she come from?'

John was surprised at the statement. 'As Joshua said, you must have faith,' he replied light heartedly.

'Faith! In the beginning there were two people, now there are billions in the world, Heaven's going to be pretty crowded if we all get converted. Chapels, churches, different denominations, everybody has a religion of his own these days. And each of them insists they have the true way to God and heaven.'

John smiled, for he too had long given up, but he had a simple thought that he always said in such a situation. 'One thing is for sure in my mind, I'd rather see a world full of chapel and churchgoers than a world full of warmongers and the exploitation of humble folk.'

'I'll say one thing about you, John, you're different.'

'Is that a compliment?'

'Take it as you wish.'

'I'd like to think it's a compliment. I'd like to think you are softening to me.'

'I soften to no man.'

'You've got to get help from somewhere, unless you're thinking of remaining in the Rolling Mill all your life.'

'Anna's stomach turned over at the thought. 'I could go back home.'

'Where is home?

'It's a small town in mid Wales.'

'Does It have a name?'

'Its name is of no consequence.' Anna pictured her home town and the loneliness she'd experienced after her mother died. She was a second-class citizen in a town of proud people. She was an orphan. Worse, she was born out of wedlock, patronized with false smiles

42

and degrading charity. She'd been in a small town with little people, tolerating it for her mother's sake. Her father was to be her saviour and benefactor in a new town with a new start in life. Her mother had always said he'd never have deserted her. Well the outcome is the same, he's dead.

John broke into her thoughts. 'Sorry if I was too inquisitive. I wouldn't hurt you deliberately, I like you too much.'

'So you like me, do you?'

John stopped and caught hold of her hand. 'I'm very fond of you Ann.'

'What are you trying to say?'

'As I said, I hardly slept last night thinking of meeting you today. I feel a little shocked at my own feelings. I know I'm a bit too old for you, but...'

'Too old for me, how young do you think I am?'

He was holding both her hands now and looking into her eyes. He had a feeling her eyes were playing with him. 'You're just a slip of girl, aren't you? Eighteen at the most, I would guess.'

'I've told you before. I am twenty!'

'I know. But I would never have taken you for that age. That's just a year younger than me.'

'I look young for my age.'

'That's good news.'

'You'll put three years on me and tell me it's good news? What's that supposed to mean, that you'd take me at twenty but not at seventeen? I suppose that's your moral standing is it?'

'Not in the way you say it.' But I'd take you for my wife.'

She stopped and he did too. 'You propose to me only knowing me a short time?'

'Would you take it as a proposal?'

She looked at him seriously thinking things out. 'If you want me to.'

'I do, earnestly,' he said, hardly knowing what was happening.

'I make no pretensions about it. 'I don't love you, and I doubt if I ever will. If you take me on those conditions it will be a marriage of convenience.'

'You mean you will? You really will marry me?'

'If you agree to the conditions, I will.'

'I do, I will.'

She bent forward and kissed him on his lips. As she withdrew she said, 'John, I will marry you, but a kiss is as far as I'll go.'

He pulled her to him and gave her a lasting hug, as those passing by turned their noses to the September sun, and so did Anna.

They strolled on down Lower Union Street, Anna silent in a new security, John proud and elated not believing he had such a beautiful creature to be his bride. And thinking, he did not deserve her.

Six

It was drizzling rain early on Saturday evening as the hordes of tired workers descended the steep stone steps leading from the coal tips that surrounded the drifts and patches. Among the crowd were David Davies and his children Rebecca and Emlyn. As they alighted onto the Goat Mill Road the steel workers joined them coming from the mills, creating an exodus. Dodging and weaving through the occasional dumper or ladle, they called greetings to each other. Behind the protective fence the transport train was chugging and rumbling parallel to the road carrying components between the mills. David extended his arms around his children looking around for possible hazards at such a vulnerable time. He was thinking of a month ago when, two youngsters horse-playing, got pushed into an oncoming debris ladle, unaware the crowd was parting to let it through. One suffered a broken arm whilst the other was pulled away before the wheels ran over him. His thoughts were interrupted when he felt someone tap him on the shoulder and call his name.

'Dai, I've been looking to see you.'

David turned around. 'John boy, how are you getting along?'

'I'm fine, thanks.'

'Haven't seen you since your Dad died.'

'No, I've had my hands full the last few weeks.'

'I was at the funeral. I don't suppose you saw me.'

'No, sorry, there were so many there, and my mind was not my own.'

'Aye, I know what you mean. You say you wanted to see me?'

'Aye, it's a big favour.'

'If I can help I will, you know that.'

'I need a place for my girl to stay.'

David, a good three inches taller, stopped in his tracks, looked at him and grinned. 'Your what?' he asked in his deep rich voice.

'I'm engaged, Dai. I want somewhere for her to stay until we get married.'

David hugged his two children tightly. 'Did you hear that, children? John is getting married.'

'Not so loud, Dai, I don't want the whole workforce to know.'

'Who is she, Mr Hughes?' asked Emlyn.

'You wouldn't know her, son.'

'A woman of mystery, that's romantic,' quipped Rebecca.

They began to walk again, David with an enigmatic smile on his face. 'When did all this come about John?' he asked, looking his friend in the eye.

'I'll tell you all when I have more time. It's important that I find a place for her immediately.'

'But there's just yourself and your sister at your house.'

'I know, but Liz, being a Chapel woman, and the house needing some attention, well, anyway, it's a bit awkward. Besides, Ann doesn't want to share the house with my sister twelve hours a day.'

David stopped again which caused a little buffeting from the moving crowd. 'Out of the damn way,' someone yelled. 'Are you going backward or forward?' another boomed. David decided to continue.

'You have three bedrooms as I remember?'

'The one bedroom isn't so free, is it? It's full of old furniture and junk since the family moved off, a bit musty too.'

'Where's...Ann staying now?'

'Nowhere. She was at the Rolling Mill, working, but Dick finished her. I've been sleeping on the couch for a couple of nights. You can fit her in, can't you, Dai?'

He looked down at Rebecca. 'Would you mind having her in your room?'

'I don't mind but Ruth may not like it. What's she like, John?'

'Well...she's beautiful, but she has a sharp tongue. I think she's had a hard time which has made her a bit sensitive to questions about where she's come from.'

'Mystery upon mystery,' enthused Rebecca, which encouraged young Emlyn to burst into a loud derisive exclamation: 'Well piddling puddlers, whatever next?'

'That's enough from you pair,' warned their father.

They had reached the top of the Goat Mill Road. People began to go their own way: up High Street, down High Street, the steep climb up Church Street and on to the narrow roads of Well Street and East Street. David stopped and had a good look at John.

'How long have you known this girl, John?'

'Long enough for me to know I want to marry her.'

'Obviously you haven't known her long. You say she's sharp-tongued, been fired from the Rolling Mill and you know nothing of her past. I think I'd better bail you out, boy. She can stay. I can't wait to see her.'

John grabbed David by the shoulders tightly. 'Thank you, Dai, thank you, I'll pay of course, and I'll do you a favour one day in return.'

'I think you'll need a few more favours before then—Are you still doing your drinking at the Rolling Mill these days?'

'Aye it's very convenient for me. Where are you doing yours?'

'Carmarthen Arms, that's my pub.'

'That's a decent walk for you, isn't it?'

'What? No, no, not the High Street one, the Carmarthen at the end of Walter Street.'

'Right, I know. I'll have to come up and pay you a visit properly. I'll bring Ann up tonight if that's alright with you.'

'We'll make her welcome. And later we'll go to the Carmarthen and we'll have a drink. I'll have to explain a few things to the family first though. The old man is still with me, you know, he has some funny ways and he's not too well. His coughing can sometimes bring sickly sounds.'

'As long as she gets on with your children, everything should run smoothly.'

David gave him a wry look. 'We'll go to the Carmarthen whatever.'

'I'll see you in an hour or so, and thank you again Dai.'

'Another mouth to feed', grumbled Mr Veldon, you must be mad.'

They were sitting around the table having their late meal. Ruth had prepared a large basin of broth with some spare lamb ribs thrown in. The butcher had winked at her when he'd sold them to her; `I've saved those for you and your family, just look at the meat still clinging to those juicy bones,` he'd said.

She,d grinned, `I know your sly ways, Ruth replied. 'A bucket of coal, is it?`

`You rub my back and I'll rub yours.` In a pretentious shock she'd said, `You keep hands of my back you Blackbeard.`

At the table David eyed the old man with contempt. 'What are you eating, Karl?'

Mr Veldon, surprised at the question appeared perplexed. 'The same as you, David, no different.'

'Are you sure you're enjoying it?'

'It's alright.'

'It's lovely,' snapped Rebecca.

'It certainly is,' agreed her father. 'And if Mr Veldon wants to continue to enjoy our good food he'd better mind his own business and let me run my house my way.'

'You tell him, Dad,' agreed Ruth, enthusiastically. 'He's the most ungrateful old man I've ever met.'

Emlyn, his mouth full of broth and the juices dripping down his chin looked up, shocked. 'How many old men do you know?'

'I got you some nice lamb, didn't I? You get to know the way of the world when you're my age.'

'Good God, stop talking like that,' ordered her father.

'It's only a joke, Dad.'

'I don't like that kind of joke. Anyway, Rebecca has explained to you what's happening, how do you feel about it?'

'As long as she helps around the house and makes my life easier, I suppose she can sleep in the spare bed in our room. One thing is for certain, I won't be making her bed. And she can keep her hands of the Welsh Dresser. Mam's precious dishes are not to be touched except by me. '

Her father gave her an affectionate s smile. 'I'll see to it that she helps you around the house, she'll earn her keep or else she'll be out on her ear.'

48

'She can clean the ashes out of the fire grate in the mornings,' added Ruth.

This time her father gave her a stern glance. 'Don't be so hard on her, Ruth. The girl hasn't set foot in here yet, and you're giving her a hard time.'

Emlyn looked at Ruth. 'I think she's very pretty, Ruth.'

'Have you seen her, then?'

'No, but the way Mr Hughes talked about her she sounded very pretty.'

'She also sounded a bit troublesome,' said Rebecca. 'Sounds as if she's got a short temper, to me.'

'There'll be trouble,' added Mr Veldon. 'There'll be too many people in this house.'

Ruth took the opportunity. 'Do you know what, Mr Veldon? I agree with you, there will be too many people in the house.'

Mr Veldon frowned long and hard at her.

'Hurry up and eat your food,' commanded the head of the house. 'They'll be here soon.'

John and Anna were hurrying up North Street as the proprietors of the shops on either side were shutting the doors and pulling the blinds down. Few people were around the darkening roads, but there was a faint silvery glow left in the soft clouds giving them enough light to ease their travels to the other side of town. At the same time the gas lighting man was coming down the street with his long pole to ignite the few gas-lights that stretched sparsely along the street. John was a little uncertain of the plans he'd made for Anna. She hadn't greeted them with as much enthusiasm has he would have liked. She was too quiet about the whole expedition, her face serious, her eyes suspicious, but her desperation to be independent from the Rolling Mill was of paramount importance. She was thinking. Dick had found it impossible to hold back any longer from her flouncing beauty and had grabbed her unceremoniously. She had struggled as he held her tightly to his bulbous stomach and forced a slobbering kiss on her tender lips. She'd managed to break free and kneed him between his legs which left him whimpering with bent knees and hands clasped on the painful parts. It was that act which had precipitated her dismissal; Dick telling his wife Ann had given him a packet of verbal abuse that he could no longer tolerate. His wife, already overwhelmed by his continual complaints about Anna, gave in to his arguments, and told Anna she had to go. Anna had said nothing. Nor had she told John, but it had left her without any doubt that men were truly animals. All this was going through her mind as they walked up North Street, for it had brought bad memories back to her of a similar incident when she was younger. It was the time her foster parents had invited their friends to supper. The middle aged man who had appeared to be quiet and servile to his garrulous wife, wanted to escape the constant chatter and offered to help Anna with the washing up. Anna, who had been appointed to the job by her foster father, felt sorry for the apparently browbeaten little man and allowed him in the kitchen. It was not long before the gentleman had his arm around her waist and forcing her close. She had done the same to him as she had to Dick. It had brought a howl from the man. However, it was Anna who was accused of encouraging the man into the kitchen. John interrupted her thoughts.

'You're very quiet, Anna, are you nervous of meeting the family?'

'There are women in the house, aren't there?'

'I told you so, didn't I?'

'That's all right then. I'll give it a go, I've no alternative.'

'They're a good family, I hope you'll appreciate them.'

'Time will tell won't it? But that old man you mentioned sounds disagreeable to me.'

'Well, make no judgments.'

At the top of North Street they turned left down the precipitous Elizabeth Street. A little way down they turned right into Mary Ann Street. Half way along the narrow road they came to a central house that was higher and broader than the two-up-two-down regular stone-built abodes that made up the street. Stopping at the front door of the larger house, John raised its knocker and tapped three times. It was a few moments before the door opened, but it was young Emlyn who answered the door. When he saw Anna he was dumbstruck by her beauty. He hadn't expected her to look so young. Her fresh face had pinkness in her soft cheeks from the energetic walk, her hazel eyes sparkled from the oil lamp he carried, and the waviness of her black hair curled down from her white bonnet on to her shoulders. Emlyn's jaw dropped and his eyes widened as he stood there staring.

'Well Emlyn, are you going to invite us in?' John said.

'Oh. Oh yes. Come in.'

Emlyn stood there as John brushed past him. He was still gazing at Anna when her slate-grey coat touched against him. She looked at him and smiled.

'I think I'm going to have trouble with you.'

As he watched her walk along the passage he whispered to himself, 'I hope so.'

Inside, the table had been cleared and covered with a green velvet cloth. An ornate oil lamp that had a large white globe burned brightly on the mantelpiece and gave a subdued illumination on shadowy walls, which, it seemed to John, was appropriate to the humour of the family. Anna immediately noticed a cold glare from the old man and an indifferent nod from Ruth. However, David welcomed the visitors warmly with handshakes and smiles.

'This is Ann, my fiance,' said John, as David shook her soft hand.

'Well John, you didn't tell me your future bride was so young and beautiful.'

'I'm twenty,' corrected Anna. 'Not quite as young as you think.'

'You look as young and fresh as a girl in her teens.'

Anna thought she had better accept the statement as a compliment.

'Thank you.'

'This is my home and family, Ann, and I'd like you to feel you are part of it, said David,' pointing to everyone in turn: 'Rebecca, my eldest, Ruth, keeper of the house, Emlyn who you've already met and young David who sometimes helps or hinders Ruth around the house. Last, is my late wife's father, Karl Veldon.'

Anna nodded to everyone in turn, but there was a significant silence when the introductions were finished.

'I'd like you to know,' she said breaking the hush, 'I will only be here for a short time. I hope we can be friends during that time.'

'I'll be your friend,' said Emlyn.

'Me too,' chirped young David.

'Thank you boys.' Turning to Ruth she added in a business fashion, 'Ruth, I wish to help you around the house in any way I can. I am not averse to housework, though I intend to rise above it in the future. But you can be sure while I'm lodging here your work will be halved.'

'Our food will be as well, I expect,' moaned the old man.

'Take no notice of him,' snapped Ruth, who saw Anna in a new light now. 'He's got no say in the matter.'

'I believe John is going to recompense for any extra cost I may cause, so you won't go short, Mr Veldon.'

'You tell him, Ann, but take no notice,' said the head of the house. 'This is my house so I have the last word. Would you like Ruth to show you around?'

'I'll show her around,' volunteered Emlyn.'

Anna was already amused by the admiration Emlyn was displaying. However, it was the reticent Rebecca Anna was looking at. 'Perhaps Rebecca would like to show me around.'

Rebecca didn't rise immediately, but a few seconds later she said, 'I have no objection. Follow me. She opened the adjoining door to the front parlour and Anna followed.

A hurried tour of the modest kitchen, a quick peek at the darkened garden from the back door and then she was led upstairs to the girls' bedroom and shown the newly made bed that was to be hers for the duration of her stay. It was a large bedroom with three beds and two large wardrobes. After Anna's quick nod of acceptance, they returned down stairs to John who eagerly wanted to take a break from the house.

'Well Ann, do you think you'll like it here.'

'It will be fine until we find a place of our own,' she said, a statement which indicated there was no wish to stay with John's sister after the wedding.'

John ignored the remark. 'Well, Dai, I think it's time for a celebration drink.'

'Right, I'm ready.'

'You settle in, Ann,' said John as they walked to the door. ' I'll come and say goodnight later.'

Anna followed behind. 'What's good for a man is good for a woman. I'm coming with you.'

Seven

John's sister, Elizabeth, never completely recovered from her illness which made the wedding arrangements difficult. She wanted the wedding breakfast to be in her home after being blessed in Chapel. Anna would have nothing to do with Chapel arrangements; it was her wedding and she wanted it her way. Furthermore, as far as she was concerned it was a marriage of convenience, so the idea of Chapel was grossly hypocritical. Even so, the debilitative Elizabeth, feeble as she was, was strong in her religion and determination. As the persuasions and encouragements to Anna persisted the weeks went by.

It became the practice of John to take his custom to the Carmarthen Arms after calling for Anna at Mary Ann Street. Anna had not been a drinking girl up and until she insisted on accompanying John on his nights out, but the entertainment of going with him was much more to her preference than staying in with the Rees family. She did not want the long walk down to the lower end of the town, nor did she want, what was more objectionable, the likelihood of John taking her to the Rolling Mill.

On most occasions David would accompany them which pleased Anna, for David was more entertaining than John. David was more light-hearted and would rib Anna affectionately about her feminist ways. She often made it clear to him that she was equal to any man in all respects of benefits and rights. And though Anna was deadly serious, David took it in a fun-loving way and gave her his pet name of Annie. However the habit of a threesome bothered John as Anna became accustomed to having drinks offered her from people who came to know the couple. And as she had never been a drinking lass, the regularity of it all was becoming an embarrassment for John and a crisis was beginning to loom; Anna would debate the right of women with the customers in a friendly manner, but as the night wore on it inevitably turned into a serious argument. The female customers would egg her on, whilst the male customers laughed her down.

One evening, on the way home from work, John was walking home with David, Rebecca and Emlyn. They stopped momentarily outside the Bush Hotel when John asked David for a private word before they parted company. David told his children to go ahead of him, telling them he'd catch up.

'Now, what's on your mind, John?'

'I'll come straight out, Dai. Would you mind not coming out with Ann and myself tonight? I want to try and get the wedding arrangements sorted once and for all. And I think it better if we were on our own.'

'Well, to tell you the truth, John, I was looking for an escape route myself. You see, the girls don't like it. They feel I spend more time with you and Annie than I do with them. And it's feels strange having her around the house after being out drinking with you both.'

'You're not offended, then?'

'Of course not, but the Carmarthen is my pub, so you'll have to find somewhere else. Besides, though she's pulling her weight in the house, I've noticed a cooling down between Annie and my Ruth. Ruth tells me Annie's trying to take over the running of the house.'

'That's settled, then. I'll call up as usual later on and take Ann out somewhere. I'll have to have a serious talk with her.'

'You're making a challenge you'd better be ready for.'

'I'll be ready for it, I've got to be. I love her but I'll try to be practical about it.'

'The best of luck to you, I say. Don't forget my household will have to put up with her afterwards, so don't put her in a bad mood, boy.'

'I'll try to be as tactful as I can.'

'See you later, then.'

Anna was upstairs in the bedroom preening herself in front of the long mirror set in the door of the old oak wardrobe. She was looking forward to another night in the lounge bar of the Carmarthen Arms. She had got used to the place and its fun atmosphere. Swishing her well-groomed hair, she let it swing around her shoulders and back again. Then she stroked the sides of the white, long-sleeved, blouse that John had recently bought her, running her hands over her hips and onto the flowing heel-length red skirt. She sighed with satisfaction at the image in the mirror. Turning away from the glass, she sat on the bed and began putting her shoes on. There was a doubt in the back of her mind that she couldn't quite understand. It was the seriousness of David when he'd come in. He'd mentioned quite purposely that he would not be accompanying her and John later. When she'd suggested he was having a night in, he quickly denied it with much certainty. If he wasn't coming out with us, she thought, who is he going out with, and where is he going? She felt overlooked; even snubbed. A night with John on her own could be a sombre one, she thought. Almost eight thirty, and being satisfied with her appearance, she went downstairs. As she entered the dining room she could see Ruth through the kitchen door washing the dishes.

'Do a good job on those dishes, Ruth,' she quipped in a jokingly manner.

'You'd better come and wipe them clean,' responded Ruth, tersely. 'Do something for your living.'

'It's Rebecca's turn, I did them yesterday.

'Rebecca's just finished a twelve-hour shift.'

Emlyn, sitting near the coal fire looked up. 'You look lovely, Annie, off out again, are you?'

Anna smiled with pleasure at the compliment. 'Emlyn's done the same shift,' she said, smoothly, winking at the boy. But he'll wipe them for me, won't you Emlyn?'

Emlyn got up and walked to the kitchen. 'The things I do for you,' he sighed.

'You'll have your reward one day, my love.'

David was sitting in the grandfather chair leaning forward, warming by the fire before going out. He looked dolefully at the burning coals. He didn't look up at Anna when she took Emlyn's seat.

'You're looking thoughtful, David, cheer up.'

He straightened up without acknowledging the girl. 'Oh well, I'd better be on my way, the boys will be waiting.'

'Where are you going tonight?'

'The Carmarthen, isn't it.'

'I thought you said you weren't coming with us tonight.'

'I'm not.'

'You said you were not coming to the Carmarthen tonight.'

'I said I would not be accompanying you and John tonight. The Carmarthen is my pub, and it's there I will be.'

'Where's John taking me, then?'

'That's up to John to tell you.'

David stood up and took his coat from the row of hooks near the passage door. Putting it on he opened the door and called, 'See you later, children.' They all called back in unison as he disappeared.

Anna heard the front door slam. She sat there wondering what was going on. John hadn't consulted her about any changes in the routine. Maybe he's organizing a surprise of some sort. A surprise her female intuition was telling, she may not appreciate. A few moments later she heard the front door opening, John had had the invitation from David that he need not knock anymore, so Anna knew it would be him.

'Hello Ann,' he said as he entered the room. 'I see you are all ready to go as usual. You're looking lovely.'

She stood up. 'Thank you. Now you might like to tell me what's going on?'

'Later—Hello Ruth, Emlyn, where's the rest of them?' he called to the siblings.

'In the front room,' answered Ruth. 'Rebecca is helping young David to read and Mr Veldon has been taken to the infirmary.'

John looked at Anna in surprise. 'What's the trouble with Mr Veldon?'

'I was out when it happened. Apparently he had a severe bout of coughing; gasping for breath. Ruth called the neighbours and a couple of them took him to the infirmary. That's all I know. I'd like to know where we are going if not the Carmarthen.'

'I thought we'd have a change tonight.'

'Did you consider that I might not want a change?'

58

'Let's not argue here, Ann. Come on, put your coat on and we'll sort things out.'

Anna reached for her coat from the row of hooks. 'Sort things out?'

John helped her on with her coat then turned to the doorway leading to the kitchen. 'We're off out, kids, goodnight.'

'Goodnight,' said Ruth.

Outside the air was cool but not cold; an occasional gas street lamp gave them barely enough light to see their way, but it had its necessary effect. They strolled along Mary Ann Street passing the Carmarthen Arms without saying a word. Turning up Elizabeth Street Anna remained silent waiting for John to explain himself. Down North Street Anna sighed prompting John into conversation. John reacted to the hint. He stopped and turned her to him, holding her hands.

'Ann, we must come to a decision about our relationship. If you don't want to marry me then say so, my lovely, I prefer honesty. I know you're not in love with me, but I love you dearly.'

'I haven't said I didn't want to marry you. I've accepted your proposal and will stick by it.'

'But its sounds so unusual; you don't want a Christian blessing, you don't want to live in my house, your social life seems more important to you than me...'

'I have admitted I don't love you John, but you were prepared to go ahead with the plans just the same. I have not deceived you in any way. I will marry you. I have not changed my mind.'

'But you seem so distant from me at times.'

Anna pulled her hands away and began to walk. John followed and caught up with her. Walking at her side he came to a decision. 'I'm sorry, Ann,' he said in a subdued voice. 'I see now I made a selfish mistake. It's best we part. We could never make each other happy.'

She stopped abruptly. 'What do you mean part? You don't want to marry me?'

'I want to, but it wouldn't work.'

'And what do you think I'm going to do? I have no job, no money, no friends except you and the Rees family. David appears aloof tonight. Have you two schemed up this little ultimatum to get rid of me? Men! Damned men!'

He grabbed her by the shoulders. 'Do you know how much you've hurt me these past few Months? Do you know the humiliation and embarrassment you've caused me in the Carmarthen with your feminist ways? You said you're a lady well you don't act like one when you've had a few drinks. I've been convenient for you, that is all. I've been your carriage to take you there and back. David has more conversation with you than me.'

'You're jealous?'

Of course not, I want you to myself. If I can't have you now before we are wed, I'll not be able to hold you once we're married. So it`s best to end it now and save a lot of grief for myself and Liz.'

'Ah. Liz. She's been turning you against me.'

'Don't be daft, girl.'

'Don't patronize me with your manly ways John. I don't like that. Now listen, if you want to get married tomorrow I will marry you, but I'm not going to live with your sister. She's the complete opposite to me, can't you see that? The problem is where will we live?'

'I've sorted that out days ago. I can rent a two-up-two-down in the Cwm.'

'You haven't mentioned it.'

'Believe me, I have tried several times but you've always been preoccupied with your feminist discussions and arguments. So often you have held your hand up preventing my words while you take the stage. I gave up.'

'I'm sorry, I didn't realize I had been ignoring you. I am truly sorry, John. If there is one thing I despise is someone ignoring my words, so if I have done the same to you then I`m sorry. I will marry you, please don't leave me, I'll have nobody if I don't have you.'

He pulled her close to him and kissed her gently on the lips and for the first time he felt warmth from her. She flung her arms around his neck and held him tightly. He could feel her tears trickle down his cheek. 'Maybe you'll love me in time, Ann.'

'I'll try my best. You're a good man, John Hughes. One thing is sure, you're a good man.'

And so, a woman lost but nothing to lose in life, with no security and hanging on to every hope, and a man besotted with blind love, they both agreed to get married as soon as possible.

Eight

John and Anna were married in the Registry Office, appearing to be a perfect and loving couple. John was smartly dressed in a black suit, Anna stunning in a long white dress carrying a posy of red roses, looked the perfect bride. David was the man John had chosen to give her away. Anna insisted that her name on the marriage certificate should be Ann, as she was known to all. Ruth had had the privilege of being a bridesmaid whilst Rebecca volunteered to help Elizabeth with the wedding breakfast at Horse Street, and to keep house until they returned from the service. Emlyn and young David were also dispatched to Horse Street readily smart and clean for the meal.

The afternoon passed rather stiffly with the atmosphere being over respectful and the celebrations tentative. However, as it was a cold October day, a fire burned brightly in the grate giving a warm glow to the room. The slim, underweight Elizabeth had busied herself attending to the needs of everyone aided by Rebecca and Ruth. Ruth helped with all she could which included washing the dishes and the clearing of waste from the table. Festivities came to an end early evening with the Rees family leaving first. Sometime later a knock came at the door and John gave a wry smile at Anna. Outside a one-horse cab arrived, a surprise that pleased the new bride. Bidding good night to Elizabeth they climbed into the cab and it made its way down the High Street. After travelling half a mile down the main road it turned right at the Brewers Arms and climbed a rough upward gradient. As the gradient became steeper the cab stopped. John got out and helped Anna down from the cab. As John lifted his hand to pay the cabman he received a lantern in his other hand from him. The cabman bade them goodnight, pulled on the reins and led his horse back down the hill. Little was said between the newlyweds as John gripped the hand of the confused Anna and led her up dark lanes of terraced houses. Anna was apprehensive as she tripped and stumbled up the small populated valley known as The Cwm. Eventually they arrived at the rented house, 21 The Graig, just a black shadow in the darkness. Before entering and not knowing the state of the house, she reminded John of the agreement on having separate bedrooms. John, ever optimistic, was confident Anna would come round to his gentle and devoted manner eventually. It was into a cold and dank room they entered. Anna suddenly felt an atmosphere of doom and feigned exhaustion wanting to go to bed. She was not impressed when John lit an oil lamp and escorted her upstairs to her bedroom. She said nothing then, but closed her door and looked around the room. Faded curtains, half open, hung over the tiny window. She quickly crossed the room and closed them. A wardrobe that had a mirror in its middle panel stood against the far wall. Almost touching the wardrobe, just nine inches away, was a single iron-railed bed that Elizabeth had made the day before. Anna sat on it and was relieved to find it dry, clean and fresh. A small dressing table stood at the right hand side of the door, its surface adorned with a piece of beige crochet material. Perhaps the daylight might make things look better, she thought. She undressed and got into the cold bed wondering about the water she could hear babbling in the distance. She was not to know it was the Morlais Brook rising from the culvert at the north end of the Cwm and meandering to the south where it disappeared into another tunnel.

The clear morning gave Anna a shock; the humble dwelling her husband had brought her to was far from what she expected. It was a small two-bedroom, terraced house, with fading whitewashed walls and simple windows that let in little light: four six-inch panes in a sash frame either side of the front door, the glass of which was smudged and dusty. The down stairs had a small parlour and an even smaller sitting room towards the back. It stank of tobacco from the last occupants and the black-lead grate and oven had not been cleaned for some time.

Elizabeth had volunteered to clean up and make it presentable, but John would not let his frail sister do the hard work. Gas had not been installed and the home was dated by the use of oil lamps. The house was situated in a dismal area near the bottom of the rural hollow. Tier after tier of terraced homes, some only three houses long, were built up the steep sides of the small valley. Access to the north was made by a narrow road that was arduous to ascend, but even more difficult was the poorly maintained numerous stone steps winding through back lanes up to Pant Road. To the south it was easier to gain access to Merthyr, but that would be going in the opposite direction and away from Dowlais. The west side of the Cwm was a tangle of small cottages breeding chickens and pigs, and the east side could be climbed, but only via narrow dirt-path lanes and slippery steps. Even then, it was another long ascendancy up the steep Elizabeth Street if she ever wanted to visit the Carmarthen. The Brewers Arms at the bottom of the Cwm was easily accessible, though the clientele she found undesirable. John, believing she could make it her home, as any new bride would be glad to, suggested cleaning the place up and decorating it to her liking would occupy her time. Any bride in love and gaining independence might have risen to the challenge, but Anna was not in love and greatly disappointed. She tried to decorate the place and succeeded in cleaning it up, but her hands were becoming callous and her spirit diminishing. The beautiful flower she wanted to be was not going to blossom from a house of flagstone floors and lowly surroundings.

Anna tried to be a dutiful wife but it was not in her to follow the servile life her mother had suffered. Her mother had tried desperately not to rely on the workhouse, and though she had many attempts of independence, the unqualified Agnes was good only for cleaning pub floors and washing out spittoons. The work did not pay enough for independent living, and the workhouse was the only retreat she knew.

However, Anna tried hard to please her husband and the first year went by slowly and painfully as she thought of ways to get out of the marriage. She knew divorce was impossible as John had been an understanding and compassionate husband, still favouring her with his love and devotion, even though she treated him indifferently and kept her distance by sleeping in a room of her own. However, she made up her mind to save as much money as she could and wait for an opportunity to escape, for that was her only hope. John remained respectful of her but could only envisage a life of loneliness in a house with no passion.

As the months of the second year dragged on, autumn turned to winter and the snow fell heavily in January, cutting off the Cwm from Dowlais. John, like all the workers, had to trudge through the drifts and slippery roads to get to his workplace. Furthermore, coal had to be stored and it was arduous work for John to keep 21 The Graig going as well as maintaining the necessary stock for Elizabeth up at Horse Street. Anna had to make trips down to Penydarren for groceries, keep the fire burning and the house in a respectable state. The snow didn't clear for four weeks; four weeks when Anna attempted to be a housewife and settle down, to do her best and keep her side of the marital agreement. However, her respect for her hard-working husband was dwindling; what kept her going was the memory, still fresh in her mind, when John had wanted to break up their relationship and go their separate ways. She knew she was on some kind of probationary period, for the marriage had not been consummated which was making John bitter towards her. She had noticed him becoming abrupt and demanding his food on the table when coming home from work. His visits to the pub at the bottom of the Brewers and up to see his sister, were becoming more frequent and the atmosphere in the house tenser. She would not go deprived and bought alcohol in Dowlais at every opportunity, sometimes whiskey sometimes rum. Mostly she kept her drinking a secret, but on rare occasions she'd throw caution to the wind when John was out with his mates, and cared little when he'd come home and find her sleeping on the couch. She felt he was coming close to an ultimatum again, which made her nervous. She realized something must be done to avert a serious confrontation.

John, too, realized it couldn't go on. He believed a heart-to-heart talk might help things. One day in April walking home from work, the sun still warm in the cloudless sky, his thoughts were to resolve the depressing situation, whether it was to free himself and Anna of the marriage, or find some spark of love that might grow into an endearing relationship. He entered the house with the intention of making a compassionate approach to her. However, his heart sank when he could see the table was unprepared and Anna

66

sitting at the fire grate staring into the dead fire, gloomy and silent. He threw his lunch bag on the couch, placed his hands on his hips and shook his head. She turned, there were tears in her eyes.

'Don't be angry, John,' she said plaintively. 'I know I'm not coming up to your expectations, but I have tried, believe me.'

'Tried?' he said, controlling his disappointment. 'What have you done since coming down here?'

'I've kept the place clean and respectable. More than some of the unsavoury neighbours who come home from the pub shouting, singing, fighting...'

'You've swept and laundered and made things good, but the walls are still nicotine brown from the last lot that stayed here. Can't you whitewash the place or change the curtains or do something to brighten up the place? What are you doing with the money? I give you more than enough housekeeping money to buy whatever is needed.'

Anna stood up and clutched her head. 'It's not in me, man,' she yelled. 'Can't you see that?'

He went to her and caught hold of her shoulders, calming himself. 'Ann, it's got to be in you. I work a twelve-hour shift and I've got a sick sister. By the time I come home I'm exhausted, but I do what I have to for Liz. You're a young healthy woman. All I ask is a home to come to and a meal on the table.'

She broke away from him, her eyes searing with frustration. 'This is a hole I'm living in; a hovel, a dungeon, hell itself.'

John flopped on the couch, checking his temper. 'There are people far worse off than us Ann. I've got a good job and one of the best paid. You have your house keeping money and enough left over to buy yourself a thing or two. This place is only temporary until I've saved enough for a better house. Or, alternatively, we are welcome to share with Elizabeth.'

'No. I cannot face living in a house with your sister.'

'But why? You treat her as though she's something evil. She's not. She's gentle and helpful. And she's not self-pitying.'

Anna went and stood over him, her face florid with anger. 'So I'm self-pitying, am I? One thing I'm definitely not; I'm not sanctimonious, nor do I look down my nose at people. Why do you want me up there, to look after her?'

He looked up at her, shaking his head. 'No. Though she is feeble and weak, she can do as much as you around the house. As for looking down her nose, you're imagining it, woman; the problem with you is you see Elizabeth as a threat to your pretentious grand ideas. She sees right through you but understands that you have your dreams.'

'Patronizing! Condescending! If we're going to say what's on our minds let's have the truth. She thinks I'm not good enough for you.'

John gave up. 'What about my food? You're not an invalid? Surely you could have made me a modest meal.'

'I'm sorry. I had to get out of this place. I made my way up to Union Street. I wandered around walking my feet sore.'

He looked at her untidy state. 'Like that? You went up Dowlais looking like that?'

She looked down at herself and sighed with self-admonishment. Walking to an old mirror hanging on the wall she studied her hair, frizzy and loose, she looked wild. She noted the fading of her white blouse and the grimy streaks on its collar. 'Do I really look so bad?'

'You've let yourself go, Ann. You've got creases in your clothes where they shouldn't be, and your hair—your lovely silky hair has lost its sheen.'

She swung around, angry at his comments. 'And whose fault is that? That's what I've turned into because of you?'

'You get more out of this relationship than me. You get security. I get nothing except one meal a day and poorly washed clothes. And I don't get a meal now, it seems. He held his head in his hands. 'I said it would not work. I gave you the option before we were wed. You needed me and I needed you. I've kept my end of the bargain. I sometimes wonder do I need you now. You, obviously, could do without this life, so what do you want to do? If you want to rid yourself of me and our unconsummated marriage then go.'

Her heart thudded in her breast. She would love to break from this life. It was worse that the upbringing she'd had with her foster parents. But the difference being she could always go back there and they'd take her in. But she'd never go back, she promised herself that. Would he take her back if she came unstuck? No. He would not, she concluded.

'I don't know what I want,' she said as she went back to the dead fire.

He looked up at her leaning on the mantelpiece, her head bowed, her hair hanging, hiding her face. He despised her then, but there was a mixture of sympathy and understanding too.

'Ann, listen,' he said, softening his tone, 'It's Saturday tomorrow and the weather is promising. I have a day off. We can take a trip to Merthyr and have some time together. Find a reasonable-priced café and dine out. I've saved some money so I think I can treat you to a present. Ok?'

She turned around, relief on her tear-stained face. 'How do we get there, John?'

'We're half way there already. The bottom of the Cwm is practically in Penydarren. It will be a stroll down the high street through the village. We'll be there in half an hour.'

'I'd like that. Oh John I'd like that very much.'

'It's settled then. You make sure you are as lovely tomorrow as you were when I married you. You scrub up my girl; I want to be a proud man in Merthyr.'

Nine

Anna and John strolled down the long Penydarren High Street in the warmth of the spring sun stopping at intervals to look in shop windows. Both were feeling uplifted in fresh air and away from the claustrophobic Cwm. John in his daytime grey suit with Anna's arm entwined around his, and Anna looking beautiful again after "scrubbing up" and wearing her azure, full-length dress, long sleeved with white cuffs. The pavements were busy, mostly with working men's wives, but also with children playing in the road and men too old or too disabled to work. The street was lined with diverse buildings on either side; a mixture of pubs, shops and houses. A wild-eyed, snorting workhorse struggled up the road pulling a cart full of goods, its head nodding from the strain. The owner cracked his whip and shouted something incoherent. In stark contrast, a smart hansom cab passed down, its black shining mare trotting proudly, composed and in control.

Another quarter of an hour and they were outside the Central Library in Merthyr, Anna wanting to rest for a while, so they sat on a public bench outside St David's church. The place was busier than Penydarren High Street. Shop windows were bigger and wider with a greater range of merchandise. The number of cabs and carts were many as the more prosperous people of the town came in hansoms and broughams. Other the less fortunate walked or hitched a lift with a farmer on his horse and buggy. Street vendors were selling goods from their stalls and handcarts, calling out the prices of their goods, from fruit and vegetable to cheap clothing and jewellery.

'Well, there's plenty of atmosphere down here, Ann.'

'It gives me a sense of freedom. It gives me a feeling of being someone equal to all.'

'You are equal to all. No, I'd say you are superior to many, as far as beauty goes.'

'Beauty! What is beauty? It is something you are born with, but it doesn't give you equality in life. Look at that those shires pulling that beer wagon, they are beautiful, but slaves to men.'

'All are born equal; men and women.'

'Then why are women always in the shadow of men? We don't even have the vote. No, God made us all equal but men keep us inferior.'

He turned to Anna. 'Ann, I'm not going to get into an argument today.'

'No, you're right. Anyway, I feel thirsty, maybe we should find a place to have a cup of tea.'

'I don't see any cheap cafes. A few inns and hotels that are probably expensive or rowdy.'

'No different from Dowlais pubs, then.'

'I've heard some of the drinkers down here can be very aggressive.'

'You promised you were going to treat me.'

'To something useful, though. No sense in paying for an expensive cup when you can get the same tea for half the price in a modest piece of porcelain.'

'So where is the cheap-skate place you know of?' Anna quirked sarcastically.

'I don't know. There's a good indoor market lower down, maybe there's a café stall there.'

Anna shifted impatiently in her seat. 'Well, it's good to have a day out from the Cwm.'

'Do you know of a better place, my lady?'

She turned to him with an air of superior knowledge. 'Yes, I do as it happens.'

'Expensive?'

'No, mediocre.'

'And how would a lady of your intellect and elegance know of a cheap place to have a humble cup of tea?'

'I told you of my eternal search for my father around the railway stations, well, that's where I was taught my frugal ways. Come on, let's go to Merthyr Station.'

John's face suddenly displayed a dour expression, not unnoticed by Anna.

'What's the matter now?'

He gave a forced smile. 'Nothing, nothing, lead the way.'

The locomotive on platform 5 was hissing steam from its lower valve waiting for the passengers to fill the carriages, whilst others sat on the wooden benches waiting for their train to arrive. Anna led John through the commuters, pushing past porters loading light freight and baggage on the goods van, while others stacked baskets on the platform. They found the station's restaurant to be pleasantly half empty. John went and got the teas and a bun each. Enjoying the modest treat, they sat quietly for a time. But when finished, the lack of dialogue became lengthy and moody with Anna thinking of her unpleasant past and of the dismal future. John was on another train of thought, worrying about Anna not being able to cope with life in the Cwm. A train blowing its whistle woke Anna from her reverie as it left the station. Looking through the cafe window, the departing train allowed her to see across the platform to the rear shop windows of the High Street stores. She had looked and desired the array of ladies fashion a year ago and hoped one day she would be able to purchase some. She turned to John.

'I'd like to have a look in that ladies shop, John.'

John followed her eyes and gave her a knowing grin. 'Fine. There may be something I can afford to buy you.'

'What are we waiting for? she said, standing up. 'I think you can buy me something to make this day worthy of returning to the Cwm.'

'Ann, we won't be in the Cwm forever. I'm saving as much as I can. I promised you a present and you shall have a present.'

'I know, providing it's within your pocket pack.'

'Providing you don't expect gold from a steel worker.'

Over at the display window Anna's eyes searched the dresses, the hats, the coats, the jewellery and all else that were on display, but everything seemed too expensive to ask. John waited patiently and apprehensively hoping she would find something reasonable. Anna took a couple of steps to the side because there was something colourful a little out of sight. Now in full view, she could see it was a red boa, reasonably priced. It was a piece of fashion she had taken a liking to for some time. She turned to John but he had left her side. Looking behind her she could see he was standing at a small stall where books and newspapers were being sold. She called him over and he tucked the purchased newspaper in his coat pocket. Entwining her arm through his she pointed to the red boa.

'I really would like that red boa John, it's beautiful.'

John nodded his head. 'I'll buy it for you, but how you can call a scarf beautiful, I don't know. Though, I must admit, it will look nice around your delicate neck.'

'Thank you, John, but it is not a scarf, it is a boa.'

Later, the pair went and walked around the large market, Anna flamboyant with her ruby boa tickling her neck and feeling as though everybody was noting her.

As John helped Anna down from the backless cart he had cheekily hailed down, he thanked the old owner, who kindly tipped his cap and whipped the reins. The mare trotted off towards the main road it had diverted from. Anna and John strolled up the dirt lane to their house hardly saying a word to each other. Inside, John took off his shoes and lay on the couch with feet up, reading the newspaper he'd bought. Anna's light-hearted day soon faded into a quiet sombre mood. She changed her clothes to more appropriate attire for making a meal; other than the cup of tea and buns they had at the station, they had had little else. Anna made a modest meal of potatoes and cabbage with some pork John had bought in town. They ate in silence, John looked up at her occasionally, but Anna had her head down and John knew she was lapsing into an unfavourable mood. Not wanting to have the occasion spoiled by an unhappy wife, he thought a night out would complete the day's outing.

'You haven't said a lot since we came in, Ann. Lost your tongue?'

'You're not very observant,' she said, without looking up. 'I haven't said *anything* since we came home.'

'Right, correction, not one word have you said. Don't spoil the day, we've had a very pleasant time, I think.'

'I can't help it. This place has that effect on me.'

'Ann, I earn a reasonable wage and I'm saving hard. We'll have a better place in a year or two I keep telling you. If I can wait and be patient, so can you.'

'You're at work all day. I've got to suffer this place all day and every day.'

'And I've got to suffer loneliness all night and every night.'

This time she looked up at him with defiant eyes. 'I'm not ready for that. I've got to be happy and feel for you. I'm sorry.'

John, though frustrated about the situation, had learnt to be cool and rational. 'I can put up with our unusual relationship, but to have a depressed wife who has no interest in home life, makes matters much worse. Anyway, to raise the gloom, why not come with me tonight for a drink?'

'I'm not going down that pub at the bottom of the Cwm, once was enough for me.'

'I didn't think you would. So you stay at home and I'll go on my own, I don't mind.'

'Why not go up to Dowlais and make our way to the Carmarthen. I used to enjoy myself there?'

'I didn't. You were so involved with other people I felt as though I was on my own. Besides, I didn't think you'd want to walk so far after our trip to town.'

'You have no right to think for me, I'm quite capable of thinking for myself.'

'So you're not too tired to walk up to Dowlais?'

'This hole would give me strength to walk to Cardiff.'

'Right, if you want to go up to town, we can make a call to the Rolling Mill.'

A picture of the lecherous landlord immediately came into Anna's mind and her heart hardened. 'No! If we can't agree on a place let's try somewhere new we haven't been before.'

John smiled to himself. 'I must confess there isn't a pub in Dowlais I haven't tried sometime or other in my life.'

'Then you should know a place where a lady can go without the raucous locals deafening your ears with crude jokes and sickening laughter.'

He thought of the times they spent up at the Carmarthen where she got involved in politics and womens' rights when it was she who evoked such behaviour. He wanted to call into Horse Street to see if Elizabeth needed anything. 'I must call in to see my sister. There are a couple of pubs in Horse Street besides the Rolling Mill. I used to go to the Forge and Hammer, that's a pub which hasn't got a bad reputation, and there used to be a few women going there.'

'Oh? I see.'

'You don't see at all. Make up your mind or I'll be going on my own.'

Anna thought about it, but not for long. 'I agree, but if the pub turns out rough, I'll be looking for another one on my own.'

'I agree. You go and freshen up.'

'Aren't you going to get ready?'

'It won't take me long. I'll finish reading my paper while you make yourself beautiful so that I can make the boys envious of me.'

'There'll be boys there?'

'Young men. I'll have to watch you carefully.'

The lighthearted statement warmed Anna. She skipped up stairs, her mood had lifted, her expectations for the evening favourable. She didn't take long, and when she returned in a red dress with her boa round her neck and her wavy, raven hair hanging down her back, John could only stare in wonderment.

'I don't know if I should expose you to the lads up there, I might lose you,' he said.

'I'll stay by your side all night if you wish,' she said, though her mood suddenly changed when she imagined a smoke-filled pub with noisy working men.

'You'd better, or I'll throw you over my shoulder and carry you home.' John left his paper on the couch. 'I won't be long,' he said, and he disappeared through the door.

Anna did a twirl in the middle of the room casting the pub images from her mind, flicked her hair around her neck and flopped on the couch to wait for John. But then her spirit took a dive, in sombre realization she was fooling herself as she pictured being in small pub culture again. Looking around impatiently, she picked up John's newspaper and began to turn over the pages. Her eyes caught a short report in one of the columns with the headline: Women Demand The Vote. Anna was immediately engrossed in what the leader was demanding:

Millicent Fawcett, founder of the National Union of Women's Suffrage, is demanding the right to vote. She recommends peaceful protests and marches through London to achieve the democratic rights for women. All women are welcome to join her and her followers to march the streets of London to Parliament and lobby the politicians. She argues that a woman can hold responsible posts in society, such as sitting on school boards, but could not be trusted to vote. Wealthy mistresses of large manors employ gardeners, workmen and labourers who are allowed to vote, but women cannot. That women have to pay the same tax as men but do not have the right to vote…

'Reading my paper? I didn't think you'd be interested,' said John, coming through the door.

Anna looked up. 'I thought it would be our paper. You're very possessive sometimes.'

'You know what I mean. Don't be so sensitive.'

Anna threw the paper to one side. 'Sorry, I suppose I am tired. Maybe I'll stay in after all. I don't think I can face the walk up to Horse Street.'

John looked surprised. 'That was a quick change of mind. You're all ready to go now, looking lovely and elegant, just like a lady.'

'Thank you, but I may not have the right frame of mind for your friends at the Forge and Hammer.'

John huffed impatiently and pulled some money from his pocket. Counting what he had in his hand he cheerfully said, 'Well, I suppose I have spent enough on you today.'

'Yes, you have John. Thank you for a lovely day.'

He gently lifted her chin and looked into her eyes. 'Are you sure you're alright?'

She gave a faint smile, 'I'm positive I'm all right. Now you go, I've got things to do.'

'Things to do?'

'Please, John. Just go and enjoy yourself.'

He bent down and kissed her on her cheek. 'I'll go, but I swear I'll never understand a woman.'

John gently closed the door behind him. Anna sat there for a while, excitement in her eyes and vocation in her heart. Then she whispered to herself, 'I don't belong here.'

Ten

The next day John was briskly walking along Mary Ann Street, his mind in confusion, his legs not going fast enough to find answers to his bewilderment. The Sunday morning sunshine didn't warm his cold feeling just then, though he didn't know whether to feel guilty that something had happened to Anna or feel enmity towards her. All he could remember was that he'd come home late from the Rolling Mill last night after he'd made a brief visit to the Forge and Hammer. Anna was not in the sitting room when he'd got in. Believing she had decided to have an early night, and not wanting to disturb her, he went straight to bed without any supper. When he rose she still had not appeared from her bedroom. He'd made himself some breakfast and waited a little longer until his curiosity got the better of him. Arranging a cup of tea and a few biscuits on a tray, he'd gone to her room hoping she would appreciate tea in bed. He'd opened her bedroom door and stood there speechless at the neatly made bed that had obviously not been slept in. After searching the house and the surrounding area he'd come to the inevitable conclusion she had left him last night and could be anywhere. The only person she knew intimately locally was David, so it was plausible that she'd gone to his home, but why he could not understand. Reaching the front door of the Rees family he noticed that the curtains on all windows had been drawn closed. His confusion doubled as he gave a respectful tap on the knocker. Rebecca opened the door and looked surprised to see John standing there.

'John! We didn't expect you so soon.'

'Is she here Rebecca?'

'Who?'

'Ann. I can't find her anywhere.'

'No, John. We've hardly seen her since you moved to the Cwm.'

He stood back and scanned the façade of the house. 'The curtains…why are….'

'It's Mr Veldon. He passed away last night.'

John dropped his shoulders, embarrassed by his thoughts of treason. It had been so apparent to him that they might have been hiding her. 'I'm very sorry.'

'That's all right, you weren't to know. What's this about Ann?'

Before he could answer, David called from inside. 'Who is it, Rebecca?'

'It's John.'

'Well bring him in, don't stand on the doorstep gossiping; show respect, girl.'

'Come in, John.'

He followed Rebecca into the back room where the curtains were open and the sunlight lit the place up. David was sitting at the table, official papers spread before him. He looked up as John entered. 'Haven't had the pleasure of your company for some time, John. It's good to see you, sit down.'

John sat at the table opposite David. 'Sorry to hear about your father-in-law,' he said, rubbing his forehead. I didn't realize.'

David looked up from his papers. 'Thanks. Bad news travels fast, as usual. Who told you?'

'Rebecca. I knew nothing of the death until a moment ago.'

Just then Ruth came into the room from the kitchen, followed by Emlyn, both hailing hello.

'Haven't seen you for ages, John,' said Ruth. You've been a stranger since you moved to the Cwm.'

'I see him often coming from work, don't I John?' Emlyn said with an air of a mature man.'

'Aye, that you do, Emlyn.' He turned to David again. 'Listen, I'll call another time when the circumstances aren't so sad.'

David stood up. 'No, no,' he said cordially. I've done as much as I can for now; funerals take some organizing. You've had the experience, so you'll know all about it. Well, what brings you up to our part of town? Just passing, John, or is there something you wanted?'

John looked around; with the whole family being there he didn't want to give the humiliating news. He hoped he would have seen David in private. He stood up and tried to change the subject. 'Where is the old man?'

'In the front parlour. The doctor signed the death certificate last night. He'd expected the worst for some time. It's a relief really. His chest was giving him hell the past few weeks; he hardly slept and was in pain all the time.'

'That's what you get for twenty years working in the coal dust.'

'Don't remind me.'

'I might be able to get you a job in the steel works, Dai.'

'I'm too old to learn new tricks. Anyway, you're not looking too happy, what's the trouble.'

Rebecca intervened, casting away any doubt John may have had leaving their home without the whole family knowing. 'He's looking for Ann, Dad.'

Emlyn moved closer to the table, and so did Ruth. They all looked at John for an explanation.

John sat back down again and dropped his head. 'She's gone. Can't find her anywhere. She was in a strange mood last night before I went out for a drink. When I got home she was in bed, so I thought, but when I got up this morning and took her a cup of tea, the bed hadn't been slept in.'

The room went quiet as everyone looked at each other with some confusion. Not because Anna had left John, but it was apparent Anna and John slept in separate bedrooms. John's heart dropped a few inches lower when he'd realized what he had said; He had shame upon shame. After a few moments of silence he raised his hands and slapped them on his knees.

'Well, now you all know. I was hoping to keep it private, but I've gone and said it now.'

Rebecca came to him and touched his shoulder. 'It's a secret we'll all keep, John'

Her father looked at each of his children in turn. 'If any of you breathe a word of this outside this house, I'll take my belt to you and you won't sit down for a week.'

Young David looked up at his father. 'What word is that, Dad?'

'Never-you mind, young one.'

'If I don't know which word it is, how do I know not what to breathe?'

'It doesn't involve you, Davey,' said Rebecca, placing her arm around his shoulder. 'But I'll tell you one day when you're older.'

Young David searched the faces of everyone but could not make sense of it all, he went and stroked his toy dog.

'Rebecca, will you and Ruth carry on with the dinner preparations? John and me will have to have a talk.'

'Aye, right Dad. Come on Ruth, back to the bosh, out here Davey boy.'

Emlyn glanced at his father who gave him a questioning look.

'Right, you want me to leave you in private. You only had to say; though I'm old enough to understand these things, you know.'

'Leave the lad stay, Dai. As long as he keeps everything confidential.'

'It's all right, John, I was about to go and meet my mate anyway.'

Emlyn disappeared through the front door as David stood up and quietly closed the kitchen door. Then he went and sat at the table again and looked across at John. 'Well, what's this all about?'

'It's a long story, Dai. It's sufficient that you to know she never loved me. It was a marriage of convenience as far as she was concerned. On my part I loved her and still do. I was hoping she'd come to love me, but I know now that she couldn't.' His voice died to a whisper, 'The marriage was never consummated.'

David thumped his fist on the table. 'You treated her too well, man; too lightly. A woman's place is to look after her husband in all respects. She had a duty to share the same bed as you.'

John sighed heavily. 'Maybe that's one of her characteristics that attracted me to her in the first place, she believes her first duty is to herself, Dai. She says that she has the right to be equal to all; man, woman, lord or lady. She's an independent woman who cares for no one.'

'She would have had my hand across her cheek if she had treated me in such a way, I'll tell you.'

John stood up. 'Well, she's gone and I can't do a thing about it. I'll be the laughing stock of the locals if this gets out. So please, Dai...'

82

David grabbed hold of John's hand. 'Don't worry, John. If there's one thing I can do is control my children. Besides, they have a great sympathy for you, believe you me.'

'Thank you. I'll see you around.'

'You'll see me tonight or I'll never see you again.'

'That'll be good, Dai. I'll appreciate some company tonight.'

'Right then, I'll come down the Rolling Mill. I haven't been down there for some time.'

'Right, I'll be there at eight o'clock; wait for me at the top of the street, you don't know the right knock for a Sunday.'

* * *

The previous night, when John had left her alone, she had read the account of the fight for the right of women to vote over and over again. She saw herself marching along the London streets carrying a banner with the real women of the country. The more she'd thought about it the more excited and convinced she became that her vocation was to join the fight for women's right. It would give her a purpose in life and, most of all, it would be a kind of revenge for the way she and her mother had been humiliated and treated with indifference in her earlier life, particularly by men. Yes, she would march to the Houses of Parliament if necessary with the London Ladies. Those intelligent and educated females who were undoubtedly equal to any man. She'd gone upstairs, collected the money she had saved over the months, packed her suitcase and left. That night she had made her way to Merthyr and booked into a cheap hotel. Early on Monday morning

Anna had made her train connections at Merthyr and Cardiff and joined two elderly women and a young man in a compartment.

Approaching the Severn Tunnel, of which she had heard adverse gossip about it since it had opened in 1886 made feel a little nervous. The thought of travelling four miles under the Severn estuary where flooding had been reported at earlier stages, and huge pumps were necessary to clear the lines, filled her with horror. But then her rational mind evaluated the situation and she came to the conclusion that the authorities would never allow such danger to its passengers. Besides, the other passengers sat there cool and confident, so why should she worry. No, it's best to concentrate on her new start in life and forget the slow, degrading existence of the eternal pub culture that was dominant in the industrial towns of south Wales. The more her mind built up pictures of a sunny future the more her heart grew with pride and expectation.

She discreetly studied the young man who sat opposite her when he was looking out of the window. He was quite handsome with fair hair and fine features. His blue eyes occasionally glanced at her but quickly turned away again. His casual tan plaid jacket, plain tan trousers, along with his white shirt and brown tie gave her the impression he was quite well off. Though his anaemic complexion suggested he was of a delicate nature. Then the whistle of the train screamed out as it raced into the darkness of the tunnel. She couldn't help giving a muffled cry as her stomach turned over. The train rumbled a lot louder in the tunnel, the closeness of the wet walls could almost be felt, and the dank smell was nauseating. A mixture of locomotive smoke, spilt oil and slimy railway sleepers, came into the compartment even though windows were closed. She expected some sort of illumination but there was nothing except pitch-blackness. She wondered how the others were feeling, but no one was saying anything. She closed her eyes in the pretense it was she who was controlling the darkness. It worked for a while, but then images of her past began to rise and she became glued in a time warp. When she was a child she believed that the workhouse was the natural process of life; being reared in such a place she knew no different. She could see the pale, lined face of her frail mother after a twelve-hour shift of scrubbing and attending to the menial tasks of the workhouse. And then getting permission to leave and find work outside, only to fall weak and ill and forced to return several times; their only possessions a uniform and a bed. Being low class of paupers they were segregated from those who had had higher positions in life but had fallen on hard times. She could see the workhouse as though it were in front of her: The brick buildings, the cobblestone yards and flagstone floors, the iron beds with straw mattresses lined either side of the cold long dormitory. The clanging of the large bell on the outside wall that woke them in the morning, called them to prayers before breakfast, and again for other meals of the day. She could see her first day at the workhouse school when she was six and the severe-faced teacher with mean staring eyes; of her mother's whispering, dying words, "Tegwyn, Tegwyn Morgan…foreman of engine fitters…Merthyr, find him my little darling…he'll have to look after you now…deserted me but won't desert you, he's your father." Later, fostered out to a middle-aged couple who were paid to look after her and educate her. Remembering her foster father who was a religious fanatic and made her attend services three times a day, memorize the scriptures and quote them time and time again; of his servile wife who would give her a weak-supporting smile. But freedom came when she fled her foster home. At seventeen she heard her mother's words echo in her mind and went in search of her father. Why? she asked herself. Why? Because of a man she answered…

The train's whistle screamed, echoing through underground as the engine driver saw the light at the end of the tunnel. Anna involuntarily whimpered audibly with it and sat up, happy to see a glimmer of light coming through the window.

'Are you all right, miss?' the young man asked, in a cultured English accent.

'I'm fine, thank you,' she said sternly

'Is this your the first time through the tunnel?'

'Yes. I didn't know what to expect.'

He smiled at her, understanding her anxiety. 'There will be a couple more shortly, but they are of a short duration, we'll be out the other side before you can count to twelve.'

The ladies said nothing but stared at Anna, their eyes inspecting her. Stone-faced they turned away and looked directly to their front. Anna ignored the coldness of them. Soon they arrived at Temple Mead Station where they had to change for their connection to London. However, the ladies were going south, but the young man was continuing on to the Capital. He assisted Anna to the London train and sat opposite her in the same compartment. She didn't seem to mind as there were four others there, three men and a lady. As the train sped along mile after mile, the young man, who appeared to be in his mid-twenties, tried to begin a conversation several times. Anna was polite to him but reserved And so, they eventually arrived in London.

Eleven

Later that afternoon Anna said goodbye to Timothy (the young man on the train) outside Paddington Station. The young man's courtesy and general mien had eventually softened her toward him and short intermittent conversations had ensued throughout the remainder of the journey. She had had reservations when he'd offered her a room at his flat. She couldn't make up her mind if he was being very caring or had devious intentions. However, her joy at shedding all the shackles of industrial life in the south Wales gave her an elation of emotion she believed she'd never would have experienced had she not made that impulsive move from the Cwm. She gave Timothy the benefit of the doubt, offered polite gratitude to him and shook his hand. She explained she was determined to stand alone and only wanted the respect that any young lady of independence was entitled to. She then waved goodbye and immediately felt the excitement of being in the capital of England. She was free and was not going to be beholding to anyone, especially the opposite sex. It was true she had doubts on the train concerning her rash behaviour. It crossed her mind that it would have been prudent had she thought more of it. However, she'd quickly cast those negative thoughts from her mind and decided to plan her future in London. All she had to do was to book into a hotel and find the lady suffragette she had read about in the paper. She could then join the campaign for women's' votes and begin a new life in a respectable and higher class of people. She had enough money to last a few weeks but intended finding a suitable position her education demanded. She had flattered herself with the teachings of the workhouse and the personal tuition she'd had with her foster parents, and the humble school they had sent her to. And though she was an excellent reader, had beautiful handwriting and had sufficient knowledge of the scriptures, she had not had the opportunity to undergo any scholarship and, therefore, had no formal certificates or references to support her verbal claims.

It was late afternoon when she made her way past St Mary's Hospital wearing her long red dress creased after the long trip and her sad-looking red boa, with a few broken feathers, hung round her neck. A round flat hat, cream with a red ribbon circling it, kept her rolled-up hair firmly in place. Carrying her brown suitcase and coat over her arm, she proceeded to Edgware Road, looking around in awe at the impressive buildings and their admirable architecture. As she approached the busy road the distant sounds of traffic grew to a cacophony of clip clopping horses, rumbling cartwheels, roaring omnibuses and the chugging of the newly created automobiles. She did not know her destination just then, for her eyes flicked from huge shop windows to tall hotels, from animated street traders to the hansoms, broughams, horses and carts and public transport racing down the broad road. All that animation, together with the hustle and bustle of the busy crowds frequenting the pavements, made her head dizzy with excitement and adventure. She twisted and turned her hips and swung the small brown suitcase as though it was merely a handbag. Nearing Marble Arch, she rested for a while at the crossroads and gazed over at the wide expanse of Hyde Park. Deducing that there would be seats and scenery there, and with some trepidation, she crossed the busy road and entered the renowned attraction. Looking around she saw a vacant seat and gladly sat down. It was near the serpentine, and there she rested and composed herself planning her next move. She remained there for half an hour, but the respite had made her feel tired and reluctant to continue. This frightened her, for she could not despair so easily. Steeling herself, she stood up quickly and made her way back towards Marble Arch where she thought she might gain suitable lodgings for the night, perhaps somewhere in the side streets behind Edgware Road. Each hotel she checked was found to be expensive. Though she had enough money to spend a few nights in a hotel, the luxury would use up too much of her savings, so she diverted into the back streets to find cheaper places. The streets and buildings greatly contrasted with the main roads. There were shadowy lanes and sordid alleyways, the houses plain and unimpressive. However, some abodes that had sets of stone steps leading to their front doors appeared satisfactory. These mainly offered bed and breakfast, but she had to vacate the room for the day and return to it in the evening unless she booked it for a week. She thought this very inconvenient for it would mean carrying her suitcase around all day and she would rather find a cheaper place to stay. Finally, with the daylight fading and she becoming weary, she came to a squalid area that had narrow lanes with two and three storey dwellings. Her depression was leading her to despair with pictures running through her mind of curling up in a shop doorway to sleep the night. There were several businesses with their lights being turned on making the place appear warm and friendly. But people who crossed her path said nothing, and those who smiled at her were men wanting her company. Her eye caught sight of a small tailor shop across the road that had a side entrance to the premises and she wondered if it led to a room. Crossing the road she went into the shop where a middle-aged lady dressed in a black blouse tight to the neck and a long black skirt, gave her a shallow smile. Her cold eyes climbed from Anna`s shoes to her red boa with intent suspicion.

'Yes, dearie,' she said, through smudged red lipstick. 'What can I do for you?'

'I noticed the side door to your shop and I wondered if you have a room to let above it.'

The lady turned and began to busy herself with a rack of clothing behind the counter. 'And what if I do? What has that got to do with you?'

'I'm looking for a place to stay for a few days…or maybe weeks.'

The lady turned around and faced her. 'And why would you want to rent a flat around here?'

'I need accommodation for a short time.'

'Have you come from the smallpox area?'

'Smallpox? I don't know of any smallpox. I've recently arrived from south Wales and need somewhere to stay.'

'Are you sure you haven't been evicted from your old lodgings because of some kind of misconduct?'

Anna was struck mute for a time wondering why she should be accused of such a thing. It was then she realized the woman's face looked hard and lined. 'I arrived from Wales a few hours ago, Anna replied, forcefully. 'I've walked the streets for ages looking for somewhere to stay. The hotels are too expensive, the boarding houses have inconvenient rules and…and I'm very, very tired.'

The woman made a comprehensive inspection of Anna's clothes once more and her well-used brown suitcase. 'You'll pardon me, my dear, but it's walking the streets that worries me. What kind of work do you do?'

'I haven't had chance to find any work, but I'll be looking for a teaching situation. I imagine a big place like London must have hundreds of schools.'

'Are there no schools in Wales?'

'I want to live in London. I didn't come solely to find a job. I came here to join the suffragettes. I need a job to pay my way.'

'You're a suffragette?'

'That's what I want to be.'

'I don't know whether I'm in favour of that lot. Anyway, I should bring to your notice your unfortunate selection of clothes.'

Anna inspected herself, dropping her case on the floor and brushing her hips with her hands. 'What's the matter with my dress?'

'It's rather loud, your boa is common and you look, unfortunately, rather like a girl of the streets. Do you know what that means?'

'You think I'm…I'm…'

'A prostitute my dear.'

Just then a bald-headed man came in from the back room, a measuring tape hung around his thin neck and draped down the front of his chalk-smudged waistcoat. He peered over his thick-rimmed glasses at Anna and then at his wife. 'What's all this talking I hear, my dear? Is it a customer?' he asked with a cockney accent that had sharpness to it.

'No, no, Matthew. This…uh, young lady, is wanting our upstairs room, but I feel she may not be suitable for a respectable abode such as we have to let out.'

He gave Anna a thorough visual inspection. 'And why not, may I ask? She appears to be fine from what I see.'

'She claims to have come up from Wales today, though her attire seems a little odd for a Welsh girl.'

90

Anna thought she had better defend herself. 'I have been travelling all night and walking for hours. Obviously my clothes are not in the clean and tidy state they were when I first started out.'

'I am not referring to the state of your clothes but to your choice.' She turned to her husband. 'Matthew, do you see what I mean?'

'The London fashions have not reached the valleys of south Wales, woman. The girl is quite innocent to your insinuations.' He turned to Anna. 'What's your name?'

'Ann.'

'And do you have a second name?'

'My name is Ann Morgan.'

'Have you the money to pay for such a room, Ann?'

'I need to know how much you charge and what I am paying for.'

'The shop is locked up at night but you'll have access to the back downstairs room that has a washbasin. It also has a fire grate, and a portable gas ring, but you'll have to supply fuel if you want to light the fire. But you'll have your independence with a key to the side door. There's a lavatory out in the garden which must be kept clean. As for your room, it has bed, a couch, and a wardrobe and an easy chair. It goes without saying that you'll have to keep it clean and tidy. There's also a gas ring there if you want to boil the kettle for a cup of tea, but there are no cooking facilities. Take it or leave it.'

'How much is it going to cost me.'

'As long as you've got a little money we can agree the terms after you've settled in and made yourself comfortable.'

'She may be gone before we get to open in the morning,' warned his wife.

'I'm a woman of honour,' snapped Anna.

'Stop squabbling,' grinned the man. 'Come on, I'll show you to your room.'

'You will not,' said his wife. The woman looked Anna up and down again. 'Right, I'll take your word. Come with me and I'll show you the room.'

Anna followed her out of the shop, through the side door and up the stairs. The woman opened the door to the room, then ushered Anna in. 'Do you think that will please you?'

Anna wasn't impressed with the gloomy room or its musty smell. 'It will do for now,' she said, dolefully.'

'Beggars can't be choosers, dearie.'

Twelve

Anna spent a couple of days settling in and smartening up her sparse wardrobe. The nights were lonely but she managed to utilize what little amenities were in the downstairs back room. There was a flatiron she warmed up on the gas ring, a cold-water tap, a small kettle and a few pieces of crockery. The door leading to the tailor's premises was always securely locked. She was glad. It gave her security from the landlord and his suspicious spouse. The first couple of days she gave her room a lot of attention and made it more homely than she had felt when living in the Cwm. It gave her the satisfaction of being completely independent. The landlord had demanded a month's rent in advance, which she gave him on the second day, after that she saw little of him or his wife. Sometimes when going in and out they would meet, on which occasions there would be a show of reticent respect from both parties. Soon she began to explore the surrounding areas, and as she gained confidence she would catch an omnibus to travel further from her lodgings.

The more familiar she became with London the more she realized how careful she had to be crossing the busy roads and the need to avoid the dark alleys where undesirable-looking men lurked. She became more excited every day searching and listening for any information about the rights for women. After two months of wandering around, and money beginning to diminish, she knew a job was imperative. One day she noticed a street boy's newspaper headline on his board stating, "Suffragettes an embarrassment to the government." She bought a copy and read it avidly learning that a demonstration was being organized for Thursday at The Wharf. Suffragettes would lobby the Houses of Parliament and would welcome anyone who would like to come along and support. Taking in every syllable of every word, she read the article over and over, even so, the more she read the more she was puzzled by the meeting place. She asked herself, how could you lobby the Houses of

Parliament from The Wharf? Nevertheless, she was aware that this was her opportunity to acquaint herself with the kind of lady and society she wanted to be part of. She decided she would make her way there first thing on Thursday morning, take a packed lunch with her and wait until the women turned up.

Thursday morning turned out to be cool but fine. She had got out of bed and looked through the window as the sun rose over Holborn. Had she been nearer the river she would have witnessed the sunrise creating a blinding golden reflection on the Thames. Full of excitement and expectation, she quickly washed and dressed and catered for the day ahead.

The City had already created a confusion of horse-drawn traffic, commerce and street traders, Anna, dressed in her purple long dress and her red boa around her neck, jauntily made her way to the Thames via the side streets. Emerging near Westminster Bridge she suddenly realized she didn't know which side of the Thames the Wharf was situated. There was a barrow boy just across the road shouting his wares and juggling three of his apples expertly above his flat cap. If anyone knew London and the Thames, surely he would, so she made her way to him and gave him a sweet smile as she approached. He stopped juggling and looked at her with some surprise.

'Hello, darlin' you're out early.'

'I'm on my way to a meeting.'

'Ah, ah. I ain't heard that one before. I bet it's not a séance.'

'I'm on my way to attend the Suffragette meeting, but I'm not sure which side of the Thames it is.'

'Cor blimey, they're all at it. I thought they were only up for votes.'

'I don't know what you mean.'

'Ne'er mind, luv. What can I sell you?'

Anna thought the man, who appeared to be in his middle twenties, a little cheeky, but his light-hearted tone, impressed her favourably. 'Nothing, thank you, but you may be able to direct me to The Wharf, if you know it.'

'If I know it? I was born wivin the sahnd of the old bow bells. The Wharf? These 'ere suffragettes, they going on a romantic cruise or somefink?'

Anna sighed at the silly remark. 'It's going to a demonstration.'

The barrow-boy wasn't amused by Anna's lack of humour. 'I'm not political, darlin' I'm a business man, but for you I'll give yuh directions free of charge; it's a bit of a jaunt, I warn yuh. Nah, cross over Westminster Bridge and turn left up river. Follow the river rahnd the bend until yuh see Blackfriars Bridge in the distance. About fifty yards before you get to Blackfriars you'll see The Wharf. What yuh do there is your business, darlin'.' He picked up an apple and threw it to her. 'Catch, a rosy apple for a pink peach. Look after yourself.'

Anna smiled at him with much pleasure. 'Thank you, if you're still here when I come back I'll see if I can afford some of your fine fruit.'

Half way across the Westminster Bridge she stopped and looked up the river, savouring an experience she never thought she'd have. She was staggered by the amount of activity on the water. There were numbers of paddle steamers belching smoke from their funnels and pushing great waves to the banks, barges apparently sliding along in silence with animated crews, and tens of small boats of different sizes manoeuvring and fighting the disturbed angry waters. Klaxons were hooting and men were shouting protests to no avail at inconsiderate sailors. She was convinced the Thames was as busy with maritime traffic as any London road was with the vehicles. The fumes from the boats soon got the better of Anna, so she went on her way.

Reaching the other side she followed the directions the barrow boy had given her and soon realized he had not been exaggerating when he'd told her it was "a bit of a jaunt." She walked on for what seemed to be a mile before she came in sight of Blackfriars Bridge. Her heart gave a nervous bump when her eyes focused on a group of women some distance beyond the wharf. They appeared to be standing at a jetty, carrying banners and calling loudly; they were so noisy their verbal protests could be heard above the river traffic. It soon became obvious to Anna they were using loud hailers. As she neared them the slogans they carried became quite clear, and she realized they were calling out in unison, "We demand votes for women." When she reached them she could see they were a group of twenty or more of mixed classes, but mostly elegant ladies attired beautifully in a variety of heal-long dresses of various colours. The loud hailers rang out and the banners were lifted up and down energetically. Some loafers, a safe distance away, sat on unused upturned boats grinning, while others, standing, waved with derisory gestures, but the ladies were completely oblivious to them. Anna bravely joined them and mingled, getting caught up in the excitement and then bursting with a scream she yelled, 'We demand votes for women. We demand votes for women.' This went on for a time until a small boat pulled up to the jetty. A deafening cheer erupted when they saw the transport. It was then a graceful lady who had been screaming through her loud hailer, and who appeared to be in her thirties, turned to Anna with some surprise.

'Pardon me, my dear, but are you a member of our group?' she asked Anna with a cultured but hoarse voice.

Anna, flushed and excited, was taken aback for a second but soon recovered. 'I certainly would like to be a part of your protest. I feel the same as you do when it comes to women having the vote.

'Ah, you are new to our cause. Are your convictions so profound and dedicated that you are prepared to make great sacrifices?'

'I think I am.'

'Think? Think? Dear Lord, you must be decidedly positive.'

'Anna called out loud. 'I am decidedly positive.'

'That's the spirit. What is your name?'

'Anna.'

'Hannah. A wonderful scriptural name who is a heroine of history and the mother of Samuel.'

'No. Not Hannah…

'Marjorie, Marjorie,' the lady called. A word please.'

A rather stout lady dressed all in white and clutching a loud hailer came pushing through the crowd of suffragettes. 'What is it, Felicity?

'We have a new member here; Hannah is her name, and a beautiful name it is. Do you think we have room for her on the boat?'

Marjorie offered her hand and Anna eagerly accepted. 'How are you, my dear?' she asked in a deep voice, giving Anna a thorough inspection.

'I'm very well, thank you.'

'You look a little ashen to me. Forgive me for being forthright and blunt, but I can take it that you are not a government spy, by any chance, are you?'

'Certainly not,' said Anna,' defiantly. 'I came from south Wales few weeks ago to join your cause.'

'Ah, you are Welsh. Sorry to give you a ribbing my dear but we cannot be too careful. Well as you have come so far I can safely take you on board, so to speak. Have you a banner or hailer?'

'No, I haven't had chance to organize myself that way.'

'Here, take my hailer and get on board. You'll have to look after her, Felicity.'

'I'll do that.'

'Well, welcome Hannah, and I want to hear you screaming abuse at the politicians when we near The House.'

Anna wanted to correct the two ladies concerning the mistaken spelling of her name, but she thought it not important. Besides, Hannah sounded much more in keeping with the society she had joined. They all pushed forward and precariously stepped on to the small steamboat that puffed out black smoke from its little funnel. On the way down river they clung to the handrail for dear life as the wash of the big paddleboats buffeted the sides of the boat mercilessly. The captain had had his orders to cross towards Parliament as and when he could. Nearing the Houses of Parliament Marjorie yelled out.

'At the ready ladies; hailers to your feminine lips, banners held high. I want to hear your thunder and see the windows crack from your vehemence. Hannah, use that hailer with all the volume you can muster.'

Passing The House there erupted in a clamour of screaming and wailing, swearing and damnations of all politicians. Through the howling of the loud hailers could be heard the disrespectful condemnation of the "hypocrites of Westminster, chauvinist pigs hiding behind locked doors, the bigoted brutes of power, we demand votes for women, votes for women, votes for women." In the middle of them was Anna, red in the face, lips pressed hard against her loud hailer, yelling as loud as her vocal cords could possibly stretch. The tumult was maintained until the river turned a curve and took the boat of protest out of sight of Parliament. On reaching a calmer stretch of bank, they alighted and peacefully settled on the grassy area in small groups some distance away from the Thames. Marjorie thanked the captain of the small boat and waved as it chugged away down river, calling, 'See you later'. Anna settled with Felicity and was shortly joined by Marjorie and a couple of other protesters. Sitting quietly on small rugs they brought with them, they opened bags and brought out modest parcels of food and bottles of soft drinks. As they enjoyed their lunch, Marjorie introduced Anna to the other groups in between bites of sandwiches. Some called welcome to her, others with full mouths raised their hands in recognition of the newcomer. Anna, at last, felt part of something worthwhile.

'Tell me, Hannah,' said Marjorie, taking off her hat and patting her shock of red hair, 'what did you think of the demonstration, and how did you feel?'

All eyes turned to the new recruit. Anna had cooled down, and to answer such a question in front of such an illustrious gathering made her feel nervous.

'I…I felt as though I achieved something; As though I did something worthwhile.'

'And so you did, my dear,' said Felicity.'

'You felt no shame?' asked Marjorie.

'Of course not; I…felt proud. Yes, I felt proud. Proud because as a woman I made myself heard to the right people for the first time in my life.'

'What do you mean, the right people.'

Well, I have made arguments back home to ordinary people stating that women are equal, but I was laughed down. But that was in pubs mostly. Today, I made my protest to top people and they couldn't answer back, that made me feel good.'

'So you've made your point back home, as well?'

'Oh yes, many times.'

'Good. Then I truly welcome you into our honourable campaign. I wasn't quite sure of you in the beginning, but now I trust you.'

Felicity turned to Anna. 'We accepted a lady with fine bearing and meticulous appearance into our group a few weeks ago. However it was not long before we discovered she was an informant who told of our movements and our forthcoming protests to the authorities.'

Anna nodded. I see. I understand. I promise you I am not an informant but very sincere in my convictions.'

'We can all see that now,' said Marjorie. 'Tell me, Hannah, do you have a slogan that underlines you contempt for the male domination of our lives?' Something we can use on a placard or of a graffiti nature.'

Anna pondered for a while. 'I've never thought about it. What sort of saying?'

'Women are expected to be teachers, governesses, sit on school boards, be mothers, run the homes etc. Some in higher classes manage a large domestic staff, and yet, they are not allowed to vote, even though several of their male staff is allowed the privilege. Now, you need a placard with a stinging caption.'

'I'm not very good…although if I was in charge of a large staff like you mention, I could write boldly, MY BUTLER CAN VOTE BUT I CAN'T.'

The ladies chuckled, finding it amusing but crude.

'Perhaps, Hannah, you should stick with the majority and just have, VOTES FOR WOMEN.'

Anna was disappointed. 'I know what I would say if I had enough room on the banner. I would quote from the New Testament.'

'Ah, of course, inspired by you biblical name, what would you say, Hannah?'

'Well, you know what hypocrites men are? I would quote the words of Jesus saying to his disciples: "Beware of the scribes which desire to walk in long robes, and love greetings in the markets, and the highest seats in the synagogues, and the chief rooms at feasts." Do you think they'd get the message?'

The gathering cheered loudly at Anna's quotations inspired Marjorie to place her arm around Anna's shoulder. 'Hannah, my dear girl, a truly wonderful passage, but we had better not get involved with religion at this stage. Maybe, just maybe, we will shake the conscience of the clergy with such quotes one day. Today, and tomorrow, we march on politicians. Now ladies, before we return to the shores of the Thames to catch our humble captain on his way back, I shall distribute the list of actions we will be taking for the next month.'

Marjorie dipped her hand into the large, deep pocket, inside her coat and pulled out a brown paper bag. She went round each suffragette in turn and gave a small sheet of paper. She came to Anna last and pressed an identical piece of paper in her hand. 'There are four locations where action will be taken, Anna. You may think this method a little bizarre but it is essential for the sake of security. Now you see why I had to be sure of you. Each lady present, with exception to you, is a leader of a larger group of suffragettes. What you experienced today is of small significance to what we are about to embark on in the immediate future. Today we were in tens, next year we will be in our hundreds.'

Anna looked at the list she had been given and gasped with astonishment. One of the items on the list was to chain oneself to the railings of Buckingham Palace.

'Are you up for it, Hannah?'

'Yes. Yes of course, but the last location on the list requires chains, where do I get the chains from?'

'Hush, girl, not so loud, and don't forget a lock; they can be bought quite easily.'

'How…how much will they cost?'

'Have you no money, Hannah?'

'Yes, I'll manage that.'

Felicity, looking on, and weighing up the general attire and mien of Anna, wasn't convinced she had money to spare. 'I have an extra set of lock and chains, Hannah. You do not have to worry about wasting your time and money on such things. Marjorie, let Hannah be part of my group, I think she may need looking after, we are throwing her in the deep end, you know.'

'Good idea. You join Felicity's group, Hannah.'

Anna gave a sigh of relief; her money must be kept for essentials. 'I'll be grateful to Felicity.'

'Don't be grateful, be delighted,' quipped Marjorie. And remember, the dates on the list must be memorized. We shall adjourn until after Christmas, but then, God willing, we will march on Buckingham Palace.'

Anna's stomach turned over. 'Buckingham Palace?' I...I am delighted.'

'Right, come ladies let us make our way back to our captain.'

Thirteen

A lonely Christmas was endured with expectations of adventures when Yuletide would be over. Although she had many a sleepless night, pictures of the weeks and months to come striking blow after blow for the suffragette movement rights was her sustenance. After the Christmas period there were to be protests every week on different days. The movement around London would mean that the authorities could not anticipate the Suffragette movements. Determined not to miss out on the New Year celebrations she had made her way to Trafalgar Square and got lost in the festivities. She enjoyed the many drinks offered to her and her eyes lit up with pleasure as the fireworks took over. January came and she had to steel herself once again for practical reasons. At the back of her mind was the worry that she had not found work, and that her money would only last a couple more months if she were really frugal with her purchases of food. Therefore, she resolved to count every penny before buying. The first week in January she had restless nights worrying about finances; sitting up in bed for long periods before snuggling in, but even then pestered by images of oncoming events and financial concerns. She would often get out of bed and make herself a cup of tea.

Rising late one morning after a few hours' sleep, she washed and dressed and decided to have a bite to eat at a snack bar up at Edgware Road. Then she would begin her search for a job. Outside she found the weather foggy and cold as she made her way to Edgware Road. Going through the side streets she came across a little café. She stopped there and had a cup of tea and a round of toast. Eating her toast and sipping her tea she watched the busy waitress coming and going with the orders. An idea crossed her mind: she wouldn't mind serving the customers until a teaching job came along. She might even get a few grateful tips from the customers. As she thought about it and watched the routine of the staff, she noticed a corpulent man, dressed in a black suit with a navy tie to match his blue shirt, appear occasionally and check that things were running smoothly. She had finished her light breakfast but lingered awaiting the return of the man. The next time he appeared, Ann stood up, smiled at him and made her way to the counter.

The man's dark eyes dropped to her ankles and slowly made their way up to her face, then gave half a smile in return.

'Excuse me,' she said, 'I was wondering if you have a vacancy for a waitress?'

'I do wish I had,' he said, brushing his thin black moustache with his index finger. 'It would make a welcome change to have a beauty like you prancing about.'

Anna was about to turn to go when he caught hold of her arm. 'Don't rush off, girl,' he said with and oily tone and a smirk on his face. 'I have a feeling that if you come back tomorrow morning one of the staff may have left. You'd be treated most generously as an employee of this successful restaurant.'

Anna gave him a chilly glare and slowly removed his hand from her arm. With a cold but calculated voice she said, 'I'm looking for a job not a bed. Thanks all the same.'

'Ah well, you win some and your lose some.'

Outside she felt she had let herself down by begging to the lecherous toad. She shook herself in a shiver realising what she could have let herself in for. At least the food refreshed her and she was soon on her way to Edgware Road. Walking up Edgware she kept a keen eye on the buildings hoping to see some kind of agency that had a register of employers. She paced up and down both sides but found nothing relevant to her cause. She turned into George Street and passed through into the Crawford area. There, in a busy broad street, she saw a brass plate at the side of a black door stating Representative of Private Employers. The door led immediately to a steep stairway, and she tentatively climbed the bare wooden steps. At the first landing there was a panelled door, the upper half being glazed with frosted glass. It read Brown and Brown Solicitors. Taking the next flight of stairs she came to another landing where she found an identical door but read, Employment Agency. Knocking quietly, she heard a female voice telling her to come in.

104

Inside, a middle-aged lady sitting behind a cluttered desk dressed in a lilac blouse and wearing black spectacles greeted her but didn't look up. She was busily writing. She gestured to Anna with a raised agitated finger to sit on a vacant chair. Anna sat obediently.

'Be with you in a moment.'

'That's all right,' said Anna. She didn't feel intimidated for the women was moderately dressed with some cheap sparkling pins keeping her greying hair rolled up around her head like the rim of a sombrero. Whilst the woman kept writing, Anna scanned the room and was impressed by the shelves of files around the walls, some in dark corners, others illuminated by the net-curtained window that overlooked the street. Then she checked herself as the woman looked up and lowered her glasses on her rather long pointed nose.

'Name?'

Anna was taken aback by the brusque question. 'Anna Hughes.'

'Address?'

Anna suddenly became alarmed, realising she hadn't made a note of her lodgings. 'I don't know the exact address. I haven't lodged there long, but I know my way there and back.'

The woman's grey eyes stared at Anna and a snort of impatience emitted from her nostrils. 'I cannot register you if you have no address.'

'I do have an address, but I've been stupid by not realising the importance of writing it down. It's in a side street just past Baker Street.'

The woman cupped her hands in her chin and leaned on the desk. 'Where have you come from, may I ask? Originally, of course, not ten minutes ago.'

'South Wales; an industrial town called Dowlais—Merthyr Tydfil,' she added quickly, thinking Merthyr may be better known.

'Right, let us ascertain your ambitions before we go any further, what kind of work are you looking for?'

'I'd like a teaching position.'

The lady sat up and opened a large black register and held a poised pen in her hand. 'Qualifications?'

Anna was becoming increasingly nervous. 'I…I haven't passed any examinations, if that's what you mean.'

She dropped her pen on the desk. 'Can you play the piano?'

Anna's head fell forward. 'I'm sorry, no.'

'Can you speak French?'

In a whisper, 'No.'

'Latin?'

'No.'

'Did you attend a private school or go to university?'

Anna searched her brain for something she could impress with. Her education came from the workhouse and her foster parents, but she could teach. She knew that. She could teach. Her foster father taught her privately; he was a teacher of religion. 'Yes,' she answered. 'I had a private tutor.'

'But not at a private school.'

'No. But I am well versed in English, I am competent in mathematics and religion, I'm quite capable of teaching children of a young age.'

'My dear,' she said with a softening voice. 'If I should include you in my register as a teacher, my employer, who is in the room behind me, would dismiss me for incompetence. Now there are certain people who have connections in society and who do favours for the unqualified, talented, pretty young ladies. However, they eventually end up in sordid little jobs with poor pay and conditions. I suggest most strongly that you lower your ambitions and seek employment in category more suited to your station: Perhaps a position in the domestic sphere such as a maid, a waitress, or a chambermaid in the house of the gentry. I may be able to assign you to such and occupation, but teaching, I'm afraid is impossible. Have you any references?'

'No. I heard there were schools that would take me on as an assistant to a headmaster or teacher.'

'They are usually schools of ill repute and poor wages that you might find in run-down districts. You would be expected to work fourteen hours a day doing little teaching, but lots of soul-destroying chores. Why on earth did you come to London to work? Was there no such jobs back in south Wales?'

'I wanted more than a job. I also wanted to give support to the suffragette movement.'

106

The woman gasped with shock. 'I suggest most strongly that you keep that ambition to yourself. You will not find anybody willing to employ a suffragette even if you had a university degree. I'm afraid you are showing a naivety that goes beyond the bounds of credibility. Now listen, you have two options, either you go back to Wales, where you may or may not succeed in finding a teaching job, or you allow me to find you modest employment somewhere in the vicinity of your lodgings. That will be difficult enough. Now, tell me what work experience you have so that I may assess you.'

Anna kept looking at the face of the woman wondering if she were a friend or foe. She could only see the paleness of an office-bound woman with creases in her face, but a mixture of sadness and honesty in her eyes. She sighed with an air of defeat.

'I have only worked in a public house serving behind the bar. I've done a little housework: cleaning, washing and ironing and that's all of my working experience.'

'I was under the impression that the industrial south was a place where employment was an easy target for anyone who wished to travel there.'

Anna could feel her blood rising. 'I could humiliate myself digging down a drift mine, or suffer the indignity of working in a pub serving beer and cleaning out spittoons, scrubbing floors...or I could become a mistress of an ironmaster... '

Right, right, I see your dilemma. I can understand your wanting to make something of yourself. I suggest you go back to your lodgings, make a note of the address and the name of your landlord and return here in a week or so. I will see if I can find a private family who needs a nanny, or a companion for a young child who needs to be taught writing, reading and arithmetic. The odds, I'm afraid, are against you, for piano playing is very popular with parents, but that's the best I can do.'

Anna stood, thanked the lady and walked dejectedly out of the office.

Outside there was much activity as people were rushing around and calling to one another. She observed many women breaking down in tears as the news spread. Desperately wanting to know what it was all about she stopped a man in the street and asked him what all the excitement was about.

'Haven't you heard, girl? The Queen is dead, long live the King.'

'Oh. Yes, look after the King. I hope he's qualified for his new job.'

'Oh he won't be as good as Victoria. She`s done us proud, Empress of India and all our lands abroad,' the man said with a tear in his eyes, then he ran off.

Fourteen

She turned the corner from Oxford Street into Regent Street, hurrying but trying not to be conspicuous, her hat in her hand. She had donned her oldest clothes for the occasion; her black skirt had lost its darkness, her white blouse clean but greying and her shoes scuffed at the sides. Having had no response from the Employment Agency for three months, she had found a generous friend in Felicity who always made sure Anna always had financial support without any commitments for reimbursement. The demonstration on Buckingham Palace had been respectfully postponed for a later date. However, since then her time had been spent breaking the law with hundreds of Suffragettes, aiding and abetting with a number of illegal acts. She and her colleagues had set fire to church buildings because the Church of England did not recognize the aims of the Suffragettes. They had shouted abuse at MPs outside the Houses of Parliament and attacked politicians as they went to work. Each time she narrowly managed to escape the law with the group she had been with at the time. But now, she was devastated knowing one of her close friends had apparently been apprehended. Her face was red from exertion and the adrenaline was pumping through her body after hurling stones through the windows of Oxford Street and running off. The police had come and the Suffragettes had scattered in all directions. She had escaped with Felicity and Miranda but Felicity had disappeared, and she'd lost Miranda half way down Oxford Street when Miranda could not keep up with her. Anna had briefly turned around and saw her disappear down an alley. She couldn't stop to follow for there was a constable running after them. Fortunately for Anna, but unhappily for Miranda, the policeman turned down the alley in pursuit of her friend.

Anna slowed down believing she was in the clear and sat on a bench in Regent Street catching her breath. The street had many shoppers, vendors and horse-drawn traffic, giving her some semblance of cover as she attempted to adopt a nonchalant attitude. She used her hat as a fan giving her a cool airflow on the warm April day. Looking furtively up and down the road she saw nothing to suggest she had been followed. It was then she realized how close she had come to being arrested. Her stomach turned over from the thought of being manhandled by the "government's lackeys" and dragged into a police horse-drawn security van. She pictured the probability of fifty-year-old Miranda, breathless and exhausted collapsing into the arms of the law in a grimy alleyway. Anna bent her head and almost broke into tears for her friend, but steeled herself as a resolute and stout-hearted Suffragette. No, she would not be weakened into tears, for that is how the male opposition would like to see a woman; frightened and wanting protection. It was then she felt someone sit beside her. She didn't look up for fear she would give herself away. But it was a gentle, quiet voice that asked: 'Are you all right, Hannah, my dear?'

She turned to the soft voice knowing it was Felicity who sat at her side. The delicate but pale complexion of Felicity had an understanding expression on her refined face. She reached out her hand and clasped Anna's. 'You were lucky again this time, Hannah. You look exhausted. Do you think it is time you rested for a week or so?'

'I musn't give up, Felicity. I don't know what's happened to Miranda. She disappeared down a narrow street with the police chasing her.'

'She has been caught, unfortunately. Poor Miranda, she is such a fervent follower, but too reckless and careless. You will also be caught if you should pursue these extremities of actions.'

Anna looked into Felicity's eyes with confusion. 'How can you say that? You do the same things as we do?'

'No Hannah, I am not an advocate of violence. It is true I accompany you on all the demonstrations, but I do not partake in any of the aggressive activities. I never have. Marjorie, Miranda and all my close Suffragettes know of my passive methods, and accept my principles.' Felicity lowered her head and whispered into the ear of Anna. 'You know the postponed demonstration at the palace has been rearranged for next week? Well I shall chain myself to the railings in peaceful protest with the rest of our followers. I shall allow myself to be cut free by the authorities, but I shall not strike out at anyone.'

Anna was silent for a time, thinking. Eventually she responded to Felicity. 'I hadn't noticed your peaceful protests. I suppose I was too engrossed in my violent ways.'

'Don't take it personally, my dear. I admire all you are doing. The fact is, I'm not cut out for violence. I was never one to accept a rough challenge, even when I was in school. It is not because I am a coward. It is because I do not believe in violence.'

Anna could only smile at the gentleness of her friend. She was a friend who had always treated her with respect and equality; a friend who had seen through her poverty without saying a word to the others.'

'I suppose I have bitterness in my soul. I get excited and vengeful, I know that, but I can't help it. You see, I haven't had a life like you, Felicity. I had a bad start in life which I can't seem to shake off.'

'I know, my dear, and it has not gone unnoticed by me. Hannah, I do not wish to be patronizing, but I can afford to give you a little money to help you through.'

Anna's emotions welled up and there was a tear in her eyes. 'You are a true friend, Felicity, but I wanted very much to stand on my own two feet and not be owing to anybody. But it's true, I have only a few shillings left and the rent is due at my lodgings.'

Felicity pulled the strings of her black purse apart and placed her hand inside. She pulled out some money and handed it to Anna. 'I am quite well off Hannah and I do not require repayment. However, if your principles will not be satisfied unless your believe it to be a debt that needs to be settled, then take as much time as you like. But please be logical about it, the money is yours to keep.'

'I don't need all that, Felicity.'

'Take it, it is yours. You do not need to spend it all on rent, treat yourself to some clothes and adornments to make you feel good.'

'You're very kind, Felicity, I won't forget you as long as I live.'

'And you shall have a place in my heart. There are some who join our group because they enjoy the excitement and thrill of adventure, but have no interest in gaining equality or achieving the vote. When the protest is over, they go home and we see no more of them. I have observed Hannah that you fight and argue for these things whether you are on a protest march or in the quiet of our company. For that, I hold you in great esteem for your sincerity shines like a beacon. I pray to Jesus for your safety.'

Anna looked at Felicity with some surprise. She had not heard her talk religiously before.

'You pray to Jesus?'

'I am reluctant to air my views in the company of many as it sometimes encourages ridicule. But to those whom I believe can understand my convictions, I am quite open. I am sure, Hannah, that you are one who understands.'

'I feel very close to you. You are a true friend. I have had a strict teaching of the Bible, and, I'm sorry to say, I find the stories and the experiences of the Israelites in the Bible hard to believe. But I respect your beliefs whole heartedly and would never make fun of you.'

'I am a Christian, Anna, not an Israelite. The Old Testament is full of myths and legends that can be hard to swallow. The New Testament has not been disproved. I only have one hero in history, and He is Jesus, for He is the only one who teaches me love—I see from the corner of my eye there are two policemen walking down the road. Fold your arm through mine my dear and we shall walk slowly down Regent Street and enjoy the pleasant day.'

Anna stood with much perplexity but obeyed the soft powerful words of Felicity.

Fifteen

The dawn was breaking through light clouds when the women came from many directions carrying banners and chains muffled in cloth bags. It was imperative they did nothing to alert the police before they were in position. Their shoes were soft and modest to give as little noise as possible. They came in twos and threes, groups of fives and tens; they came from Marylbone, Mayfair, Bloomsbury, Holborn and Lambeth, within the sound of bow bells and outside the sound of bow bells. Some came from Maida Vale, Knightsbridge and many small areas too many to mention. They obediently walked speechless and whispered only when dialogue was necessary. Occasionally there was a quiet chinking sound when someone carelessly allowed her chain to become loose from her cloth bag. Anna came alone but met up with Felicity and her group at the arranged meeting place in Green Park. From there the hundred or so Suffragettes marched as quietly as they could until they reached the formidable iron railings that protected the front grounds of Buckingham Palace. As they took up their places along the railings and secured the chains, chatter was then permitted; chatter that became louder as chain after chain was secured to the ironwork. As the light got stronger and the sun rose higher, the excitement began to grow among them until they could hold their emotions no longer. One began to call for the freedom to vote, and then another and another, until the freedom to vote became a chorus and wooden stakes that held the banners cracked with force on the royal metalwork. Crowds began to gather in a mixture of ages and gender from school children to pensioners, from tourists to locals, from beggars to the society sections of the capital. Some onlookers cheered in support, others jeered with derision. Soon the word had reached the police and the horse-drawn vans of the central emergency yard came galloping through the streets to the sounds of equine neighing, whips cracking and drivers yelling. They broke through the crowds scattering innocent people in all directions, evoking curses of damnation from those who got injured and loud boos from those who chose to show defiant fists.

The sudden presence of the police inspired the Suffragettes to shout their slogan, in unison and repetitiously as loud as their voices could reach, Votes for Women, Votes for Women. Within them there was a festering frustration and enormous tension that exploded into bombardment of verbal abuse at the police. The crowd began to challenge the unnecessary severity of the police action by yelling any crude expletive that came to mind, for the protectors of the law grabbed the women tightly by their arms and tugged at them as though they could rip them from their chains by sheer force. The Suffragettes screamed and protested by kicking at the enemy. Metal saws were brought from the police vehicles and the women were being cut free unceremoniously and taken to the vans. Women in the crowd came forward in support of the Suffragettes and were given the same treatment. Felicity remained calm as she waited for her turn to be freed. When she had, she made no attempt to protest, but merely stood up, straightened her back, thanked the policeman and walked calmly away. Anna, however, had worked herself up into a frenzy. All the bitterness of her past erupted with vehemence. She kicked and spat at her official escort breaking away several times only to be brought down by an officer diving at her legs. It took four policemen to take her to the van as her violent outburst included kicking bruising and injuring the arresting officers; officers who strained and gasped and eventually bundled her into the police van. The Suffragettes were separated into groups and driven to several different police stations. Anna's group ended up in a nearby station where the women were roughly pushed on to wooden benches in front of a senior officer. The officer was steely-eyed and with an intolerant expression, spat out the charges of assaulting an officer, affray, causing a disturbance and inciting a riot. The Suffragettes, surrounded by a host of constables, hissed at the charges and continued to call out their slogan until they were manhandled into the crowded cells. Anna, looked around for Felicity, finally realized she had lost her friend to another part of the city and at a different police station. She sat in a corner in the cell that smelled strongly from a mixture of perspiration and a multiple array of stale

114

cosmetics emitting from the exasperated women. They were given nothing for hours, but eventually offered the mandatory rations to keep them fit and healthy. The majority refused these survival tokens of sustenance because the Suffragettes leaders and their followers had agreed to undergo a hunger strike if jailed. When exhaustion took over they slept as well as they could, sitting on the cold hard floor.

Many awakened early in the morning, others who had previous experience remained slumbering knowing nothing would be done until the police had prepared their case against the offenders. Then they would be taken to the court and sentenced. Anna had sat up all night drifting in and out of semi-consciousness feeling bruised and aching in every limb. Squeezed against Suffragettes either side of her there was little room to move, the musty, humid atmosphere sickening her. The woman on her right roused and, with difficulty, stretched her slender arms up in the air, then dropped them on her bent-up knees. She turned to Anna and noted the sadness on her face.

'Are you all right, lass?' she asked, brusquely.

Anna looked at the fair, untidy hair of the woman, automatically guessing her age at thirty-something. She could see by the smudges on the woman's chin that her lipstick had been crimson.

'I'm as right as the rest of this motley lot. How can anyone be all right in a stinking cell?'

'You'll get used to it. Don't let them get to you.'

'Don't worry, they won't get me down.

'That's the spirit, darlin'. If they see a weakness in you, they'll play on it.'

'I've got no weaknesses.'

My, my, you are a strong girl, aren't you?'

Anna looked at her closely and changed her mind about her age. She had many lines in her face for a woman who she had estimated at thirty. 'Are you a Suffragette?'

'Sometimes.'

'Sometimes? You're either a Suffragette or not.'

'It's according to my luck at the time, dearie. It ain't been very good lately. No customers if you see what I mean; got a little hungry, saw the opportunity to have free grub and lodgings for the night, jumped on the band wagon so to speak.' She then turned from Anna and began to talk to her other neighbour who appeared to be one of the same.

The woman on the other side of Anna nudged her and whispered. 'Woman of the street, dear, ignore her. We get quite a few of those at times; unsavoury lot.'

'She must have been desperate to want to spend a night in this place.'

'Probably a palace to what she is used to. Some of her kind don't survive the night, you know; either die of heartbreak, suicide, or even get murdered. I take it you are a fellow Suffragette? The work fellow intended metaphorically of course.'

'I am. And a lady like you, I should add.'

'Lady in lower case, I take it.'

'I don't understand.'

'Oh come, dear, I'm not a lady, I'm merely a respectable woman who believes in equality for the female gender.'

Anna looked with some surprise at her. 'Well, I believe in equality for women, too, but I also look upon myself as a lady.'

'Oh, you do surprise me. Please do not be offended, but I was under the impression by the lilt in your voice that, perhaps, you were from one of the regions of the Celts; Welsh, perhaps, and among the proletariat of that beautiful country.'

'Are you making fun of me?'

'No, no dear, please, I am only setting out the class of gentry to which you claim to be part of. I intend no offence, I assure you.'

Anna was disturbed by the sudden increase in volume of chatter from the women as they roused and began to exchange their experiences of their arrests. However, she was intrigued by the woman's language and her confession that she was something lower than a lady, as well as intimating that Anna was the same.

'In my world,' said Anna, 'you're either a lady or you're not.'

'No, no, no. You do not seem to grasp the social divisions of the situation. You cannot design yourself into a Lady when born a commoner. And when a person is born into the social class of

Ladies and Gentlemen, they will always have those titles. Would you class yourself as a princess?'

'Of course not.'

'That is because you were not born into royalty. You See?'

'I don't claim to be aristocratic, but I am a lady—with or without a capital L.'

'Right my dear. Let us leave the discussion there. Incidentally, what is your name?'

'Anna.'

'My name is Pricilla,' said the women, holding out her hand of friendship. 'I can see that you are a true Suffragette by the way you refused food, and in that vein, we are equal, for you may have observed that I too, did not partake.'

'I did notice,' said Anna, shaking the woman's hand gently. 'Sorry if I sounded a bit abrupt.'

'Understandable under the circumstances, let us be friends. We will need the company and moral support of each other when we are convicted and moved to prison.'

'Do you think we'll be convicted?'

'Most certainly; I have experience in these matters. But do not fret. We shall comfort each other and pray together in times of great need.'

Anna dropped her head and felt she would have liked to pray, if the image of her austere and bigoted stepfather did not cross her mind every time religion was mentioned. She wondered if there was anyone there who could give her strength. If only she could believe, she may feel she belonged somewhere.

Sixteen

Anna was numb with shock in the crowded police van as it bumped along with a dozen other Suffragettes. The decisions of the courts had varied; those bystanders who aided and abetted were shown leniency and given only official warnings. But others who were found guilty of more serious offences had custodial sentences that ranged from a week to six months according to the severity of their actions. Those who were responsible for organizing the demonstration, or assaulting the police, had longer sentences than those who merely chained themselves passively to the Palace railings. Anna was one, who resisted arrest, was punished with others to three months in Holloway. The judgement spawned hatred in her and she and other Suffragettes planned an immediate hunger strike as soon as they were in prison. The strategy was intended to make their stay as difficult as possible, and hoped to gain favourable publicity in the press.

As the van pulled up outside the castle-like prison the bedraggled prisoners were bundled out, screaming at their male escorts who were bullying them along. They were led in single file to the arched entrance where the wooden door opened. A piercing scream suddenly cut the air when one of the prisoners lost all composure and tried to escape. She was easily overpowered and dragged by two escorts through the open door.

Inside the women were soon silenced by the orders of the wardresses. Anna, like the others, was locked in a reception cell. After being examined by the doctor, she was searched to ensure she concealed nothing. Taken to another room she stood before a female prison official; a stout woman dressed in dark clothes with a severe face, and high cheekbones, sitting behind a great polished desk. Her cavernous black eyes peered at Anna with contempt. Standing behind the formidable woman, keeping a close eye on Anna, was another wardress staring at her.

'Name?'

Anna, defiant and indignant didn't answer for seconds but then replied abruptly, 'Anna Hughes.'

'Age?'

'Twenty three.'

'Address?'

'21 Andover Street, Holborn.'

'Religion?'

'Atheist.'

'What? What did you say?'

'I said I'm an atheist.'

'You're a devil, that's what you are. You'll burn in hell, girl.'

'I'm in hell, where's the fire?'

'You're making life hard for yourself, girl, don't be brazen.'

'I've had nothing but hardship all my life, and why? Because of inequality, that's why. Women are equal to men and you're a disgrace to your sex.'

'I shouldn't be saying this, but I do have sympathy with your cause but you're going about it in the wrong manner. '

'Know them by their fruits.'

The woman was surprised at the New Testament quotation. 'I believe that is taken from the Bible.'

'My mother's Christian advice.'

'And you're an atheist?'

'Maybe. Maybe agnostic, maybe a believer. What's the difference? We're all making each-way bets; sitting on the fence, let's go to church just in case there is a hereafter. But "you can't serve two masters." I serve no master, it's less hypocritical.'

The wardress lost patience. 'Profession?'

'Suffragette.'

'Don't be ridiculous, that's not a profession. Now give me a proper answer or you'll go straight into solitary confinement.'

'I'm unemployed.'

'Can you read and write?'

'Don't you be ridiculous, of course I can.'

'Can you sew?'

Anna squinted her eyes at the woman. 'Yes, I can sew,' she said reluctantly. 'But I'm not going to slave for this place.'

The interviewer stood up and turned to her colleague. 'Take her away and make sure she has a bath.'

Anna was marched through a corridor and into a room that held a row of cubicles each having a bath. The room was reverberating with grumbling and the splashing of water from Suffragettes who had already undergone the interview. There was a medical smell from the dark brown common soap that the women were given. Two wardresses walked up and down outside the area looking over the row of low doors inspecting the bathing prisoners. In the middle of the passageway at the front of the cubicles was a pile of clothes.

The wardress who had ushered Anna there said nothing until they had reached the bathhouse and located a vacant bath. It was then she barked out the orders with a hoarse asthmatic voice.

'Undress and bath yourself thoroughly. When you're clean you can pick some clothes from that pile.' She pointed to the clothes. 'You have been designated as a third class prisoner. Therefore you'll wear a brown dress. The green are for the second-class prisoners.'

Anna was startled. 'I can where my own clothes.'

'You'll not see your clothes again until you leave here. Now do as you're told or you'll be scrubbed by me and another.'

'And who are they who have the privilege to be first class prisoners?'

'We have no first class prisoners here.'

There was growing contempt within Anna but she knew she could not take on the warders. Inside the cubicle she undressed and handed her bundle to the woman without another word. After she had bathed, watched occasionally by the wardress, she went to the pile of clothes and donned course underclothes and a brown serge dress. The shoes were ill fitting and heavy. Like the others, she was given a white cap, blue apron and a large handkerchief. On the clothes, in contrasting colours, were large broad arrows. They were also given shapeless stocking with red hoops. They were given nothing to keep the stocking up. When she and the others were taken to their cells, they were given bed sheets, toothbrush, a Bible, prayer book and a hymn book. They were also given a book on cleanliness. In the cell she was given a badge bearing the cell

120

number, a number that was to become her name for the rest of her duration in prison; her name: number SG113.

The days went by slowly and SG113 sat in her solitary cell and dreamt of her release, refused food but sipped water to prevent dehydration. The terrifying screams of those who were being force-fed haunted her through day and night. She was getting weaker and dreaded the day they would come to her. She would push her fingers in her ears, but the strident screaming penetrated just the same. Sleeping was almost impossible, for her mind wandered and fretted. When exhaustion finally put her to sleep, it was just a couple of hours before the five-thirty bell rattled its raucous tone through Camden Castle—pet name for Holloway. One day, she could not tell which, but it was some time into her sentence, she suddenly found herself quoting the New Testament loudly. It gave her some kind of power; a resistance against authority. She found comfort in the knowledge that there had been many in history who suffered greater than her and could still believe in God. Is that what belief is all about? She asked herself—suffering. She answered herself: No, believing in God gives me the strength of an irresistible force to deny the dictatorship of civilization. 'I believe in God but not the churches,' she called out. She sat down on her three planks of wood that was her bed and took her mind back to the workhouse where her mother used to nurse and hum hymns to her. To a later time when she waited for her mother to come to her after slaving twelve hours scrubbing floors. She had Images of looking out of windows seeing men breaking stones in the workhouse yard, the sledge-hammer cracking the rocks and the granite splinters spitting through the dust: The monotony of the prayers every morning asking God to take pity on them for their sins. 'What had we done? We were deserted. I thought nothing could get worse, Lord, but the screaming of these poor women in this place; the agony of their torture, the degradation--' NoSG113 looked at her locked cell door, for she heard the key turning. The door opened slowly, three wardresses came in. One carried a bucket another carried tubes and a third carried a bottle of green liquid.

'No! No! I will not be force fed,' she screamed. 'Get out of here, you animals.'

The wardresses easily overpowered her. One forced her mouth open; another held her legs whilst the third callously forced the tube down her throat. She gurgled, coughed and kicked but she could not prevent the tube scraping her tender flesh. Her body convulsed and heaved trying to vomit up the tube, but it was held tightly as the brown liquid was poured down through the funnel attached to the tube. The torture lasted for ten minutes until the last drop of the foul sustenance had gone. Already weakened by her days of voluntary starvation, she collapsed as the tube was withdrawn.

'No SG113, when you have digested your food, slop out your bucket, make your bed and tidy up your room,' was the last words the wardress said to her before slamming the cell door.'

Anna laid there her throat burning, her stomach heavy and her head throbbing. Though weakened, she struggled to the floor and held her head over her slop bucked. There, she forced her fingers down her painful gullet and brought up the disgusting meal. This she did as often as they force-fed her, her body deteriorating, her mind regressive, her spirit constant, until the day the prison officials concluded that the treatment was doing more harm than good. The new policy was to let them starve, but release them before they died. If they want to die, let them do so on the outside.

Seventeen

Five prisoners were released the same day as Anna, all weak and disorientated after being ejected for not consuming their food. Those who accepted the daily prison rations, and still inside, were given a pint of sweet tea, a small brown loaf and two ounces of butter. But Anna had been resolute in her protest and maintained her struggle against the tormentors until they'd given up. She was victorious in her stand, yet dispirited and lacking confidence, for her physical weakness had taken its toll on all senses. It was not just the hunger strike that took away her strength, it was the struggle trying to prevent the force feeding; the violent twisting of her head as she turned away from the tube, the heavy hands on her wrists, the pulling of her legs as they prevented her from bending her knees. All this pressure day after day made her an exhausted weakling. She walked in the drizzling rain across the outside of the prison appreciating the coolness of the gentle shower, her mind wandering and wondering would she make it to her lodgings. Ten weeks and three days she had served before the authorities finally concluded she'd be hailed as a martyr if she should die in the custody of the law.

She lifted her tired head and peered through dark-rimmed eyes at her fellow prisoners, some of which had friends or family meeting them. She had nobody. But reconciled to the knowledge it had been her choice to escape small-town drudgery and seek a life in a higher society. She knew being alone would be part of her quest until her time came. She'd fitted into a stylish group of people, now she wondered of her station in life; a lowly individual. The grave of her mother flashed across her mind, remembering the scene. She'd knelt on that bare piece of soil, void of gravestone and flowers, that she would have an ornate headstone made in her honour or die in the attempt to be a lady. And that Suffragette, who without malice but rationally, had called her a commoner, had spoken candidly. The truth was hitting home. However much her education and foster upbringing had benefited her, she was still a commoner. She flopped down on a low wall with her back arched forward facing the ground. She took little notice of the busy traffic nor was she aware of the hubbub of daily life. It was all a hum in the distance. She was unresponsive to the trotting of a horse that stopped at the kerbside. She was too tired to raise her head, but then a voice called out.

'Hannah. Hannah my dear.'

An arm around her shoulder.

'Hannah, what have they done to you? You poor, poor darling.'

The pronunciation of the aitch and the soft voice she'd come to know so well; that delicate compassionate voice of her friend. She strained her neck and looked up. 'Felicity?' she whispered. 'Oh Felicity, is it really you?'

Felicity, dressed in a cream ankle-length dress covered by a white three-quarter length raincoat and pink flowers in her hat, appeared to Anna like an angel.

'Let me help you. This drizzle will penetrate you clothes. I have a hansom standing by. I'll take you to your lodgings. You are far too weak to make it alone. Don't worry, I'll get you fit and well again.'

She struggled to her feet with the help of Felicity. 'You're a kind lady, Felicity. Where would I be without you? God bless you.'

Inside the cab Felicity gave the instructions to the driver to make for Anna's lodgings. The horse trotted off as Felicity cradled Anna in her arms.

'Don't Felicity or I will cry, and I don't want that.'

'It is no shame to cry, Hannah. It will relieve some of the anger within you. Listen, I have brought with me a basket of food that will help you gain your strength. I have tea, bread, cheese eggs, fruit; everything you need to bring you back to health. You must not overdo it, however, for eating too much at one serving will give you pain. I will not be able to come into your premises, as I must not be seen in the area. I shall wait in the cab until I see you safely through your door.'

'I don't know what I would do without you.'

'I will probably surprise you when I tell you I have given up my involvement with the Suffragette movement.' Anna attempted to sit up, but Felicity restrained her. 'Stay, my dear and let me explain. I am a pacifist and do not believe in violence. The Suffragette cause is an honourable one, but I cannot condone violence any longer. They are planning the burning of churches, and though I have restrained myself in the past to any such activity, I feel my very presence at such extremities would be mistaken for wholehearted support. Furthermore, I suggest you do the same as I, for it will be your downfall if you continue.'

Anna began to weep softly. 'Thank you for telling me, I want to leave it as well. I'm afraid I've given all I can give.'

'And you have borne it bravely and with great credit. You need not feel that you must do more. You have made me very happy to know that you will not be treated with such brutality again.'

Felicity suddenly realized Anna had slipped into a shallow sleep, so she said nothing more as they journeyed on to Holborn. On reaching Anna's lodgings, Felicity gently woke her. Anna sat up and looked around. Realising she had reached the building in which she lived, sadness overcame her. The thought of being in her sparse musty room meant loneliness again. It would be solitary confinement on a higher level.

'I'll see you again, won't I Felicity?'

'Of course you will. I shall send a messenger to arrange a meeting in a few days. I shall keep in touch with you, but I'm afraid it will have to be a meeting of some discretion.'

Anna did not understand why discretion had to come into their friendship, but she asked no questions knowing that Felicity knew best.

Felicity called the cabman to help Anna out of the hansom and instructed him to take the basket of food up to Anna's room. Having helped Anna onto the pavement he waited until she opened the side door. Being weak, she was unable to turn the mortise key, so the cabman offered to do it for her. He tried but failed. After several attempts, he realized the key did not fit.

'I'm sorry, but the key is not the one for this lock,' he told Anna.'

It was then the woman came out from the tailor's shop carrying Anna's humble suitcase and a few modest belongings of hers. 'Your room has been let, dearie. We don't want the police around here asking questions again. We're respectable around here, we are, and we don't want troublemakers.' She threw all of Anna's things on the pavement and marched back into the shop.

Felicity peeped out of the cab window. 'Cabbie, cabbie, bring the belongings in here. Hannah get back in cab, quickly.'

Once in the hansom they drove away, Anna in a confused stupor, Felicity thumping her clenched fist on the side of the seat.

'The gall of that woman, she is undoubtedly an inhuman feline.'

'Don't worry yourself, Felicity, you've done more than I expected from anybody, I'll find somewhere to live.'

'I fear not, my dear. I fear not. You'll perish in the attempt.—Hartnell,' she called to the cab driver.

The cabbie opened his trap door and pushed his thin features through. 'Yes, My Lady?'

'I told you not to call me that today. But you could redeem yourself greatly if you would just do me a kindly service.'

'Anything you say my…missus.'

'You can see the poor medical state of my acquaintance, would you and your good wife be so benevolent as to give her board and bed for a few days until I can arrange an alternative. I shall recompense you generously. You will not go without reward.'

'I dare say my wife would be grateful for the opportunity to help someone in need without reward, but if a monitory expense is offered to prepare the spare room she would be pleased about that, too.'

'Let us make our way to your home at full speed.' She turned to Anna. 'Hannah, my dear, I would love to take you to my home, however, domestic friction prevents my doing so.'

'You're a Lady, a real Lady,' Anna whispered. I didn't realize that, but I understand. You should not be seen with a commoner like me. I don't mean that as a complaint, I mean it sincerely. You've done so much for me and I appreciate all you've done. The last thing I want is to make life difficult for you. Please, let me find my own way, I won't to trouble you again.'

'Hannah, you are not a commoner. Be proud my dear for you are special. Now listen, I will see that you are made well again, and then I shall find you employment so that you can keep yourself from hardship. From then on I shall remain in the background but communicate with you to learn of your welfare. Hartnell will see you right for as long as it takes. He and his wife are good people, so you must not fret. He will take me home and then you will abode with he and his wife until you are well and fit for employment.'

'I am not qualified for employment. I am no use to anyone.'

'I will find you some menial job to begin with. I know you will work yourself up to a higher standard and a respectable situation. Now do not fret. You have earned yourself a better life.—Hartnell, take Hannah into your home and then return me to my premises.'

Eighteen

How grateful she was lying in the clean comfortable bed, the sun illuminating the brightly decorated bedroom of the Brown family. The relief was overpowering and tore at her emotions bringing tears of relief through the peace of the night. It seemed to Anna that Hartnell Brown and his wife Mary were the salt of the earth and treated her like one of the family. A couple whose children had grown to maturity and left home just a few years prior, having homes of their own not too far away. Near enough for them to visit with their grandchildren. The Browns were zealous in their sympathy with homeless Anna, almost to the point of servility, and gave her the same care and attention they would their own. They were recompensed generously by Felicity who used Hartnell as her private transport in a clandestine way, keeping her secret life hidden from her relations. Communications to Anna were made through written correspondence, Hartnell being the postman. After two weeks Anna, feeling she did not want to extend her stay or take advantage of all concerned, sent a message to Felicity saying she was feeling well and could be independent again. Felicity, however, new better and insisted she stay for another two weeks, stating her ordeal in Holloway would take longer to repair. Furthermore, the only employment Felicity could acquire for her was a job as a scullery maid, which would be strenuous work, but added the experience would lead her to higher positions in the society of domestic service. Anna had no choice but to accept the lowly position and put her trust in the wisdom of her aristocratic friend and benefactor. During the time Anna lodged with the Browns she became attached to the family and to the grandchildren, and although she felt she had never been so comfortable and secure, she had to tear herself away and find another path in life. Besides, there was something surreal about the situation; it was as though she was in some kind of drama production and everything was being acted out. The day came when Felicity called to take Anna to her new position. Felicity waited in the hansom while Hartnell escorted Anna to the cab and helped her in, placing her suitcase on the floor.

It was an emotional moment as Felicity put her arm around Anna's shoulder and gave her a reassuring hug. Anna's head was bowed as though embarrassed at all the charity and care she had been given. The cab gave a jerk and the horse trotted off creating a gentle bounce as it rumbled along the road. Felicity lifted Anna's chin and looked in to her eyes.

'Well, Hannah, you are looking yourself again. Colour in your cheeks and a shine in your tearful eyes. Is that a new dress you have?'

'I bought it out of the money you gave me before the Buckingham Palace demonstration. I had been keeping it for a sunny day out, perhaps with you.'

'You've changed your choice in colours; I think it is a beautiful option. Quite frankly I think your change to primrose suits you a lot better. Darker clothes are fine for demonstrations. However, bright colours give you radiance.'

'Thank you Felicity. I can't say how much I appreciate all you've done for me. You've been more than a friend. You've been like a loving sister to me.'

'We are related in common ethics and the belief that all human beings are equal. Furthermore, I have had greater satisfaction and a feeling of fulfilment helping you than all my passive activities with the Suffragettes. I believe Jesus taught equality for all when He said, "He who is without sin let him cast the first stone" for all are flesh and blood and have human weaknesses. The birth of a king is no different from the birth of a beggar, and death treats us all the same.'

'You really believe in God, Felicity?'

'Of course, my dear, it is quite simply the question: if there is no God what is there in life to live for?. Life is but a drop in the ocean of time, time flies and Death is around every corner.'

Anna felt a depression looming. "What does it profit man if he should gain the whole world and lose his soul?"'

'You know your Bible Hannah, so come out of that hard shell you sometimes hide in.—Now listen, the people whom I am taking you to is a Mr and Mrs Darlington of Mayfair. They are of middle class and are returning a favour, for I have helped them in the past when their ill-advised financial investments let them down. However, they are well off now and their experience has made them quite strict monetary wise. They have a grown son of their own. They like to be called Sir and Madam and keep their employees at a distance. So be respectful at all times and treat them as your superiors. You may find them strict but they will treat you with respect, although, perhaps, on a patronizing scale.'

'They sound frightening.'

'Fortunately, you will have little to do with them. Your supervisor will be Mrs Goodwin, the cook, and head of the kitchen staff. You will find her fair and strict, but always expecting the best of you and the rest of the kitchen staff.'

Anna held Felicity's hand. 'Does this mean our friendship is over?'

'I will always hold you in great esteem and as a friend in my heart forever. I want you to know, and I do not patronize you in any way, but you are the first working class lady that has ever shown the same fervour and sincerity towards the Suffragette movement. In my estimation that makes you a peer to all women.'

'You are a first class Lady, Felicity. I will never forget you. If, in the future, there is a possibility that we may meet and have tea together, it will give me something to look forward to.'

'I am sure we will meet again someday, somewhere. However, my last piece of advice: save your modest wages and seek reconciliation with your husband. I am convinced you will find your ambition to be a teacher of children somewhere in your native Wales far more rewarding than menial employment here in the competitive city.'

'I shall have to think about that.'

The cabman brought the mare to a standstill outside a detached, four-storey house in a broad road. Half a dozen steps ascended to the front door, glossy with black paint and shining brass knocker and letterbox. Another ten paces to the left hand side descended another set of stone steps to the basement.

'Here we are, Hannah. You have Hartnell's address. If you ever find yourself in dire need of help, send him a note and he will communicate with me, God willing. And so, you must not feel abandoned in any way. Hartnell will take you down to the kitchen and introduce you to Mrs Goodwin.' Felicity kissed Anna on her cheek. 'No tears, now; off you go.'

Hartnell came and opened the cab door and helped her out. He took her case as she looked back and lifted her hand with a reluctant goodbye wave, and then followed Hartnell down the stone steps.

Hartnell knocked the basement door and was let in by a smartly dressed young lad.

'Come in Harty,' he said in a loud cheerful voice—Oh gosh, who is the beauty with you?'

'You mind your own business, young Archie and less of the familiarity. Is Mrs Goodwin there?'

'Where'd you expect me to be at this time of day, Hartnell?' came the strong authoritative voice of the cook.'

'I've got young Hannah here to begin her duties as arranged by Lady Felicity.'

'Ah Lady Felicity, God bless her soul.' How is she?'

She's as well as can be expected,' replied Hartnell, gruffly, as he escorted the hesitant Anna into the heat of the busy kitchen.

Anna took little notice of the conversation, although the phrase, "as well as can be expected," did seem odd, as she had just left her friend looking well and cheerful in the cab. But Anna, the new scullery maid, had a heavy stomach just then as she looked around the room and pictured herself slaving in the hot kitchen. Her eyes were glued to the formidable cooking range that had a large frying pan crusted with the remnants of bacon, egg, and pieces of black mushrooms stuck around its sides, accompanied by a king-sized kettle and teapot on two other hotplates. She felt somebody grab her hand and shake it. It was Mrs Goodwin giving the newcomer a big smile and friendly tone.

'Hello, Hannah, I'm Mrs Goodwin; I am fully in charge of the running and everything you see in the kitchen, so you'll be answering to me.'

Anna's eyes turned to her supervisor; the stout woman looked genuinely happy to see her.

132

'Pleased to meet you Mrs Goodwin, can I just put one thing straight, my name is Anna without the aitch.'

'Oh right, now we know.'

'And I'm afraid I haven't had any experience in such a place.'

Mrs Goodwin let go of her hand. 'Not to worry, the jobs you'll be doing will need elbow grease not experience.' She turned to Archie. 'This is Archie who does a number of jobs and errands; he will help you now and again when he's idle.'

She looked at the thin-faced boy who was beaming at her. 'Hello, Archie,' she said softly.

'Anything you need I will see to it, Anna. And don't you worry about the skivvies work, I'll help you out. I'm going to enjoy working with you—Am I her boss, Mrs Goodwin.'

'I'll clip your ear if I hear you bossing her around. Now off with you down to the post office and get those stamps for the master.'

'Well, I'd better be off,' remarked Hartnell. 'My Lady will not be kept waiting.'

Anna looked at him to give her farewells, but Hartnell Brown gave her a sullen expression and a cold nod. She had a strange feeling she had done him a disservice, but what she could not recall.

'Bye, Hartnell,' called Mrs Goodwin. 'You mind you look after Lady Felicity,' she warned, as he disappeared through the door, followed by Archie. Mrs Goodwin turned to Anna. 'Now Anna, I'll make us a cup of tea. Don't worry about any chores today; I want you to settle in. Daisy and Charles – maid and manservant, are upstairs clearing away the breakfast things. We usually have a little breakfast ourselves once all the washing up and cleaning is done.'

'Does Lady Felicity often visit here, Mrs Goodwin.'

'No, no. She is not the visiting kind. You can be sure if she does make an appearance it will be for some charitable reason. Now once Daisy has finished upstairs and had a bite to eat, she will take you to your room and help you settle in.' Mrs Goodwin went to the range and picked up the large teapot, brought it to the table and poured Anna a cup of tea. 'There are biscuits in that barrel, just there, if you should want one. I'll start on the chores until they come down from the dining room.'

Anna sipped her tea in the heat of the room, grateful for the kindness but apprehensive about the future. Her sad eyes scanned the room with warning signals of present labour. The numerous pots and pans hanging on the greasy walls and the huge sink below them in which they would be scrubbed spotless did not inspire thoughts of a dignified life. The long wooden table, at which she sat, was covered in dirty crockery and greasy cutlery freshly brought down from the dining room, and looking down at the flagstone floor which, presumably she would have to get on her hands and knees to scrub, threw her spirit back into the workhouse where she could see her mother doing the same menial chores.

'What exactly will my duties be, Mrs Goodwin?'

'Don't go worrying about your duties. I have had some advice notes about you via Hartnell from Lady Felicity. I know what you have been up to and how Lady Felicity has praised you in all you've done. I'm not of that particular calling myself, such activities I leave to those who have strong views, but I do respect those who suffer because of their convictions. It is best you never mention your vocations or beliefs in this house, for the master is very much against such demands by women. Now you will have a free day today and begin your duties in the morning but I will start you on washing up pots and pans. There will be no scrubbing floors until you are quite fit and strong.—would you like breakfast?'

'I had breakfast at Hartnell's.'

'Have you noticed our cooking range?' Anna nodded. 'Well you'll be pleased to know it was converted to gas just a month ago. Prior to that the scullery maid had to alternate with Archie to clean out the ashes and relight it every morning. Now you just have to put a match to it.' Mrs Goodwin scanned the serious face of Anna and felt the girl was not responding, as she would have liked. 'Anna, don't fret about living here. You'll share a comfortable room with Daisy who is a nice girl, if not set in her ways. You'll settle in.'

'Thank you Mrs Goodwin, I'm sure I will.'

'Now drink your tea and cheer up.' The far door opened. 'Ah, here are Daisy and Charles.'

Nineteen

Not wanting to let Felicity down she braced herself for the indignity of the menial hard work that she was about undergo. She minded her own business and took her orders from the amiable but strict Mrs Goodwin with reluctant obedience. During the first few weeks she got into the routine of domestic work and spent seventy to eighty hours a week carrying out her duties. She had alternate Sunday off and sometimes an afternoon in midweek, that was if Mr and Mrs Darlington were dining out or socializing at the homes of friends. She saw little of them as she worked mainly in the kitchen, making beds and generally cleaning the house with Daisy. Occasionally, when cleaning the hallway, Jeremy, the twenty two-year-old son of the house, would make an appearance on his way out or when returning from his idle social life. It was noticeable that he would eye Anna with an with a one-sided smile on his handsome face. Anna tried not to be impressed but thoughts went through her head of better things. After a hard day's work she would go to her attic room, compact with two beds, two wardrobes, a table with a mirror that served as a dressing table, and flop into bed. She would nurse herself to sleep with hopes and aspirations of becoming a real Lady if ever Jeremy showed sincere interest in her. Rising in the early hours to attend the kitchen, the night's thoughts would soon evaporate when her eyes fell on the slovenly scullery-maid clothes hanging over the back of the chair at the side of her bed. The weeks went by quickly and soon turned into months. After eighteen hard and tiring months she was as efficient at her job as any of the domestic staff. Daisy was her roommate but said little and kept herself to herself. The slim, small-faced, demure maid, though working often with Anna, gave little away. Her placid demeanour and quiet ways gave an air of secretiveness that Anna couldn't understand. Perhaps being a maid she might have considered herself to be a step up, Anna thought. Nevertheless, she was always ready to help Anna learn the routine of the household, even if it was in a patronizing manner.

On a wet and foggy August night, the kitchen staff was working late, because Mr and Mrs Darlington were entertaining some of their upper class friends. They had arrived back at the house late afternoon after attending the coronation of Edward VII and brought the entourage with them. The guests remained till late and enjoyed a celebration dinner with their hosts. The dinner table had been cleared, the ladies had had their conversations and the men had smoked their cigars in the smoke and games rooms. It was time for all to go to their homes. Several hansom cabs were outside as well as a couple of landaus and a chaise. Charles was up at the front door assisting the departure of the guests by opening and closing the door after handing them their hats and coats. Once outside they clutched their open umbrellas and fought against the blustery drizzling rain as they made their way to the waiting transport. Mr and Mrs Darlington shook hands with all those leaving and smiled gratefully at their compliments of a fine social evening they had enjoyed. When the last guest had left, the Darlington's retired to the lounge and sat gratefully on the floral upholstered easy chairs either side of the open log fire, the corpulent Mr Darlington fell heavily in his chair and gasped with relief that the entertaining had come to an end.

'Well, I must say it was a colourful and enjoyable coronation,' he said. ' A decidedly historic occasion, I am confident he will make a good king.'

'He will if he shows a little more decorum than when he was a prince,' replied his wife.

'He may have been a little indiscreet at times, but I am sure he will prove to be a great leader.'

'Yes, men must do the leading, but we ladies sometimes have to show them the way.'

An irritable movement came from her husband. They said nothing to each other for some time. Mr Darlington's clean-shaven, florid face wore a serious expression. His thick lips puckered on and off as thoughts of what to do crossed his mind. His wife sighed several times waiting for him to speak, her colourful heavy make-up could not hide the severity of her expression as it turned from anxiety to impatience. She habitually patted and caressed the light-blue material of her long, low-cut gown. She could tolerate the suspense no longer as her crimson lips suddenly burst with the pertinent question.

'Well, Hedley, I did mention decorum in expectation that it might inspire some movement of brain within that head of yours. Have you come to the right decision?'

Hedley leaned forward to the small table before him and opened his cigar box, took out a thick six-inch Havana, clipped off its end with the adjacent tool, struck a match and leaned back in his chair.

'You are not going to pollute the lounge with that disgusting firebomb are you? We have a decision to make.'

'We?' He questioned, his gruff voice breaking the plumes as he puffed away, his full cheeks dimpling with each suck. 'What you mean exactly is that I have to make the decision not you.'

'Well, you are the man of the house.'

'Only when it comes to some unfortunate ruling that requires someone to carry out an execution.'

'Oh don't be so dramatic. It is not a woman's job to dismiss a member of the household staff for dishonourable behaviour'

'The situation is dishonourable on both sides. Jeremy took advantage of the poor girl in his privileged position.'

'And did she not take advantage of her freedom of the house and encourage him into rooms in which she was pretentiously going about her duty?'

'She was doing her work and not being pretentious; the same work she does every day of the week. It was Jeremy who should not have been there at that time of the afternoon. I shall have to find him some work in the factory. He can work on the filing cabinets or something. The boy is becoming a continual embarrassment.'

'Then get rid of the girl before the scandal emerges from this respectable abode.'

'It is so unfair on the girl, but I know it must be done. I shall summons her tomorrow and pay her off.'

'Pay her off? Pay her off? She must not be rewarded for seducing our son.'

'Would you have her go to her relatives and plead poverty? Would you have her relatives ask why she was dismissed? Would you aggravate the situation to the extent that hostility would raise its ugly head and bring them around here protesting? Would you like the scandal to be publicized woman?'

Mrs Darlington shook her shoulders in frustration. 'Do what you may, but I will not sleep tonight unless she is out of this house. We have church in the morning and I don't want any unpleasantness tomorrow. Tonight, Hedley, tonight if you please.'

Hedley puffed some more at his cigar and blew a stream of smoke towards his wife. 'Very well, I shall deal with her tonight.' He reached out and pulled at the bell-pull and waited for Charles?'

Down in the kitchen the last pots and pans were being dried by Daisy as Anna handed them to her from the large sink. Once they were considered dry Daisy handed them to Archie who stood on the portable steps. He took them and hung them on the required hooks in such a way that they were in the same order each day. If one should not be on the required hook, Mrs Goodwin would get a superfluous poker from the range and clang the irregular pan while giving Archie a stony stare.

'Are you all right, Daisy? Anna asked.

'Yes. Why do you ask?' replied Daisy, her pale, oval features serious, mistiness in her eyes.

'You seem in a bit of daydream lately.'

'I'm fine thank you,' Daisy replied, unconvincingly.

'Well, that's the last saucepan, thank goodness. I'm ready for bed. I could sleep for a week.'

'It has been a long day,' agreed Daisy.

Mrs Goodwin called to them. 'I've prepared supper for you lot, so come and sit around the table.'

'I'm not hungry, Mrs Goodwin, replied Daisy.'

'Come on. Keep your strength up, urged Anna.'

'Why should I want to keep up my strength?' Daisy snapped.

'That's what eating is all about, Daisy. You'll get ill if you don't eat properly.'

'I can look after myself.'

'Please yourself, then.'

Archie jumped down from his steps and hurried to the table. 'I could do with something to eat. And if Daisy doesn`t want hers I'll eat that too.'

140

'If I listen to you, you can always eat something. I don't understand how you keep so thin, seeing all you eat. Look at me, I've only got to look at food and I put weight on.'

'Ah but you're cuddly Mrs G.'

Mrs Goodwin smiled. 'Get on with it you flatterer or I'll clip your ear.'

Just then Charles came in, stood at the door in his usual imperious air and scanned the kitchen. 'Ah, I am just in time for the evening repast.'

'You time it well, Charles,' quipped Archie, with a suspicious tone.

'I'll have you know I have been extremely busy conducting the evening's proceedings.—Daisy, the master wishes to see you.'

Daisy's head dropped and she took in a deep breath. Without saying a word she left the room.

Anna gave a lasting look at Charles for some hint of explanation, but said nothing as Daisy left the room.

'Come on Charles, what does the master want with Daisy?' asked Mrs Goodwin as Charles sat.

'It is not my position or business to enquire the reasons for the master's requests. I am a butler not a female inquisitor.'

Anna sat at the long table and helped herself to some cold mutton, bread and butter and a glass of leftover wine. There were spare pastries and savouries also for the kitchen staff that Archie enjoyed. When Anna's appetite was satisfied she stood up and looked at Mrs Goodwin.

'If there is nothing more to do, Mrs Goodwin, I'll be off to bed.'

'Yes, off you go, Anna. Be here at six prompt, there's a lot to do in the morning: laundering and mangling to say the least, and the kitchen floor will need a clean over before we prepare breakfast. If Daisy isn't coming back down, make sure she is aware of the morning's work.'

'I'll be here and I'll let her know. Goodnight all.'

'By the way, Anna, I know I remind you at regular intervals, but do you adhere to the advice? The advice I gave you on your first week here?'

'And every other month, Mrs Goodwin, no I do not go too far from the house. You can be sure I have no desire to go Hyde Park Corner or White Chapel or any other place where there maybe danger. Besides, I don't get the time off for such travels. Good night.'

'Good night, Anna.'

Her joints were aching from the long day and pained her as she climbed the servant's stairs to the ground floor. At the landing she opened the door to the hallway and listened. No, she could hear no voices coming from the sitting room, there was either a pause in conversation or Daisy had gone to bed. She closed the door quietly and climbed to the first floor and continued up to the garret where she and Daisy slept. She was about to open the door when she heard weeping from inside. She stopped not wanting to embarrass Daisy by bursting in. She retraced her steps down four stairs, emphasized her tread and sighed aloud as she walked back up. Pausing a little at the door she heard no sound so went in. Daisy sat on her bed looking dazed and red-eyed. Anna pretended not to notice.

'I thought you might have come back down for a drink. There was half bottle of wine there for the offering.'

'I'm not in the mood for anything,' she said, quietly, turning her back to Anna.

'But you like your drop of red.'

'I don't want anything tonight.'

Anna began to take off her grubby clothes she'd worn all evening, while Daisy sat on her bed still dressed in her plain black dress and full length white apron uniform. Anna put on her nightgown and went over to Daisy and sat aside her on the bed.

'I know you don't like talking a lot, Daisy,' she said with a sympathetic tone, 'but it's obvious something is wrong. You can confide in me, and if I can help in some way I will. I've been in some awful trouble in the past and could not have got through it all without the help of Lady Felicity. I've even served time in jail.'

Daisy turned around and looked at Anna, shocked. 'You've been in jail?'

'I was sent to prison for demonstrating with the Suffragettes.'

'I didn't know you were a suffragette.'

142

'I'm not anymore; anyway, what is the trouble?' Tell me.'

Daisy said nothing for a short time, then buried her head in her hands and wept. 'I'm going to have baby.'

Anna could not believe her ears. It seemed incredible that this tacit, demure girl should get into such extreme trouble. Daisy, the one who always seemed so in control, had succumbed to an apparently secret love affair. Trying to be positive she put her arm around Daisy's shoulder. 'It's a terrible blow, Daisy, but it's not the end of the world. Does he love you?'

'He certainly does not,' she sobbed. 'He's a selfish brute.'

'But he'll stick by you, surely.'

'Huh! You don't know the half of it. He told me he loved me just to get his way with me. I fell in love with him and have been over the past two years. But all he wanted was me in his bed. Now that he knows I'm pregnant he wants nothing to do with me.'

Anna's blood began to heat up as pictures of her deserted youth came back to her. She was the baby Daisy was going to have. Daisy was her mother who would fall into poverty and despair. Her little child will grow up with shabby clothes and fatherless, shunned by those small-minded puritans who preached love and charity to their own kind.

'I can sympathize with you, Daisy.'

'What do you know?'

'I'm illegitimate; I've never told that to anyone before.'

Daisy looked amazed at Anna, but controlled her emotions. 'You mother never married.?'

'I didn't even know my father. He died before I could track him down. Have you got family to help you out, Daisy?'

'Yes, I've told my sister, she said she would take me in when I was ready. I dare not let my parents know just yet—He paid me off, you know.'

'Who paid you off, the father of your child?'

Daisy gave a hysterical laugh and turned her head away. 'Oh no not him haven't seen him for days. It's the baby's grandfather who just paid me off.'

Anna was confused. 'Who just paid you, Daisy?'

Daisy turned back to Anna, wiping her eyes. 'Mr Darlington; Jeremy is the father.'

The words took Anna's breath away. 'Typical, spineless member of the masculine race, men of honour; men from the sewers of London, more like.'

Daisy opened her hand to Anna. 'That's what I'm worth to keep my mouth shut: twenty pounds.'

Anna shook her head in disgust. 'That will tide you over for a time, I suppose, until you sister can arrange something for you.'

'Oh it's not for spending on myself—he suggested it could find me a place to get rid of it.'

'God, these people are beyond belief. You're not going to have an abortion, are you?'

She tightened her thin lips and spat out the words. 'Oh no, I will rear my little aristocrat and return one day when the time is ripe.'

'You do that, Daisy. You do that,' urged Anna.

'I'm sorry I've been so aloof, Anna, but I was afraid I might let the truth out if I got too close. Now, I don't care.'

'I can understand now how you must have felt.'

Daisy reached under her bed and brought out her suitcase and laid it on the bed, opened it and began packing her personal clothes.

'What are you doing, Daisy.'

'I've been told I have to get out tonight.'

'They've given you no notice at all?'

'Charles is to come up here in the morning to make sure I've gone; I've got to be out before they come home from morning service.'

Anna could only gasp and hold her hand over her mouth.

'How far have you got to go?'

'My sister's house is about two miles away.'

'I'll come with you and keep you company.'

'No, no, I shall call a cab and ride in dignity paid by the Darlington's money.'

'I'll be lonely up here on my own.'

'It's kind of you to say so. I know I've been little company to you. Anyway, you'll soon have a room-mate.' She looked at her maid's uniform. 'You'd better try this on for size. You'll be the

144

housemaid now. I hope you'll have a friendly scullery maid to keep you company.' Daisy picked up her case and walked to the door. 'Good luck Anna, learn from my mistakes.'

'He won't have me. Careful how you go, Daisy.'

She closed the door behind her and Anna suddenly felt very lonely.

Twenty

She was a sixteen-year-old, short and tubby with a chirpy personality and a willing hand to everything that was asked of her. She worked hard and soon became endeared to the kitchen staff. She was as happy scrubbing floors and cleaning greasy pans as helping Anna to make the beds. There was just one anxiety she expressed, and that was whenever Charles made an appearance in the kitchen, which, of course was quite frequent, especially at meal times. The stern face and receding hairline, the straight back and superior mien of the butler was the only aspect of Molly's job that took the perpetual smile from her lovely fresh face. As for Anna, she felt much uplifted in her maid's uniform for it made her appear smart and clean and gave her an air of respect. She immediately made friends with the unassuming Molly, partly from relief, for it had taken a month to find someone suitable for the job, and partly because Anna thought there was a common bond with the girl who obviously had come from social degradation.

When she had first arrived she had no money, her attire had been well used and faded and her education was near to nothing. But Molly proved to be exceptionally clean and tidy in the garret and often smartened the room on her evening off when Anna was on duty helping Charles to serve dinner. When there was time to relax, Anna would enjoy a chat with Molly, which was another aspect of her new roommate that had not always been prevalent when Daisy was there. Coming off duty at ten o'clock, Anna found Molly lying on her bed, hands behind her head staring at the ceiling. As soon as Anna came in Molly turned her head and greeted her friend with a smile.

'Glad you've finished Anna?'

'I'm ready for bed.'

'I've just come in and flopped down. Archie helped me with the washing up, he did. He's good Archie is.'

'He's all right. A bit facetious sometimes.'

'What's tha'.'

'Facetious? Oh, he tries to be funny and witty.'

'Oh yea, he makes me laugh. He calls Charles, Charlie boy. I wouldn't call him that.'

'Molly, you've been here three months now and I've never seen you go out; unless, of course you're out when I'm working.

'Oh no, this is my home now. It's lovely here in this room.'

'But you can go out in your free time. I know we don't have many opportunities for leisure but we're allowed a bit of freedom. The house will still be here when you come back.'

Molly's face turned ashen, as she sat up and dangled her legs over the side of the bed. 'What if mistress comes and finds me out? She might get somebody to do my job.'

'Of course she won't. You can go out and meet your friends during your time off.'

'Got no friends.'

'What about family?'

'No, no, I got a Mum and step-dad, but I don't like him. My Mum does, mind, but I don't.' No I'm happy here.'

Anna looked at Molly and wondered was she another girl who had domestic problems, things in common with her. She began to take her uniform off and talk in vague terms to Molly. 'I had a foster father who I didn't like much.'

'Foster father, that sounds funny.'

'He was like a stepfather, but not married to my mother.'

'Married to your mother?'

'No married to my foster mother.'

Molly looked perplexed. 'Oh.'

'You see, my mother died when I was young and I went to live with a woman and her husband who had no children. They weren't my real parents but they looked after me. The woman was not too bad, but my stepfather was dominant and very strict.'

'My step-dad is very strict. He beat me with a strap if I didn't do my work quick—an' he looks a bit like Charles, always got a sour face.'

Anna sat on her bed and stared at Molly with some concern. 'He was a horror, was he?'

'Oh he was a horror. If I go out of here and he sees me, he'll drag me back home.'

'Good God, no wonder you won't leave this place.'

'He'll be looking for me now, I guess.'

'So you ran away from your mother and stepfather and you're...well, hiding here?'

'I didn't run away from my Mum, oh no she got me the job here. She got a friend who knows Mrs Goodwin. And Mum's friend told Mrs Goodwin all about me. And Mrs Goodwin got me here, and it's all a secret from my step-dad.' Molly went pale again and clapped her hands over her face. 'Oh dear, oh dear, dear, I've done it now.'

'It's all right, Molly. I won't tell a soul.'

'You promise, honestly? You won't?'

'I promise honestly.'

'You see, I only live a couple of miles away, so if I go out and he's looking for me and he sees me and takes me back...'

Anna rushed over to her and put her arm around. 'It's all right, Molly. Nobody knows only you and me.'

'And Mrs Goodwin, don't tell her I told you.'

'I won't, really.'

There was a pause in the conversation while Anna put on her nightclothes. Molly watched her with some admiration for Anna's beauty was much appreciated by all. She had let her long black hair down much to the admiration of her roommate. Molly's mousy hair had been cropped by her stepfather and was growing untidily. She could only sit in humility and admire the slim beauty she would never be.

'You got lovely hair, Anna. I wish I had hair like yours.'

'Hair is what you make it, Molly. Your hair can be lovely if you train it the right way.'

'No. My step-dad says I'll never make a beauty, I'm too ugly. That's why Mrs Goodwin makes me wear a cap. It hides my daft-looking hair.'

'Your step-dad is a sadist, and Mrs Goodwin makes you wear a cap because it's the rule of the kitchen. It's in case a strand of your hair may drop into the food. I wear one if I've got to work in the kitchen for long periods.'

'Is that so? Well I'll be jiggered.'

'I've got a magazine that illustrates different kinds of hairstyles. You can read it if you want.'

Molly smiled sheepishly and shook her head. 'I can't read, silly. I can't write neither.'

'Oh Molly we can't have that. I tell you what, when we both got spare time I'll teach you to read and write. And what's more, you have a very pretty face. We'll do your hair as well, and when you've saved enough from your wages you can buy yourself a new dress. We'll make a new girl of you. You'll be so changed not even your stepfather will recognize you.'

Molly fell back on the bed and began to laugh. 'That'll be good, oh that'll be good that will.'

'Now come over to the table and look in the mirror. We'll start by grooming your hair and see if we can curl it.'

Molly rushed to the chair and looked in the mirror with some excitement and expectation.

And so, Anna began the recreation of Molly, both in making her attractive and using her as her first pupil in literacy. As the months wore on and Molly began to take pride in herself she learned her ABC and began to put words together. Her hair grew into waves and Anna cut strips of material from an old blouse and used to tie her hair up at night. Her hard work in the kitchen and general house duties soon had her losing weight. And the time came when Molly was transformed from a puppy-fat, illiterate sixteen-year-old into an eighteen years of age young lady, confident and attractive. During those two years she and Anna became close friends and enjoyed occasional nights out frequenting the sparse spots of entertainment that existed in their area. At times they were tempted to go into the city, but had not picked up enough courage to go that far, for the tales of attacks and murders in certain areas filled them with dread. But very happy they were for that period of time.

Twenty One

Molly, slimmer from her hard work in the hot kitchen, walked proudly at the side of Anna as they strolled through Marylebone on their way to Regent's Park. She had donned her red frock and planted a boater-type hat with a ring of flowers circling its rim on her head. Anna, attired in a long flowing lemon dress, applied her matching parasol as a pendulum, and smiled around confidently, swinging her hips, her hatless head showing off her tousled raven hair.

'You don't half waddle back and fore, Anna, I can't keep up with you.'

'I like mixing my walking with dance.'

'You don't half make people look at you.'

'Let them look.'

The pavement was busy with people, men women and children, all taking advantage of a beautiful Sunday afternoon. The road, too, was busy with traffic as carts carriages and the newly craze in automobiles made Anna feel the excitement of being in the centre of the country that was leading the way into her future.

'I saw Jeremy winking at you yesterday, Anna. I think he likes you.'

'Well he can go to the devil until he decides to make a positive gesture. He's been winking and smacking my behind for a long time. I've told him what he can do if he wants me.'

'I'm good at keeping secrets, aren't I Anna.'

'You crossed your heart, so I have faith in you.'

'I love us two having secrets that nobody else knows. If Mrs Goodwin ever found out—oh gosh'

'If Mrs Goodwin, or anybody else, finds out it would have come from you, and that would be the end of our friendship.'

'Nobody will ever find from me.'

'Anyway, you make it sound as though he's already had me in his bed. I let him give me a peck on the lips once, that's all. Then I gave him a big smile and he melted like a chocolate bar near the fire. Have you ever had a man in bed, Molly?'

Molly stopped and looked at Anna feeling insulted. 'Anna, what do you think I am?'

'I was only asking,' quipped Anna. 'You never know these days what happens.'

'And what about you, If you can ask me such a question then I can ask you.'

'I'm a virgin, and shall be until the day I die unless there is a big change in my life. And it will have to be a huge change. I just can't imagine myself lying at the side of a man.'

'Anyway, tell me more of your grand plans with Jeremy, Anna.'

'I've told you all, he just keeps making promises in hope that I'll believe him and give in to his sexual demands.'

They strolled and Anna's face took on a more serious expression as her mind drifted back to the degrading contrast of Dowlais and the man she is still married to. John is still there, she thought. But nobody in these parts knows that I'm married to him. What's a bit of paper anyway, couples are not joined together by paper. They're either joined by love of one another, or the desire of wealth and security. And this so-called gentleman has all I want. He deserves no better; he nor his hypocritical hard-hearted parents.

'Penny for your thoughts Anna.'

'There are certain thoughts that are very private, Molly, and my thoughts are top secret.'

Once through the gates of Regent's park they maintained their walk until Molly suddenly stopped and huffed.

'I could do with a sit down if I could only see a spare bench.'

'We'll walk a little further there might be a vacant one further up the park.'

'Anna, what do you do when Jeremy smacks your behind? I wouldn't know what to do.'

'I give him a hard, cold stare and call him a naughty boy.'

'What does he do then?'

'He giggles like a schoolboy then says, "I'll have you one day my beauty, I'll have you one day." And then he toddles off as though he's gained some great achievement.'

152

'Oh gosh, I don't know who to be afraid of the most, nasty-looking Charlie or the sly Jeremy.'

'Don't worry about Charles, his look is only to gain a feeling of I'm-better-than-you, but underneath he's good natured and will help you in the household duties.'

'But Jeremy?'

'Ah now, he appears good-natured, but underneath he's an irresponsible blackguard who'll desert you once he's had his way. Keep well clear of him, Molly. You're too soft hearted to get the better of him.'

'You can talk.' Molly sighed, 'I can see an empty bench up ahead, let's hurry before someone sits on it.'

They ran lifting their dresses above their ankles and managed to secure the steel-railed bench before anyone else got there. Not that there were many contenders, for the large majority of people were making for the north end of the park.

'There seems to be some attraction up there, Molly.'

'I've been up there once with my real Dad before he died, poor Dad. He took me to the zoo and showed me around to see all the animals. We could go there if you want to it's just outside the park.'

'I don't believe in caging animals.'

'Nor me. I was excited, but when I saw them all locked up behind bars and looking sad I felt sorry for them.'

'I know what it's like. I was like an animal when I was caged up in Holloway.'

Molly turned to her friend and touched Anna's hand. 'It must have been awful for you, Anna.'

Anna's eyes became glazed and distant and she gently shook her head as she thought of the experience. 'I was not only caged up but tortured as well—the sadists.'

'You never told me what they did to you Anna.'

Anna gave Molly a generous smile. 'And I never will, Molly. I wouldn't pollute your mind with the goings on in that place of hell.'

They sat in peaceful silence for a time watching the people pass by; the ladies with their different coloured dresses and hats and with perfect deportment, the men in the smart suits, some with hands clasped behind their backs, others with shiny walking canes. There were the modest working-class mothers hurrying with their children towards the north end, some with their husbands but mostly just mothers and children. Suddenly, their observations were interrupted by a smooth-talking male voice from behind.

'Hello, hello, fancy my meeting the girl of my dreams here in the beautiful surroundings of nature.'

Anna looked at Molly and raised her eyebrows. 'We have the company of a very important member of the aristocracy,' she said, recognizing the tone.'

Jeremy came round and faced the girls, raising his boater. 'It is indeed my lucky day, not one, but two beauties for my pleasure,' he said, caressing his thin moustache with his forefinger.

Anna encouraged him playfully. 'My, my, you are looking handsome today. I haven't seen that suit before, Jeremy.'

'Made to my own design and specifications,' he said, stepping back apace and bowing slightly. 'The colour I requested is somewhat between azure and indigo, enhanced by my contrasting colour scheme of a pale yellow shirt and a blue bow tie to match.'

'I have got eyes. You certainly stand out and attract the attention of all around.'

'Oh, do you think so? It is good to know that one's efforts are appreciated.'

Molly glanced from one to the other as they each spoke in turn, wondering if Anna was serious or just egging him on. 'I like it, too, Master Darlington,' she said. 'It's very pretty.'

'Pretty? Pretty? I do hope it is not pretty but exquisite and appropriate for a man of my bearing.'

'That's what I meant,' said Molly demurely and decided not to say anything more.

'Would you ladies mind if I took up a seat at your side?'

'We were just about to go, Jeremy,' answered Anna quickly.'

'Then perhaps you will allow me to accompany you. Where were you thinking of going?'

'Oh, we were about to go back to the house.'

'No, no, no, the day is far too fortuitous. I would have thought you would appreciate the new additions to the London Zoo; everybody is going there. Have you ever seen a real camel, Molly?'

'Yes, I've been to the zoo before.'

'Have you indeed. And you, Anna?'

'No.'

'Then you must make a visit and experience the wonder of Nature's creatures.'

'The little money Molly and I earn we save up and then splash out on clothes. As you can see we are in our finest, but out of wages.'

'And beautiful you are both looking. However, I will not be denied, I will treat you both to the zoo and we'll enjoy some delicacies later at a restaurant of Anna's choosing.'

'Oh, thank you Master Jeremy, that will be very nice,' enthused Molly.

Anna looked at Molly with some disapproval. 'Do you really want to go, Molly?'

'I do feel my tummy rumbling now and again.'

'Very well, we accept your invitation to the restaurant, Jeremy, but we'll postpone the visit to the zoo for another day. It must be very crowded there and the warm day might be a little too much for my delicate disposition.'

'I am surprised you have a delicate disposition, Anna; you appear to do your household duties with such speed and attractive movements. But as you wish, we will bow to your delicacy, will we not, Molly?'

'Yes, Master Jeremy.'

'Oh, and Molly, there is no need to call me Master whilst we are out of the household.'

'Right, Ma...Jeremy.'

'Very well, now where is this restaurant you wish to go, Anna?'

Anna feigned a sad expression and bowed her head.

'Whatever is the matter, Anna?'

'Poor Molly and I have been walking for hours and our legs are so aching, I feel we really should have some kind of transport. We would be very grateful if we could have a cab to Oxford Street, I'm sure there must be a nice restaurant there. And I'd love to see the new electric trams that run there.'

'These cabs are not cheap these days, you know Anna?'

'Oh dear, we'll have to find a cheap café somewhere, I suppose.'

'Oh very well, let's vacate the park and I'll call a hansom.—Mm, it might be cosy at that.'

Jeremy did so and sat sandwiched comfortably between the two girls. Anna and Molly had a grand tour of Oxford Street, Euston and Edgware Road among others. They had tea and buns in a restaurant and were treated like ladies and not servants to such an extent that she began to have a different view of Jeremy. She even understood his dilemma when they were being taken home in the hansom. He begged them to be dropped off a street away just in case "Mother might just be looking through the curtains." This they agreed to and allowed him to go on alone, with much gratitude for the most enjoyable day.

Twenty Two

Anna and Charles were clearing the long table of its china dinner set, silver cutlery, platters, crystal glasses and the floral arrangements that had made up the impressive display the Mr and Mrs Darlington had put on for their guests. All had adjourned to the respective rooms; the ladies to the guest lounge and the gentlemen to the smoke room. Molly was hurrying back and fore to the dumb waiter carrying the used dishes and discarded food. Charles stood back with a majestic air to supervise the last of the food containers being picked up by Molly; it was a domed silver dispenser its upper half being a hinged cover with an internal removable glass bowl inside.

'Be very careful with that, Molly, it's one of Mrs Darlington's prize possessions. The mistress will not be pleased if anything should happen to it.'

Molly had been cool and efficient with all she had carried, but the warning from Charles had sent a shock wave through her delicate nervous system. Her hands began to shake a little as she placed all her concentration on gripping the utensil tightly, and her normally sprightly legs slowed to a crawl. Her eyes were glued to the bowl she was carrying and her attention taken away from where she was making for. As she approached the half open door, Jeremy rushed in on the pretence that he wanted to see if all was well. It had been all well until he'd swung the door fully open and knocked the precious silverware out of Molly's grip. She screamed as it flew out of her hands and up in the air landing with a fearful clattering on the plush carpet. The hinged semi-globe flew open and detached itself from the lower half sending the glass bowl across the floor gyrating around the table leg. Molly burst into tears as she watched the nightmare happening and Anna held her hands to her mouth preventing herself from some foul expletive. Charles's cool expression turned to one of shock as he darted to the pieces and retrieved them immediately. Whilst attempting to reassemble the precious piece of tableware, Mrs Darlington rushed in, her painted face full of rage, her crimson lips twisting with disbelief.

'What was that crash?' she demanded, but then her eyes fell to Charles, on his knees and doing his best to carry out the repair. 'My God! My silver tureen; what have you done to it?'

'It was this clumsy scullery maid, Mother,' accused Jeremy. 'She just does not look where she is going.'

Anna stared at Jeremy, fire in her eyes and her face red with anger. 'It was you who burst into the room,' she said.

'Shut up, Anna,' ordered Mrs Darlington. 'When I want your opinion I shall tell you.' Her eyes turned to Charles. 'You are supervising these girls, Charles. What on earth is happening?'

Charles composed himself and got up off his knees with the assembled tureen and coolly replied, 'I fear it might have been my fault, madam. I inadvertently diverted Molly's concentration for an unfortunate moment and took her attention away from the opening door. However, the accident has not caused any damage to the tureen as the thick pile of your exquisite carpet cushioned the fall.'

Mrs Darlington was aware of the respect her husband held for Charles and of his indispensable duties and the cheap labour he provided. His workload, the hours he put in and his clever manipulation and organization of the staff could not be replaced so easily.

'Is there any damage at all to my silver tureen?'

'No indeed, madam, just a little rinse in warm water will see it at its best again.'

'Very well.' She turned to Molly. 'You be very careful in the future, girl.' Molly nodded, her hands clasped together on her chest. Mrs Darlington turned to her son. 'And what are you doing here, Jeremy?'

'I thought I would call in to see if everything is being cleared properly, Mother.'

'Cleared properly? Why do you think we employ Charles? Get back into the gentlemens' room where you belong.'

Jeremy turned and disappeared through the door, his mother assisting him with a push on his back, mumbling as she went.

Molly looked at Charles, her eyes still glassy and apologetic. 'Thank you Mr Charles for sticking up for me; I'm very sorry.'

'Molly, I do wish you would not be so nervous at such times. You must learn to be cool and collected.'

'I will try, honest I will.'

'Very well, now take the tureen to the dumb waiter and let us get the room cleared so that we can have a little supper ourselves. Anna, will you remove the tablecloths and quickly polish over?'

'I will, Charles, and thank you for helping Molly.'

'Never mind all that now, finish off here while I go on down.'

Molly placed the remainder of what was left in the dumb waiter and followed Charles down to the kitchen. She ran down the stairs but had to check herself when she caught up with the dignified waiter who took his time with great aplomb. Mrs Goodwin leaning on the kitchen table met them.

Well', what was the ruckus upstairs? I thought the ceiling was going to fall in.'

'Just a little mishap, Mrs Goodwin,' replied Charles. It is all in hand.'

'Judging by the sheepish expression on Molly's face the mishap concerned our little scullery maid.'

'I dropped the silver tureen.'

'Oh my goodness, is it still in one piece?'

'It is now thanks to Mr Charles. He fixed it back together again.'

'Trust Charlie boy to come to the rescue,' quipped Archie as he emptied the dumb waiter. 'I'll say one thing for Charles, he's a good un.'

'Ah, our saviour as always,' agreed Mrs Goodwin. 'Well, food is ready with a glass of red wine. Where's Anna?'

'She is putting the final touches to the tidying up.' said Charles. 'I am looking forward to a glass of wine.'

'You can have mine,' said Molly. 'That will make two glasses.'

'Thank you, Molly, you are kind.'

Up in the dining room Anna had just completed the dusting and polishing up. She had a last lingering look at the room, turned the lights off and quietly closed the door. Crossing the spacious hallway to the servant's stairs, she heard a loud whisper from the first storey landing. She looked up to the stairs to the bedroom floor and could see Jeremy at the top beckoning her to come up.

'I thought you were told to go to the smoking room,' she said, louder than Jeremy wanted.

He put his forefinger to his lips signaling her to be quiet. 'It is like an opium den in there, one can hardly breathe for cigar smoke.'

'When were you in an opium den?'

'Not so loud, mother will hear and investigate.'

'So?'

'Will you come up here, please, I want to apologize.'

'You've got the wrong girl, it's Molly who needs an apology.'

'And so I shall make that also, but I have a little present for you and for Molly.'

Anna felt suspicious, but intrigued. 'For Molly as well?'

'Yes, now come up and I'll show you.'

'Why can't you bring it down?'

'If mother should come out of the ladies' room whilst I am down there, I shall have a lot of explaining to do. Now do you want these presents or not?'

'Just for minute then.' Anna began the ascent but Jeremy put his hand up.

'Wait. I want a jug of water to fill my washbasin in the morning.'

'You have the jug up there, bring it down.'

'I shall come half way down the stairs, you come half way up whilst I get the jug.'

Anna was beginning to feel uneasy about his strange behaviour for he rarely bothered to use his jug and basin, preferring to go the bathroom. She gingerly climbed the stairs and stopped halfway. Jeremy appeared from his bedroom with the large jug held by both hands.

'Be careful, it's full.'

'Then why do you want it filled again?'

'It is stale, girl, stale and smelly.'

Anna went to the bathroom and filled the jug with fresh water. When she returned Jeremy was not to be seen. She slowly climbed the stairs once more and reached the top, only to find him

160

ominously in the landing shadows sitting on a chair. She stopped and waited for a moment thinking he'd come and take it off her, but he made no move.

'Well, girl, place it where it belongs. Do I have to tell you everything?'

Anna walked into the subdued gas lighting of his bedroom, the heavy olive curtains and the shadowy walls exuding a nicotine odour. She was aware he was adopting his employer's role and expecting a servant's response, but she kept a close eye on his movements. 'Jeremy, are you feeling well?'

'I have never felt better, my dear,' he said, following her into the bedroom.

'Stay where you are Jeremy until I come back out.'

He went in and closed the door behind him. 'In my own house I shall go where I want, especially into my own bedroom.'

'That is your privilege, but I have finished for the night and entitled to my supper. Now where are these presents you supposed to have.'

'All in good time, Anna, all in good time,' he said, in a harsh whisper like the hiss of a large snake. He moved towards her barring her way to the door.

Jeremy, I don't like being tricked. Now you keep your gifts and let me go down stairs with the others.'

'Oh darling, I have been thinking about you all week. I believe I have fallen in love with you.'

'I don't like the sound of your voice, please let me pass.'

'I can't get you out of my mind; I laid awake all through last night, thinking about you, dreaming about you, fantasizing about you.'

Anna thought it best to humour him. 'Jeremy if you really love me that much, surely you'll want to marry me, and we can live happily ever after.'

'You are not being fair, Anna. We live in different classes of society. I am a Gentleman, you a working girl, and a beauty at that.'

'I'm sure I can fit in nicely. I can play the part of a Lady.'

'Anna, you really must reciprocate a good turn you know. It is considered ill-bred to accept a friend's generosity and not reciprocate. That is what is called taking advantage of a good natured person.'

'So I'm ill-bred now, am I? What are you talking about, Jeremy?'

'Last Sunday, Anna; I was very good to you and Molly, taking care of you and buying you tea and buns in an expensive restaurant. Since then you have ignored me and not given as much as a smile.' He moved close to her and grabbed her by the shoulders. 'I know your little tricks,' he said his voice now course and deep. 'Feigning tiredness so that you could fool me into hiring a cab, saying how thirsty and hungry you both were so that I might buy you refreshments, cooing and smiling sweetly as you looked into my eyes. How stupid do you think I am?'

Anna was trembling, her voice quivering more with anger than fear. 'I owe you nothing. I merely employed the tactics you use to get innocent servants into bed. Well I'm not one of your Daisy girls. I'm not one to get pregnant and to be bought off by your sanctimonious parents.'

He threw her on the bed and jumped on top of her, but Anna was as strong and determined as he, raising her knees and thrusting them into his stomach, she kicked him away. She tried to make it to the door but he caught her around the waist from behind and forced her on the floor. As they struggled Anna screamed and yelled at him.

'Get off me, you perverted pig, get off.'

He yelled just as loud, forgetting where he was and who might hear. 'Stop struggling you little demon, or I shall wring your delicate little neck.'

Anna felt her apron being torn off and then her blouse burst open. 'Help me! Somebody help me from this madman.'

They had struggled to the unlit fire, and Anna felt the companion set fall across her face as it crashed from the hearth. He grabbed her hair and forced her head back. 'Got you, you common wench,' he grinned, as he pressed his lips on hers.

She grappled with him and suddenly felt the poker in her hand. There was no hesitation; she began to hit him at the back of his head but had no power in her limited swing. He raised himself to take away the weapon, but by doing so gave Anna's hand opportunity to come round in a speedy arc, the poker painfully opening up a three

162

inch gash on his forehead. He felt nothing for a moment, but then the blood began to run down his face dripping on to Anna's torn white blouse. He freaked just then and began to scream like a baby with the gripes.

It was then the door burst open and his parents ran in followed by some of their guests.

The mother went to her son and cradled him in her arms, the blood smudging her yellow silk gown. 'What have you done to my son?' she screamed at Anna. 'You are an evil common filth. Get out. Get out of this house and never come back.'

Anna stood up and glared at the woman cradling her son. 'He attacked me. He tried to rape me.'

'You are a treacherous liar, Get out! Get out! I command you! Get out of my house!'

Jeremy composed himself and shook his head in denial. 'She lured me, mother. She's been provoking me for months. She wanted me to marry her.'

'Marry! Good God is the girl insane.' She turned to her husband. 'Throw this serving commoner out now! Do you hear me? I want her out now.'

Mr Darlington placed his arm around Anna's shoulder. 'Come, my dear, it is best you leave.'

Anna shook her shoulders releasing herself from his ushering arm. 'Leave?' she mumbled, as several guests broke apart, opening up a staring gauntlet of cold eyes to the door. 'I've done nothing wrong, sir, I had to protect myself.'

'I'm afraid you were caught in his bedroom, Anna. A foolish mistake, do you not think?. I dare say he may have had some part in it, but you have no defence going to his bedroom.'

'I'll call the police. He tried to rape me, can't you see that?'

Mrs Darlington came rushing out and hit Anna on the back of the head with her hand. 'The police indeed, and whose word do you think they will take, a Lady's, or that of a common labouring girl?' Now get out before I have Charles throw you out.'

Darlington gave Anna a final nod. 'Collect your things, Anna, it's for the best, believe me.'

Mrs Darlington helped her son into the private lounge, asking the guests to make their way back to their respective rooms. The men were shaking their head in disgust, the women mumbling about the shocking incident. Anna stood there with her employer hoping to atone herself and keep her job. The doors closed and they stood there alone, his head bowed her eyes wide and expectant. The silence was ghostly and intolerable. Anna was about to offer a plea of rational reasoning when the servants' door opened and Charles emerged from downstairs.

'Is everything all right, sir? There seemed to be a disturbance coming from the ground floor.'

'Charles, I'm afraid Anna has caused my son an injury which has resulted in a rather large gash to his forehead.'

'Good grief! Is master Jeremy all right?'

'I think he will survive, however, Mrs Darlington has given strict notice that Anna must remove herself from the premises immediately.'

'Immediately sir?'

'I'm afraid so. I will leave you to carry out the necessary unpleasant formalities,' said Darlington as he turned to go.

Charles gave a tactful gently cough. 'May I make a suggestion, sir?'

Darlington turned back. 'What is it Charles?'

'Perhaps it would be prudent to allow Anna to stay until morning. The smog has drifted across our way and has made visibility very low. It is the custom of the rogues and vagabonds to take advantage of such conditions and prey on the vulnerable. I am sure neither Mrs Darlington nor your good self would want anything to happen to our innocent employee.'

Darlington stood there defenceless against the ambiguous innuendo. 'You make sure that Anna is out of the house before Mrs Darlington rises, otherwise we might have to make excuses for your failure.—Anna, I don't want to see your face around these parts again.—You Charles, come to me first thing in the morning and make your favourable report.'

'I will do that, sir. Shall I give her recompense for her loyalty and impeccable service?'

164

'Ten pounds and no more.' Darlington turned and hurried away.

Anna turned to Charles. 'Thank you, Charles, you are a true gentleman.'

Charles caught hold of Anna's hands. 'I am deeply sorry to see you go Anna, as I was to see Daisy go. One of these days the boy will have his just reward, believe me. Now go and pack your things, I shall see you in the morning before you leave.'

Twenty Three

There was no reprieve for Anna, six o'clock in the morning she left the premises, her body numb, her mind as misty as the foggy day. She had lain awake all night not knowing why she had been treated so harshly. What did they expect her to do, lie down and take it all? Let the dual personality have his pleasure of the common working girl? No, her pride and chaste disposition would not be defiled; she would rather beg for money than let herself be treated with such animal indignity.

As she climbed the wet stone steps from the kitchen she was unable to reciprocate the sincere condolences of her colleagues. Molly was inconsolable as she buried her tearful face in her apron. Mrs Goodwin held back her inner fury, for she knew Anna was the latest victim of Jeremy's manic lust. As for Charles, he had told Mrs Goodwin that the situation had become intolerable and he is seriously considering finding employment elsewhere. There were tears in Archie's eyes too, as he carried Anna's new larger suitcase up the steps in one hand and a parcel of food Mrs Goodwin had prepared for the sad departure. At the top he put the suitcase down and shook Anna's limp hand.

'I'll come with you, if you want, Anna. I really will.'

The sentiment made Anna turn to him. 'Thank you, Archie,' she said in a whisper. 'You really are a lovely lad. You've all been true friends, but I don't fit in here, you see.'

'You do, Anna. It's the crazy family who don't fit in here.'

Anna picked up her laden suitcase as Archie handed her the parcel, and then she said goodbye and wandered off, to where she did not know. Archie stood there watching her walk the long road until she disappeared in the fog, then turned and shook his head as he descended the steps to the kitchen.

In her mind there was a picture of the kitchen she had assumed would have been her permanent place of work for many years. Many pictures rose from the past as she went deeper into the smog. Images of her futile wanderings looking for a father who, unbeknown to her had already been dead, and as a child, witnessed her mother's premature death and burial, victim of consumption; of her severe God-fearing stepfather who would send her to bed at five o'clock without food when she couldn't remember a verse from the Bible. She saw the face of sincere John, angry and humiliated by her, of the Rees family, who probably despised her. There was no returning there for she is probably hated, and rightly so she thought. And then her heart lifted as she pictured the beautiful features of the wonderful Felicity. Yes. She will search for her compassionate friend and become untied again. She'll tell her about the heartless family who dismissed her so that she'd know the truth about them. Felicity is the only one who can help her in her present state. It would be wonderful again to be a close friend of Felicity. She will have to find Hartnell's house for she'd lost his address; he will know how to get in touch with her true friend. The thought brought her to her senses and she suddenly realized the noises around her, the trotting horses pulling cabs and carts, the complaining of the shoppers cursing the weather, the honking of the motor car klaxons and the general hubbub of a busy day. She waved several cabs down and asked those drivers who stopped if they knew of a cab driver named Hartnell, but they could not help her. And she fretted over those who did not stop, she still held faith she would find one of them who would know him. Seeing another hansom approaching through the mist she waved him down hoping it was not engaged. The cabman reigned in his horse and came to a stop.

'Where to, miss?'

'I don't know, but maybe you can help me.'

'If it's in the radius of fifteen miles, I'll know it.'

'Do you know a cab driver named Hartnell?'

'I certainly do. He's a right one he is. What do you want him for? I can take you anywhere you want.'

'You must have got the wrong man. He has a wife and children and lives in the Holborn area, somewhere.'

'There's only one Hartnell, he'd skin his mother for a few pounds. Now do you need a cab or don't you?'

168

'Do you know his address?'

'Of course I do, I'm telling you aren't I.'

Anna climbed in. 'Take me to his home, I want to see him.'

'If you must.'

The cab driver gently trotted his horse for twenty minutes until he turned into a side road, through a lane and into a main road again. Anna kept peering out of the cab window hoping to see familiar places, but it wasn't until they turned into Edgware Road her heart began to hope. Going down Edgware Road they turned left into a long narrow street that Anna recognized. Half way through the street the cabman pulled his horse to a standstill, and Anna knew where she was. She stepped out of the cab and knocked at the maroon door of Hartnell. Hartnell's wife answered but her face immediately gave a startled expression.

'Good God, what do you want?'

'You remember me, don't you?'

'Of course I do, you were one of Lady Felicity's homeless.'

'Can I come in?'

'What for?'

Anna suddenly saw hardness in the face of Hartnell's wife. A defiant face full of forebode and trouble.'

'I'd like to see Hartnell, if you don't mind.'

Hartnell peered over the shoulder of his wife. 'What's going on here?'

'It's one of the waifs her Lady picked up.'

'Hartnell pulled his wife behind him. 'Go and get on with the food, woman.' His wife obeyed and Hartnell eyed Anna up with a mean eye. 'Now, what is it you're after?'

'I would appreciate you giving Lady Felicity a message for me.'

'Been up to your old tricks again, have you? I don't do messages for nothing, you know.'

His abrupt voice and grave face manifested the mercenary side of the man, another who apparently had a split personality, but it didn't matter as long as he'll deliver a message to her.

'How much do you want?'

'You're out of luck this time; if she was alive I might be able to help you, but it's a hell of a job contacting the dead.'

Anna couldn't believe what she heard. She stood there staring at the crudeness of the statement. 'What…what did you say?.'

'She's been ill for an age, girl, it was just a matter of time. I miss her as much as you do, my lovely. She was a good un for paying up. Her death was a big blow to me.'

'I don't believe you. Tell me where she lives.'

'I'm not surprised she didn't confide in you, she didn't tell many, but I'm in the know. It's good business to know what's going on around here. If she didn't confide in you, well, you weren't very close to her, were you?'

'We were best friends,' blurted Anna, hurt by the coldness of the man. 'Don't you talk so disrespectfully about her.'

'She's been preparing herself for the hereafter for months. She spent a lot of money on the unfortunate, including me. I'll certainly miss her. Anyway, I can't stop talking here all day, like me you'll have to find another benefactor.'

'I have nowhere to stay. Can I stay here for a few days until I get on my feet?'

'I'm not a charity worker, be on your way and find somewhere else. Felicity is not around to pay for your digs now'

'If Lady Felicity were here you'd have a different tone of voice, wouldn't you?'

'Business is business, If Lady Felicity were here she'd be going into her purse. It's a cruel world we live in. I've got enough kids and grandkids to take my hard earned money.'

'And what if I said I would pay you handsomely?'

He smiled on one side of his cruel face. 'Now that would be different, I might be able to fit you in your old room. You know how comfortable that is.'

'I'd rather sleep in a shop doorway and freeze to death,' she snarled, and turned away leaving him growl like a dog as he slammed the door shut.

She climbed back into the waiting hansom, the shock beginning to spread through her body. The cabby looked in from his back hatch and sighed.

'Do you believe he's the same fella now?'

She looked up at him. 'I didn't believe such people existed.'

'So what's your plan now? Where can I take you?'

'I don't know. I have no place to go. The only person who could have helped has passed away. Poor Felicity,' she whispered as she buried her head in her hands and wept.

'I'm sorry things haven't turned out for you miss, but I can't drive you around all day.'

'I know,' she said controlling herself. 'Do you know of a place I can spend for a couple of nights?'

'Well there are some cheap hostels, but you'll find the conditions basic and the company unsavoury. Most decent places for the homeless are for men. There is a small back-street hotel I know of where they will give you a clean bed and a decent breakfast for a pound a night. You'd have to be in by nine and up by seven. But they're fair.'

Anna thought about the money she had, just the ten pounds Charles had tactfully forced out of Darlington's reluctant wallet and a few pounds savings. She wondered how much she'd have to pay the cabman. 'How much would I owe you if I asked you to take me there, cabby?'

He scratched his head realising the dilemma the young girl had. 'I don't want to sound like old Hartnell, but I've got to make a living, darlin'. You've run up £1.10s already. Normally I would have to charge you the same to get you to the hotel, but I'll do the return journey for just a ten shillings, that will make it a round £2.'

'I appreciate your kindness. Take me there. I'll have to stay somewhere.'

Back through the streets they went, the cab driver seemed to know every short cut and side street that existed. Eventually he got her to the destination and dropped her outside. She gave him his fare and he wished her the best of luck, and then disappeared down the squalid little alley in which he had left her. She looked at the façade of the place, it had been painted in slate grey at some time or other, but the paint was chipped and peeling in places. It stood three storeys high and was crowned by two gables partly hidden by the mist. She entered the half-glass double doors that admitted her to a dimly lit parlour room that served as a reception area. A wooden stairs covered in a thin worn carpet a few yards in led to the upper rooms. There was no receptionist behind the thick oak desk to her left, just a guest book and a brass ping-bell with "Ring please" printed near it. Anna placed her suitcase on the floor and patted the bell with the palm of her hand and waited. A slim middle-aged woman appeared from a door behind the desk and smiled at her.

'Can I help you?' she asked in a squeaky voice, her wan thin face tired but cheery.

'I understand you let rooms for a pound a night including breakfast.'

'A bed dearie, but no breakfast, those days are gone, I'm afraid. If you require breakfast it's a shilling and sixpence extra.'

'Oh, I'll just take the bed.'

'It's a good breakfast for the price; two sausages, one egg, a rasher and some toast and tea,' she persisted in her warm cockney accent.

'No thanks just the room, please.'

'How many nights?`

'I don't know how long I'll be staying. Can I have just the two nights for now?'

'You can have as many or as little as you like but you must pay in advance.'

'Anna got out her purse and gave the woman two pound notes.'

The woman took it and thanked her as she handed her the key. 'I don't know why but you'd better sign the book. Nobody ever come to see who we got staying.—Up the stairs to the first floor, round the banister to number three. It overlooks the front so you can count the traffic if you get bored,' she giggled. 'You've got old Tom for a neighbour, he's okay, a bit untidy that's all.'

'Thank you,' said Anna as she stooped down and picked up her suitcase.'

'Just a couple of things before you go, no men in the room and no eating in the room, those are the strict rules. Across the landing in number four is, Lucy, she's definitely not allowed men in her room, if you see what I mean.' She changed her tone of voice to a low husky whisper—'she's a lady of the night.'

Anna nodded and climbed the stairs. The room was sparsely furnished with a bed, a small, well-used wardrobe with fading

172

varnish and a cracked mirror, a side table with washbasin and jug, and a single wooden chair with a spindle missing in its back. The gas light on the wall had a mantel that had burnt a large hole through its top, but the bed appeared to have fresh linen even though the room had a stale smell of its last occupant who apparently smoked heavily. She had no intention of opening her case and placing her lovely dresses in the grubby wardrobe. She pushed it under the bed along with her food parcel. She sat on the bed for a while wondering what her next move would be. She'd have to find a job pretty quickly. She couldn't sit in the room, it was too claustrophobic; it would have to serve as a bed for the night and that's all. She went outside on the landing, locked her door and made for the stairs.

'Hello, missy, are you staying here?' asked a scruffy old man with a shaking voice, who suddenly appeared in the doorway of the room next to hers.

Anna stopped and turned around nervously. Her neighbour stood there in his baggy trousers and black waistcoat covering a flannel-striped shirt. 'Yes, but only for a night or two,' she said, then bolted down the stairs.

'Nice to meet you,' he said, waving his gnarled hand, but she had gone.

'I'm going out for a short while,' she called to the lady at reception.'

'Make sure you're in by nine.'

'Tell that to the lady of the night,' she mumbled, as she went out the door.

Twenty Four

Anna spent the next two days looking for some kind of work in domestic service. It was a peculiar situation, for every time she applied for a post at an employment agency she was told there was nothing at all in her line of work. She concluded her lack of references were the main cause of her refusals. She had boasted working as a senior serving maid to an eminent family, but declined to declare the name. Revealing her past employer would only lead to relating the experience she had at the Darlington's and the circumstances leading to her dismissal.

The time wasting meant she had to spend another two nights at the hotel. She continued her futile search, and came to believe there was nothing she could do but think of the unthinkable and try and make her way back to Wales. It was common knowledge that there were many small workshops in the Soho and Clerkenwell areas, with most of the heavy industry situated near the river. In desperation she made her way to Soho and applied for a job at one of the many small factories that were in full production at the time, and though it was against her principles to be a "factory girl", any form of employment had to be considered.

She didn't believe her luck could get any worse until she sat in the corridor of a factory personnel department waiting for an interview. There were three other girls sitting with her and full of expectation. She heard footsteps coming down the corridor and looked up automatically. Her heart thumped when she saw the figure of the corpulent Mr Darlington ambling down the corridor with a secretary. He held a fat cigar between his fingers and had a big smile on his full face chatting amiably to the attractive girl. As he was passing the jobseekers he glanced at them momentarily, took little notice and walked on, but a few paces further he stopped suddenly. He turned round and his face suddenly hardened. Without a word he turned and barged through the personnel officer's door. An exchange of a few muffled words sieved through the door, silence for a second or two and then the door burst open. Not looking at the row of girls, he joined his confused secretary and disappeared round the corner of the corridor.

Within minutes the door of the personnel office opened slowly and a head hung out. It was the personnel secretary who smiled broadly at the line of applicants.

'Miss Daily, Miss Smith and Miss Broad, you may come in now.' She lowered her glasses to the tip of her nose. 'You must be Miss Hughes, is that so?'

'That is so,' said Anna,' dolefully.

'I'm afraid we have no more vacancies, sorry.'

'Is there any hope for me if I should apply at a later date?'

'I'm afraid not.' She bent her head and lowered her voice, 'It appears you have an adverse reaction on our dear owner, Mr Darlington. I say this in confidence; if you want a job in factory work I suggest you move out of the area to a place where Mr Darlington has no influence. This is just a small production factory, elsewhere there are larger factories where Mr Darlington is not known. I'm terribly sorry, goodbye,' she concluded and she closed the door.'

Anna slowly stood up feeling as though she were a pariah that had no rights in such a society. Deeply hurt at the rejection she began walking away and wondered if she was guilty of some crime she was unaware of. Was I really so inconsiderate to Jeremy that the world has turned against me? Why did I go in to his room? I could have turned and gone down to the kitchen, he would not have dared complain. Those were the thoughts going through her tired mind as she emerged into the smog-filled roads of Soho.

She wandered the streets for a time and sat on several benches resting from her lethargy. Weak after not eaten since teatime the previous day, she bought a cup of tea and a bun at a street vendor's utility. Temporarily lifted by the food she made her way back to the hotel, deciding to walk the three miles and save some money on transport. When she arrived it was two o'clock in the afternoon, nobody manned the reception as she made her way up the stairs to her room. As she turned the key a female cockney voice called to her from a doorway of the room two doors away from Anna's.

'You alright darlin'? I heard you coming so I popped my head out.'

Anna lifted her head and saw for the first time the "lady of the night" the landlady had mentioned to her a few days ago. The girl leaned on the door jam, her hand on her hip, a friendly smile on the pale lips. Anna was a little surprised at the attire; the long black silky dressing gown and red slippers suggested she had just got out of bed. She could tell by the dark roots of her fair hair that she was not a natural blonde, and the multiple curlers blistering all over her head made her look comical, though her round face looked fresh and pretty.

'I'm fine, thank you.'

'Fancy a cup of tea and a little chat. I get lonely around this time of day.'

Anna was longing for a friend and this girl, she guessed to be a few years her senior, offered the first kind words she had heard in days. 'You seem a little inconvenienced at the moment, do you mean now?'

'You seem as though you could do with a good square meal, darlin'. Come on in and have a cuppa. Excuse the state I'm in, but I had a late night.'

Anna was surprised to see that the room was a bed-sit with a small kitchen, its open door revealing a small worktop and a gas ring. The smell of lilac perfume pervaded the place. She couldn't believe how the flat contrasted with hers. The walls were beautifully decorated with heavy brown-striped wallpaper on a pale yellow background. A golden eiderdown covered the wooden-framed bed, and a dressing table with a large mirror had a pink padded stool tucked under its middle.

'Sit down and make yourself comfortable,' she said, as she made her way to the kitchen. 'My name is Katie, pleased to meet you.'

Anna sat on a red leather chaise longue near the window that overlooked the same street as her room. 'My name's Anna,' she said in reply. 'Pleased to meet you Katie.' She could hear the kettle being filled and a gentle explosion as the gas ring ignited. 'You have a lovely bed-sit here, Katie.'

Katie returned with a smile on her face. 'I pay for it. All the trimmings you see here I bought myself. I've been living here a few years and made an agreement with Jim that if ever I should move out I'd leave it all behind for the next occupant. Well, I've made it my home now and had my wear out of the place. I'm not short of a few bob so it doesn't worry me wherever or whenever I go.'

'Who's Jim?'

'The owner of these digs; he likes to call it a hotel. Huh, some hotel, more like the large inn it used to be. He's made a few alterations but can't hide the fact it's still an inn without the booze. This room is the best in the entire building except for his.'

'I haven't met him.'

'He's hard to find. His wife doesn't know where to find him half the time.—you've met her of course, she mentioned you to me.'

'The lady at reception?'

'That's right. She does the work he takes the cash. Poor sod could do with a break. I expect she's told you my job?'

Anna shifted in her chair with embarrassment. 'She did say something.'

'Well, she's partly right, but I'm not a street girl; there are plenty of those half-price hags around, picking up a couple of pound. I make no bones about it. I'm the upper class type. I work in a respectful place for clients who don't want anyone to know about them. They pay plenty.'

There was a hissing from the kitchen and Katie rushed off. A couple of minutes later she came back carrying a tray with a couple of china cups and saucers, a china teapot and matching tea plates with biscuits and cream cakes.

'Pull that small table near to you, Anna.'

Anna did so, feeling as though the girl had been her friend for years. Katie placed the tray on the table and reached under her dressing table for the padded seat, placing it opposite Anna.

'Help yourself, paleface.'

Anna grinned. 'You're not exactly sun-tanned yourself,' she said, picking up a cake. 'These look expensive.'

'Enjoy them. My worn-out face is from late nights and too much drink, yours is from fatigue and hunger. I know I've been there. I've noticed you coming back miserable and tired, worn to a frazzle, as they say. Come on get it off your chest, what's your trouble?'

Anna swallowed, 'Don't be kind to me, Katie, or I'll cry, and I don't want to cry over male pigs.'

'Ah, well, tell me what you did for a job before you were down and out.'

'Yes, you are right, I am down and out. I worked as a maid for a few years holding off the master's spineless son. But he eventually tricked me into his bedroom and I had to club him with a poker to save myself. His mother came on the scene just as the blood run down his face and made it all my fault. That was the end of my job.'

'You don't know how to handle that type. You could have made a few pounds out of him in a secretive way. If you puckered your lips and talked sweetly to him you could have had what you liked out of him; money, presents, and then maybe let him into your bed.'

Anna finished her cake. She felt embarrassed as a faint smile came to her face. 'I did suggest to him that if he married me he could have his way with me, but he didn't take the bait.'

'Marriage? That was one hell of a mistake. They don't want commitments they want thrills and clandestine activities. Their perverted lust used to shock me at times, but I know them now, and they make me rich.'

'You must be very brave. Don't you fear for your life at times?'

Katie stood up and went to a drawer at the side of her bed and pulled out a little derringer pistol. 'I've always got my little faithful with me.'

Anna gasped. 'I could never shoot someone.'

'It's not loaded, but girl, it sure gets them running.'

Anna admired the spirit of the woman but did not want her to think that she was the same, though she couldn't help but warm to her. 'Thank you for the tea and pastries, Katie, I don't want to overstay my welcome.'

'You stay as long as you like, Anna. It's been a long time since I've had an intelligent female to talk to. What are your plans, anyway?'

'I don't know. I've tried to get a job but I think I've been blacklisted around here. Wherever I go I seem to pick the wrong place. I get no interviews at all.'

'You're a beautiful girl, Anna. You could work the same rooms that I work. The Madam is a friendly and fair woman and the girls are okay too.'

'It's not for me, Katie, thanks all the same. I'm not into that kind of life.

'You're too proud Anna. I was like you at one time, but I got wise.'

'Well, I haven't given myself to a man you see.'

Katie stared hard at Anna. 'You're a virgin?'

'That's right. I've never loved a man enough to go to bed with him.'

'You don't have to love them, darlin', you just take them for their money.'

'I suppose I must have a different view to life from yours.'

'You'll learn. Okay, if you want to be a labouring woman and work in a factory or washing up in a café just for bread money, then you're certainly different than I am. Do you know what I do with the money I don't spend?'

'No.'

'I invest it. And when I can live on my savings, I'll either retire or I may go into competition and be a Madam myself.'

Anna rose and smiled at Katie with some amusement. 'You certainly know your mind, Katie. Anyway, I'd better be on my way.'

Katie saw her to the door and stopped her before she left. Think about it Anna, with your looks and figure, you could earn a hundred pounds a night.'

Anna's eyes nearly popped out of her head. 'A night?'

'All you need to do is work four nights and you'll make four hundred. You'll have three full days leisure to buy yourself whatever you fancy.'

Anna hurried away calling back to her, 'Don't tempt me, don't tempt me.'

'Come and see me as often as you want. There'll always be bite to eat and a cuppa.'

As Anna opened her door she turned around. I'd like that Katie, I may call in tomorrow.'

Twenty Five

Two days later Anna was still residing in the grubby hotel, but now she was penniless. Another night's rent was required. It was eight pm and she was looking out of the window as she had done all afternoon and into the evening. Earlier, her heart was a little lighter because the brightness of the improved weather conditions had lifted her spirits; the sun had hung above the narrow street illuminating the pavement on the opposite side.

People had been chatting in a pleasant manner grateful for the change, and the trotting of the horses below had sounded jolly as though the beasts of burden were happy with their lot. But now it was dusk and her suitcase already packed should the worst scenario happen and she be evicted.

Turning away from the gloom and loneliness of the changed melancholy street, she pondered on her next move. Embittered with her unnecessary situation and Katie's words ringing in her brain, she had told her new-found friend that she could not go through with it. Katie had laughed in a friendly way for she knew Anna would never have made the grade as a high-class call girl. Katie had been unbelievably beautiful in her preparation for the night's duty, as she had called it. Her provocative working attire, her hair down and curling around her shoulders, her low-cut blouse and cosmetic make-up had transformed her into a gorgeous play-doll.

Yes, Anna thought, still hearing Katie's words, she should have been more cunning in her attitude towards Jeremy, but now she realized he had been aware of her antics and was only waiting for an opportunity to have her. No, she was convinced trying to sweet talk him would not have worked. Besides, that was over and in the past and could not be changed. She would have to go to Mrs Cavanaugh and plead for credit until she found a job. Just a couple of days would do it, she persuaded herself.

She checked herself in the mirror and run her hands down the side of her waist, touched her hair and opened the door. At the top of the stairs she stopped when she heard raised voices of a man and woman. She listened for a minute, her heart sinking, as she realized the pleas of the woman were those of Mrs Cavanaugh, and the man's voice, she guessed, was that of her husband.

'I haven't had a day off for three weeks,' she pleaded. 'You are not being fair.'

'What do you do, woman?' his cynical tones gurgled out through a congested throat. 'Maggie does all the rooms. All you have to do is keep the books and make a bit of food now and again. You don't even have to make breakfast for the guests any longer. I organize the deliveries and the finances of the business, do all the running around and ordering.'

'But I need a break. I'd prefer to be more involved with the shopping and ordering.'

'You made too many errors the last time I let you run the place.'

'I'm entitled to a couple of days leisure!' she screamed.

'Shut up, woman, do you want everyone in the hotel to hear you?'

Anna decided to casually make an appearance and walked leisurely down the stairs, but tactfully making her steps heavy and giving the banister a little slap on the way. It seemed to work, for before she had reached the bottom the altercation had stopped. However, it was obvious to her that a request for a couple of days stay with no money in hand would be futile.

Mr and Mrs Cavanaugh were standing behind the reception desk, a weak smile on both faces. It was the first time she had seen the husband but already she had taken a dislike to him. His six-foot ungainly figure, dressed in a black suit, stood arched like a huge vulture, for his nose was aquiline and his face as pale as death, in contrast to his wife's flushed appearance. He watched Anna with watery eyes as she approached them.

'Good evening,' said Anna with a disinterested tone.

'My dear,' he said, his voice weak and apologetic, 'Am I right in thinking that you be our new guest, Anna Hughes?'

'That's right,' said Anna, politely.

'Oh dear, we have made a bad impression I'm sure.'

'In what way?'

'Well, you may have overheard—Inadvertently, I'm sure, my wife and I having a little domestic difference as married couples often do. Please don't take the impression we are generally like that.' He turned to his wife. 'Are we dear?'

'Of course not, I'm sure Miss Hughes does not think so.'

'Of course not,' mimicked Anna. 'I heard raised voices but thought nothing of it. I've heard noisy guests in many hotels and find it part of a busy, thriving business.'

'Ah then, our innocent little difference is forgotten. Are you enjoying your stay with us, my dear?'

She wanted to tell him what a rotten little slum she thought it to be, but there was no point. 'I find it adequate.'

'Oh dear, just adequate?'

'Pardon me for saying so, but this hotel was recommended to me by the cabby who brought me here. I thought it a fair price at the time as there was a breakfast included in the offer. I was very disappointed to learn that breakfast was no longer part of the deal.'

He turned to his wife. 'Did you not tell the lady breakfast could be served for an extra nominal fee?'

'Your wife did indeed,' intervened Anna, not wanting his poor wife to get any blame. 'However, I feel you should make it clear by printing boldly on your notice board that anyone requiring breakfast will have to pay extra.'

'My dear you are right, we have inadvertently misled you and I shall put it right. Tomorrow morning you shall have a hearty breakfast free of charge.'

Mrs Cavanaugh quickly presumed the offer could not take place. 'I believe the lady is not staying the night, for she has not paid in advance for another day.'

The husband feigned a mild expression on his lined face. 'I am ashamed that we have not been as welcoming as to force you to leave so soon. Can we not make it up to Miss Hughes?'

Anna was delighted with the unexpected invitation. 'Well,' she began sadly, in an embarrassed stance. 'I am between jobs at the moment and have currently run out of ready cash, but I'm sure to get a job soon, so I would appreciate some credit for a few days.'

She looked up at him. 'I'll be able to pay my way then and stay for many months with you.'

The woman's eyes darted to her husband's shocked face which had suddenly lost the faint smile that had been there. The man's interrogating eyes burned into Anna's, and she had to turn away to avoid her shame. He began wringing his blue-veined hands to control his wrath, then forced a twisted smile. 'My dear, you ask for credit? Do you know how many tricksters have tried that in the past? I will tell you, too many for me to fall for the same cunning little ploy again. If you have no money, make sure you and your baggage are out of here within the hour.' It was then he turned and shuffled through the door behind him.

Mrs Cavanaugh stretched out her arm and touched Anna on her shoulder. 'I'm sorry, miss, I didn't realize you had no money. I thought that you were moving on.'

'That's all right. I didn't really think he'd give a starving dog a bone, anyway.'

'I think you're very perceptive. You don't have to rush out. He'll be gone to join his cronies in the pub in a few minutes and won't be back till midnight.'

'Thanks—hope you have a day off soon.'

'I'll get my way eventually. If all fails I'll walk out, that usually does the trick. He can't get a head-cook-and-bottle-washer as cheap as me.'

Anna gave a half-hearted smile and made for the door. 'Bye.'

'Good bye miss, remember you can stay till morning, he won't be in a fit state to know who's in and who's not.'

Anna wandered the streets again, every step washing all hopes from her brain. She prayed in a meditating manner for some wave of kindness to bring about a miraculous happening, and then asked herself why she is seeking God? She recalled that passage in the New Testament: "Your Father knows what things you have need of before you ask." That's what Jesus said, she remembered. So what's the use of praying? Can you see what state I'm in, God? Can you see what needs I have? In a capitulating reverie she made her way through the streets, sometimes smiling to herself or nodding in a mocking fashion. Yes, I've made a fool of myself. I suppose the cynics back home would say I'm unable to cope with the demands of contemporary life. Well I can't, I'm a labouring woman's daughter not fit to be a lady and two proud to be labourer. I could keep looking for a job, and she nodded again to herself. But I won't. Oh no, what kind of employment am I suited to? A labouring job! I'd rather die than demean myself for the rest of my life. And she nodded in agreement. People passing by gave her a wide berth, unsure of the strange girl. They saw her, but she didn't see them nor could she hear them. Too engrossed in her stupor, deprecating herself, she could only hear the voice of her inner conscience. She suddenly giggled to herself when Katie came into her mind. I could do what Katie suggested. Oh yea, I'd be sitting there in the middle of painted-up, glorified girls-of-the-street waiting to be chosen by a client, and who should walk in?—She laughed aloud startling pedestrians—Fatty Darlington with nicotine around his lips and a fat cigar in his chops, that's who would walk in. Then she stopped. I could go back to compassionate John, but would he have that much of compassion? Not even John could forgive my desertion. Besides, I have no train fare, you stupid girl—Oh grief of hell, what did that women see in that monster Cavanaugh? She must be desperate. There was a long pause in Anna's brain, she wasn't talking to herself anymore, she was just walking slowly picturing the ultimate consideration. There was a bridge she saw in her mind, a bridge with a river underneath busy with boats. Yes, she thought, that would solve everything. She smiled again. Why that would be so simple. And then God could choose where I should go: up for safekeeping, or down to Satan. Either way God it must be better than this. Darkness had fallen and she began to hurry, firstly taking long strides and then running at a gentle pace. She knew where to go and how to get there for the place was very familiar to her. She was in the illuminated Charing Cross Road slowing down to a quick walking pace brushing past people. She continued on until she reached Charing Cross Station. There she stopped breathless and panting involuntarily. Leaning against the wall she became aware of the familiar place she had so often met up with the Suffragettes. Now the street girls were out. She ignored them with distain, flaunting themselves, selling their dignity so cheaply. There they were, smiling and trying to catch the eyes of men, hoping for an agreeable smile in return, and then the furtive follow-on until they were away from the pick-up zone, going to a place arm in arm. Anna knew not where but imagined a disgusting den of filth. Now she felt sympathy for them. They had nothing but their bodies to sell. At least there is some pride in an honest job as a labouring woman. I can hold my head up high. She crossed the road and went on to the Thames embankment and made her way to Blackfriars Bridge. Hardly anyone about as she began to cross, just a few people up ahead of her making their way to the other side. She stopped at the middle of the span between gas streetlights and leaned over the parapet gazing down at the dark quiet water. No traffic at the moment. The river was inviting; the answer to all her misery, the beautiful painless peace of death. Shall I, shall I not? she thought playing a game with herself. Suddenly everything seemed settled and all the anguish left her. She was at peace as she attempted to climb over the steel structure. She managed to lift herself up until her stomach crossed over the top, her head hanging over the waters, her legs dangling on the bridge side. It was strange how the sounds of life came back to her, for she heard the noise of trotting hoofs and a man's voice calling her. Is that you, John? she mumbled. Things happened quickly just then, for the clip clopping stopped and she felt hands on her dragging her back off the parapet.

'Come on now, miss, things can't be that bad,' said the cabbie.

'Please let me go,' she pleaded.

'I will not,' he said, as he manhandled her away from danger.

'Bring her into the cab,' someone called.

'I'll do that, sir,' said the cabbie, and he escorted her firmly to the hansom.

'Where are you taking me? Get your hands off me. I'm not going back to prison.'

The man inside the hansom helped her in and sat her down. 'Drive to the next gas light,' he ordered the cabbie.'

'Where are you taking me?'

'Please don't be afraid, I am not taking you anywhere. I want to help if you will allow me.'

188

'I know what you want but you won't get it off me,' mister.
'Damn men!'

'I assure you I want nothing from you, and all men are not damned. I just want to help.'

'I don't need help.'

'Then I shan't detain you, but first please let me try.'

The cabbie pulled up as near as he could by the streetlight. Anna averted her face away from the light so that the stranger could only see her profile.

'Now lady, what is this all about, we cannot have young ladies throwing themselves off the bridges of London, you know. Please let me take you home, I'm sure you and your family can work things out.'

She was still confused in her despair but coherent and responsive. She spoke in a whisper. 'I haven't got a home to go to, nor a family to work things out. Leave me alone.'

'Oh dear, that is very sad. What about your friends?'

'The only true friend I had died!' she blurted, as the fury in her suddenly erupted and she turned full face to the stranger and screamed. 'I have nobody! Nobody! So let me go.'

The stranger gasped, astonished at the familiar face before him. 'Good Lord in Heaven. It is Anna, if I am not mistaken.'

Anna's eyes widened as she stared at the man. 'Who are you? I don't know you.'

'You've forgotten me, Anna, and though you are a little thinner in the face you are still as beautiful as ever.'

'I don't know you. What tricks are you playing on me?'

'Anna, have a good look at me.'

She scanned his face deeply for a few seconds. 'You look familiar.'

'You came up on the train with me some years ago. It's Timothy, don't you remember me?'

His face blossomed in her memory and for a moment she was elated and wanted to scream with joy for the wonderful reunion. But then her face turned away again as shame spread through her soul.

'It's good to see you again, but I'm afraid I'm not the girl you believe me to be.'

He stretched out his arms and his soft hands gently turned her face to him again. He didn't understand her statement. 'You cannot fool me. We were on the train far too long for me to make such a mistake.' Now, where are you staying?'

Emotions welled up in her and she could not restrain the immense relief inside her. She relented and lost all her reserve. 'I have no place to stay, nor do I have any money. I can't find a job and I have no friends to go to. The friends I had were in my last employment. I was dismissed from there because I wouldn't let the son of the house have his way with me. His father is quite powerful around these parts and has blacklisted me. Now, do you see my predicament? I have nothing left in life. I belong nowhere.'

'Anna, would you like to know where I am bound for tonight?'

'Tell me,' she said in a dismissive way.'

'Well, you will remember my saying on the way up from Cardiff that I commute regularly to and from the city often in the execution of my work. The cabby is presently taking me to Paddington station to catch the night train to Cardiff. I shall be delighted if you will join me on the journey.'

'I have nothing. No money. Nothing.'

'Not even any belongings?'

'I left my suitcase in my last lodgings.'

'Then we shall go there and regain them. And then you shall accompany me to Wales paid by the expenses of my father's company in Cardiff.'

'I'm a mess; ashamed of my appearance.'

'You have a change of clothes, surely?'

'Yes, or course.'

'Then I shall wait for you to brighten yourself up.'

'What do I have to do to repay you?'

'It is a high penalty, I'm afraid. I will have the pleasure of your company all to myself for the duration of the journey. Agreed?'

She could feel the tears running down her face and she brushed them away with her fingers. 'Why are you doing this, Timothy?'

'Purely for selfish reasons; firstly I would be truly lonely on the night train, and secondly, it may help me to get into Heaven when I die.'

'You deserve to have a wonderful wife.'

'Ah. That is another matter. I am a confirmed bachelor. I have need of no woman, except to admire those who have unique personalities. I think you are a brave lady to go alone into the big city and seek independence. You have much to tell me and I am sure the journey will fly by.'

She burst into an uncontrollable fit of tears sobbing, 'Thank you, oh thank you Timothy.'

Twenty Six

By the time Timothy had made the detour to collect Anna's suitcase, waited for her to change in to fresh clothes and then on to Paddington Station, the train had just left. However, he had a relaxed attitude to it all and took things as they came without stress or strain. Anna was troubled by the inconvenience she had caused, but Timothy waved his hand to the wind as though it were no problem.

'There'll be another in an hour or so,' he said, as they stood in the subdued lighting on the empty platform, the smell of the departed locomotive still pungent in the vicinity. 'It will give us more time to relax and have something to eat.'

It was then Anna managed to catch her breath after all the hurrying and become more aware of the man who had come to her rescue. There was a lilt in his voice she hadn't noticed before. A voice that was clear and confident. Timothy was certainly an individual and stood out from others with his beige coat and tan cravat. Thin featured and handsome, his pale cheeks needed a little colour. He was aware she was inspecting him. He run his hand through is mop of fair hair and smiled at her.

With a mischievous expressive face he said, 'Do I pass the inspection?'

'I'm sorry, I just can't believe how things have happened and so quickly.'

'Don't be sorry. How are you feeling now?'

'I feel much better now, thank you. You're going to a lot of trouble and expense on my behalf.'

'Think nothing of it, wait here and rest while I go to the ticket office and find the time of the next train.'

Anna waited obediently, her mind spinning in an eddy of confusion. I'm going home, she thought with trepidation. What am I going to do when I get there? Look up John and say, I'm back John, how are you? God I can't do that, he'll murder me for sure. Maybe I will be able to get a job as a housemaid in one of the managerial establishments or waitress in a Merthyr café, if there is nothing else I'll just have to get a job as a barmaid.

'We have an hour and a half to wait which means we have time for a meal,' announced Timothy as he arrived back.'

'Oh Timothy I can't keep accepting all this charity.'

'It's not charity. It's paid for on expenses. Besides, this little adventure takes me away from my routine tedium. Come, I know of a place we can have a quiet meal and chat. You can tell me all about your experiences in London.'

Anna winced at the thought. Telling of her years in London and all the activities she had been up to, did not fill her with joy.

He picked up her suitcase and they left the station making their way on Bishop Road. Half way down Bishop Road they turned right into a side street and walked another two hundred yards where they came to a cafe, brightly lit and cosily laid out. Inside, Timothy demonstrated his familiarity of the place by making for a two-seater, partitioned cubicle where they sat opposite each other on cushioned seats at a polished oak table. Anna immediately noted the tablemats had pictures of the Tower of London printed on them.

'Is this place special to you, Timothy?'

'Not really, but whenever I'm at a loose end waiting for a train I come here to pass the time away. It's got that inner city feel about it, yet distant from the claustrophobic centre.'

'It's very private in its layout. I like it.'

'Good, then we shall order.' He turned around and caught the attention of a waitress who immediately came over.

'Good evening Mr Brown,` she said, with an Irish accent and an enigmatic smile as she glanced at Anna. 'What can I get you this evening?'

Timothy slit his eyes at her in a playful manner. 'For the present, you can keep you mind on the job, Mary.' Then he gave her a big smile. 'However, for me, I shall have my usual, a fillet of bream, saute potatoes, peas and matelote sauce.'

'And for the lady?' asked the girl as they both waited for Anna.

Anna shifted with discomfort. 'I'm not quite sure what I want,' she said.

'I can recommend the speciality I have just ordered, Anna. It really is both simple and delicious.'

'Then I'll have the same, thank you.'

'It will take a little time,' the waitress said, as she left, twisting her lip at Timothy.

Timothy turned to Anna and smiled kindly. 'Now Anna, tell me what you've been doing these past years.'

A frown spread over her face and some lines appeared on her forehead. 'I'd rather you tell me what you've been doing since the last time we met.'

'Only if you promise me you'll respond by favouring me with an anecdote of your time spent on this world of ours'

'That will be my life story.'

He touched her hand. 'You interest me, Anna.

'It will take more than an anecdote, but you first.'

'Very well, let me see now, where shall I start. The problem is my repetitive life guides me to exercise the same things over and over again. I keep the books and documents at my father's business in the office at London docks, then I travel to the smaller, though busy, docks at Cardiff and do the same there. I am a commuting financial wizard, so my father tells everybody, but in reality I'm a glorified accountant. My father has a good business importing and exporting. I have a month in Cardiff, but most of that time I am imprisoned in an office down the docks.'

The word, imprisoned, shuddered her heart. 'It must be very complicated,' she quickly said.

'Not really, over the years I have had a lot of experience. I managed a first in economics at Cambridge, and then joined my father's business. Very boring, you know.'

'What do you do for leisure? I expect you go to the theatre.'

'Rarely. I like to get out and about when I'm not working. I'm more the artistic type than the sporting type, you know. I like painting and writing and have had modest success in local circles. Alas, I am unable to pursue my literary ambitions as my father relies too heavily on me, even if I do say so myself. Oh, and I attended the funeral of Queen Victoria in 1901. If I had known you were within my circle of communication I would have got in touch and taken you to Windsor.'

'I'm not a royalist, Timothy; I live in the next galaxy.'

'Ah but you would have been impressed. She was taken to her resting place on a gun carriage pulled by some magnificent horses and escorted by the Royal Horse Artillery. Her son Edward VII walked behind the carriage with the German Kaiser followed by hordes of dignitaries and foreign officials, it was very moving. But I digress; I was talking about my father's business.'

'And your writing. Can't you employ an accountant so that you can further your ambitions?'

'I do have an understudy for when I am unable to work, but my father, God preserve him, likes me to be close to his business and trusts nobody else—Enough of me, what of you?'

Anna lowered her head. 'My background can't compare to yours, Timothy. You were born into a secure family. I was dropped from somewhere out of space and landed in a void. My education is minimal.'

He rested his elbows on the table and his head in his cupped hands. 'I assure you I was born in a modest street called Whitefriars near the docks, nothing grand.'

'That is grand compared to my birth.'

'You intrigue me more and more. I shall have to write a book about you. Come now, we made a bargain.'

Believing she will never see him again, and wanting to know what an outsider really would think of her entrance into the world, she leaned forward. 'If you insist: I was born an illegitimate child on a flagstone floor in the basement kitchen of a second rate hotel.' She waited for a response, but he didn't take his eyes off her. 'My mother had worked at the hotel as a dish washer and skivvy, but couldn't hold down the job because she had fallen in love with my father who I never knew. Because she left her duties to meet up with my father, her work was neglected, as a result she finally ran away with my father. This she told me when we lived in the workhouse.'

This time, Timothy' jaw dropped hearing the word Workhouse. But he declined to comment and there were no words between them until he recovered. Anna waited.

196

'Go on, Anna, I am still listening,' he said softly.

'I was fostered out to a religious couple of extreme views; a puritanical foster father who demanded the highest in obedience. He had me read the New Testament over and over until I could find a text that he randomly chose. I could stand it no longer so I ran away when I was seventeen, hoping to find my father who worked somewhere in Merthyr or Dowlais. After many months of searching I was told he had died. I then got married.'

Timothy sat up and laid his back on the rear of the seat. 'You are married?'

'Yes, Timothy, does that shock you?'

'It made my brain turn over. Yet you came to London on your own.'

'We lived in a little grubby cottage in Dowlais in a place called the Cwm—you'd probably call it something beautiful like a dingle or dell. I suppose before it was crowded with small terraces of houses and cottages and inhabited it might have been a lovely green valley. Anyway, we rented the cottage while my husband John saved for a house of our own. We were there over two years, him in work all day, and me a lonely skivvy growing calluses on my hands and knees. The only entertainment was to go to the local pubs and drown my sorrows. I saw myself growing old before my time with no independence; a steelworker's wife to fetch and carry and be a dog's body. Then I read in a newspaper of the wonderful work the Suffragettes were doing in London.' She looked him straight in the eyes and forcefully said, 'I upped and came to London and joined those glorious women.'

Timothy's eyes widened and his mouth dropped open. 'You're a Suffragette?'

'Fully paid up with a jail sentence and forcefully fed to ensure my survival.'

'Heavens above have mercy on this poor tortured soul. Anna you are a magnificent specimen of womanhood.'

'You're not embarrassed or ashamed to know me?'

'You are a free spirit akin to me. I am proud to be your acquaintance.' He reached over and shook her hand enthusiastically.

She suddenly felt clean. She had told of her stigmatic past and was actually accepted.

It was then Mary arrived. 'Here's your meals Mr Brown and the, uh, lady's,' said the waitress as she placed the meals on the table.

'Mary, may I introduce to you a Welsh lady and a Celtic cousin of yours. This is Anna who you may be proud of, she is a martyr and a Suffragettes.'

'Is that so, then let me shake your hand, for I, too, am a woman of the good cause. May God bless you and keep you, me darling. Many of my kin have gone to Wales for work in the coal and iron industries, personally, I prefer the big city.'

'I'm afraid I've had enough of the city, I'm going back home.'

'Well, safe journey, then, and look after yourself for this cruel world won't look after you.'

The waitress left, but the enthusiastic Timothy wanted to know more about Anna. 'Tell me to mind my business if you want Anna, but how are you going to reconcile yourself with your husband? I imagine he will be extremely hostile towards you.'

Anna's thoughts went back to the Cwm and the gentle man she married. 'John was never a hostile man, though he might have changed after the way I treated him. I'll just have to stand in front of him and say, I'm back, I don't deserve you but if you want me I'm yours.'

'"The boss's son," as you called that cowardly miscreant who tried to bed you, you fought him off admirably. That goes in your favour. Have you had interest in any other man whilst you've been in London?'

'Of course not; my passion has been with the Suffragettes, my job has been a necessity.'

'Well then, it all goes in your favour. If I was a judge and you were up before me, all this evidence would be mitigating circumstances. I would put you on probation for an appropriate time for you to prove to your husband that you are a respectable and admirable lady; chaste, faithful and honourable, who had an overwhelming desire to put right that which you believed to be wrong. A woman who chanced everything to fight that part of society which deemed women to be inferior; reconciliation, in my humble opinion is just and acceptable.

'You make it sound so simple and light-hearted. You have a talent for saying the right things at a crucial time. You've made me feel so much better. I haven't betrayed him, that's for sure. That mad moment to go to London may have been foolish, at least, that's what I tell myself.'

'Anna, you may go home and ask forgiveness on those grounds and, if your husband truly loves you, he will forgive. Furthermore, you say you have not the education that I possess, rubbish; you have the education of life itself.' He pulled a pocket watch from his waistcoat and gave it a glance. 'My word, we had better stop talking and eat our train is half an hour away from us.'

Twenty Seven

In thoughtful mood and the train to Merthyr chugging along up the gradient, Anna's heart had lost its lightness when she left carefree Timothy at Cardiff station. With great kindness he had given her ten pounds telling her, with a grin, it was an advance on her story royalties for giving him permission to write it. His optimistic attitude and logical reasoning had given her confidence to face the consequences. She had resolved to be honest and penitent with John, intending to ask forgiveness and to take into consideration her mitigating naive impulses, and the fact that she had been a faithful wife, if not a loyal one. However, a great sigh burst from her in the empty compartment as she neared the terminus, and she began to doubt the encouraging words of Timothy. The train came to a hissing halt and she stepped down on to the familiar platform. With suitcase in hand and dressed in lemon blouse and tan skirt, she handed her ticket to the porter amid the rush of the buffeting crowd. The drizzling weather outside the station was consistent with the whole journey, though she had managed to have a couple of hours sleep on the London train thereby having a short respite from the window-weather. Unfolding her raincoat that hung over her case, she quickly put it on and donned her boater hat. The place had altered a little over the years she had been away. New buildings had gone up, stores and shops had changed hands and she was surprised that tramlines stretched up the High Street as far as she could see. The town was as busy as ever with traffic and pedestrians, street traders and idlers. As she strolled passed the Castle Hotel she heard a rumbling behind her. It was a tram coming up the street and stopping near the hotel. She quickly made for it.

'Excuse me, could you tell where this tram is going?'

'Now wouldn't I be a poor conductor if I didn't, my lovely. Where do you want to go?'

'Dowlais.'

'This is the one for you, then. Last stop Bush Hotel.'

'Do you stop near the bottom of the Cwm?.'

'That'll be two stops before the Bush Hotel.'

'Thank you, I'll get off there.'

'As you please. Hold tight now, here we go.'

Anna had intended to go straight to Horse Street, but changed her mind hoping that John still lived in the terraced house down at the Cwm. It had crossed her mind he might have moved back in with his sister, but if a confrontation could be avoided with Elizabeth, it would be less stressful. Going up through Penydarren it seemed only yesterday she and John had walked the same road to Merthyr where he had bought her the red boa she had prized so much and still had in her suitcase.

She could not believe five years had gone so quickly; like an hour in her life that had been filled with drama, happiness and suffering. And now, she was on her way back to the humble dwelling she had escaped as though London had been a dream. With ambivalent emotions running through her soul, she heard the conductor shout out, 'bottom of the hill, your stop, my lovely.' She thanked him and made her way up the muddy lanes and rickety paths of the Cwm, passing through the lowly terraced houses, climbing ever nearer to her previous home. Up the flagstone steps she eventually reached 21 Cwm Graig.

The front door and windows had been painted chocolate brown and flowery curtains hung behind white net-curtains in the clear-clean panes. His sister Elizabeth has been keeping the house spic and span, she thought. I hope she's not here and him in work. Plucking up courage she knocked the door and waited for the worst. A few seconds later the door opened and a stout woman stood there with her sleeves rolled up and a turban on her head.'

'Yes, me darlin' what can I do for you? If it's a room you'll be wanting you've come to the wrong place. I've got a lodger and there's only room for her.'

The Irish accent took her by surprise, and she stood there speechless for a time.

'Has the cat got your tongue or something?'

'I'm sorry I was expecting to see Mr Hughes.'

'And who is Mr Hughes when he's at home?'

'My husband.'

'And what would your husband be doing in a respectable house like mine?'

'It's your house?'

'My God the girl's got a fever. Would I be standing here answering me front door if I didn't live here now?'

'Oh. I see. Ho…how long have you been living here?'

'The cheek of the girl. That's my business.'

'I only ask because I used to live here with my husband. I've been away for some years and I foolishly thought he might still be living here.'

'I'm not going to get any deeper into this conversation, me head is beginning to spin. I rent this house from a Mr McIntyre and have done so for the past two years. Who lived here before, I do not know nor do I care. Now if it's a room you're wanting my friend, Mary O'Neil, has a spare one up at number 41 Top Cwm Graig. She lost her husband in that drift explosion a year ago. She'll be needing the money. Tell her Widow Mahoney sent you. Off you go now before me head explodes.'

Widow Mahoney closed the door, "41 Top Cwm Graig" echoed in her ear. Anna stood there realizing thinking Mr McIntyre still owned the house. She stood there long enough for the curtains to twitch and a hand shooing her away. There was only one place left to go and that was Horse Street where John must have moved back in with his sister. Feeling things were beginning to go against her she held her hand up to the window and moved off up the winding lane to Lower Elizabeth Street making her way up the steep road to Dowlais. She stopped at the entrance to Mary Ann Street and was tempted for a while to call in and see if the Rees family still lived in the centre house, but the thought of the reception she might have changed her mind; it would probably be hostile. The Carmarthen Arms stood there, and the memories of her drinking bouts with John and David, the friendly arguments about womens` rights…no, she must go on and get things settled. She made her way down North Street, turned left at the top of South Street, passing the Oddfellows Hall in Upper Union Street, and then rested on a short stone wall near the top of Horse Street. There before her stood the new building on the corner of Horse Street and upper Union Street: the Constitutional Club. As she watched the world go by she realized the road rose steeply in areas too irregular for trams. Nevertheless the place was busy with pedestrians and shoppers, some working horse and carts and an occasional horse and buggy. Two old ladies, Welsh shawls sheltering their heads, gave her a polite nod and smiled as they passed. Dowlais had hardly changed over the years. St Johns Church still stood proudly at the top of the road, the huge stone-block wall of its perimeter following the road all the way up and around the left to its entrance. The same old bigwigs still go there, I expect. Praising God on Sundays and working their men to early deaths on weekdays. For all I know John may be dead. Always a death or two in this town; collieries, iron works, fever and a few from drunken brawls, I shouldn't wonder. Come on, Anna, she admonished herself, you're stalling. Get down that road to his sister's house.

She stood up and slowly made her way down Horse Street until she arrived at the door. She doubted her sanity just then, but she knew she had to knock. She stood there for two minutes as people went by and gave her quizzical looks, though she hadn't noticed. She took a deep breath and knocked. She could hear a woman's voice inside giving instructions to answer the door. When it opened she was shocked to see a little girl who appeared to be at and age of four or five.

'Mammy said my Dad's in work and she's busy washing clothes, and if you're a gypsy she's got plenty of pegs.'

Anna couldn't figure out what the situation was. 'I see. Tell your Mam that 'I'd like to see her for a minute and I'm not a gypsy.'

'Mammy said Dad's in work and she's busy washing clothes.'

'What is your Dad's name, please?'

It was then the mother came to the door wiping her hands in a rough piece of cloth. 'Who is it Megan?'

'She says she's not a gypsy.'

'The mother brushed in front of the little girl. 'What is it you are wanting, my lovely?'

'I wanted to see John Hughes.'

204

'John Hughes. 'I'm afraid he moved away with his sister three years ago. My husband has this house now, you see, he bought it off Mr Hughes before he left.'

'Oh, I see. Did Mr Hughes say where he was moving to?'

'Not as I know, no, I'm sure he didn't. Are you belonging to him then?'

Anna turned away. 'Thank you for telling me.'

'You look tired, my lovely, would you like a cup of tea and a Welsh cake?'

'That's very kind of you,' said Anna as she left. 'But no thank you.'

'Why doesn't the lady want a cup of tea, Mammy?'

'I don't know child. Come on in, this is no weather to be standing on the doorstep, let alone tramping the roads looking for somebody that's not here.'

Anna tiredly strolled back up the road to Upper Union Street and went into a café for a cup of tea and a light meal to think things over. The clock on the wall was showing 12.30. There was plenty of time left in the day to ask around for the whereabouts of John, but the few hours she'd had slept on the train had not prepared her for an arduous search for information, besides she didn't know where to start. It would be more sensible if she found a place to stay, or even a place to work, before exhausting herself. Then it crossed her mind that widow Mahoney had given her an address at Top Cwm Graig. Was it 21? She asked herself. No that was our old house. 41, that's it, Mrs O'Neil. It will do for a couple of days.

When she found 41 Top Cwm Graig she realized it was more convenient to gain access to Dowlais than that of her previous abode in the Cwm. There were children playing around the area with smudged faces and dressed in old clothes. Mrs O'Neil was a friendly woman in her mid-thirties. Her slim appearance and pale features suggested she was not a strong woman. She welcomed Anna with a tired smile and blue expectant eyes. Anna explained her situation and an enthusiastic acquiesce gushed from the woman who obviously needed the money.

'Of course, yes, yes, God bless you and widow Mahoney. I'm a widow too, you know. It's been over a year now, but the children and mee-self of course, miss him dearly. You look tired. I'll put the kettle on and make a nice cup of tea for you now.'

'I've just had a meal up at the café thank you. I would like to see my room so that I can unpack and settle in.'

'Of course, of course, I'll be showing you the room then. I hope you'll approve of it Mrs...?

'Call me Anna.'

'Fine, fine, and you can call me Mary, named after the Mother of God, would you believe it. We'll be friends, I'm sure. Now there are only two bedrooms here, me four children sleep in the large one and the small one we keep for guests, but it's cosy and clean and warm in the winter. And you won't hear a pip out of the kiddies at night, you can be certain of that. I've told them if they frighten away me paying guest they'll have nothing to eat for a week.'

Anna inspected her room with the anxious landlady looking on. The room came up to Mrs O'Neil's description. Clean curtains hung at the small four-paned window, the single bed appeared comfortable and the small dressing table and single wardrobe were polished to a fine shine.

'It looks quite suitable Mary, I'll take it.'

'God bless you. I'm sure you'll be comfortable. Would you be paying a week in advance, Anna?'

'How much, Mary'?

'Would five shillings and sixpence be alright with you?'

Anna took her purse out. 'There you are, there's seventeen shillings to cover three weeks, I'm sure you can do with it.'

Mary's tearful eyes lit up at the money, and the gesture was overwhelming. 'My God, you're a saint to be sure.'

Mary, one thing puzzles me, where do you sleep at night?'

'Oh don't you worry about that; I'm late to bed and early to rise, so I have me sleep at night, and sometimes an hour in the afternoon, all on the comfortable sofa in the living room. I'll leave you to it now Anna.'

Twenty Eight

Anna spent the next few days feeling lost and alone again. She had breakfast each morning with Mary and the children who grew in steps from a two-year-old to a nine year old, two girls and two boys, but it was not what she wanted. Once more the priority was to find a job so that she could provide for herself and, most importantly, to find where John had gone. Her homecoming would not be complete until she was reconciled with her husband.

The two older children, one boy one girl, attended a small school run by volunteers who had other means of income. When Mary had told her of the school Anna thought she might apply for a post helping out, but then Mary added it was voluntary organization with no pay, Anna's hopes were dashed once again. Then one day widow Mahoney called to have a cup of tea and a chat, by which time Anna's dilemma concerning the whereabouts of John was known by both the widow and Mary. Mrs Mahoney suggested she get in touch with Mr McIntyre the landlord, for he might know where John may have moved to. Anna hadn't thought of that and decided it was worth a try, though deep in her heart came a fear of meeting John again and how he would react. However, the outcome was negative. Negative as far as knowing where her husband had gone. However, she was informed by Mr McIntyre of a man who knew John and was once his colleague when they both worked together. He didn't know where this man lived but could tell her he was quite a popular individual who was known by most people in the drinking fraternity. He was sure that most publicans would know of a Spaniard by the name of Miguel. Anna knew what she had to do; go to the most popular pubs and make enquiries. She told Mary of her plans, plans that shocked her newfound friend.

'Are you sure you know what you're doin'? There's many a pub around Dowlais where only the Devil his self will go.'

'I can look after myself, Mary, don't you fret.'

'But there have been robberies and beatings, terrible at times; drunken men have no respect for nobody. And a girl like you will have no chance with the likes of those brutes. If you must go then go early when it will still be light and come home early.'

'There would be no use going early, half the men will still be in work.'

'Shall I go and fetch widow Mahoney? She can look after the little ones and I'll come with you.'

'No, no, I will be alright.'

'May God protect the innocent,' Mary whispered.

At eight o'clock that night she came down from her room. The children cheered and applauded as she made her striking appearance. Mary came in from the kitchen to see what all noise was about and gasped at the lady before her.

'Surely, surely, you're not going out like that.'

'I'm not going to dress like the dowdy working girls, if that's what you mean.'

'You'll be raped for sure.'

'I looked after myself in London, and I can look after myself in Dowlais.'

'Be careful me darlin,' said Mary as Anna left.

She ventured into the twilight of a clear sky, ignoring the concern of Mary. Her all-white dress was immaculate; a pink floral border skirted round her ankles matched by a short pink shoulder cape and a white floral hat. She might have been going to a society occasion not around the pubs of Dowlais. Her pride at being a lady and not some course barmaid outweighed any dangers she might be heading for.'

She made her way up to Elizabeth Street and stopped outside the Pembroke Arms. It seemed a friendly-looking place, small and cosy and no bawdy sounds coming through the doors. Not too many drinkers inside, she assumed. All she wanted from the first pub was someone who had heard of a Spaniard known as Miguel. She made a graceful entrance that made the sleepy barman look up sharply, and the four drinkers jump off their benches as though royalty had come in.

'Yes, lady, can I help you? asked the bemused barman.'

She placed a coin on the bar. 'I'll have half measure of ale, please.' Then she looked around the room. 'Good evening,' she said with great confidence. 'It's a lovely evening.'

'Aye, it is,' said the one and the others nodded in agreement. They sat down, staring at her.

'They wouldn't know what sort of evening it is,' said the barman as he handed Anna her drink. 'They've been here since this morning. Here's your ale my lovely and here's your change.'

'Thank you,' she said as she lifted the tankard and took a drink. Placing the drink back on the bar she weighed up the barman. A stout, five feet six-inch man with a determined face, not to be messed around with, 'It's a bit quiet in here,' she said.

'They'll be pouring in within a half an hour, it'll be noisy then, for sure,'

She took another drink from her mug and daintily placed it back on the bar.

The barman gave her time to catch her breath and wipe her pretty lips with her laced handkerchief before his tentative enquiries began. 'I haven't seen you around here before, in fact, I've never seen anyone like you in this pub since I took the lease twenty years ago.'

'Twenty years, maybe you can help me.'

'You can have me any time you like,' he said as a chuckle rose from the onlookers.

'During the years you've served pints in this pub you must have come across a man by the name of Miguel.'

Maybe.'

'Do you know where I can find him?'

One of the drinkers intervened. 'You'd be better off in Spain, lovely. There's hundreds of Miguels' there.'

'Shut up Maldwyn or you'll be out on your ear. Then he turned to Anna. 'There has never been a man by that name in my pub since I've been here. The Pembroke Arms is open to everyone, but the different employment of the workers go to pubs they feel more relevant to their jobs. Now these thirsty…drinkers are originally from Pembroke. They're not on shift at the moment which gives them the opportunity to spend some of their money here. If I'm lucky they'll move on to the Farmers Arms, because that's the work they did prior to leaving their agricultural homes.'

'Don't they have wives?'

'That's the reason they're here. They need a break from the chores of employment, wives merely find them more to do.'

Anna finished her drink and gave the man a wry look. 'I'll be on my way, then.'

'Your best hopes of finding the man you're looking for is to ask in the Horse and Harriers. You'll find an Irishman there who knows everybody and everything. Sorry I can't help more.'

'Do you know where that pub is, my beauty?' one of the drinkers asked.

'I'll find it.'

'I'll come with you and show you.'

'Have you heard of a derringer?'

'Good God, have you got one of those?'

'You follow, me, my beauty, and you'll find out.'

'Well, be careful, cause they'll all be coming from the afternoon shift.'

She decided not to continue up Elizabeth Street but walked through the side streets. The words of the drinker in the Pembroke Arms echoed in her ears as the place became busy with the sound of men changing shifts in the distance. Floating on the evening breeze she could hear music and laughter and decided to make her way towards the happy sounds. A violin was playing and people were singing. Locating the place, she was surprised to see that the stonewall that fronted the pub had a row of men sitting on it. Above the door, embossed with mortar was "Horse and Harriers." Around the back was a larger drinking area with benches full of men and women and some lively girls dancing a reel. A gate gave entrance to the rear half and Anna made straight for it. As she approached, the fiddler still playing his lively tune came to the gate and smiled at her, his tilted head snuggling his instrument.

'Welcome to the Horse and Harriers me darlin', come in'

'Thanks for the invite.'

The fiddler ceased to play as a hush came over the crowd and all eyes turned to Anna.

210

'If it's not Lady Charlotte herself, I'll buy yuh all a drink,' a voice muttered in the crowd.'

'She's passed on, you fool. More likely to be a spy for the gaffers, indeed she might.'

'Anna straightened up and looked around. 'Haven't you seen a lady in this area before.'

A short man with a flat cap perched on the side of his head came forward. 'I'm not known to the gentry me lady, but would you be the ghost of great Lady Charlotte by any chance'

'I'm Welsh, you fool.'

'Ah, yes of course, the Lady herself was English so you can't be she. Would you be representing the ironmasters or the colliery owners?'

'I take it that you are Irish?'

'I am indeed and proud of it.'

'Would you as an Irishman be representing the masters?'

'I'd hang me-self first.'

'But you insult a Welsh lady by suggesting that she would?'

'Beg your pardon, I would not and I apologize profusely. Can I buy you a drink as a gesture of goodwill?'

'I would take that as sealing a friendship between the Irish and The Welsh,' she smiled.

'And I would take it as a privilege. What would be your liking?'

'I'll have a straight gin.'

'Will you indeed, I mean you will indeed – Mick, go and get the lady a straight gin, it's your round. Pat, what are you doing staring at the lady, get up and give her your seat.' the man obeyed and Anna sat on the wooden bench, the interrogating Irishman taking the liberty of sitting at her side. Meanwhile, the crowd began to chatter among themselves and continue with the drinking.

'You seem to have some authority around here,' she remarked. 'I've met Mick and I've met Pat, but I missed your name.'

'Ah, first I want to know what a lovely lady like yourself is doing in these parts. It's a mystery to me and I don't like mysteries. Furthermore, I don't have your name in me memory.'

'You can call me Ann. I am looking for a Spanish man known as Miguel. He used to work with my husband and I need some information from him. Now I have been told an Irishman who drinks in this pub may know of him and where I can get in touch.'

He gave Anna an enigmatic grin. 'Now who would be telling you of this Irishman?'

'The landlord of the Pembroke Arms informed me.'

Ah, that would be Ivor himself, do doubt. Well you may be surprised to know that I am that very Irishman he tells of.'

It was then that Mick returned with a glass of gin and handed it to Anna with a big smile. Anna thanked him and turned back to the man who had not yet given his name.

'Well, would you know of Miguel's whereabouts?'

'Well now, Miguel's is a very proud steelworker and is loyal to those pubs that reflect that industry. And so, me little searcher of Spaniards, you'll find him in that kind of pub.'

Anna looked disappointed and shook her head at the man. 'I gave you my name in good faith and expected your name in return. I need your name so that I can call you the cunning little scoundrel that you are.'

'You gave me a name.'

'My name is Anna Hughes, but my friends call me Ann.'

'That's better, me beauty, I think I can believe you know so I'll put me trust in you. There are four pubs the Spaniard might be in tonight, and I'll tell you the names and what street you'll find them in. There's the Puddlers Arms in High Street, and in the same road there be the Smith And Anvil. I wouldn't be seen dead in either, the landlords let anybody in, I tell yuh, so be careful. Now the next two are pretty respectable and they're both in Horse Street – do you know where Horse Street is?'

'Anna searched his face wondering if he was playing with her. 'I know it.'

'Good. The two in that street will be the Forge and Hammer and The Rolling Mill. If he's not in one of those pubs then he's gone back to Spain, I tell yuh.'

'Thank you for your help, Mr...'

'Huh, don't worry your darlin' little Welsh brain about it, it's been a privilege talking to yuh.'

'Drink up and I'll buy you one.'

'No, no, it be my round now, you'll offend me if you don't have another with me.'

'I wouldn't want to offend you so I'll just have another gin.'

'That's me girl, hu, hu, did you get that? That's Miguel.'

Anna gave him a cursory nod of approval as he went for the drinks. She remained there for another twenty minutes being pleasantly entertained by the fiddler and the singing and dancing. And then she thanked her host and made her way to the High Street.

Twenty Nine

Anna departed, darkness had fallen and the drinks began to take her clarity away. She felt light-headed but relaxed as her shaky legs struggled up the High Street. She emotionally shook herself knowing that she always felt that way on her initial drinks. It had been the same in the kitchen surrounded by the servants; Charles would pour the remnants of the bottles into the glasses and pass around the wine. And then to surprise them all he would produce a full bottle of the cheaper wine and pass more around. It was the second glass that always made her head light and her legs feel weak, but the feeling would fade within a half hour and she and Molly would go to bed content in the peaceful privacy of their bedroom and sleep till morning. But now in the dimness between gaslights economically placed here and there, she could hear the occasional explosion from the blast furnaces of the steelworks and the distant sky illuminating. Yes, she was back to familiar surroundings. Workers were still coming off shift and exiting the steelworks from the main gates situated on lower High Street. The smoke from the stacks was choking the crescent moon, and between those giant structures she could see the glow of the smouldering mountain, the pungent smell of the huge fearsome slagheap drifting across lower Dowlais. They laughed at her in the Rolling Mill, she remembered, when she got her initial shock of it. That was the first time she met John. She shook herself again and looked around, and there it was, the Puddlers Arms. She went into the crowded room, full of raucous thirsty men, laughing and bragging about their jobs. There were boisterous women too who uttered remarks; Oh look at her then, she must have lost her way.' Some men showed their appreciation with a wink or whistle, but generally they were happy to be away from twelve-hour shift and not waste valuable drinking time on other subjects. The men made way for her to the bar. There she bought half measure of ale and inquired the whereabouts of Miguel. The barman knew of him and told her he frequents the place at times, but was not present. She drank her ale and left. The Smith and Anvil was also negative and so was the Forge and Hammer in

Horse Street. The only place left was the Rolling Mill, a place she was hoping she would not have to enter, but by this time, having had a drink in each pub, she had little reservations about meeting the randy Dick Thomas.

She strolled slowly and began to wonder about her existence; her attitude towards life, her uncanny bad luck and the discontentment that turned into a mad moment of despair when she ran and deserted John. And Elizabeth, the pious sister-in-law whom she despised for some reason she could not remember. In her mental soliloquy she asked for the first time, why Lord? If You are there, why couldn't you make me like other woman, simple with a faith, believing in a myth? Why give me a brain that asks questions nobody wants to answer. I trust nobody. Christ said, "I am the way, the truth and the life, only through me will you enter the Kingdom of God." Huh, so what happens to all those other souls? What happens to the Muslims and Jews, Buddhists and Shinto, all the other religions of the world, and all those who can't understand any of it, anyway? And how big is Heaven? Since Jesus died there has been billions and billions of people passing through this Earth, and before Jesus came many more billions that could fill every planet in the cosmos—

'Annie? God is that you lovely Annie?'

Shaken from her reverie she stared at the handsome young man who had walked up to her; a clean-shaven stranger who appeared to be familiar, though not fully recognizable. Then she asked in a quiet but determined whisper. 'Who are you? Only one person as ever called me Annie, and he was a young lad.'

His excited voice was playful yet sincere, his handsome face carefree. 'That was when I was ten, Annie, before you married John. I'm a big lad now.'

'It can't be. Is it really you, Emlyn?'

'It is me, Annie, Emlyn Hughes.'

She fell into his arms and began to whimper, slightly incoherent from the drink. 'I've made a real mess of my life since I went away, Emlyn. I've hurt so many people in this town. Tonight I realized I should not have come back.'

216

'I knew you'd come back some day. When you left I was depressed for months.'

'You were?'

'Of course, I needed you.'

'You…you needed me?'

'I used to dream about you and think about you. You were always in my thoughts.'

'I was too busy to notice. Can you forgive me?'

'I have nothing to forgive except for you marrying the wrong man. I was hoping you'd wait for me to grow so that I could have shown you my true feelings.'

She slowly pulled away from him and looked up into his eyes. 'How can you joke about such strife I've caused?'

'I'm not joking Annie,' he said with a serious tone. 'I was in love with you when you lived with us. You can't have missed all the attention I gave you, the little jobs I done to save you doing them, the long looks I gave you.'

'I took them as a boy who had mischief on his mind.'

'Oh no, when you went away the depression I felt lasted for a long time, but then one day it drained from me when I realized you left because you didn't love John, and the expectation you would return one day so that I could have you all to myself.

'You're a handsome man, Emlyn. Tall, fresh and handsome, any girl would be proud to have you for a husband.'

'I don't want any girl.'

'I'm sorry to disappoint you, I'm looking for John. I'm still married to him. Do you know where I can find him?'

'You won't find him, he left years ago. He briefly came back after his sister died, but you weren't here. We tried to look after him, you know, but it was no good. Then one day he came to our house and shook our hands and said he was going back to live near his family. He came to terms with the truth and realized, of course, you didn't want him and left. We haven't heard from him since. He could be dead for all we know.'

'I must have hurt him deeply.'

'He knew what he was doing. He told us all about your little arrangement. It was doomed from the start. Come on, I'm taking you in for a drink.'

She looked up and read the name above the door the, Rolling Mill. 'I don`t want to go in there.'

'Come on, it's different now.' His strong arms ushered her in.

The gaslights were bright and the walls had cream panels with brown frames and brown ceiling beams. Anna was relieved to see there were strangers serving behind the bar; a man and a woman, apparently in their mid-thirties. The place was tidier and well looked after. The clientele, a mixed gender, spoke in low murmurings and were workers who had obviously gone home for a bath and clean clothes. But then she remembered John was just like that whenever he came to the pub. Emlyn caught under her arm and led her to a vacant table. As they sat down she pointed to the bar.

'Where is Dick this evening, night off?'

'He gave it up about a year ago. Decided to take on a bigger pub in Merthyr that had living quarters for guests. Haven't seen him since, but then I rarely go to Merthyr.—What will you have, Annie?'

'I think I've had enough tonight, my head feels very confused, but I'm so relieved to have found a friend at last.'

'Your worries are over, have a small one?'

'No, I'll have half of ale, I can manage that.'

'Half of ale it is. You won`t go will you?'

She shook her head.

When he came back he brought a full tankard for himself and half for Anna. They were quiet for a while, Anna looking into her drink and Emlyn adoring her face. She glanced at him and gave him a gentle smile.'

'How is everybody at home? Is your Dad still down the drift?'

Emlyn dropped his head. 'Things have changed drastically,' he said, sadly. 'My Dad was caught in a roof-fall at the face. We needed to change some roof beams, me and a couple others were bringing the chocks to support the roof...'

Anna's face turned pale at the news. 'Oh no, not another, Emlyn, don't say the worst.'

'Aye, as we approached with the chocks there was a sound like thunder. Black dust came rolling up the drift billowing like storm clouds. We were too late.'

'If you had got the...chocks there you would have saved them?'

'Oh yes, it's a cubed steel framework with handles. It's used to hold up any weaknesses in the roof until it can be repaired. It was kept a little distance from the coalface. Five of the face workers were buried, Dad was one of them.'

'Oh God Emlyn! You could have died yourself.'

'I felt nothing just then. Everything was automatic. We grabbed our shovels and picks and swung and kicked and dug and burrowed for an hour. We got them all out, but none survived.'

'There's death written all over this place.'

'Not just here but all over the industrial country.'

'I'm lodging with a lady who lost her husband in a roof-fall a year ago, Mary her name is, was it her husband in the same disaster?'

'Does she live down the Cwm, four kids?'

'Yes.'

'Aye, that's the very same cave-in, though it was eighteen months ago not a year.'

'I feel so useless in life knowing how hard people around here are living and me deserting...'

'Hey, don't be hard on yourself. If I thought I could better myself somewhere else, I'd be off with no conscience. Life doesn't last long round here, here today and dead tomorrow. Have to make the best of it when you can. Anyway, let's not talk of all that, tell me where you've been and what you've been doing.'

'You just said it, let's not talk of it.'

'Was it that bad? Where did you go?'

'London. When I'm feeling in the mood I'll tell you all about it.'

'It's not a bad night, why don't I take you to your lodgings and you can tell me on the way.'

She touched his hand. 'You're warm and tender, Emlyn, can be friends?'

He held her hand firmly and brought it to his mouth kissing it gently. 'I've not been out with a single girl, only bought one or two a drink in a pub. I've lain in bed many nights seeing your face in my mind. You've been a lasting dream to me. Friend? I'm going to be your protector, friend and, if you can find it in your heart, I'll be your love forever.'

'Oh Emlyn, there is a difference in our ages.'

'Same difference as it was when I first met you, I remember, I was nearly eleven and you were twenty-one. I could not bear to see you with John those years you lived with him. Then when you broke away and John told us of your arrangement and that the marriage had not been consummated—I think I was fourteen at the time, I knew I would see you again one day.

'I haven't been very honest with people around here but I'll be honest with you Emlyn. I lied about my age so that people might respect me more, but the truth is when I came here I was nearly eighteen. People kept telling me how young I looked and that my appearances made me look like a teenager. Well, I was a teenager but I didn't want to be treated as one.'

'So how old are you? Pardon me for asking.'

'I was born in 1879. That makes me twenty six.'

That's even better. I'm nineteen, just seven years between us.'

He made her smile broadly. 'I think you are a romantic lad, Emlyn.'

'Hey, you didn't like being put down because you were of a certain age, did you?'

'Sorry. You are a romantic man.'

Emlyn pulled his hands away and clasped them to his chest. Looking uncomfortable with himself, his eyes looking into his empty glass, he said. 'Annie, can I ask you a personal question.'

'No, I haven't been with any man. I'm as pure now as I was when I came to Dowlais, I'm still a virgin. Does that help you prevent asking an embarrassing question?'

'Oh yes. That means you are a perfect angel. Come on, I'll walk you home. From now on you're my girl until such time as you reject me.'

Thirty

Emlyn came home from work with his brother-in-law, Luke, and young David. Ruth had noticed his change in demeanour the past few weeks and wondered at the cause. Not wanting to appear intrusive she had said nothing to him, but her curiosity was getting to breaking point. When they walked in she got up and took the saucepan off the fire and poured its contents into an earthenware basin, and then placed the basin on the readily prepared table. She had been in bed when he came home the last few nights but now eyed him with a quizzical look, and he in return gave an enigmatic grin before going to his bath. Luke, her husband of nine months, pecked her on the cheek and then went to wash his hands. Luke, quiet and laid-back, had managed to secure a job for young David in the steelworks maintenance shop. The position had given the lad a feeling of adulthood, which together with his recently reaching his thirteenth year had made him a serious and proud young man. He had got to the washbasin before Luke and cleaned himself up. They waited for Emlyn, who was singing in the outhouse scrubbing the coal-dust off his blackened skin in the wooden tub, prepared earlier with hot water by his devoted sister.

'Come on Emlyn or we'll start without you, called David'

'Just wiping down,' came the tenor's voice. 'Be there in a minute.'

'Where did you meet him?' Ruth asked her husband.

'Meet who? Oh Emlyn. He was coming down the Goat Mill Road steps as we were walking up the road. Waving and calling, he was, as though he had been given a rise in pay.'

'He's in a good mood,' said David. 'He didn't stop whistling all the way home.'

'I tried to get the reason out of him,' said Luke, 'but he just kept on whistling.'

Ruth squinted her eyes. 'Yes, he's in high spirits for some reason. I'll have to take him aside and coax it out of him.'

'My ears are burning,' he said, as he came into the room. 'I've got a feeling somebody's talking about me.'

He sat down at the table and Ruth took the cover off the earthenware bowl of cawl, the steam rising and the savoury smell immediately spreading through the room. She dipped the large ladle into the wholesome broth and drew out an ample serving of vegetables and meat, filling the soup dish in front of her husband, and then continued to serve the other two.

'You've been very happy lately, Emlyn,' Ruth said, filling his dish. 'What's come over you?'

'Oh nothing really, you might as well be happy as miserable, don't you think, Luke?'

'You've got it,' said the agreeable Luke, who was happy to assent to anything, unless Ruth thought to the contrary.

David reached for a thick slice of bread from the pile Ruth had cut.

'But you're different today than usual, Emlyn,' Ruth persisted.

'Well, things change Ruth, don't they? Can't a man be happy without all this interrogation? Anyway, has Rebecca been today.'

'I can take the hint, boy.' said Ruth. 'No she hasn't.'

'Less of the boy, girl, I'm the man of the house now and don't you forget it.'

'Huh! Nineteen and man of the house, that`s because women haven't got the same rights.'

'Oh yes, and who have you been talking to?' he said abruptly. He swallowed a mouthful of vegetables. 'Do you know something you shouldn't know?'

Ruth was about to put a spoonful of broth in her mouth and suddenly realized she had hit on a relevant point. To what she didn't know, but she noticed Emlyn's face turned a little pink. All she alluded to was womens' rights, nothing to get annoyed about. 'I haven't seen anyone to talk to.' She continued eating, her mind going over what she had said. Emlyn made her feel as though he had something to hide.

David was gulping his food down. 'David, love, take your time please. You bring memories of old man Veldon slopping your food like that.'

222

'You shouldn't make it taste so nice.'

When David finished his food he looked at Emlyn who had gone suspiciously quiet. 'Emlyn, what was that tune you were whistling on the way home.'

Emlyn looked up and stared at the boy. 'Don't you start, David, just let the subject drop.'

David looked to Ruth wondering what he had said to deserve such rebuke. Ruth shook her head. 'Do you want some more cawl, love.'

David patted his stomach. 'No thank you, I'm full, he said, then turned to Emlyn again. 'Where are you off tonight Emlyn?'

'I'm going out Davey, sorry if I snapped at you.'

'You're my big brother aren't you? You can snap at me anytime, but I'm getting to the age now where I might snap back.'

The remark made Emlyn smile and Ruth gave a giggle. 'You snap back at him Davey boy.'

'Don't forget I'm working now, Emlyn,' so I'm entitled to ask you a few questions.'

'It's private David. I don't want to go into it now, but when the time is ready I'll tell you all.'

'Emlyn,' began Ruth in a quiet, pleading voice. 'Just tell me one thing, is it a girl?'

Emlyn sighed. 'Yes it is a girl.'

'That's all right then. I'm happy for you.'

'Talking about going out,' said Luke. 'Maybe we should have an hour or two relaxing in a nice cosy lounge, my love.'

'We could do. What are you going to do, David?'

'I'll go up and see Rebecca and family. Maybe I can be helpful with the kids.'

'Rebecca would like that. It will give her a break.'

When they finished their food Ruth and Luke did the washing up while Emlyn went upstairs to change in readiness to go out. David thought a quick exit would relieve him of any potential cleaning up duties.

A half hour later Emlyn came down from his room looking very smart dressed in his second best suit. The grey waistcoat that matched the suit was buttoned up holding in the chevron-pattern tie. His sandy hair was combed with not a strand out of place. Ruth, who was sitting by the fireplace knitting, looked up at the fine five-foot eight-inch of her brother and believed for once that he was indeed the man of the house.

'You're looking very handsome tonight, Emlyn. She'll be proud to walk out with you.'

'You're presuming a lot aren't you? I'm going to the Dowlais Constitutional Club.'

'They won't let you in there with a girl on your arm, women aren't allowed.'

'You're still presuming.'

'Well, what's the big secret? Is she a society girl, or something? Not belonging to the steelworks owners, is she?'

'Don't be daft.'

Luke thought he'd make a light remark. 'Hey, she isn't married, is she? A lot of these married women get lonely when their other halves are on nightshift.'

'I'm going out now, I've heard enough,' he said as he slammed the door.

The remark had downed his spirits. He knew that he would have to reveal all one day, but he wanted to be sure of Annie. If she could love him as much as he loved her, he could face any backlash that might come about. He didn't lie to Ruth, he was going to go to the Constitutional Club first, and then on to meet Anna. The August weather had been favourable the past few days and they had arranged to meet and keep company and maybe go for a drink. Emlyn had suggested they go to the Oddfellows Hall where a concert was being held, thinking it would be a right and proper place for a lady, but Anna declined the idea. She wanted privacy until such time as she knew her own mind and feelings, but she agreed to meet him near the Oddfellows Hall. Her affections towards Emlyn were becoming more confused as each day went by. At her lodgings she thought about him most of the day and looked forward to seeing him at evening time. Now she was hurrying up Lower Union Street on her way to him.

He had a tankard of ale in the club at a strategic window where he could look down Union Street. He realized she had quite a walk from her lodgings and offered to meet her there. However, she wanted to make her own way under the comparative cover of dusk. She had considered the time Emlyn finished work, would have had his meal and then made his way to meet her, it would be getting dark. One tankard of ale led to another and he was beginning to think she had reservations of the meeting. But half way through his second tankard, he could see her coming up in the distance. A large brimmed hat, low on her forehead, gave her an air of mystery and her long hair curled round her front almost hiding her chin. She couldn't hide from Emlyn for he knew her walk too well, and if she wanted to go unnoticed she was unsuccessful, for her jauntiness and her city attire stood out. He hurried out and met her as she was passing the Oddfellows, turned and walked along at her side.

'Slow down, Annie, you're not in a race.'

'I just want to be away from the shop-window lights and gas streetlights as quickly as possible. Some people may remember me around here.'

'You didn't always care what people thought.'

'I'm not thinking of myself; it's us keeping company may have repercussions on you.'

'Annie, I don't care a damn what people think.'

She relaxed, put her arm through his, and they both went boldly and brazenly on up towards St John's Church, Emlyn looking down into her eyes.

'I thought we were going to the Oddfellows Hall,' Emlyn reminded her.

'Too many people in there.'

'That's all right with me.'

'Well, where are we heading for?' she asked.

'Where do you want to go?'

'If we were in London I might be able to answer that, but as we are in Dowlais I can't imagine where a lady could go.'

'Dowlais has had some very notable people in the past?'

'You must humble me with the news,' she said, elbowing him.

'What about the Grand Duke Constantine? He was so impressed with the rails we made for his country he wanted to see the mills that produced his Russian railways.

'I seem to have heard that before,` she teased. And then she remembered John had told her.'

'It was in 1847. And then not so long ago Lord and Lady Wimborne—'

'I don`t want to know.`

'And if that doesn't impress you Lord Nelson himself visited Merthyr in 1802.'

'I give in, where are we going tonight, Emlyn?'

'Oh you'll be surprised there are nice places in Dowlais.'

'Surprise me then.'

'Right, we'll have a nice walk in the dark first.'

They walked past the top entrance of the closed market hardly saying a word, happy to enjoy each other's company. Anna, however, had things on her mind wondering what Emlyn's family would say when they eventually found out. Then suddenly the apprehension left her as quickly as it had come. She realized the affection that grew for Emlyn since he came back into her life out-weighed any objections they might have.

'Did you tell Ruth about our relationship, Emlyn?'

'Relationship? If you mean the love I have for you, no I haven't. I don't want them to know because I'm not sure of your feelings towards me. If I tell them and then you leave me, it will be a double blow; the loss of you and the scorn from them.'

'Tell them tomorrow, Emlyn, it will only be one blow.'

Emlyn pulled her to a stop and looked down into her eyes. 'What does that mean, Annie?'

'It means I think about you all day. I've never felt like this for a man before. I never believed I could or would. As long as you know what you are doing and what we will have to face, I want you. I suppose I love you.'

Impulsively he pulled her to him and squeezed her tightly, burying her head in his chest. Then she drew away and clasped her arms around his neck her emotions welling up and her eyes filling

226

with happiness and her heart experiencing enormous relief. Then he cupped her face in his hands and kissed her, again and again.

'I can't believe my fortune, Annie. I can't believe you said that wonderful word.'

'I'm full Emlyn. My cup of love runneth over.'

'Let's go somewhere and make our plans.'

'Right, where is this place we can go?'

'I will take you to the warm and friendly comfort in the plush lounge of the Bush Hotel.'

'I'll believe it when I see it, but I don't care where.'

Thirty One

They had been seeing each other for two months as the pressure built up on Emlyn to bring his new girlfriend home. Ruth had told Rebecca all about Emlyn's romance and the siblings insisted they would be delighted to meet any girl who would make Emlyn happy. Even Luke and young David added their eagerness to meet the mysterious lady. As the weeks wore on and Emlyn's reluctance to reveal his love began to appear suspicious, Ruth and Rebecca became concerned. They had asked Emlyn to help them understand the reason for his secret, telling him that his refusal to allow them to meet his girlfriend was unreasonable and approaching the ridiculous. That they were worried there was some underlying, unacceptable reason why he was reluctant to disclose. He eventually gave in and said he would reveal all on his day off, which was the following Sunday. But first he had to talk to his girl and have her agreement. Naturally they understood the girl would have to be consulted. Emlyn laid down one condition, and that was only his two sisters should be present when he tells them of his secret love. They agreed. However, Rebecca explained that her layman husband, Aled, will be carrying out certain duties in the chapel all day Sunday and that there will be nobody to care for the children. Emlyn reminded them it was the business of his two sisters and nobody else. But if need be the children can come and play in the back yard supervised by David. This Rebecca agreed to and was happy to have the children near her in the back yard.

On Saturday night Emlyn and Anna were having an evening in the quiet lounge of the Bush Hotel. The cosy room with its upholstered chairs and small polished tables was half full of respectable courting and married couples. The conversations were quiet and the decorum befitting to the prestigious hotel. Anna had had two glasses of red wine and Emlyn two pints of ale. They had said little sitting there, content to have each other for company, secretly holding hands under the table. But then he began inspecting his beautiful lady and complimented her smartness of attire; for she had donned her primrose dress that Felicity had given her. Changing the conversation from Emlyn's flattery, she turned to him and asked the question Emlyn knew was coming.

'Well, have you told them yet?' she asked quietly.

'I promised them I would reveal all tomorrow. I've arranged for Rebecca to come down after lunch, when the explosion is ignited I want my eldest sister to be there.'

'Why in the afternoon? It will be a long morning, waiting.'

They all go to chapel in the morning; Rebecca and her children, Ruth and her husband, and even little old Davey. I'm the black sheep in the family.'

Anna raised her voice unintentionally. `Are you a black sheep because you don't attend chapel?'

'Not so loud, love. They've given up trying to convert me, and maybe I feel guilty not pleasing them. It's not that I'm against it. It's just so pretentious and theatrical. All that dramatic preaching of fire and damnation, the animated arms of the reverend reaching up to the roof threatening brimstone and hell; and then there's Aled, Rebecca's husband, he's a lay preacher who gives a sermon now and again, well...'

Anna's heart dropped to her stomach. 'I can see that our relationship is going to be met with great approval—they`re going to crucify us.'

'I'm my own man. Nobody tells me what to do or where to go. You are my love for life and nobody is going to break us up.'

'I feel the same Emlyn. It's just that I didn't realize there was so much piety in the family. And poor young Davey being brainwashed when he`s not knowing the world.'

'He's fourteen now and working in the steelworks.'

'And the Christians agree with that?'

'Your voice is going up a tone again. It's the way of society at the moment.'

'But is it the right way? It seems a bit exploitive to me.'

'Davey wouldn't give it up for the world.'

Anna sighed. 'I'll be glad when it's all out in the open.'

230

'Whichever way they take the news Anna, we'll have each other. So let's enjoy ourselves and I'll tell you how it all went when I see you tomorrow night.'

Anna looked at him with some astonishment, afraid to speak in case she blurted. Controlling herself, she gripped Emlyn's hand. 'Tomorrow night? I won't let you face the hostility on your own, Emlyn. They've got to see me sometime so it might as well be with you. We'll face them together and share whatever they have to say about me.'

Emlyn put his arm around her shoulder and kissed her cheek. 'You're wonderful woman. I'll pick you up at three o'clock, but now let's have another drink.'

`Yes, lets, people are watching your advances.`

They remained in the Bush for another hour and had a couple more drinks, by which time Anna was in a merry mood and Emlyn as carefree as a pirate on the Spanish Main. When they left they wanted to be with each other as long as possible, so Emlyn took her the long way home: up High Street, where the glow of the pub windows and terraced houses gave them a warm feeling as they went by, then to the Guest Memorial Library built out of huge blocks of hewn stone and sporting pillars at its entrance. Across Gwernllwyn Road, round the curve to the stables, past the market and the gas "ring lamp" at the top of Commercial Street and into the popular Upper Union Street where the pubs and cafes attracted the evening revellers.

'It's very impressive, isn't it? He said to Anna.'

'What is?'

'St John's Church.'

'You haven't travelled very far, Emlyn Rees. You should see the buildings in London, then you'll be impressed.'

'I'll show it from another angle, come here.' He ushered her into the recess of the Boot Emporium's darkened doorway directly opposite the church. There he pulled her to him and gave her a lasting kiss. She responded by holding him as tight as she could and reciprocating. Pulling away, she looked again at the church.

'Yes, I suppose it does look better from here.'

'If you come into the doorway a little further down it's even better.'

'Why is that?'

'It's the co-op doorway, I pay out dividends there.'

She dug him in the ribs with her elbow. 'I don't take dividends in doorways. Come on let's go before you take advantage of me.'

When they had past the Constitutional Club there could be heard in the distance a lone voice booming out expletives, too far to comprehend.

'Who's that shouting?' Anna asked. 'I hope it's not a drunken brawl, I can't stand the sight of grown men hitting each other around.'

'It's only Joshua on the steps of the Oddfellows Hall giving his warning of the dangers of sin.'

The name thudded in her heart, another reminder of John. 'Good God, doesn't he ever give up?'

'He hasn't been here for some time. He's been doing his rounds. Loyal to the end, is Joshua. He'll preach anywhere and at any time when he has a few listening to him.'

Being in a jovial mood Emlyn decided to have some amusement from the preacher. Anna was not as enthusiastic but she agreed to join the small crowd that was giving him a respectful hearing.

'He's still wearing the frock coat,' noted Anna. Doesn't he ever change his clothes?'

'He's got a few of them, it's his status symbol. The Chinese laundry helps him out with his Monday wash. He's a nice man, is Joshua. Let's hear what he's got to say.'

'And don't be fooled by believing that only adulterers, boozers, murderers, thieves, slave traders and fornicators and all the rest will be judged,` he raved to the small gathering, arms in the air, face illuminated by the Hall's light. Oh no, all kinds of profanity will be judged. Those hypocrites who preach but do not practice will also be called before the Lord and asked why they worship false idols? Why they hide great riches in their vaults? Relics of gold and silver they will not part with at any cost. Oh yes, they do these things in their own foolish ways with the pretence that it is for the glory of God.

The altars they polish and dress in lace, the artistry in their leaded windows they admire so greatly, the pride they exhibit in their ceremonial resplendent regalia, colourful ornate vestments, the crucifix symbols they flaunt, their repetitious prayers and superficial offerings are patronizing and superficial to the Almighty and too easily performed. They are humouring God by raising Him on an infantile pedestal of immaturity. They tear flowers from His earthly garden and place them on a man-made wooden table as a gift to Him. They offer Him any triviality but will not part with their wealth or earthly status. They have made additions to their religion and the additions have become their religion, and Jesus trails in the wake of their vanities. There is a saying that beauty is skin deep, I tell you that clothes have the same misleading value, for God can see the ugliness that lies within the sinner. Jesus says, Lay not up treasures upon earth where moth and rust corrupt but lay up treasures in Heaven ...'

'You tell them, Joshua,' Anna suddenly blurted. Tell them to read the New Testament and stop practising the Old Testament.'

Emlyn was struck dumb by her outburst, but Joshua looked down and smiled at her.

'And what is your name, sister?

'Just call me Ann.'

'Bless you Ann. Follow the way of Jesus and be happy.'

'Blessed are the meek for they shall inherit the earth, but what about Heaven?'

'Don't you worry about Heaven, Ann. blessed are the pure in heart for they shall see God.'

Anna was struck by warmth spreading through her body. She smiled at Joshua and turned away. Did she have a pure heart? 'Come on, Emlyn, I've heard enough. Though I must admit, he does make a bit of sense,' she said, as she pulled at Emlyn's arm, walking away. 'Sometimes I feel ugly inside whatever fine clothes I wear.'

He stopped and pulled her to him. 'You surprised me talking to Joshua. But don't worry you have beauty in every bone in your body, in every drop of blood, in every faculty and breath you make. Don't put yourself down, Annie.'

They kissed and Anna felt a tear come to her eyes. She had many compliments in the past from admirers and lots of sympathies and help, but the sincerity of Emlyn was the warmth that moved her with deep emotion.

'I don't want to go home just yet, and I'm tired of walking.'

'Fancy another drink? We can call in to the Miners Arms in the High Street. It's one of the better pubs down that way.'

'Anything you say. I could do with a drop of ale, that wine was a bit strong.'

'You can have as much ale as you like, I'll carry you home if need be.'

'I think you would too.'

She gave a little scream as he suddenly swept her up in his arms and began to carry her. 'Put me down, put me down,' she pleaded. But he didn't, he decided to carry her to the Miners Arms. 'This town is full of extremists,' she lightly complained. 'There are drunkards, slave drivers, religious fanatics, and love-sick miners.'

'By the way,` said Emlyn, `don't you say a word about God when Aled's around.'

'If there is a God why chose fools to spread His word?'

'Joshua is no fool, believe me.'

'I wasn't taking about Joshua I was meaning the ecclesiastical hierarchy. Anyway, I have nothing against God, really. Joshua is right, you know…'

Emlyn pulled her head to him and pressed his lips on hers. He kept them there for some considerable time until she forgot what she had been saying.

3.30 Sunday afternoon Emlyn and Anna were walking across Mary Ann Street ready to face his family. The overcast day added to the heavy feeling Anna had in her stomach. Though it was unusual for Emlyn to have a dull feeling in his spirit, he too, appeared serious, business-like, as though he was about to meet a stubborn adversary who was asking over the odds. They reached the door and Emlyn breathed in and pushed out his chest, Anna closed her eyes and sighed heavily. Emlyn grasped the doorknob.

234

'Right, stay a little behind me my love, I'll lead the way,' he said as he opened the door and walked down the passageway, Anna's white dress swishing against the wallpaper, and she adjusting her pink hat as a last nervous gesture.

Emlyn opened the door leading to the sitting room and stood in the doorway for a while inspecting the gathering. They were all there. Ruth stood up in anticipation to shake the girl's hand, Rebecca sat with her two young children at her side and David walked to Emlyn to see who was behind him in the passage.

'Well, family, this is the girl I love,' he said as he stepped aside and caught the hand of Anna, escorting her inside.

All prepared smiles dropped from the faces of the family. There was nothing. No movement, no sound, but a great atmosphere of disbelief as everyone stared at the sophisticated, beautiful woman in the doorway, the sisters showing horror on their faces. Luke being the husband of Ruth had only heard about Anna and wasn't sure who stood there, but he had a softness for the lady who had come in. The silence lasted for some considerable time. It was David who leaned his head to one side and then to the other.

'It's auntie Ann,' he suddenly blurted. 'I remember you. You used to come here with uncle John.' He went to her and caught her hand. 'Pleased to see you again.'

'Thank you David, it's very kind of you to say so.'

'David,' said Ruth in a controlled voice. 'Take the children out the back yard and amuse them some way.'

'Oh Ruth...'

'You promised you'd play with them once Emlyn came, he's here, now keep your promise.'

David huffed in disagreement, but took the children out.

'Well, aren't you going to offer Annie a chair,' snapped Emlyn.

Rebecca pulled at a chair near her. 'Have a seat, Ann. Sorry if we seem a bit surprised, we didn't realize you were back and you look so...different. How long is it since you returned?'

'I'd rather stand thanks. I've been back a number of months.'

'You're not welcome in this house,' blurted Ruth, in a low guttural sound. 'John went through hell because of your betrayal.'

'I never betrayed him until I met up with Emlyn, I swear. I have never loved a man in my life until I met your brother.'

'That's no excuse for abandoning John when he did everything he could to make you happy,' she said, as she went to the fireside and held on to the mantel piece.

Emlyn intervened. 'There's no point in raking up the past. We know John was a decent man and that he loved Annie dearly. She tried her best to love him but found she couldn't so she did the next best thing and left.'

'She used him!' continued Ruth. 'She took him for everything he could give and then left when she could get no more.'

'That's not true, Ruth,' Anna said, hurt at the remark. 'I tried to keep to the promises and agreement we made, but I was depressed, very unhappy. I couldn't stand it any longer.'

'Whom God has joined together let no man put asunder.'

'God did not join us, it was a certificate that the registrar made out. A piece of paper that had no meaning or bond; something that John believed would tie me to him.'

'And who joined you to my brother, not God nor man.'

Trying to remain calm, Emlyn broke in again. 'Love united us Ruth. Love joined us. And if God is a God of love, then he made us one; a greater bond than a marriage certificate.'

'But she's married legally to John, can't you see that?'

'She didn't love John, can't you see that?

'Then why in Heaven's name did she come back, to taunt him to hell?'

'I don't know why I came back. I realized what a good man he is...and I thought we could make it up.'

'Make it up? I suppose you suddenly realized how much you were in love with the man you left behind; a man in despair and on the verge suicide. Or was it you couldn't find another fool to foot your bill? Well he's back with his loved ones now, God bless him, and I thank the Almighty that he hasn't witnessed you coming into our house with my idiotic brother.'

'That's enough of that Ruth,' thundered Emlyn. Try and be reasonable, woman.'

'Reasonable? How could she be so cruel as to take advantage of a man's love when she knew she had no affection for him?'

'That's not fair Ruth,' Anna said. 'I know John loved me and he knew I didn't love him. He was prepared to come to an arrangement just to keep me with him. I didn't have a mother or a father to turn to for help. Yes, I used him, but in his own way he used me too. I was vulnerable and homeless and didn't know what to do. I tried to please him but he took me to a hovel to live. I tried to please him but it wasn't in me. I freed him from his obligation to me and mine to him.'

Rebecca looked at the venomous Ruth, but could understand both sides of the argument:

'Ruth, I'm not supporting Ann in any way, but it seems to me that both parties had something to gain from their arrangement. It seems to me it was a mutual agreement that just didn't work out however daft it was.'

'That's right,' agreed Emlyn. 'Annie was a free spirit who realized her mistake.'

Anna gave Ruth a pleading look. 'Ruth, I thought it would work out at the time but it was a disaster. A disaster I will never forget.'

'Nor will John. And how long will it be before you treat my brother the same way?'

'No. I love Emlyn, the only man I've ever loved in my life.'

Ruth turned to Emlyn. 'I don't want her in this house.'

'This is my house too, Ruth,' he said firmly. 'I'll say who's to come in and who's not. Annie has had a terrible time in London and needs understanding.'

'I'll live on the coal tips rather than share the same house with that Jezebel.'

'It's all right, Ruth,' said Anna. 'I wouldn't want to live here and have you hurt or embarrassed.'

'Maybe you'll feel different in time, Ruth,' said Emlyn.'

Ruth sneered at her brother. 'Oh no, I'll be like that festering slag tip, burning constantly, I'll never cool down—brother.'

'Then we'll find somewhere else to live. Come on love, let's go.' He turned to Ruth, 'I'll move out when I find a friendlier place to live.'

'Have you considered how old my brother is? He's still in his teenage years, you harlot.'

Emlyn stood in the doorway and looked back at his sister. 'I'll have trouble forgiving you for that remark, Ruth. It will take a long time.'

Ruth buried her head and wept as Emlyn slammed the door.

Thirty Two

Emlyn remained living with his sister for some time until he finally found a double room to rent at the Cross Keys Inn situated in Church Street, a terraced road of stone houses that had a sharp incline from St John's Church down to the High Street. Anna agreed to move to the bustling area, for it was convenient to the shops and entertainment. It had been agreed with the landlord that she do the shopping for the Inn and was happy busily going to the bakery, market, Co-operative and any other outlet that served the needs of the Cross Keys. Everything was convenient to her, the chemist on the High Street, and merchants at the top of Horse Street, the cafes and public houses, all in easy walking distance. She kept herself behind the scenes at the Inn and her labour was rewarded with cheap board and lodge for her and Emlyn. She was pleased to join the Dowlais Library at the top corner of Church Street and borrowed books to pass the time away when Emlyn was at work. She was a lady of leisure, nicely dressed, respectable, responsible occupation and greatly satisfied with life. But then the inevitable happened, she became pregnant, a condition that gave great joy to Emlyn, but mixed feelings to Anna. However, she accepted the responsibility and looked to the birth with some concern. The Innkeeper looked upon the coming event as an inconvenience, he was about to lose an efficient employee that cost him very little. Furthermore, the inn was not a place to give birth to a baby; though it was not a big establishment, it did have commitments to other guests who might be disturbed by a noisy baby in the middle of the night. After giving Emlyn and Anna due consideration, he told them of his concerns. Emlyn agreed with him, he didn't want his child to be born and grow up in a public house. And so when the time came nearer to the birth they parted on friendly and mutual terms. Emlyn had sought accommodation prior to their leaving. It had been difficult for him because the friends and colleagues he was closely acquainted with had nothing to offer in the way of suitable lodgings for a family of three. He had always been a good friend and neighbour to the widower old Dan who lived next door to him in Mary Ann Street. Living alone in a modest house and having spare rooms with ample space would be ideal for a temporary stay. However, he had reservations moving in next door to his sister, and it had been those worries that had held him back. But as the weeks went by he had become desperate and had approached his old neighbour. Having agreed with Dan that they would find a permanent place to live elsewhere as soon as possible after the birth, they moved in to an upstairs room with a double bed, wardrobe, two chairs and a small table, Dan giving them the freedom of the kitchen.

Rebecca soon heard of the move and came to visit Anna with the promise that she would help with the delivery. She would bring with her the lady who had delivered her own two children and together she assured Anna everything would be fine. Ruth however, wanted nothing to do with the embarrassing situation, and could only imagine that the name of Rees would be ridiculed and degraded in the community. Her brother living with a married woman who was expecting her brother's baby was too much for her to accept, and the thought of her being an auntie to a child born out of wedlock was a case for feigning illness and not attending chapel until it had all blown over.

Anna gave birth to a baby girl a month later to the great happiness of Emlyn and somewhat bewildered pride of Anna. The pregnancy she had looked upon as inconvenient and disruptive to her equilibrium now turned to a serious kind of joy. The sight of a defenceless baby crying into the world, made her realize the responsibility she had before her. Mrs Pugh, the woman who delivered the baby, had left with the gratitude from all concerned, satisfied she had done a good job. Rebecca remained and helped to tidy up the place. As the perspiration dripped from Anna's face in the temporary bed of a house belonging to a genial old man, the child in her arms, a husband with a secure income and prospects of a house of their own, she looked up at Emlyn wanting a positive resolution from him.

240

'Our baby needs security and love, and you'd better see that she has both,' she said in a weak but demanding voice.

'I will be her cradle and her shelter. She won't want for anything.'

'We can't stay here. The baby will need more than a dingy bedroom.'

'Just one calendar month, that's all we need stay here. Just one more month and we'll have a place of our own.'

Rebecca looked at her brother with some scepticism. 'You've found somewhere to live, Emlyn?'

'It's a two up and two down, just the job for a family like ours.'

Anna's face lit up. 'That's wonderful, Emlyn, where?'

'Now I know you don't like the Cwm but I've been to see this house and the people who live there are moving to a bigger house because they have four children. The house is as clean as an Ironmaster's parlour and as fragrant as a field of roses.'

'Your poetry had better live up to the description you gave it, Emlyn Rees.'

'It's got a small garden at the rear of the house with a lawn I can build a swing on. On a sunny day we can sit there and watch our little girl swing to and fro.'

'Dressed in a beautiful pink dress,' added Anna, 'with ribbons in her…' She looked at her baby's hair, 'with ribbons in her hair.' And then she looked at Emlyn. 'I don't mind the Cwm if it has a house as nice as you say it is.'

'You'll like it, I'm sure.'

Rebecca stood up and looked at the three with sympathy. 'I'd better be off now. I'm sure the three of you are going to be very happy.'

'Thank you for all you've done, Rebecca,' said Anna. 'I only wish that Ruth would be as kind as you.'

'She may come round eventually, but if she doesn't you'll just have to get on without her. Do you mind if I come down and visit you sometime?'

'You're welcome anytime. Bring the children if you want.'

'Thanks, bye now,' she said and made for the door.

'Hey, where's my kiss, Sis,' asked Emlyn as he followed her to the door. She gave him a kiss on the cheek.

'Thanks for all you've done, especially accepting Anna as you have.'

'It wouldn't help anyone if we took an alien attitude, would it?'

'I can always rely on my big sister then, can I?'

'I've always looked after my little brother, from the day he picked up his shovel at the age of ten and entered the drift. I can leave that to Ann now, but you need to look after her too.'

'I will, and thanks again.'

'That's all right, brawd,' she said, and then she left.'

Thirty Three

It was Emlyn's father who had given his son the paternal advice when he had started work nine years ago. And though his father had died in the tragic accident in the same drift Emlyn worked, the death only gave Emlyn stronger resolve to adhere to his late father's shrewdness, and that was to "spend a little and save a little." This Emlyn had done religiously over the past years until he had accumulated a sizable sum, enough to purchase the affordable premises that had come up for sale. They moved into the place when Anna had gained her strength. It was a detached cottage situated near the north end of the Cwm. Though it was a modest building, it had been maintained in good condition. The front of the house was in natural stone but pointed by a craftsman who was obviously proud of his work, with each line and curve of every joint filled evenly and neatly with grey mortar. The rusty hues and tans and the mixture of light greys of the hewn blocks were brought to prominence by the four window frames and front door that were painted in a contrasting brown. The rear garden with its small grassy area had a dry stonewall surrounding it. Opposite the front door, across the narrow path that was built past the house, was another dry stonewall with a wicket gate that gave access to a piece of neglected land that belonged to the cottage, which Emlyn said he would cultivate one day and plant vegetables.

Anna had been impressed when they moved in, for Emlyn had been true to his word. The place smelled of a fine polish, and the previous owner had cleaned the patterned linoleum in every corner, though the imprint of the flagstones beneath showed through. The fire-grate and side ovens had been given a good coating of black lead. Emlyn had spent his money well, but most of it had gone on the house and there was very little left. However, having a secure job with reasonable wages he was able to buy the necessary second-hand furniture on hire purchase, which meant they had a double bed and wardrobe, table and chairs and a cradle for the baby. The house had been left with some small rugs that gave a warm impression to the floor, and there were neat floral curtains on every window. And so, they settled and were happy.

As the months wore into years Anna dutifully, and with love, cleaned, laundered, shopped and did all those chores a wife was expected to do as well as tending to the needs of her precious little girl they named Hannah, inspired by her thoughts of Felicity and the Suffragettes when they assumed the wrong spelling of her own name. She was polite to her neighbours though kept her distance in rather an independent way for there was a stigma hanging over her head. She was aware that news travels fast in a small town, and she was convinced all around her knew of her marriage to John. She felt safer keeping a wide berth ensuring people would not get too friendly and ask personal questions.

Emlyn, however, followed the tradition of having a drink with the men after a hard twelve hours in the drift mine and often came home late, satisfied and jolly. Anna accepted this way of life for two years until one autumn evening she was sitting at the fire after putting Hannah to bed. She began to meditate on her situation. It was the first time since they had moved to the Cwm that a wave of mild depression came over her. It was not so much the feeling of being neglected, but she was three months pregnant with her second child. The thought occurred to her that once the child was born she would be imprisoned in the house for some considerable time. She did, natural to her nature and habits of past employment, buy alcohol when she shopped and indulged in a few drinks when Emlyn was out at nights. At such times, in those dreamy periods of intoxication, she counted her blessings. And though Rebecca and David made frequent visits to her, she began to miss the social life that she had enjoyed so much when she was unattached. One Saturday night, after Emlyn had bathed and was dressing to go out, she decided to share her thoughts with him, but he just shrugged his shoulders.

'That's the way life is for a respectable couple, my love. The man brings in the wage to keep things ticking over financially and the woman keeps the house going while bringing up the children.'

'I was thinking, David seems quite a natural with children caring for Rebecca's two, do you think he would mind Hannah for an evening for us to go out together?'

'Well, he's a young man now, and though he's been enthusiastic in the past, he goes out with his mates a lot, and has grown out of that big-uncle fad he had. As you know, he and his pals often go to Merthyr for some excitement.

'But he could look after Hannah for just one night now and again.'

'Looking after a two-year-old is much different than looking after kids you can reason with. No, Hannah is too young for David to take the responsibility. Why don't you ask Rebecca to have Hannah up at her house for an evening?'

'I couldn't bring her out in the night air after having a drink.'

'She's only a sprig of a thing. There's plenty of room for her to sleep up.'

Anna thought about it. 'Well, if Rebecca wouldn't mind, I suppose it would be all right.'

'There you are then,' said Emlyn as he laced up his shoes. 'Why don't you take a walk up sometime and see if she'll agree, I'm sure she will.'

'Yes, I'll do that.'

Emlyn pulled on his coat, gave Anna a peck on the cheek and left.

The following Monday Anna made her way up to Victoria Street pushing her pram with little Hannah sitting up, all eyes on the busy streets of shoppers and traffic. It was quite a way from the Cwm, but being a fresh and clear morning it helped to keep her cool from the exertion. She nodded frequently to people who bid her a cursory good morning, some stopping to look at the baby and paying her compliments, others hurrying by. She had a momentary thump in her heart when an old man on the opposite side of the street wearing a flat cap and having a scarred face stopped and stared over at her. He touched his cap to her and moved on. Anna's mind began to wonder who he was and why he looked at her in such a way, but then it struck her; it was John's friend, the ex puddler. Suddenly her mind was full of those years with John, and she wondered is he still alive. The thought frightened her. She shook herself and quickened her step, blanking out the past.

After twenty minutes of walking she eventually came to Rebecca's house and knocked, hoping that she would be at home. She was, and invited her in with a smile from Rebecca, wearing her pinafore and her hair tied back in a bun.

'You look busy, Rebecca.'

'No no not at all.'

'Are you sure it's convenient?'

'Of course, sit down, Ann it's nice to see you. I didn't expect you that's all.'

'I'm not intruding, am I?'

'Of course not—cup of tea?'

'Please. It's thirsty work walking up here.'

Then Rebecca bent down and chatted to the Hannah. 'And what is my favourite niece going to have to drink? A drop of milk, I think. Yes, a drop of milk will do you good—the kettle's on the hob, Ann, so it won't be long,' she said as she went to the back room.

Anna had promised herself the luxury of the carpets that graced Rebecca's floor, and the book display cabinet that made the room appear where educated people lived. And so it was, for Aled loved his literature, reading being his favourite pastime. The room was bright and cheerful with a glass vase of carnations sitting on the table that was covered in a thick olive protective tablecloth. But it wasn't as private as her cottage. Rebecca's small front window was always flashing from the effect of people passing by and momentarily blanking out the light.

Rebecca came in with the baby's beaker half full of milk.

'She's fine with a beaker is she?'

'Normally, but I expect she'll let me down.'

'Not to worry.'

'How are William and Emma getting along at school, anyway?'

'They're getting along very well.' Rebecca looked at Anna knowing something was on her mind. 'Is everything all right with you, Ann?'

246

Anna sighed. 'I'm bored with being in at nights. Sundays are not too bad because Emlyn and I go out walking with Hannah when its fine, but in the evenings when I'm alone I get…well lonely.'

'I'm not surprised. I'll have to have a word with that brother of mine, he's neglecting you.'

'I feel that too, but he works twelve hours a day and I can see his point of view when he says he wants to clear his lungs of coal dust.'

'Huh! They all say that. I know, I've worked in the drifts, remember. I had to clear my lungs with water.'

'Yes, I suppose I could argue that point with him.'

'Won't get you anywhere, it's a collier's religion; got to clear their throats got to spit up the dust, got to wash out their system. They've got some dirty habits; chewing tobacco to keep the dust from getting to their lungs is one. They chew tobacco all their working lives, but they still get the dust. You won't change them, Ann. What you need to do is get him to take you with him once in a while.'

Anna looked at Rebecca with sheepish eyes. 'That's the true reason I came up to see you. Could you possibly look after Hannah for me to go out one night?'

'Of course I will. She can sleep up here and you can pick her up the next morning.'

'Oh, you're a true friend, Rebecca and a wonderful sister-in-law…well almost a sister-in-law.'

'Sister-in-law by love but not by law, never mind. Well, I may come back to you and ask you to look after my two in exchange,' she laughed.

'I'd do that for you, I wouldn't mind.'

'I'm just joking, Aled and I find our own entertainment. And if we need to go out we all go out together. Besides, Ruth has the job of minding them for me when necessary.'

'How is Ruth, Rebecca? Has she forgiven me and Emlyn yet?'

'She doesn't talk about you, so I wouldn't worry.'

'I think of her now and again, but I don't worry about it. It's our choice and our lives.'

'Well, there you are then. Now that kettle must be on the boil by now. I'll get a couple of cups and some of my Welshcakes.'

Anna looked down at Hannah, 'Auntie Rebecca is going to look after you for Mam to go out, I hope you're going to be good for her.'

Rebecca came in with a tray laden with some cups and saucers, Welshcakes and a full teapot.

'Right, we'll have a cup of tea and then we'll make plans for your night out,' she said as she tilted the pot and poured the teas.

Thirty Four

Five months later Anna and Emlyn had become accustomed to having Saturday night out together. The social evening had become an event that Anna looked forward to each week, and took it for granted that it would last right up to the birth of their second baby. Emlyn, however, had a different view of the immediate future and was hinting to Anna she should slow down and take it easy for the next couple of months until the baby was born and weaned. It was ten o'clock on Saturday night in the Dowlais Inn and they had been drinking for a couple of hours in mixed company, Anna making the most of the one night-a-week out.

'Besides, Annie, you've gone seven months now, the drinkers pass comments, girl.'

'You're too sensitive, that's your trouble. Besides, it's your friends that pass the remarks not strangers. Strangers have more respect.'

'Strangers are embarrassed.'

'Let them be embarrassed.'

'Listen, this is the last night out together until the baby is old enough to eat solids.'

'Emlyn, don't tell me when to go out and when to stay in. I will not take orders from you or anybody else.—Here,' she handed him her empty glass. 'Make yourself useful and stop ordering me about.'

He stood up and glowered down at her. 'Who's giving the orders now?'

She looked up and smiled a silly smile making her look half-witted. 'Get on with you and don't forget to get yourself a fresh one.' Then she caressed her abdomen feeling movement there. She looked around and waved at a couple of familiar faces, some waved back and stuck up their thumbs communicating a question and answer at the same time. Anna raised her hand and pushed her thumb up. 'Yes I'm fine and so is the baby.'

At the bar Emlyn was being served with a pint and a gin.

'Is the missus all right Emlyn?' asked the big barman. A man who could pull a full dram of coal with one hand before his lungs filled with dust.'

'Aye, Llew, as right as she thinks she is.'

'She looks a little bit...' Llew animated his hand in a seesaw fashion.

'Yes, I know.'

'It's none of my business, but I didn't let my missus out of the house after six months.'

Emlyn paid for the drinks and picked them up. 'I'd do the same Llew, except there's a bit of a problem, she don't take orders.'

Llew shook his head as Emlyn walked away.

Emlyn sat down after placing the drinks on the table and looked at Anna who had taken the drink immediately and began sipping it.

'Annie, I wasn't ordering you I was just giving you a little advice, that's all. And don't be disappointed if Rebecca doesn't want to take on the extra child to care when the baby is old enough to be minded.'

'I don't think you are in a position to advise me. Anyway, you can look after the children a couple of nights a week while I go out for a break.'

Emlyn stared hard at her, but she wasn't looking so she didn't notice. He took hold of her hand firmly 'Listen, Annie my girl, I'm the man of the house and I'll say what's best for us.'

'You, call me a girl? You're a half-ounce hauler, young man.'

'I'm a top miner, Annie, and proud of it...a mother's place is at home with her children.'

Anna took another sip of her gin and frowned the same time. What about the father? Where's his place when he's not in work?'

'Don't be daft. I think you've had too many of those gins. A man's place is to bring home the money to keep his family. I'm doing my bit, so don't go finding fault with me.'

Anna stood up unsteadily with glass in hand, and addressed the women that were drinking, some alone, others with their husbands or friends. 'Did you hear that, ladies,' she yelled, and the place went quiet. 'A man's place is to bring the money in and have no other duties. From work to pub, from pub to bed, from bed to work, hey that's a damn good life.'

A cheer went up from the men, and they raised their glasses in sardonic agreement.

'You tell him Annie,' shouted a middle-aged woman hanging on to her bald-headed husband.'

'It's all right for you, Peggy,' Emlyn shouted in defence. 'You've raised your kids and are free of them. And if Annie can do as good a job as you have, I'll be very pleased.'

'Oh, he'll be very pleased,' shouted Anna. 'The boss has approved of you Peggy. Let's hear a cheer for the boss.' Then she sat down with a bump.

It was the womens turn to raise their voices in mock approval with screams of delight.

Anna stood up again. 'Are we lackey wives or equal humans.'

There was a cheerful response, but muted when a voice shouted from the back of the room.

'You're not a bloody wife, are you? Get married and give your offspring a name, woman.'

'She is a wife,' came a gruff voice from another corner. 'But she's not living with him.'

Emlyn shot to his feet. 'Who said that?' He began to walk to where the voice had come from. 'Who said that? Show yourself you cowards.'

'The burly landlord came running from behind the bar. 'Right, I've had enough. Emlyn, take your missus home. I'll not have a brawl in my pub.'

'I want to know whose hiding behind those comments.'

The crowded room was still and quiet as Emlyn looked around.

'You won't find them, Emlyn,' said Anna. They're men aren't they? Now if they were women they'd show themselves.'

'Shut up Anna.'

'I won't shut up for you or anybody else.'

The landlord breasted up to Emlyn, taller and heavier. 'Now Emlyn, I don't want to throw you out, so I'll ask you, if you please, to leave the premises.'

Emlyn looked at the pleading on the man's face. 'Right, Llew, but if you know of the men I want, I'll expect you to let me defend the lady's honour.

Outside in the darkness the heat of the burning tip filtered through the main gates of the steelworks assisted by a light breeze. The silhouette of the nightshift locomotive dragged trucks of burning debris to the precipitous edge. Sparks cascaded in the air as the trucks dumped the molten slag and dross. Emlyn and Anna walked slowly accompanied by the humming of the iron works machinery pervading the area, she hanging on to Emlyn for stability. Occasionally some passer-by would bid them goodnight, Emlyn would give a quiet response, but Anna could only raise a weak hand. Her head was very hazy and her thoughts distant as they made their way down the gradient to home. She was thinking through a brain of mist, of the time her foster father told her that he was the man of the house and he will be obeyed at all times or else. His wife would utter, "Yes dear, you are our saviour and champion, without you the devil would be our downfall and we would be cast into eternal fire." Anna could never tell if her foster mother was humouring him or terrified of provoking him further.

'Are you going to cast me into eternal fire, Emlyn?'

'What? What the hell are you talking about, woman?'

'Ah. I'm a woman now, not a girl, nor am I lovely Annie anymore.'

'You're drunk. I hope this will be the last of your ranting. I hope you are going to show a more responsible attitude soon.' He stopped and grabbed her tightly by her arms, his face almost touching hers as he looked down on her. 'I tell you what Annie if you embarrass me in public again I'll drag you outside by the hair and thrash you.'

'Oh you old caveman—sorry young caveman.'

He spun her round and pushed her forward. 'I'll talk to you when you're sober.' But Anna could not keep her balance after the forceful shove and she fell to the ground, prostrate and groaning.

Emlyn rushed forward, 'Oh my God, the baby. Get up, drunk and lying on the floor what will people think? You'll lose the baby acting like this' He picked her up and supported her, his arm around

252

her upper back. Will you please pull yourself together and stop whimpering?'

'You threw me to the ground,' she cried. 'Pregnant and you threw me to the ground. Nobody has ever treated me that way, nobody!'

'I didn't mean it…I'm sorry. Come on let's get home before anymore mishaps.'

The following morning, the day being Sunday, Emlyn was first up and decided to go and pick up Hannah from Rebecca's, leaving Anna still sleeping. He had only slept a few hours during the night turning things over in his head. He thought about last night, how he had to help her to bed after she had fallen asleep on the rug; how he had pushed her to the ground and made her look so helpless lying in the road. How she had turned from a loving, caring partner to a cool, single-minded woman who had given the impression she had grown distant from him. He kept telling himself it was the drink, but for the first time she had brought to his notice that his own drinking habits had festered latent grievances in her. Grievances he had neglected to notice. Furthermore, she had chosen to vent her feelings in public. Yes, it was the drink that brought it all to the surface, but her inner stifled depressions had obviously been growing for some time. He suddenly felt guilty and wanted desperately to make it up to her. How could he have been so blind? There is only one way, he thought; he will have to change his ways. After all, many of his fellow miners, if not the majority, would go out once or twice a week. And those who were religious would not be out drinking at all. Yes, he had taken her for granted and will tell her so. He hoped news of last night hadn't travelled to his sister and brother-in-law.

When he arrived at Rebecca's Aled had already gone to chapel having duties to carry out before the congregation should arrive. Emlyn gave a short tap at the door and walked in. Rebecca was finishing dressing her two children by giving them a final inspection and touching a loose hair of Emma's that had gone astray. Hannah was sitting up in her pram having had the benefit of being attended to first in readiness for her parents.

'I'm glad you've come now, I'm just about to go to chapel.'

'I timed it right, then'

'Avoiding Aled, are you?'

No, why should I?' said Emlyn picking Hannah up in his arms and giving her a kiss.

'Afraid he might use his powers of persuasion and play on your guilty conscience.'

'What do you mean by that, Sis?'

'Don't get all annoyed, I'm only playing with you. He might persuade you to come to chapel. What do you think I meant?'

'Nothing really, just wanted to know what you meant.'

'Right, children, say bye to your uncle Emlyn.'

They both said goodbye in unison. Rebecca caught them by their hands. 'We are ready for your father's prayers. Sorry I've got to rush off, brother, but I musn't be late.'

Outside, Emlyn put his arm around Rebecca's shoulders. 'Thanks Sis, for looking after Hannah, we really do appreciate it.'

'Don't mention it. See you later, perhaps.'

When Emlyn got home Anna hadn't risen. He was worried she might be feeling ill after last night so he climbed the stairs to investigate, carrying Hannah. In the bedroom Anna was sitting on the side of the bed, her back arched, her head drooping and her face hidden by her hanging hair. She was shaking her head, groaning and mumbling to herself. Emlyn placed Hannah on the floor and pointed to her mother.

'I don't think Mammy is feeling too well, little one. Sit there a minute.'

Anna slowly lifted her head and looked up at them. 'Give her to me.'

'No, get yourself sorted first. You're not fit to hold her at the moment.'

'I think I had too much to drink last night.'

'I don't think, I know, you definitely had too much. Listen, get yourself dressed and I'll go down and boil the kettle. Then we can have a quiet, sensible talk. And I mean quiet.'

'I made a fool of myself, didn't I?'

'You were the entertainment for the night. I've never been thrown out of a pub in my life.'

'We weren't thrown out, were we?'

Emlyn picked up the baby. 'Not physically, just with a great deal of humiliation, get dressed I'll see you downstairs.'

'Oh God, I'll be there in a minute.'

She dressed lethargically for every movement gave her head a jolt, and then she faced the painful descent. Downstairs she had a cup of tea prepared by Emlyn. She sat sipping it and kept taking furtive glances at him, wondering when he was going to begin the manly reprimand. But it didn't come which made her feel worse.

'Hannah, come to Mammy? Give Mammy a hug.'

The little girl went to her mother and sat on her lap, Anna hugging her overwhelmingly.

'Did you have a nice time up at Auntie Rebecca's last night.'

'I played with Will and Emma,' she explained in baby talk.'

'Good, and did you sleep all right?'

'I always sleep in the cot that Emma used to sleep in.'

'Of course, I just wondered if you slept all night or did you wake up in the night.'

'Daddy said you were bad.'

'Ill,' said Emlyn, 'She knows I meant you weren't feeling very well last night. I've been thinking, Anna; maybe I haven't been as attentive as I should have in the past. I realize I've been a little preoccupied with my work and leisure time and, I confess, I've been neglecting your needs and feelings. I've decided I am not going out so often for a drink. If I go out just twice a week, will that be all right you?'

Anna's face gave an expression of minor shock. 'Does that mean that I've got to stay in seven nights a week?'

'Of course not, at least, not after the baby is born, but I would like you to stay in until then.'

'I've got to go out; shopping and all that.'

'I meant drinking.'

'Don't worry, I've learnt my lesson. I'll be a model of pregnancy and will look after my baby until it is weaned. But I expect you to do your part by minding them to give me a break once or twice a week.'

'Right, I agree. We'll see how it works out after a couple of months.'

Thirty Five

Their second child was born without complications in the month of January when the Morlais Brook was frozen over and the snow had fallen hard and the Cwm had a white sheet thrown over the scattered houses, a wintry scene glistening with virgin-white lumps and bumps and only the smoking chimneys poking through. The healthy baby girl proved to have a strong pair of lungs, she wailed for some considerable time without any physical encouragement from the local deliverer of children, Mrs. Pugh. And for a time there was a deal of contentment as Emlyn and Anna maintained their resolutions and dutifully cosseted their children. Young Hannah adored her new baby sister and helped as much as she could in her own infantile way by having her sibling on her lap whilst her mother did the housework. But as the seasons came and went with sun-blessed summers and snow-covered winters, the baby grew into a toddler, from a toddler to match the energetic activities of her sister, and the two playful girls were making physical and emotional demands on Anna. However, she made demands on Emlyn and insisted he look after them more often for her to have longer leisure time, which really meant more visits to the local pubs to enjoy the company of other drinkers. And though Anna was given freedom to have a couple of nights out each week, the chores and responsibility of motherhood was beginning to tire her. She descended into a mode of life not unlike Emlyn. For his habitual ways was almost copied by Anna. He would do his shifts and return home tired and dirty, with the demand that a bucket of hot water be readily boiling in preparation for his bath, put clean clothes on and go out to relax with his colleagues. Anna would do the drudgery of housework motherhood and shopping. She would perspire over the oven, her skin drying tight and thin, her hands sore and callous from scrubbing clothes on the washboard. Then there was the coal to bring in and cleaning the fireplace in the morning before bathing the energetic and squabbling children. With these chores pulsing through her mind she too found the only respite was to go out and have a drink. They both got entrenched in this kind of life and the years rolled on. She became pregnant again and another baby girl arrived two years after her last. The birth took place the same year royalty visited Dowlais. King George V and Queen Mary visited Dowlais House and entered the grounds through the coal arch, an imaginative structure built with blocks of coal and surmounted by a full dram. Anna was too weary to line the streets with the crowds, and Emlyn had little interest in the visit.

And so her tedious life went on to 1914 when war broke out and Anna was well into her fourth pregnancy. She gave birth to a baby boy and shuddered as her imagination drew a picture of her bringing a son into a war-torn world. Men from all walks of life and of all ages were volunteering to enlist, bringing fear into the hearts of mothers, and a falling of morale into communities. This gave Anna a new impetus to follow her philosophy of living for today and let tomorrow look after itself. She was often reminded by Emlyn that other colliers' wives accepted the traditional way of life. But Anna could only think of the time when she was dressed in a smart maid's uniform and served the upper class. Sometimes she wondered how things would have turned out had she been as cunning as Katie had suggested and entrapped the sex-mad Jeremy into marriage. It seemed the right thing to do in retrospect. Her second thought about that situation was the family who were too devious and sophisticated for her to fool. The conclusion always depressed her, though the possible scenario returned time after time.

There was no way out of her present situation and she had to accept the many painful duties and obligations she could not turn a blind eye to. Each day she looked in the mirror she saw a pale face getting paler, fuller, lined and plain. Her hair got duller losing its sheen, wiry and wild. Her eyes had lost their sparkle and had grey swellings under them. She could do nothing but forget it all under the influence of drink. In company she laughed and derided the male sex, which made her popular with the women, but the men had heard it all before and just ignored her. In time the women found her boring and humoured her, more than she was amusing them.

Furthermore, Ruth was despising her more and more for continuing to have children outside marriage, Rebecca's husband called her the Harlot of Hell who continually degraded the Rees family and all associates, and even Rebecca found it difficult to tolerate her. Emlyn, defiant and steadfast hoped that somehow a miracle would come along and straighten things out, but it never did. The contact with his family became less frequent and finally deteriorated to a state of estrangement. Anna and was an abandoned unit with no friends except those who had little or no moral aspirations; the boozers, the lay-a-bouts and those who preyed on susceptible and gullible people. Emlyn became very sensitive when anyone should mention Anna in the slightest derogatory fashion.

One evening when he left Anna with the children, and before going for a drink, he decided to walk up to Mary Ann Street and call in to see Ruth in an attempt to bridge differences. He knocked at the door and walked in. Ruth was sitting in the granddad chair near the fire, staring into the flames unaware it seemed, of Emlyn's presence. She had developed from the sturdy fourteen-year-old whose energetic enthusiasm looked after the family all those years ago, to a serious disappointed woman who, through no fault of her own, had no children because of her husband's infertility.

'I realize I'm not welcome, Sis, but I need to see you and be friends again—nice savoury smell, maybe I'll stop and join you,' he joked

Ruth looked up, tears dribbling over her prominent cheekbones. 'I never thought I'd say this, but it's good to see you.'

'What's the matter, something wrong?'

'I just wish we were all together and as happy as we used to be.'

'And that's why you're crying?'

'No. I'm crying for my baby brother.'

Emlyn came to her and sat on a chair and lifted her head. The tears had been profuse for her flushed cheeks were wet. 'What do you mean, baby brother? David must be twenty-three or four by now. I haven't forgotten him, you know. Even though I'm not welcome in my own house I still think of you all.'

'Well, you're welcome now, because I don't understand life anymore. I just want my family to be together again, but that's impossible now.'

'It's only me you're keeping away. You've still got Rebecca and David.'

'Rebecca keeps to herself with that preacher husband of hers, and David is gone.'

'Ruth, what are you talking about?'

'He enlisted. Left this morning and joined the army. Fed up of the steelworks, he said. Going to do a man's job and serve his country.'

Emlyn had to let the news sink in. He just couldn't believe his ears. 'The stupid, stupid boy, what the hell did he want to do that for?'

'As you said, he's twenty-three years old now. He's a man.'

'Where did he go?'

'Brecon Barracks.'

'I'll go there. Maybe I can get him out before it's too late.'

'He's as stubborn as you; I tried to talk him out of it until my brain was buzzing from frustration. Besides, it's all signed and sealed. Nobody can get him out now.'

Emlyn stood up and paced back and fore for a time. 'It's all this Lord Kitchener's propaganda. Him and his damn posters. "Your county needs you." Huh, wants you to have your head blown off for some Austrian Duke that's been assassinated. We've only been in the war a few months and already there have been massive casualties. Youngsters can only see glory and medals.'

'David believed it was his duty to serve and defend his country.'

'That's what he was doing in the steelworks. As I am doing in the mine; the country needs steel and coal as much as anything else.'

'He didn't see it that way Emlyn.'

'I'd rather be buried under twenty tons of coal from a roof fall. At least my body will be found and I will have died as a collier and be interred in my country.'

'I wish you would have been here, maybe you could have persuaded him not to go.'

'Maybe,' he said, calming down. 'Where's Luke anyway?'

260

'In work, he's due home any minute.' She stood up and went into the steamy kitchen. 'I'd better check on the potatoes and greens.'

Emlyn followed her and put his arm around her shoulders as she stood over the kitchen fireplace with steaming pots over the coals and oven. 'I'm as unhappy as you, Sis. Things have all gone wrong with me, too. Anna's drinking too much, the children are growing and in need of things...I don't know what to do for the best, myself.'

'Why don't you get married, it might make things easier for people to accept.'

'She's already married, you know that.'

'Isn't there some rule or law that frees a man or woman from marriage if the husband has been missing for—I don't know, six or seven years, presumed dead, desertion, or something like that. For all we know John could be in the army too. He could be dead for all we know.'

'I didn't think of that. And there's a law covering it? I haven't heard of that.'

'Well, find out. At least I'll have a married brother and with children that are legitimate.'

'I'll do that.'

They heard the front door being closed and Luke walked in. 'Hello, hello, Emlyn. You're the last person I expected to see here, but you're welcome all the same.'

'Thank you, Luke, I was just going, did you know about David?'

'I did indeed. Tried our best to deter him, but his strong-will defeated us both. There was no changing his mind.'

'No, I don't suppose there was,' said Emlyn. 'I'm thinking of making more visits up here in future Luke; Ruth and I intend to make things up.'

'That's splendid news, and about time too. Bring Anna and the children as well. I'd like to see them other than passing when shopping.'

'Yes, it is a bit silly, isn't it? Well I'll be off now. Cheer up Sis. He'll come back safe and sound, you'll see.'

Emlyn kissed his sister on the cheek and shook hands with Luke as though there had been an agreement he had to abide by.

He stood by the bar in the half-full Miners Arms next to a jovial Irishman who insisted on buying him a pint. Emlyn wanted to brood into his pint but the Irishman persisted.

'Will you be having a drink with me now, my fine man?'

Emlyn looked at the man, who was roughly the same age and stature as himself. 'I'm not in the mood for socializing tonight, Paddy.'

'Now how did you know I was Irish?'

'You've got a brogue as thick as the washery sludge.'

'Ah that's good to know. You say you're not in the mood, but one should always be in the mood to make friends. If I can make a friend a day I think my life has been worthwhile. Don't you think that now?'

'It's better than making enemies I suppose.'

'Well, there you are then.—Landlord, loosen the tap on that keg and pour the man a pint of your best.'

Emlyn huffed. 'I'll get the next one.'

'There's no need, I don't buy to have the same compliment returned you know. But I know a lot who would exploit the situation and drag the last penny out of a leprechaun's pouch.'

'Aye, well those kinds of people have no pride or conscience and are not worth the soulless skin that covers them.'

'Tis a terrible time for us with this war going on, don't you think?'

'I don't know why we're in it.'

'Oh some Duke Franz or other got himself assassinated in Austria.'

'I mean I don't understand why we got involved.'

'Well one thing led to another and before you know it everybody is killing one another. It's inhuman I say. Ah there are some devilish stories coming back from the front of men dying needlessly in the trenches. Being blown to smithereens they say, others being mown down going over the hill, so to speak.'

'I'd rather not think about it.'

'Ah here comes the man with best drink in the world. Thank you landlord—I like your sentiments. We'll say no more. Is it this pub you always drink in?'

Emlyn shuffled his feet and straightened his back in an impatient manner. 'Mostly,' he said, thinking a brusque answer might deter the man.

'Oh I like to travel around you know, meet new people, make new friends. Ah, a good conversation takes away the tensions of life, you know. Don't you ever think of changing your pub now?'

'I do when I take my wife out. We go to the Bush Hotel, or the Dowlais Inn. Sometimes we go a little further up to the Patriot or up to Pant to the Codiver Arms; but that's a summer pub, too far to walk in the evening.'

'I'm more of a Merthyr man myself, but I thought I'd try my luck up here. I've heard they are friendlier up here.'

'Don't put your tam-o-shanter on it.'

Paddy looked at Emlyn with some surprise. 'Now wouldn't that be a piece of Scottish headwear?'

'Is it?'

'My word man, you are in sombre mood. You need cheering up. Do you know what cheers me up when I'm down like you? Well I'll tell you; it's the company of a friendly colleen. Ah, the ladies are prettier up here, you know. Oh yes, you can find many ladies of the night down below but I don't see many up here. Though there were a few ladies in here the other evening, mostly friendly and jovial, but there was one, a devil of a woman she was, running the men down she was, and cursing at religion.'

The landlord, leaning on the bar listening, banged an empty tankard on the counter. 'There's a lot of talking here tonight and not enough drinking.'

'What's the matter with the man? Conversation is good for relationships,' expounded the Irishman, by which time Emlyn had turned to him and looked him straight in the eye

'What night did you say you were here?

Paddy stroked his chin. 'Let me see now, aye, it was the night before last.'

'And who was this female, you called a devil of a woman?'

263

'I don't know, I'd never seen her in me life before.' He turned to the barman. 'What was that banshee's name that was spouting all kinds of profanities the other night, could you tell me that?'

The barman shook his head. 'Leave it, leave it!'

'No, no. Let me think now…was it Mary…no, Fannie. No that wasn't it…Ah, Annie they called her. I remember now. Sit down and shut up, Annie, they called, you're making a foo…'

The Irishman was stopped by a right swing to the jaw, which floored him but did not put him out. He sat up and shook his head clear. 'Now what in St Peter's name did you do that for? Oh well, if that's what you'll be a wanting. He stood up and run at Emlyn, diving at him from a few feet away. Emlyn was knocked over and hit his head on the counter but soon got up and took up a boxer's defensive pose, fists up to his chin and his left leg forward. Paddy advanced and struck out a right hook, but it was easy for Emlyn to anticipate. He ducked and shot out a straight punch flattening Paddy's nose, drawing blood. The Irishman was not one to give up and he took a run and dived at Emlyn again. This caused some tables to be knocked over as the two of them fell to the floor grappling and rolling in all directions. Women were screaming, drinks were tipping, chairs were skidding and the men made a ring around the brawlers. The barman could only do what was judicious, and that was to call upon his hefty regulars who assisted him to clear the pub at such times. He ran to the two, who stood there smiling, arms folded waiting for the inevitable call for help.

'Two pints on the house if you throw them out immediately, the landlord yelled above the hubbub.

'There are two of them, Tom,' one shouted back. 'It's worth at least four pints.'

'I'll give you both three each, but you've got to do it now before they wreck the place.'

They looked at each other and nodded. One grabbed Emlyn by the scruff, and the other grabbed the Irishman. They dragged them through the front door, took Emlyn ten yards down the road, and Paddy ten yards up the road and let them fall flat on their faces.

'Now which one of you would like to cross the line first?' said the stocky six-footer.'

264

The fighters, both breathing heavily, looked at the muscular evictors and decided to go their separate ways.

'Nobody calls my wife a banshee,' grunted Emlyn.'

'Was it your wife now?' said Paddy. 'Well send me to hell for my foolishness.' Then he walked away calling back, 'Tis my apologies you'll be deserving and I'll give them to you freely, g-night now.'

Emlyn strolled down the street mumbling to himself. 'She`s not my wife, though, that's the trouble. Maybe if she was it would make things easier all round.'

Thirty Six

When Emlyn came home from work the following day he was in sombre mood. Anna nodded her head as a welcome and then continued preparing the evening meal. She had sent the children out the rear garden to amuse themselves, telling eight-year-old Hannah to look after them until food is ready. Anna went into the kitchen and filled a bucket of water, struggled with it into the living room and hung it on a bracket over the coals. Emlyn sat down on a wooden chair and began to take off his boots. He looked up at Anna.

'I thought the water would be ready by now.'

'Well you thought wrong. I've got four children to feed besides the man of the house.'

'Don't be caustic Anna. I've had a bad day.'

'Huh! You've had a bad day? What do you think I've been doing while you're in work, lazing around? What went wrong with you, anyway?' She gave the fire a shaking up with the poker causing a few sparks.

'I don't know,' he said demurely. 'I've been unable to concentrate on my work.'

'Huh! If you got to bed earlier your brain might work better. You came home at midnight like a pickled puddler. Your eyes were half closed man. Red-raw they were as though you'd been stirring white-hot pig-iron.'

'I got into a fight.'

'And I thought you'd been crying, poor thing. And what was the fight about?' she asked, placing a cloth on the table.

'You.'

She leant her hands on the table and looked at him, puzzled. 'Me?'

'There was a Paddy in the Colliers Arms running you down. He called you a raving banshee.'

'I don't know any Paddy.'

'He knew you. Everybody knows you, from Abergavenny to Cardiff, and now you've got a new name, Raving Banshee.'

Anna sat down on the sofa. 'Raving Banshee, am I? The trouble with people around here is they can't see how women are servile and downtrodden. Womenfolk pretend to put up with it, but the truth is, they're brainwashed into believing they're second-class citizens.' She went to the dresser and took some plates to the table.

Emlyn stood up, frustrated, his boots in his hand. 'Don't start that again or I won't be responsible for my actions.'

'Going to fight me now, are you? Maybe you'll have a better chance with me than Paddy. What's the matter with you lately, can't you take the rough with the smooth anymore? A bit of gossip never hurt you before.'

'It's not just the gossip. Everything's coming on top of me. I went to see Ruth last night.'

'Good God, your brain is puddled. Did she tell you to go back to your whore of a wife?'

Emlyn growled like an irritable dog, his eyes staring through red eyelids and his coal-dust face streaked where sweat had run rivulets. 'Stop using such language woman! Ruth welcomed me. She had bad news. David enlisted in the army. He's going to Europe to fight the bloody Germans, would you believe it!'

Anna audibly gasped and caught Emlyn by the shoulders. 'I'm sorry, Emlyn, that is utterly disastrous. Whatever got into the young fool?'

'Time has flown, Annie. As Ruth said, he is not a teenager anymore; he's an adult with his own stubborn mind. Ruth said she'd pleaded with him but he wouldn't waver from his commitment. It seems that pig-headedness runs in the Rees family.'

Anna let go of him and walked to the bucket on the fire, dipped her finger in and quickly pulled it out again. 'He's no more obstinate than a lot of us, including me. You say that Ruth welcomed you?'

'She's had enough of the family squabbling all the time. She wants the family to be together again, as it was.'

'As it was before I came along, you mean.'

'No, she accepts you now. She said she doesn't care anymore if only we could all be together again.'

'What does Rebecca think of it?'

'That's another heartache for Ruth. Rebecca hasn't been to see her in months, which gives more worry. Ruth seems to think that Aled has something to do with it.'

'Aled! Aled! He's got her where he wants her, under his thumb. It's strange how people change from one ideal to the next; Ruth is waking up and seeing life as it is, Rebecca is finding it easier to obey her husband in a fantasy.'

Hannah came running into the living room, her sandy hair following the colour of Emlyn's. 'Mam, Bronwen won't do as she is told.'

'What's she doing now, Hannah?'

'She won't do her sums. I'm the teacher and she's the pupil, but she won't do as I tell her.'

'Play something else, Hannah, something that Bronwen won't mind.'

'Huh! What's the point in me trying?' she exclaimed as she run back out again.'

'There's another one with a chip off the old block,' said Emlyn.

Anna flopped on the sofa. 'I'll have five minutes while the bucket's warming.'

Emlyn sat back on the wooden chair and faced her. 'Anna, Ruth made a suggestion last night.'

'Oh, you look quite serious about it.'

'She seems to think, and I agree with her, that it would be quite legal for us to get married.'

Astonishment spread over Anna's face but soon disappeared as she broke into laughter. Emlyn thumped his knee with closed hand. 'It's not funny, Anna,' he yelled. Ruth thinks it will make life easier for the family if we were wed.'

Anna stifled her emotions and controlled herself. 'I don't know who it will make life easier for, you or her, but you're both forgetting something, I'm already married,' she said, as she found it difficult to stop herself laughing.

'Will you hear me out woman? You haven't seen John for years. His disappearance can be judged to be desertion.'

'Emlyn, I deserted him!'

He jumped to his feet again and began to pace back and fore clearly annoyed. He looked down on her. 'It doesn't matter! It doesn't matter! He left town and disappeared, didn't he? He could be dead, or maybe he joined the army. We can go and seek legal advice. Ruth is sure there will be no problem. You left a long time ago. It'll be 1915 in a couple of months. We needn't wait longer.'

'Emlyn, Emlyn, stop parading. Listen, if you want us to marry, then I'll marry you. But signing a piece of paper to make it legal won't change anything. And if you think I'm going to go opening my soul to some solicitor and go through the legal channels, you can think again.'

'What do you mean?'

'There'd probably be some kind of investigation. The Registrar will ask, has anyone got any objections? I wouldn't be surprised if Saint Aled would get involved and poke his holy nose into our affairs. No! All we need do is go to the registry office and say we want to get married. Don't tell anyone we can't trust. I shall have to give my married name and probably my maiden name, I shall say my husband passed away some years ago—deceased. If Ruth wants to see us married, she and Luke will have to play along.'

'You're a cool one, Annie. By damn you're a cool one.'

'Look at life as it is, Emlyn, not as society has made it. Their way is pretentious and hypocritical; my way is how Nature has made us and how life has treated us. I'll marry you. At least the kids won't have a stigma hanging over their heads.'

'I'll book a couple of days off and we'll go and see the Registrar.'

'Wait a minute. Now that you've brought up your concerns about our life, I might as well tell you mine.'

'What now?'

'I can't cope with my existence as it is now. I've got to have a little more freedom and independence.'

'Emlyn sat down again, complexity written all over his face. 'One minute you're going to marry me, and the next minute you

270

want your freedom. You have your nights out while I stay in with the kids, what more do you want?'

'I want to earn some money. I know you're regular with the housekeeping, but it's not enough. I've served behind a bar before and I think I can get a job at the Puddlers Arms in the High Street.'

'Since when have you been going to the Puddlers?'

'When I go out, I either go to the Puddlers or the Colliers. The Puddlers is a busy pub and Jim the landlord offered me a couple of nights a week.'

'Did he indeed? That was very kind of him.'

'Don't be cynical, there's nothing in it except money.'

'I've been to the Puddlers, there's quite a raw bunch there at times.'

'Emlyn, I'm not the woman I was, look at me. I'll just be a middle-aged barmaid.' A mischievous gleam came to her eyes and an enigmatic smile to her lips. 'But I'll take delight in deriding those who take a fancy to me, don't you worry it will be fun.'

'Will you ever grow up?'

'Will I ever stop feeling young?' she said, the smile persisting.

'Jim's all right, I suppose,' said Emlyn, already reconciling himself to the scenario. 'Who's going to look after the kids? You'll be out four or five nights a week if you intend to continue with your social life as well as your working nights.'

'Hannah is very good with them now. She's eight and mature for her age. She looks after them when I'm busy or when I'm out shopping, don't she? Besides, if Ruth really wants us to be a family again, I'm sure she'll enjoy the children. After all, she's missed out on that side of life far too long.'

'You've got it all worked out, haven't you?'

'I've been thinking about it for some time. The unlikely Ruth has helped me make my move sooner that I intended.'

'I'll agree to a trial run for a few weeks and see how things work out.'

'Very magnanimous of you, I'm sure.'

She went to the fire and checked on the bucket. 'It's hot enough. Am I going to carry it into the scullery or will you?'

Emlyn thought about it. 'Leave it to the man of the house.'

'Have you ever thought about leaving the world to women? There wouldn't be wholesale slaughter in Europe if women had their way.

Thirty Seven

Anna and Emlyn took their time in getting married, but they eventually did in early August 1915, declaring to the Registrar that she was a widow of many years and that her late husband had died in a blast furnace accident at the Dowlais Iron works. She also decided that it would be prudent to register her name as Annie, and not Ann, the name that was declared on her last marriage certificate. She spent the following months revelling in the pub atmosphere working as a barmaid in the Puddlers Arms, teasing and ribbing the male customers, but praising the virtues and sufferings of the womenfolk whenever an appropriate opportunity arose. It was all taken in good humour and nobody complained. Life was fine and looking up for her as she turned a blind eye to all the grievances Emlyn put her way, for he was an unhappy man.

Emlyn became disgruntled and embarrassed, forced to spend more time at home with the children as Anna took on less domestic responsibilities and more employment duties. It was not the local culture that woman of the house should be out working whilst the man of the house be doing woman's work. She should be at home looking after her kiddies and the man having his well-earned relaxation with his colleagues in the pub. That was the gossip spreading through the Cwm and the working community. Emlyn was continually having his leg pulled in work as well as those times he had his nights out. "Where is your pinafore, Emlyn? Not wearing it tonight, are you?" Another would respond, "He's washed it in case the missus gives him a row for not keeping it clean." Things came to a head when Anna agreed with Jim the landlord to work extra hours. This she did and still demanded her nights out enraging Emlyn, and also Ruth, who had agreed to help out with the children whenever possible. Ruth began to believe she was being taken advantage of and that her brother was too lenient with Anna. 'You are the man of the house, Emlyn, for goodness sake put a stop to it,' she would often say, but Emlyn would shrug his shoulders and tell her he will sort things out when he's ready. But Ruth could not wait, her patience had been spent and a confrontation was imminent. It was a Sunday morning when Ruth came down to see the two of them knowing that Emlyn was not in work, and that Anna was at home.

Anna opened the door, surprised to see Ruth. Emlyn hadn't mentioned her coming and it was usual to make arrangements. 'Hello Ruth, I didn't expect you this morning, but you're welcome.'

The buxom Ruth walked in with a rigid back and a serious expression, her full lips tight and determined. 'Thank you,' she said tersely. 'Is Emlyn about?'

'He's across the road in the front garden building a chicken run, to the delight of the children who are being amused helping him.'

'I wanted to see you both together, but I can speak my piece just as well to one of you.'

'Oh. It sounds serious, Ruth. I hope we haven't offended you.'

'Offended could be the word; exploited would be a more accurate one.'

'You'd better sit down and we'll talk about it,' said Anna, with an indifferent tone.

'I'd rather stand thank you. There's not a lot to talk about. I'll come straight to the point. You'll have to find somebody else to mind the children. Though I find them lovely and well behaved, and I'll miss them, I will not be an accomplice to humiliating my brother whilst his wife is carousing and belittling him in private and in public.'

Anna was taken aback at the sudden attack. 'Well, I think I'll sit down,' she said finding the nearest chair which was at the table. 'That's quite a statement Ruth and an offensive one if you don't mind me saying so. What's brought this on?'

'Ann, you seem to be quite indifferent to the needs of others.'

'Good grief, it gets worse. Be my guest and tell me more, don't worry about my feelings.'

Ruth turned around and eyed up the stool near the door. 'I think I will sit down.' She sat and looked at Anna for some sign of understanding, but there was none. 'You just don't realize how much you expect off others do you? Or the little you give back.'

274

'If you want some financial reward for looking after the children, I already offered some months ago.'

'I don't want financial reward, I want more time to myself and less time coming down here, which is sometimes completely unnecessary. When I offered to help out I thought I'd be coming down here once or twice a week, but now I'm coming down four times a week to accommodate, not the essential needs of you and Emlyn, but to give you both leisure time.'

Emlyn and I work hard, Ruth. We're entitled to some pleasure in life.'

'Not at my expense.'

'You were enthusiastic in the beginning?'

Ruth stood up, frustrated at Anna's replies. 'Can't you see you're not giving me a thought when you make your personal plans? I have a life to live, you know.'

'With all due respect Ruth, you have very few interest that take up your time. I mean, what would you do if you stopped coming down here?'

'What I would do or what I wouldn't do is none of your business. If I chose to sit down and knit, which I have done for your children and Rebecca's, though I've never seen your children wear a thing I've made for them, then that is my prerogative. If I should spend hours reading a novel which you might find amusing, then it's my prerogative. I just like to have the time to do such things. Take Thursday of last week for instance, Luke had bought two tickets as a surprise to take me to a concert in Merthyr, but when he told me of it, it was too late. I had already promised Emlyn I'd come down for him to go out with his workmates for a drink, because you had decided to work an extra night. Can't you see? I have to fall in with your plans whether I know of them or not.'

'Well as woman I wouldn't put up with it from a man. You'll have to have a word with Emlyn.'

'I have, he wanted me to have a word with you first.'

'That's typical of a man. Incidentally, it's a shame Luke didn't realize that under the circumstances he should have consulted you. He can be a bit naïve at times.'

'It was supposed to be a surprise!' shouted Ruth.

The door opened and Emlyn came in, his sleeves turned up and his hands and face dirty. 'I thought I heard voices, had a word with Ruth have you?'

'More like Ruth has had a number of sentences with me. Why didn't you bring the subject up, not man enough?'

Emlyn dug his thumbs into his belt and stood there akimbo. 'I've brought the subject up time and time again but you don't listen to me. I've given up on you. I thought woman to woman chat might open your ears.'

'Ruth says she's not going to mind the children again. What are you going to do about it?'

'Ruth will mind the children, but only when it's essential, is that right Sis?'

Ruth nodded but said nothing.

'It's essential that I work,' smirked Anna.'

'It's not essential you work four nights a week and go out another two for your pleasure.'

'I'll go out when I want to and work when I want to.'

'No you won't because I'll tie you to the bloody chair unless you do as you're told.' He turned to Ruth 'Now Ruth, If you're in agreement, I'll go out two nights a week and Annie will stay with the children, Annie can go out twice a week for leisure and I'll mind the children, then Annie can go out working two nights a week if you will come down for an hour until I come home from work.'

'We can try it for a trial period,' said Ruth'

'Ruth will only be down here for a couple hours on a couple of nights,' observed Anna with a complaining tone.

'She doesn't have to come down here at all, and if she decides not to you'll just have two nights out for work.'

'How do you work that out?'

'Because I'll be going out the rest of the bloody week while you do your duty as a mother.'

'That suits me,' said Ruth.

Anna jumped to her feet. 'Well it doesn't suit me!' she yelled. 'I believe in equality so I'll go out four nights a week and you can go out three nights. Then you go out four nights a week and I'll stay in three nights, that way we won't need Ruth to trouble herself at all.'

276

Suddenly the door burst open and all four children came running in. 'Guess who's coming down the lane,' shouted the breathless Hannah. 'I'll tell you, it's auntie Rebecca and uncle Aled.'

There was an amused expression on Emlyn's face, but Ruth and Anna appeared shocked. They all stood in silence until a knock came on the door and Rebecca called out unnecessarily, seeing as she had just witnessed the children run into the house. 'Anybody at home?'

'Come in, do come in,' said Anna, a forced tone of acceptance. 'We are one big jolly family at last,' she said, remembering the phrase a Suffragette used to use frequently.

Rebecca entered, her slim figure swishing her dove-grey gown that covered her ankles, her hair curled up under her white wide-brimmed hat. She was followed by the corpulent figure of Aled, his face grave, his dark square-cut beard well trimmed six inches beneath his chin in contrast to his balding head.

'This is a surprise,' remarked Emlyn.

'We thought it high time to make a visit,' said Rebecca. 'We don't see the children often, and Aled wanted to give you some spiritual advice on their welfare.'

There was silence for a time while everybody took in the presumptuous words of Rebecca.

'Everybody seems to be so diplomatic this morning,' said Anna, eventually. 'That's very nice, isn't it?'

It was Aled who spoke next.

'Would you mind if I take a seat?' he asked gruffly. The walk down here can be quite fatiguing.'

Anna pretentiously rushed to the table and pulled out a dining chair. She drew the sleeve of her cardigan down to the palm of her hand and polished the seat.

'Please, do sit down,' she said, as she pulled out anther chair for Rebecca. Rebecca looked at her and gave a questionable smile knowing that Anna was being facetious.

'Maybe we should all sit down,' said Emlyn, and took a chair.

'There's not enough chairs for us all,' reminded eight-year-old Hannah.

'Well go back out the garden and amuse yourselves, her father said.'

'Don't want to, I'll have to look after these three again,' she said pointing to her three staring siblings.

'Then be quiet.' Turning to Aled, he gave the layman a cold eye. 'I'll hear you out Aled, but I don't think your proposals are going to please me.'

Aled, dressed all in black except for his white high-collared shirt, sat stiffly in the chair, his black tie shining from constant ironing, his right hand lay on top of his left hand resting both on his protruding stomach. He gazed around his silent audience and sniffed deeply. In a deep and tremulous voice he began the prologue to his admonishment. 'I had no alternative but to carry out my duty as a Christian and call upon you. I am hoping I can appeal to your better nature and bring you to your senses.'

'I don't know whether I've got senses other than the ones I use every day, interrupted Anna. 'You make it sound as though I have a split personality; one for weekdays and one for Sundays.'

'Give me grace to hear me out please Ann.'

'Please, be my guest, I am all ears.'

'When Rebecca used to take care of your children some years ago—'

'Child,' said Anna. 'Just the one, when Bronwen came along it was too much for Rebecca.'

'Just be quiet, Annie,' urged Emlyn. 'You can have your say when Aled has finished.'

'Thank you Emlyn,' acknowledged Aled.

Anna twisted her lip. 'Sorry, I didn't know this was a court of law, the guilty shall have her say later, I suppose.'

'Right,' emphasised, 'Aled. I'll come straight to the point. Your children need spiritual guidance and also parental guidance, both of which appear to be missing at the present time. This neglect is the talk of the area and an indictment of the poor treatment you both deal out to your children. If you are not careful they will grow up lacking respect for the community in which they live and not knowing the word of the Lord. That cannot be tolerated in a civilized society such as ours. I implore you to allow them to come to chapel at least twice on Sunday and once in midweek before they go beyond the limits of redemption. By allowing this reasonable interlude in their unnecessary prolonged outdoor playtimes they can learn to be good Christians and hold their heads up high in society.'

Emlyn stood up. 'Right, I've listened to what you had to say. Thank you for calling. Goodbye.'

Anna stood up. 'Emlyn dear, where are your manners? We can't leave Aled and Rebecca go without offering them our hospitality. 'I shall put the kettle on and we'll all have a nice cup of tea. Besides, Aled has a duty to swell his congregation. I hear it's becoming depleted.'

'I'm trying to be tolerant, Annie.'

'What do you think I'm holding back, an Amen to all what he's said. We must be Christian-like and give them tea and a buns.'

'Don't think I want to go to chapel, Mam, if the people there are all like uncle Aled, said Hannah.'

'That was out of the mouths of babes. Well done, Hannah,' rejoiced her mother.

'Don't bother making tea for Aled and I, Ann,' advised Rebecca nervously. 'We aren't staying very long, are we Aled?'

'We shall only stay as long as necessary.' He turned to Anna. 'It is not my congregation, it is the Minister's. If we have lost any members these past months, it is because they have left as consequence of the war in Europe.'

'And how many Christians have you advised not to go to war and kill others, Aled?' Anna asked.

'They go to serve their King and country by their own virtue of duty.'

'But shouldn't they be serving Jesus and professing love to all mankind?'

'You must learn to live in the real world, Ann, and not in a dream.'

'I didn't dream the words of Jesus. He knew that futile wars had been going on from the beginning of time. "When ye hear of wars be ye not troubled," He said. There'll be many things to test you, Aled. Read Mark chapter 13 verses 7-9' And in other verses Jesus said: "You cannot serve two masters," those are the words of our true leader.'

279

'Do not quote the Bible to me unless you know all of the scriptures, Ann. Remember the tribal wars of the Old Testament when God guided the Hebrews to glorious victory against the Hittites.'

'The Hittites, the Hivites, Semites, Gittites, Philistines, where did all those tribes come from? Considering the Israelites were supposed to be the first people on Earth, isn't it strange the Israelites should be taken into slavery by the Egyptians who had been around a lot longer than them and were far more civilized and advanced. For goodness sake, Aled, how long can you preach such fallacies before the people wake up and drain from the chapels and churches?'

Aled shot to his feet, his face red with rage. 'Blasphemy! That is blasphemy and you'll burn in Hell for your ungodliness, you self-righteous harlot.'

'And you're a hypocrite. You'll see Christians slay Christians, men women and children. Has William reached the age of volunteering yet?'

'William will do according to his conscience. If he should enlist, I'll support him.'

'God, you'd swap your son for a medal'

Emlyn grabbed Anna and forced her to sit down. 'That's enough. Shut up the pair of you, I'll not have this brawling in front of the children

Anna adopted a composed attitude and said in a sweet voice, 'But Emlyn, dear, did you not know that Jesus came to dispel all those legends? He gave us two commandments that cover all others: "Love thy God and Love Thy neighbour as you would want him to love you." Isn't that right Aled?'

'You are a Devil's disciple for sure.'

'And you Aled, with all the other sanctimonious hierarchy, are the modern equivalent of the High Priests, Scribes and Pharisees whom Jesus despised so much. Nothing has changed over the two thousand years Jesus died for. There is more wisdom in the words of our local Joshua.'

'Ah! That is where you obtain your Biblical guidance, is it?'

'I was taught the Scriptures long before I came here, and the man who educated me was not unlike you.'

'Come, Rebecca, out of this house and into the fresh air.' Rebecca turned her head and raised her eyebrows to Ruth. Ruth sighed and shook her head.

'Your country comes first, your God comes second and Jesus is bottom of the list!' yelled Anna as they disappeared through the door.

The room was silent for some considerable time until Hannah, who had been thinking to herself suddenly said, 'I don't know what you and uncle Aled were shouting about, Mam, but I'm going back out. Dad, are you coming to finish the shed?'

'Aye, it will be therapeutic for me.' He turned to Ruth, 'We'll do it Anna's way, Ruth. We won't have to trouble you then. I'm sorry we've been so wrapped in ourselves.' He and the children left.

Ruth stood up and looked at Anna with a mixture of contempt and admiration. 'You surprise me, Ann. I didn't realize that you felt so deeply about religion.'

Anna was staring at the floor. 'I try not to be, but I get infuriated when those parts of the Bible where Jesus is speaking of love and what He wants from us are ignored, and those sections that are easy to follow are spouted regularly.'

'I suppose I shall be cast aside now. It will be from one extreme to the next.'

Anna, trying to recover from her heart-thumping ordeal, went to her and clasped her hands. 'Please come down anytime you want, whether I'm at home or if Emlyn's at home. I'm a bit hot-tempered at times Ruth, but I do have a conscience. You're right, I have taken you for granted and not shown enough gratitude, but I do have lots affection for you. And I will feel so guilty if you should stay away. I've exploited you and I want to make it up. Please, please, I'm sorry.'

Glassy eyes were welling up in both women. 'Thank you Ann, I shall be here, not just for casual visits but for the children as well. I didn't want a complete break. Now I've got it off my chest is doesn't seem so important.'

'Good. Let's have a cup of tea. Let's talk about practical things that are relevant to our humble existence. Like clothes and society outside this town.'

Ruth smiled affectionately at Anna. 'I don't quite know what you mean, but anything is better than a family feud.'

Thirty Eight

She regretted the day when she claimed equality and demanded her idea must be agreed to. The rota system worked against her and she could do nothing about it. It was her idea and she did not have the humility to admit it. She now realized why Emlyn had been so enthusiastic accepting it for it was advantageous to him, but over the months she realized she had fewer days to herself than the previous arrangement. The summer months had been made easier by fine weather; sometimes sunny, other times cloudy or light rain. But things were frustrating for Anna, her free time evaporated quickly when she was enjoying herself, but her nights at home became stagnant and intolerable as each hour dragged. After five months she became moody and irritable, and the talk of terrible suffering and deaths from the front line depressed her. Four nights staying in with squabbling children, bathing them, putting their nightclothes on and shouting at them before they would agree to go to bed, was upsetting her and taking its toll. She had not experienced such stressful work and responsibility on her own; two nights had been the maximum she'd had the children at their present ages. Had Hannah not been so helpful with her big-sister authority, she would not have been able to cope. Ruth occasionally made visits, but they were brief, only lasting half hour or so. She stayed longer when her brother was on duty with the children, and Anna suspected she helped Emlyn with the kids.

When out shopping, she would walk from the market with bags heavy in her hands and stop at the top of Church Street. There she could see the smoke stacks of the iron works beyond the Goat Mill Road, their smoke drifting down the valley. And higher up the hillside the coal tips growing into mountains, one of which named The Blackie, for it was the commander of all tips, overlooking the landscape for miles and rising higher than the rest. Its infertility proved to be the death of all vegetation, for not a blade of grass or weed grew on its black surface. She felt Dowlais was closing in on her and she would one day suffocate from dust and smoke. She tried to count her blessings when she heard the shoppers talk of neighbours and friends who had lost relatives in the war, but it did no good. At those times she'd look down and tap the side of her shopping bag to ensure the bottles were safe, for this would soothe her depressing thoughts of life. Alcohol had become her dependency giving her pleasure relaxing her and drifting her into a make-believe world of temporary splendour. She could manage the days without too much trauma, but always returned home with a bottle of something, whether it was some of her favourite spirit or a few bottles of stout knowing there was a supplement of gin in the house. The drink would give her comfort in the evening. It was then, when the time fell silent and the children asleep in bed, she would sit with glass in hand and hear the distant humming of the steelworks and be reminded of the industrial activity outside. As the alcohol slowly took over, outside sounds decreased and thoughts of London took over and transferred her to her glory days she loved and had grown to exaggerate. If only she had persisted a few more years in the excitement of the city. Then maybe…just maybe things would have turned out differently and she would be a lady in the company of society.

The greatest relief was when her four night duties were finished and her pleasure time had come. A great change would manifest itself; dressing up and going to work for two nights and having the third to do what she wanted. She would be transformed from a depressed lethargic housewife to a frivolous feisty attractive woman once again, older but still desirable. And the luxury of the following week would not be so disheartening when she would have four days off and Emlyn the responsibility of the children for four evenings at home.

February came in with a fierce snowfall and the Cwm had to have its lanes and paths cleared. Fortunately it was not a lasting blizzard but one heavy, blustery fall over night. The following morning everybody was out with shovels doing their bit to keep things moving. Children were off school and sliding headlong down the slopes of the Cwm. A happy and friendly atmosphere spread through the area making a pleasant change from the gloomy autumnal weather when the thick mist that hung deep in the Cwm persisted through to winter. Emlyn was in work. Hannah and Bronwen were laughing and screaming riding their sledges down the gentle slope into the front garden, Carin and Emrys threw snowballs at them. They had dressed and scurried out after their mother had given them their breakfast. Anna stood at the front doorway in her thick dressing gown hugging herself, her hair hung untidily as she viewed the wintry scene. There were stained holes in the snowdrift in front of the house where the kids had struggled through. Her head was heavy and painful from last night's late social evening. She decided she would have tea with a drop of gin in it to give her strength, and then clear the drift, for she knew that Emlyn would not clear it after a twelve-hour shift. Besides, the kids would carry the snow into the house on their shoes.

She went in, grimaced at the dead fire, entered the kitchen, made a cup of tea and dropped a generous amount of gin in it, sat down and looked around the chilly living room. It was not just untidy, it was scruffy, and she thought she could detect a stale smell about it. There were children's nightclothes on the settee and chairs, and shoes were on the floor where they had left them when they'd dressed to go out. She had left a sink full of dishes behind her when she made her cup of tea. She pictured the upstairs and thought of the beds she needs to make in the cold room where ice was spreading up the inside of the windows. A drop more gin was required in her tea and soon the alcohol began to burn delightfully in her stomach. Then she heard the scraping of a shovel outside her door. She went to the window and saw a man clearing the drift away from her front door.

'Now that's what I call a Good Samaritan,' she whispered to herself. 'Who on earth is he?'

She waited awhile for him to turn and face her, but he kept his back to the window, He was a brawny man and, strangely, in clothes a person would not wear to clear snow. Not suitable for shovelling the snow at all, she thought. Anna finished her tea and made sure the belt of her dressing gown was tied securely around her. Then she went to the front door and opened it slowly.

'That's very good of you. I wasn't looking forward to clearing that lot away.'

Not turning around but continuing the job he said. 'Once I've finished this, I'll sort other things out including you.'

Anna's mind was not clear and she asked the man to repeat what he'd said.

'I said I'll sort things out. I'll be taking you home soon.'

'What are you talking about? Who are you, anyway?'

He turned around, his face hard, his eyes cold. 'Do you know me now?'

She lost all colour and her knees suddenly felt weak. Her head began to spin as she hung on to the doorjamb for support. She stared hard not believing the apparition before her. 'Good God! Good God! Where did you come from?'

'From hell to hell, it seems. Get dressed, and clean yourself up. I'll make you into the beauty you were before you left me.'

Holding her hand to her temple and staring at John trying to clear the confusion in her brain, she eventually managed to force some words of sanity. 'I'm married and have four children, man. It's too late for anything.'

'You're married to me. But I'll take you back and make you a respectable woman. Your time with the Rees boy is over.'

Anna's knees gave way and John had to go to her and hold her before she fell. He carried her into the house and sat her on the settee. 'Now, woman, maybe I didn't give you proper understanding when we wed. After all, you were just a slip of a girl that had no fun in life. Why you ran off I don't know, I can only assume it was for a better looker than me. But I'm no saint, so we'll start over again.'

Anna's head began to clear and see things as they were, she would not be misunderstood or accused of things she didn't do.'

'I kept myself pure, John. Pure as long as I could, but Emlyn was kind and young and I had a soft spot for him in my heart.'

'And where's that soft spot now?'

'I have no soft spot for anyone.'

'Well I have. Every day, every month, every year I've been away from you I've tried my best to believe you were dead. I remained in Dowlais two years hoping that you would come back. When I left I

286

returned as often as I could, but your never came. But lately I learnt that you were back, so, fool as I am, I packed my bags and made my way to you.'

'I don`t understand you John, it's been a long time. Are you saying you've not had anyone else all that time?'

'Nobody serious; Every time I went close to a woman I felt you in my arms, but when I looked into her face it wasn't you and I felt repulsed with myself.' He grabbed her arms. 'Where did you go, Ann? Why did you leave? You are my wife I could never be unfaithful to you.'

She gently pulled his hands from her arms and held them in hers. 'It was nothing you did John. It was the place, the conditions, the hopelessness of it all.'

'Huh. And now you're in the same boat with four kids to help you along.'

'Yes, and I hate it now as much as I did then. When you're at low ebb, mentally and physically fatigued, and emotionally drained, when you feel the whole world is against you, that is when you make desperate decisions.'

John put his arms around her and held her close. She did not pull away. Anna's mind began to picture an escape from the Cwm. Her love for Emlyn had long died. There was nothing left in the marriage. Bitter feelings and quarrels only upset everybody including the children. Besides, present circumstance mean she is no longer legally married to him, never had been it seems, and John appears to be in no mood to let things stay as they are. She was ashamed to feel hope rising in her heart to a new door that was opening for her. The children will be fine with Ruth, and Hannah will give support to the little ones. She's almost like a mother to them, and Bronwen is growing too. The thoughts flashed through her mind as though she had rehearsed them for some time. She squeezed John, pulled away and looked at him.

'You really forgive me, John'

'I can't deny you a place in my heart, and I can't refuse you a room in my home. I've been back two months thinking things out. I have a job in the steelworks where I worked before. They were glad to have my experience and skills and needed a supervisor. I'm renting a house at the top of the High Street, a house you'll be proud to live in.'

'It's been a long time, why now? Where have you been till now?'

'I'd given up on you, thought you had gone forever. I had settled down with my family in the west wales and then a few months ago I heard about you. Our roaming preacher was in Carmarthen town centre giving a sermon in the market place. He'd been there before, reminding me of you and me together, but I always walked away. This time I went on to him and asked him about the old town as I hadn't been there for some time. One thing led to another and he inadvertently told me the place livens up when he preaches. A strong-willed young lady who gives him a pleasant challenge to his beliefs, he said. I asked him to describe her and I knew it was you. I told him your name and of the first time you saw him on the Oddfellows Hall steps. He nodded to me.`

Anna stared into open space. 'Joshua! My mind is swirling around. I don't know what to do. The children are out playing, I can't leave them alone.'

'I know that. It was a great shock when I learnt of your circumstances, but I've thought it all out. Maybe I was as much at fault as you.'

'No. You were faultless in the matter.'

'I'm not so sure, but I can't go into that now. I don't expect you to come this minute but go and pack your things and I'll come for you when you are ready, and if necessary we'll take the children as well. What time is Emlyn home?'

'He'll be here at half past seven.'

'I'll come then.'

'No! I'll meet you at the top of the Cwm…Half past eight. I'll need time for him to settle. I don't know what I'll say to him.'

'Leave it to me. I'll have a few chosen words with him.'

'No. I don't want any violence.'

'Have it your way, but if you're not at the meeting place as arranged, I'll come for you.'

Emlyn came home and was surprised to see a bucket of water was steaming on the fire in readiness for him, the smell of roast meat and his supper keeping warm in the oven. What was more the place was clean and tidy, looking like a well-kept house should be.'

'What's happened here, woman? Has Ruth been down and told you what a man expects when he comes home from a shift?'

'Ruth hasn't been here.'

'Then you've come to your wifely senses.'

'Just go and have your bath, Emlyn, the water is ready.'

'I can see that. 'You'd better go and call the kids in, and prepare them for bed.'

'The children have all had a bath and they are in bed; not asleep I may add, so I don't want to hear any shouting from you.'

'Shouting? I've got no need to shout. I haven't had such little need to shout for years.'

It only took him fifteen minutes to have a bath, change his clothes and sit at the table for his meal. Anna placed a full plate of dinner in front of him then sat on the settee. He dined in a motionless, quiet room, occasionally glancing at Anna who watched him chew ravenously at his pork chops and vegetables. Something was wrong for he felt a foreboding. It wasn't going to ruin his appetite, the food tasted too good. And there was nothing serious in his life to worry about otherwise he would have known about it. The children were fine because they were in bed, though why so early he couldn't figure out. They've been extremely mischievous, that must be it, and she's going to let him know it any minute. No. Things look too grave for such a triviality. He made his mind a blank and concentrated on finishing his food.

Anna couldn't help but weigh him up as though she was going to bury him and give him his deserved eulogy. He was smart man when dressed. His job ensured he kept a sinewy frame, and his oval face and determined chin gave him a proud countenance. He looked a little immature with his sandy hair combed into a wave at the front—yes he was quite handsome as I remember. Never let me down financially, and his chauvinist pretence never really established itself with me. So why should I leave him? He's no ambition to leave the Cwm, that's why, which makes him…common.

When Emlyn had swallowed his last mouthful he sat back in his chair and wiped his lips with his handkerchief. 'Well, Annie, I must admit that was a very tasteful meal; you must have taken your time over that one. Now, what's all the attention about?'

Anna looked at him, steeling herself for the violent altercation that must erupt. 'You could call it the last supper.'

'One of your quotes again, what's that supposed to mean?'

'It means that is the last supper I am going to make you.'

He sipped the last of his glass of water and placed it back on the table. 'I don't like what you are saying, Annie. Talk sense woman.'

Anna stood up and pointed to the dark corner of the room. 'You're not very observant, are you? My cases, I'm leaving you,' she said with a cool indifferent tone.

Emlyn left the table and walked to the two suitcases, picked them up and felt the weight. He dropped them down again and looked at her, stunned. 'Don't be ridiculous Annie. Unpack them and stop talking nonsense.'

'I'm not legally married to you.'

'Of course you are. What's brought all this on?'

'John.'

'John? He's probably dead and buried.'

She pulled her suitcases to the front door and went to fetch her coat. 'If he is then it must have been his ghost who turned up today.'

Emlyn stopped her in mid-room, gripping by the shoulders. 'John? Here today?'

'Here, and determined to take me away from you. I haven't much choice have I?'

'We've been together for ten years, woman.'

'Hannah is nine and apparently illegitimate, I'm a bigamist because of your smooth talking.'

He let go of her. 'You didn't take much talking to wed me. You loved me, remember?'

'Did I love you? Or was I just infatuated with you? Whatever, it's all in the past tense now,' she said, putting on her coat.'

'Annie, sit down and be logical about this. You've got nowhere to go and we've got four children to look after. I won't give up the children.'

'I have already explained to the children that I can't live with you anymore and that I shall always love them and take them with me when I've settled.'

'You cold bitch! I've tried to cater for your extreme ways but each time I give into you I get nothing in return. How can you expect me to keep down a twelve-hour a day job and look after four kids? One thing for sure, you won't have them.'

'Well then, you're going to find it hard. I'm sure your relatives will help you out. I can't cope with living down here anymore. I was destined for better things. Well, if I don't do anything else in life, I'll get out of the Cwm. I've got my rightful husband back.'

'Where are you going to live? Tell me!'

'That's my business.'

Emlyn caught hold of her and threw her on the settee pinning her down. 'You're not leaving here. If I have to tie you down and make a prisoner of you, you won't leave here.'

Suddenly the front door flew open and John came in. 'I've been listening at the door long enough. Now we can either come to blows or do this in a civilized manner. Which is it to be? Whichever way you choose, the law is on my side. I could bring them down here tonight and have the family in all sorts of humiliation and embarrassment.'

Emlyn let go of Anna and looked at the thickset John with astonishment. 'I don't know what devil brought you back to life, but if you want to do the decent thing you'll go back to where you came from.'

'Emlyn I am truly sorry for this situation, but I love Ann and can never forget her. I'm taking her with me, violently or peacefully.'

'We've got four children, man, doesn't that stir any compassion in you.'

'I will take on the four children as well if need be.'

Emlyn went and faced up to John. 'You lay a finger on any of my children and I'll fight you to the death.'

'I'm glad to hear it Emlyn, you are truly a good man. There'll probably be a custody battle. Now, Ann, let's go,' he said as he picked up her suitcases and made for the door.

The children had been listening at the top of the stairs and Hannah could listen no more. She screamed down, 'Mam, don't go! Don't leave us, Mam!'

Anna rushed to the bottom of the stair. 'Listen Hannah, I'm not going far, just up the High Street. You'll be able to come to me every day if you want to. I'll come and see you all as often as I can. Now go to bed and I'll see you tomorrow. Mam loves you all.'

'You'll come down to see us tomorrow?'

'Of course I will, and you can come up and see me.'

'Where will you be?'

'I'll tell you tomorrow.'

'Promise!'

'I promise. Now go to bed.'

Hannah reluctantly led the children back into the bedroom as John pulled Anna to the door.

'Take her!' snarled Emlyn, she's no good anyway. Good riddance.'

'Good luck to you, Emlyn,' said John. 'It's better this way than doing it through the law, believe me. Then they left.

'Don't you dare come back, Jezebel! You won't see the children again I'll make sure of that.'

Thirty Nine

John had rented the terraced house from the landlord when the previous tenant, a foreman in the steelworks, had moved away after he retired. Foremen and puddlers were well esteemed in an industrial community, for they were well paid and looked upon themselves as middle class citizens. The house Anna and John moved into reflected the respected position of the previous owner, for he and his wife left behind floral carpets, colourful curtains on the windows and several pieces of furniture that they believed were too inconvenient to take with them. Puddlers, however, were lucky if they reached the age of forty; their stark work and burning heat from the white-hot molten streams they had to guide into pools known as piglets and sows drained their strength burned their skins and caused them to have very poor eyesight. Evidence of this was on the face of Anna's next-door neighbour, Bill Evans. His thin face was scarred and crimson from years of being a puddler, his sinewy body worn lean and veined. It was his skill and high wages that had bought Mr and Mrs Evans their home, a high price to pay for such luxury, for it would not be long before Mr Evans would be forced to give up his job through ill health.

The cordial but childless Mrs Evans had welcomed the newcomers to their home and offered to help move them in. And though she was a strong-looking thirty-five-year-old lady with a stout build and round cheerful face, independent John declined the offer, knowing that her husband was a puddler and was wearied enough when his shift was over. Anna made friends with Mrs Evans, the only neighbour she could attach herself to, the others being polite but aloof. The friendship grew between the two and they often called into each other's homes to have a chat and share their ups and downs.

The façade of Anna's new home was rendered and painted cream with light brown window frames and door, and had the advantage of the morning sun. The house had a large parlour, a middle dining room and a generous kitchen that lit up with the early evening sun. The three bedrooms were bigger and brighter than those of the Cwm with large sash windows. There was one significant drawback, however, and that was the sounds of the heavy machinery and motors from the nearby engine house, also the cranes and locomotives, and the blast furnaces lit up the night sky. There was the trotting of the horses pulling carriages, the occasional motorcar that drove past and the hundreds of men going to work in the mornings and home in the evenings; the Cwm, though humble, had its advantages, for its remoteness from the Dowlais Works could only be heard as a distant droning. The good points being of the new house was it being closer to the shopping area and the indoor market.

Anna settled, not daring to complain about anything. She was delighted with the house and its up-market pretence, feeling, as she always wanted, a lady of some distinction. Often she would arrange to meet Hannah and her siblings as a good mother should, but it was always a strained atmosphere. Her children could not have the same feeling towards her, though Hannah tried hard to understand the situation. They were told to make their own way up to their mother, with Hannah being the guide. Emlyn had sent a message to his ex-wife that he would not be responsible for his actions if she should set foot in the Cwm again. Hannah, when going home from her daily lessons at the prestigious Dowlais Central School, would pass her mother's new house, stop and look through and wave if she should see her mother, though if it was John's face she saw, she'd quickly move on.

Anna began to feel the days long and lonely when John was in work, and though she tried to abstain from her alcoholic ways, a bottle of gin was always at hand to see her through. John was not as heavy a drinker as Emlyn, a night or two would suffice. Anna suggested she go out once or twice an evening on her own and let him stay home and rest, seeing that he was weary after his long day in the works. The idea appalled John, for he'd rather stay in and have his wife at his side. The thought of her drinking on her own in some pub would not be tolerated. He expected his food be ready when he got home and assured her that the two nights they went out together was adequate for a respectable married couple, for any nights extra to that would be extravagant and a waste of money. Any spare money should be saved or spent on the upkeep of the house. He was generous when furniture was wanted for the house or when Anna sighed she needed a new dress. Time quickly went by. Their home was filled with new furniture and up to date appliances and Anna's wardrobe filled. The gas stove lightened her housework, the laundry tub needed an energetic agitation when stirring with the wooden pole, but the method washed the clothes in bulk rather than the old way of scrubbing on a board. But the freedom wasn't there, and the new clothes John had bought her in the Emporium required showing off more often. Though Anna did not love him she did, what she had refused before, her wifely duty, and ten months after they reunited, Anna gave birth to a baby boy, named Daniel. His birth was the turning point for Anna as memories of rearing children rose in her mind. She promised herself she would do her utmost to look after the child and make John proud of her, though her heart was not in unison with her mind. The handsome baby grew into a healthy twelve-month old when Anna gave birth to a baby girl, and they named her Cerys.

It may have appeared to all those looking upon this balanced family that contentment and harmony prevailed, but it was not so, for both parents feigned a life of a happy family; their marital differences suppressed for the sake of society. John would take them out walking on a sunny Sunday afternoon dressed smartly in a suit and hat, as a foreman of the goat mill workshop should, and proudly holding Daniel's hand. Anna, regaled in her bright Sunday best and smiling to all that went by, pushed Cerys in the pram and displayed an air of importance. John had long concluded and assured himself that if Anna had children to look after and nourish she would find her vocation in life, blanking out of his mind his and Anna's earlier partnership. But she had not stopped drinking, and though John had begged, persuaded and chastised her for her habit, he could not make her give up. Nevertheless, they remained carrying out their married obligations and parental duties with a united and respectable front. Anna's four children by Emlyn, estranged and alien to her, had finally been pushed into the back of her mind, blanking out the adverse circumstances of the unfortunate past. But Hannah was faithful to her brief tapping of the window, and when John was in work she would knock the door and go in.

It was on a sunny but chilly day in the autumn in 1919 and the country was slowly forgetting the evils of the war. Anna left the children with Mrs Evans to go shopping. Knowing Mrs Evans wouldn't mind how long she was away, Anna thought it a good idea if she should change her route and do some window shopping in the lower High Street. Normally she would avoid such a place for it was noisy and smoky being near the works. However she hadn't been that way for some months and was bored with the same routine of the market and Union Street shops. Walking briskly down High Street she was greeted many times by people who had come to know her since moving. The ladies gave a warm smile and the men lifted their flat hats, those who wore bowlers touched the rims. Passing the Wimborne Institute she neared the Bush Hotel and could see lower down the slight breeze was blowing the black smoke from the works stacks across the road and spits of soot fell to ground. Thinking that the greasy spots might tarnish her light grey outfit, she quickly made a right turn up the steep Church Street and decided it was best to adhere to her usual route. At the top of the street she turned right to go to the Co-operative and indoor market, but hearing a familiar voice in the distance she walked on. Reaching the brow of Upper Union Street she put a spring in her step, for the sight of Joshua waving his arms and booming his bass near the ring lamp lifted her spirits. His old attire he had disregarded and his black suit, though not new, was much smarter along with his waistcoat and white shirt and navy tie. As she neared, she realized his beard and hair, though profuse, had turned to a shade of grey, and his face looked worn and lined. There were four women paying him attention and a group of giggling mischievous children. Anna joined them and listened to his words, for she had grown to like and respect the man, though she never told him so.

'...and because I sinned a great sin that I could not reconcile myself to, like a coward I ran away from my sin where I was ridiculed and shamed, to places where I could face strangers who

296

knew nothing of me. Two years I made myself an abominable outcast and begged on the streets for survival, but I could not run away from myself. And then at my lowest ebb, when all was lost, a spirit was sent to me and I saw a light, not in the Heavens was this light, but in my soul, my mind, my heart, making my body whole and clean. Look to your Saviour a voice within was telling me. And so I prayed to God that I might be forgiven. Yes, in prayer and meditation I talked to God night and day learning more of the Lord, I read the New Testament, and His words taught me the new beginning of my life. And then one cold night in the hills of Carmarthen, I felt the warmth of God spread through my body, and push the heaviness of guilt out of my soul. God gave me the freedom from sin that I had craved. His words came into my mind and I heard them clearly: "You have done with your foolish youthful days and have drawn into your mind the wisdom of love and benevolence and changed your ways, now go into the multitudes and preach the truth I have extended to you. Let the Old Testament be for the Israelites, and the words of Jesus you must impart to the world, for it is to My Son I gave the new commandments. Remind the world of those commandments for they embrace all other commandment." And so, I have made it my life to pass on the words of God to the people. Jesus said, "Those who have ears to hear let them hear, those who have eyes to see let them see." But still, the world chooses to be deaf and blind to the true love that Jesus preached. I now remind you of the two Great Commandments of which the first is, Love Thy God With All Thy Heart, and the second, Thou Shalt Love Thy Neighbour As Thyself. On these two commandments hang all the law.'

The sight of Anna had silenced him and his tall lithe figure looked down on her. 'Is it not Ann my earthly tormentor?' he playfully said.

'How are you, Joshua? I haven't seen you for about a year.

He clasped his hands to his chest. 'I have had my work to do around the country. My evangelism took me to mid Wales where I believe I saved one lonely soul.

'What did you do, jump in the river and pull him out?'

'You may jest, woman, but you'll need the Lord's help one day. The lonely soul I saved, just like me, had a troubled mind and a depressed spirit. He told of his guilt and we both knelt down and prayed for forgiveness. When we arose the man had been made new and was troubled no more.'

'Tell me, Joshua, what was the great sin you committed that brought you to God?'

'That, my dear lady, is between The Creator and me. And, Ann, our life is but a drop in the ocean of time and soon passes. Eternity is forever, don't you think it's time you asked the Lord for your sins to be forgiven.'

'I read somewhere in the New Testament Jesus said, "Before you seek the mote in thy brother's eye first seek the mote in your own eye."'

'Ah you torment me again, but you are right, I shall right my own faults first.'

Anna smiled at him and gently caught hold of his hand. 'Don't take me seriously, Joshua, I'm only teasing you.'

'I know, but what you say is true. I bring your attention to the fact that time is essential. When I first saw you in my gathering many years ago you were a sweet innocent-looking young girl. Your time is passing, and your countenance and body are changing to an older woman. It is because I have taken a liking to you that I beseech you to change your ways and repent for no-one knows when the time has come.'

'Thank you for such cheerful words Joshua. Anyway, I've got to believe first, haven't I?.'

'I can see that you've been deeply hurt. You must get that bitterness out of your heart. Remember, temporal misery, like temporal riches, is short-lived in this world. But the spiritual happiness is for eternity. Kneel down with me and let the bitterness be taken away.'

Anna laughed and moved on, calling back, 'I'll think about it and come back to you some time.'

Joshua shook his head. 'Lord I feel that woman has goodness in her, please give her time.'

He called after her, 'Be an enigma to others if you must, but know yourself. Deep down you are desperate for His love.'

Anna moved on thoughtfully. Joshua could see into her heart and soul, but Anna could not open the door to God. How could she? She asked herself. I don't believe in him.

John was called to the casting mill from a meeting he was attending. The familiar dry smell of burning iron, coke and limestone coming from the blast furnace and the smouldering ladle hit his senses as he entered, but he was not prepared for the scene he witnessed. Ten minutes earlier the two-and-a-half-ton white-hot ingot had been taken out of its pit and lifted in the air by the overhead crane. As it was being taken to the tilter in readiness for the cogging mill the crane's motor had stalled as it traversed along the gantry. The sudden stop caused the ingot to sway, straining the joints at the most vulnerable points: the clamps holding it. It hung and creaked precariously between the soaking pits and the tilter. At first John couldn't understand why the machinery and live rollers had been shut down. Seeing the workmen at a standstill with eyes locked on the crane, he looked up and immediately knew the reason. If the ingot should fall over the tilter and hit it at an angle, it could roll in any direction. With the conveyer rollers in motion and underneath it, it could be conveyed and burn up all in its path. His face paled at the thought. For a few minutes he and the rest waited for the precarious load to settle hoping that the crane could hold on to the blistering lump of fire. John could wait no longer, the loud creak coming from the ingot's holding caused a shower of white sparks. It was obvious that the sudden jolt it had received when the motor stalled had increased the pressure on the clamps weakening them and partially dislodging the ingots. The fear was, as it hung there like an incandescent monster, it could drop anytime.

'Edgar,' he yelled, to a senior fitter, 'clear the mill of all personnel except for yourself and the crane operator.'

Edgar carried out his orders in double time. When only the three were left, John made his way to the crane controller who was stationed on a platform that gave a clear view of the overhead crane, the soaking pit, the tilter and the rollers. In front of him was a panel of switches that could manipulate the crane up and down, and backwards and forwards.

'What happened, Islwyn?'

'There's a phase down feeding the gantry and its motors. It could be the triple switch or a fuse blown. I had to shut down when it stalled because the motor was struggling to turn on two phases, it could have burnt out completely. The engineer's gone to the mains panel to find out.'

'He'll have to hurry, that ingot is going to drop any minute as it cools and contracts. How long ago did it happen?'

'About fifteen minutes.'

'And the engineer?'

'He was carrying out an inspection on the end rollers when it happened.'

'He should be able to tell us the problem soon, then.'

They waited another fifteen tension-filled minutes listening to the creaking on the weight of its load, the white-hot ingot sparking each time it moved in its clamps. In the doorways the workers watched in silence, their faces wet with perspiration mainly from the nature of their work, but also from the drama before them. Then the engineer came hurrying out of the main electrical distribution control room at the far end of the mill. They waited for him to cross the floor and climb the six steps up to the remote control deck.

'One of the contacts on the triple switch had burnt causing a bad connection,' he said catching his breath. 'I've fixed it temporarily until we can get the ingot down. So it's over to you, John.'

John took in a deep breath. 'Islwyn, I want to lower the ingot closer to the ground; at least if it slips it will lessen the impact. Don't move the gantry. I'll go down and guide you the best I can, so keep a sharp eye on me.'

'Right, John,' obeyed Islwyn. He made sure the traverse motors were isolated and the lifting/lowering motor was at the ready. He switched in the main rheostat so that he could control the motor in slow movements. He then energized the motors with sufficient voltage but not enough to make them turn. John left and made his way to the rollers hearing the motor hum into life.

300

John stood ten yards away from the tilter and rollers; even there he could feel the heat of the blistering two-and-a-half-ton moulding hanging fifteen feet in the air. He looked back at Islwyn and moved his hand up and down indicating he wanted the ingot lowered slowly. As it was neither fully over the tilter or the rollers the gantry would ultimately have to be moved, and that was the danger point. Islwyn energized the motor for lowering it and turned the rheostat for a slow descent, and then gasped and shook from shock not believing what was happening. The temporary lay-off had settled the motor and its connecting tackle making it difficult to move, plus the essential low voltage to keep a slow movement was not enough. More power was needed to give it initial momentum. Instead of moving smoothly, the crane could only judder. The ingot slipped its holding, hurtled down and crashed into the side of the tilter. Though it tumbled into the receptacle, it had caught its edge. A cascade of sparks flew in all direction and a ball of fire the size of a child's shoe hit John straight in his chest. John was thrown backwards and fell to the ground in deathly silence. In seconds workers ran from all directions calling for assistance. Reaching John they could only gasp in horror. Those who were not stunned in shock ripped the burning clothes off their foreman revealing raw skin and fleshless broken ribs.

Islwyn had sprinted the distance to John and took command. 'Hugh get the stretcher, Will, get the slag barrow, we'll take him to Dr Clarks hospital. Juan move that break-off out of harm's way.'

John was conscious moaning from excruciating pain. In weak whispers he was asking for Ann.

'Save your strength, John. We'll get you out of this,' promised Islwyn, though the open wound in John's chest gave him grave doubts of keeping his word.

They conveyed John to the small hospital situated in the High Street opposite Wimborne Institute. There they carried him up the stone steps, for the hospital had been built on a grassy bank that had no pathway for the humble transport they used. Placing him in the care of the nursing staff, they waited. However, the manager of the works soon arrived accompanied by works officials. They thanked the men for their quick action and advised them to go back to their work. The officials waited for the doctor to do what he could for John. After half an hour, the nurse appeared and informed those waiting for news that John was conscious though very weak. In a low whisper he was and asking for his wife. She shook her head and told them they had better hurry and fetch her before it was too late.

Anna was coming down the High Street from her shopping wondering what all the commotion was about further on down. Obviously some accident had occurred for there was a crowd of people on the pavement outside the hospital. Mrs Evans was on the door, baby in a shawl and holding Cerys`s hand.

'What's happening down the road?' asked Anna.

'There's been some kind of accident in the works, it seems. I've seen this sort of crowd gathering before, it's never good news.'

'Let's hope it's better news this time,' remarked Anna, acidly. 'That place should have a danger sign written over the entrance gate.'

'There's someone coming out of the hospital. Looks like one of the officials.'

They waited on the door for a time and saw the man who had left the hospital turn up the street and make his way hurriedly towards them.'

'We'd better go in,' said Mrs Evans. 'I believe it's one of the managers. I don't want him to see me on the doorstep, it's a bit common.'

'You might as well bring the children in to me. We'll have a cup of tea.'

Inside Anna put the kettle on the gas stove, but before she had time to take her coat off there was heavy rapping on her door. She looked at Mrs Evans whose face had suddenly turned ashen.

'My God it's for one of us Anna.'

Anna rushed to the door. The man standing there was panting. He had his spectacles in his hand and was cleaning them with his handkerchief. Anna waited for an explanation from the well-dressed man whose flushed face was full of alarm.

'What is it?' demanded Anna.

'Mrs Hughes?'

302

'Yes.'

'I'm sorry to tell you that your husband has had an accident, it's serious I'm afraid. He's asking for you. I suggest you come immediately.

Mrs Evans, standing behind Anna, gasped with fear knowing that an accident in the works could mean imminent death. 'Go Anna. Go straight away. I'll look after the children.'

Anna swept out of the door and ran down the street. She pushed her way through the small crowd outside the hospital and ran up the steps. There was a nurse waiting to escort her to the room where John lay, his breathing getting weaker as each minute past. The doctor stood and looked at her with dour expression and shook his head. She winced as her heart thudded against her chest. She leaned over him and whispered his name.

'John, I'm here, it's Ann. John can you hear me.'

He opened his heavy eyelids and spoke in a whisper.' Ann...I have...I have a confession...' he attempted to breath but could only give a weak cough.

'Don't talk, John, save your strength.'

'No I must...clear my con...conscience. Years ago I loved you so much...I'd do anything to keep you...even stop you looking for your father.'

Anna's face turned to suspicion. 'What do you mean?'

'I told you...your father was dead...he wasn't...he left his job sud...suddenly...no explanation...left the town.'

Anna straightened up, her mind clouding over with a thousand misty pictures; of John investigating for her at the works, his conclusion that her father had died, his wanting to marry her at any cost, his blind love promising her anything, the years in the Cwm with him—stupidity selfishness, cruelty. 'My father is alive!' She yelled.

'Yes. Forgive me, Ann...please forgive me.'

'Where is he? Where is he?'

'I don't know...I...' John gave his last three breaths and relaxed into death.

Forty

Mrs Evans volunteered to look after the children whilst her husband was doing the necessary running around contacting the essential officials for the burial. Anna was grateful for she never had the experience of organizing such a harrowing event. She spent the next few days in mourning waiting for the funeral to take place. She mourned mainly for herself and to herself: such selfishness John had shown all those years ago when he had lied about her father. The deceitful trick was unforgivable. Had he told the truth at the time she would have traced her father. Life would have been so much different then. She would have been settled as a young lady with dignity and respect. She would have been the daughter of a Foreman of Engine Fitters, a father who was highly paid and much esteemed. Her mind couldn't stop retracing the past as the long hours turned to interminable days waiting for the funeral; it gave her mind opportunity to travel back over the years and blame all her suffering she had experienced on John. Her mind turned from sadness to a bursting anger, from thoughts of a penurious future to a renewed search for her father, from hating John for dying on her and leaving her in such a dilemma to suddenly having a pang of guilt and pitying him. How would she cope financially, what John had saved would last a few months only, she suspected. Not ever taking interest in her John's affairs, she was completely in the dark about his financial assets. The most serious concern she had was the two children. She could not envisage a life struggling along tied down twenty-four hours every day of the week in a lonely house without the support of a man. The scenario was out of the question. No. After the funeral she would have to make some plans. One crucial undertaking was paramount and must be seen to the end at all accounts—she must find her father before it's too late. Already she could see the child-starved Mrs Evans and husband eagerly taking on the responsibility of temporary foster parents. Anna thought of the time she was fostered out, it never did her any harm, she convinced herself. Yes, once the funeral is over she would take a few weeks in respectful lamentation, get what money there is and take the open road to search for her father.

The sight of the coffin coming through the door when they brought John's body home depressed Anna as it emphasized the finality of it all. They placed it in the front parlour where the curtains had been pulled shut. The undertakers bowed to her and left. Anna took a drop of gin.

The body had been retained for three days at the Funeral Director's whilst an enquiry took place. The evidence of the works officials was taken into consideration and the verdict by the coroner was accidental death. She stood there, her back to the coffin, her mind in a fog of low visibility. And then a gentle knock on the door. She went and opened the door. There was a man and a women standing all dressed in black, solemn faces, tight lipped and staring eye; in their forties she guessed. The woman wore a broad brimmed black-laced hat, the man a black bowler and a cold expression. Anna was struck dumb for a few seconds wondering who they were. The man spoke.

'I believe you must be Ann,' he said.'

Anna detected a patronizing tone, almost like an accusation. 'I am.'

My name is Owen Hughes. I'm the younger brother of John, this is my wife Caroline.'

Anna managed to prevent her mouth from dropping open, but only just. 'Oh. Sorry. John did tell me of you years ago, but of course we've never met. Please come in.'

The husband and wife were invited to sit on the sofa; they did, resting their hands on their knees.

'It's unfortunate that we have to meet under such sad circumstances,' Caroline said.

'Yes, it is a sad time for you and all our family,' added Owen.'

'I still can't believe it,' said Anna. 'It happened so quickly...so quickly.'

'Is there anything we can do?' offered Caroline.'

'No, everything has been attended to, thank you. I would have notified you myself, but John did all the corresponding. I just haven't got round to looking through his desk for addresses.'

'That's all right,' said Owen. 'Ruth informed us. When I lived in Horse Street the Rees family was friends of ours.'

'Of course, David was a friend of John. Can I get you a cup of tea or something?'

'Thank you,' said Caroline. 'We've been travelling a great distance from Carmarthen today, so a drink would be very nice.'

'I have something stronger if you prefer.'

'No, no,' interjected Owen. 'A cup of tea will be adequate.'

Anna hurried nervously to the kitchen and remained there until the kettle boiled. She set the tea and waited while it brewed. She called softly through the door to the couple.

'Milk and sugar for both?'

'Just the milk, please,' answered Caroline, 'same for Owen.'

While Anna was in the kitchen the man and wife whispered their observations.

'Do you smell alcohol, Caroline?'

'There's a small glass over on that table, dear, and there is a bottle of gin nearby, but don't jump to conclusions, the woman is under a great deal of stress.'

'According to John's letters she is always under stress.'

'Don't be cynical.'

Anna came in with a tray laden with teapot, two cups and saucers and a plate of biscuits. She laid them on the table where the glass and bottle of gin were. Her heart thudded against her breast when she realized she left them in sight. She filled the cups and gave them to her unexpected guests, and then she removed the glass and bottle. She then sat down.

'This is very kind of you, Ann—you don't mind me calling you Ann, do you?' said Caroline.

'Of course not, after all we are kin.'

'Have you no-one to help you at such a time?' asked Owen.

'Oh yes, Mrs Evans next door. She's looking after the little ones.'

'Ah, I wondered where my niece and nephew were.'

Anna thought him to be over familiar. 'The death of John must have come as a great shock to you as it did to me,' she said.

'I have learnt to accept death in this place,' remarked Owen. 'One of the main reasons for leaving Dowlais was because of the death rate and accidents. It has improved lately I suppose, but too late to save my parents, my sister and now John.'

There was a hush for some interminable minutes as Anna waited for the two to finish their tea and biscuits; just the sounds of gentle munching and smooth sipping broke the insufferable silence. Eventually they put down their empty cups and Caroline gave a thankful smile to Anna.

'That has refreshed me, thank you Anna.'

'Yes, very nice,' agreed Owen.

'That's alright…my pleasure…Would…would you like to see John?'

'No, no,' stressed Owen. 'I would rather remember him as he was and not in a coffin. I would like to see my nephew and niece, if that's possible.'

'That would be really lovely,' said Caroline.

'Yes of course. I'll go and fetch them from next door.'

The well-attended funeral finally took place and there were moving hymns sung by the works choir. The harmonious mixture of tenors, baritones and basses singing hymns shook Anna's spirit and she held on to the arm of Bill, overcome by the unexpected moving atmosphere. Owen and Caroline and those workmates most close to John were invited back to Anna's house where Mrs Evans had prepared a light buffet and some beverages. Regrets and condolences came from many quarters of the community, but it was noticeable that nothing came from the Rees family, though Ruth did attend the internment at the cemetery standing unnoticed some distance away from the mourners. She was determined to attend in memory of her own father who was a close friend of John. When all the civilities were over and the people had gone back to their work and homes, Anna was left with Mrs Evans, Owen and Caroline and the two children in the living room of Anna's sombre abode. No longer could she see it as a home without John. Besides, the huge lie he had kept secret through the years had killed all feeling and respect she held for him.

She was watching Caroline bouncing Cerys on her lap while Daniel looked on bemused at the stranger, and confused by the sad occasion. Owen had an enigmatic smirk on his face as he observed his wife entertaining the baby girl. Mrs Evans busied herself tidying up and occasionally asking everybody if there was anything they could do. But there was always a polite negative answer. Occasionally she'd sigh sympathetically as she noted the daze Anna was in. The white face contrasted by the black mourning attire, the lost look in her eyes staring.

'Have you any children of your own, Caroline? asked Anna.

'Oh yes, I have two boys, James is ten and Edward is twelve. My mother is looking after them until we return. They're quite well behaved when mother has them. Well, like grandmothers she spoils them.'

'Which brings me to the time, my dear' interrupted Owen. 'I think we should be getting along, we have a long journey in front of us.'

'I'm sorry,' said Anna. 'I would have put you in the spare room if I knew you were coming.'

'No need to be sorry, Ruth put us up last night.'

'Oh, did she? She's very kind. I've always liked Ruth,' said Anna solemnly.

Owen cleared his throat. 'Yes, well, we don't want to outstay our welcome, do we Caroline?'

'You can stay longer,' Anna insisted. 'There's no hurry on my part.'

'No, no, it's very kind of you but we do have a long way to go. Caroline, are you ready?'

Caroline stood up and lifted the baby high in front of her. 'She's a beautiful little girl, Ann. Absolutely lovely.'

Owen gave her a wry glance. 'Maybe you should adopt her.'

'I would, too,' she said, looking at Anna. But Anna's throat was longing for a drink, and was not fully attentive.'

Caroline carried the child to Anna and handed her over. 'Oh well, I'd better give her back.'

'Thank you for the funeral tea, Mrs Evans, you did a fine job,' said Owen as they moved towards the door. Mrs Evans smiled politely and said goodbye to them both.

Anna walked to the door with them and shook their hands before they went on down the street. She waited respectfully until they were far enough away, then returned Caroline's wave when she turned around. Anna was about to go back in when her eye momentarily caught the movement of someone across the road half hidden by a lamppost. She waited for the person to show. When she did it was Hannah, staring seriously at her mother.

'Hannah, what are you doing over there?'

'I looked in the window but the curtains are closed.'

'Come in for five minutes, Mam could do with a friendly face.'

Inside Hannah sat down not looking around. There was a sickly smell of something she had never smelt before, but she knew it was to do with a dead body. Mrs Evans gave her a drink of Dandelion and Burdock with a couple of fairy cakes she had made. Hannah felt a great sympathy for her mother but could not think of anything to say. There was eeriness about the place and her mother looked so sad. She and her mother looked at each other but said nothing for some time. Hannah turned to the two children, the baby in a playpen the two-year-old outside it amusing his baby sister.

'They seem happy enough,' she said, quietly.'

'They're fine. Mrs Evans does a good job looking after them. How are your brother and sisters?'

'All right, I suppose. I'm the one who has to look after them mostly, but Ruth does come down and help out.'

'I've made a mess of things. It's all down to me. I expect my name's mud.'

'We're not allowed to mention you Mam.'

'Oh God!'

'Cup of tea, Ann?' whispered Mrs Evans. 'It might help.'

Anna raised her head as though waking from a dream. 'Did you say tea Mrs Evans? I don't think so. No. I have something more appropriate in the cupboard.' She stood up and walked weakly to the

310

kitchen. When she returned she had two glasses in one hand and a bottle of gin in the other. She offered Mrs Evans a glass. 'Would you join me in a stress-breaking drink, Mrs Evans?'

'No thank you Ann, you have a glass by all means. And don't you think it's time you called me Mary. We've known each other long enough now.'

Anna's face flickered a one-sided smile as she filled her glass. 'Strange, I always thought of you as a kindly neighbour with great respect, but you're more than that aren't you? You're a true friend Mary, a true friend.'

The compliment brought a happy smile to Mrs Evan's face. 'That's kind of you to say so Ann. You're going to find the next few months difficult, but I'll be here for you at any time of night and day, you can be sure of that.'

'I'll help out if I can, Mam,' offered Hanna. 'But don't tell anybody in case Dad gets to know.'

'That's not necessary Hannah, Mrs Evans is very kind.'

'Oh alright then, anyway I'd better go. I've been standing outside some time. Dad will be wondering where I am—Mam, don't drink too much of that stuff, please.'

'I'll just have a small one. Off you go then, love, and Hannah, call in more often.'

'I will. Goodbye, goodbye Mrs Evans,' she called back just before the door slammed.

'Hannah's a nice girl, isn't she Ann.'

'Yes, she's the only one who cares for me, I'm sure.'

'I care for you, Ann.'

'Yes you do. I can depend on you Mary. I would like to explain something to you that is very confidential, but I'm not sure whether the present is the right time.'

'If it helps to ease your mind by all means tell me. You can be sure of my absolute discretion. Tell me, it might lift your spirits.'

Anna took a sip of her drink then lowered the glass, cupping it in her two hands. 'Do you remember me telling you of my father?'

'Of course I do; he deserted you and your mother. You went in search of him with the help of John, but John discovered he had died some years before.'

'Well, John told a terrible lie in hope that it would keep the one he loved so dearly?'

The smile on the face of Mrs Evans disappeared. 'What are you trying to say Ann?'

'I am saying that my father is alive and living somewhere, probably nearer than I can believe. Could be next door or in the next street. I may have past him in the market or served him in a pub. I thought I knew John, but I didn't. He was a damn liar.'

The full lips of her neighbour parted with a gasp. 'John lied about your father? How do you know this Ann? It can't be true, surely. He wouldn't do such a cruel thing.'

Anna drank her glass dry then stood up. 'John's last words before he died were, "I told you that your father was dead, he wasn't, he left his job suddenly, no explanation." John said he had lied because he loved me so much he couldn't bear to lose me.'

Anna went into the kitchen to refill her glass. Mrs Evans sat there, shocked. When she returned her glass was full again. She sat back down in her chair and sipped her drink, her eyes slipping into a thoughtful daze. There was silence for some considerable time. It was Mrs Evans who spoke first.

'What can I do to lighten your sadness? I want to help in any way I can.'

Anna slowly undid the first three buttons of her black blouse, her face becoming flushed from the gin. 'If only he had told me the truth back then there would be no need of this,' she said holding the glass up. 'Things would have been so different.' She turned to Mrs Evans. 'Mary, I've just got to search for my father.'

'But so many years have gone by surely there is no hope of finding him now.'

'I have an intuition that he is still within reach of me. May be Merthyr or Aberdare or he could be working in Fochriw or Neath. He could even be as close as Penydarren Iron Works. He's not in Dowlais, I would have heard of him, but he's not too far away, I feel it. I feel it!'

Mrs Evans suddenly felt a positive surge come to her spirit as though Anna was willing her to see the same vision as herself—the happy reunion of father and daughter. 'Then you must go Ann, my dear, you must get it out of your system.'

Anna looked at her through glassy eyes. 'It's the children, you see, Mary. The children, I can't leave them just anywhere.'

'I understand, Ann. Yes I will look after them for a time. You'll never rest until you've satisfied yourself one way or another. You must find the truth about your father whether he is alive or dead, though God only knows how you will do it.'

Anna went and knelt by Mrs Evans and clasped her hands. 'I'll always be indebted to you Mary. Are you sure you want to do this?'

'I don't know if I can because God never blessed me with children, but I won't let you down. I'll be their Bopa Evans...or Aunt Mary, whatever they want to call me.'

'Thank you Mary. I'll stay a few weeks in respect of John's passing, though God only knows if he deserves it. When I'm away I'll keep in touch with you and send you some money when I can. I won't forget you Mary.'

'You must look after yourself, and if you get into any kind of trouble you must come back to us straight away, do you hear?'

Anna rested her head on Mrs Evans lap and wept with relief.

Forty One

John's modest savings amounted to £175 15s 9d after Anna had paid the funeral costs and other miscellaneous outstanding bills such has the credit she had at the Co-operative. She gave Mrs Evans £25 0s 0d believing she would be returning before the money would run out. She left Dowlais three weeks after the funeral with doubt in her mind, wondering if she was on a futile journey into a void of stupidity and hopelessness. She did not intend to carry out a wide search for she knew it was only the surrounding area she could hope to cover. When she had first imagined her quest it felt like an adventure of discovery and reconciliation. But now alone on a tram going to Penydarren, she didn't know where to start, for she had done the same rounds years ago when she had first left Hay-on-Wye. But maybe she had overlooked some simple clue staring her in the face, she thought. She would ask questions in places she had never been before. She decided she would begin with the management of Penydarren Works, and then she would go to the Merthyr Works and onto Plymouth Works a little further down the valley. Getting off at the General Hospital she suddenly felt a sense of freedom and took in a big breath of air. As she made her way up to the works she could already hear the discordant clatter and humming of the diverse sounds of the machinery and furnaces. Approaching the gates the noise became louder, but her attention was taken away when an official with a gruff voice and a stout figure challenged her. He was dressed in a grey suit, its coat wide open and a waistcoat bursting at its buttons. He had emerged from the small building of the security lodge.

'And where do you think you are going my good woman?'

'I'm here my good man,' she mimicked. 'I am looking for a close relation of mine who I haven't seen for many years, and I hoped that I'd fine some clue here.'

'And why would there be any clue here?'

'Because his title was Foreman of Engine Fitters, a position that would make him stand out from others.'

'Oh I see, stand out would he? Griffiths,' he called, turning his head to the security kiosk. 'We have a lady who has a relation of notable position.'

A short man wearing a flat cloth cap emerged from the lodge holding a pipe in his hand.

'Don't be hard on the woman Reg, the lady is clearly in mourning.'

Reginald was taken aback. 'Many women wear black these days. It doesn't mean they are in mourning.'

Anna pulled her coat around her widening waist, the coat now a little too tight for her. 'I lost my husband a month ago up at the Dowlais Works. He was involved in a fatal accident.'

'My God,' blurted Griffiths. 'Was he the unfortunate man in the rolling mill who was crushed by a white-hot ingot?'

Anna raised her head with annoyance at the exaggeration of the ill-informed man. 'He was fatally injured by a chunk of the metal that broke away when the ingot fell from the crane. He died an hour later from his injuries.'

Reginald had gone beetroot with embarrassment. 'My apologies missus, I'm so sorry, I didn't mean to offend. The news of the tragic accident has spread throughout the industry.'

'The news collected a lot of false details in such a short distance.'

'You have our deepest sympathy,' Griffiths apologized with great sincerity. 'Who are you looking for in particular? We'll help in any way we can.'

'I'm looking for my father.'

'Your father,.' repeated the man, surprised. 'When was the last time you saw him?'

'I have never seen him. He left my mother when she was with child—me.'

Reginald's eyebrows flickered from shock. 'When she was pregnant with you? With respect lady, you appear to be a mature woman.'

Griffiths also had his mouth agape. 'Goodness me, you took your time looking for him.'

'I don't need to relate the history of my family, nor do I want you to poke your noses into my affair. It's a simple question. My father's name is Tegwyn Morgan. He was foreman of engine fitters at the Dowlais Iron Works years ago. I searched for him at that time but was told he had died. Recently I have learnt that the man who told me my father was dead, lied, and that my father merely left the works.'

'Good God, that's cruel,' spluttered Reginald.

'That's evil,' agreed Griffiths. 'Tell me how long ago did you say you began looking for him?'

Anna sighed suddenly seeing the situation may be impossible, and this is just the first stop she's made. Her head dropped, as she felt so silly. 'Just over twenty years ago.'

The men fell dumb and they stood there looking at Anna for some moments, it was the blowing off of the blast furnace that shook them to their senses. Griffiths went into his waistcoat pocket, pulled out a match and lit his pipe, staring at the woman in front of him and turning the name of her father over in his head. Tegwyn Morgan…Tegwyn Morgan…sounds familiar, though. Don't you think so, Reg?'

Reg stroked his chin and looked to the sky. Something in his brain was ringing a bell.

'Well?' said Anna.

'I'm sure there was a man we called Morgan labouring for us in the yard for a time, years ago.

'Yes, said Griffiths. 'I'm sure we had a Morgan here many years ago.'

'His name was Tegwyn,' Anna reminded him.'

'Yes, yes. We get into a habit of calling the workers by their second names, makes them show a little respect for their betters, you know.'

Anna gave the man a look to kill.

'Well,' said Reg, 'the man I knew as Morgan was a labourer, but I remember him saying that he had worked as a fitter. He didn't say where, but he wouldn't have worked for Cyfarthfa because Dowlais and Penydarren boys don't like the bosses down there. As he didn't work here as a fitter, he must have worked up at Dowlais...yes.'

Anna was about to turn away when Griffiths exploded with an exclamation.

'Got him! 1890 or 91 it was. A fitter finished on ill health and Morgan was hopeful he'd have the job, but the manager gave it to one of his cronies even though he was inexperienced.' He turned to Reginald. 'You remember, Reg, Morgan moped about the yard for weeks, depressed he was.'

'That's him. Kept complaining he was being punished. He went a bit strange. Said he knew what he had to do.'

'That was him. He suddenly disappeared without giving his notice.' He turned to Anna. 'Sorry my dear, but that man was alive as you and me, then. He said he had something to do, but what I couldn't tell you. But I know what I will do for you. I'll go to records office and find out what his first name was.'

'Thank you, thank you, I'd really appreciate that. Can I come along with you?'

'No, no,' asserted Griffiths as he hurried away. 'That would not help the situation.'

Anna waited, slowly pacing back and fore outside the lodge impatiently.

'Can I offer you a cup of tea, missus?'

'No thank you, I can only hope that your friend brings me some positive information.'

'I've a feeling the man you are looking for is the same man who worked here. Did you say you never saw him?'

Anna stopped pacing and turned to Reg. 'That's right, I have never seen my father. What did this man who worked here look like? Was he small, tall, fat, thin?'

'Well the fellow, who I think is your father, was a good-looking man. I'd say he was about five-foot ten-inch tall, quite athletic-looking really, but a bit moody, as though he had things on his mind, you know? He kept himself to himself.'

Anna pictured her father, tall handsome, athletic. She became intolerably excited and cried out. 'Oh God let it be him. I must find him.'

318

Reg sniffed loudly and shrugged his shoulders; it seemed the only thing to do in such a situation. It was not long before Griffiths returned with a hand written record he had quickly copied on a small piece of paper no bigger than a notepad sheet. He read it out to Anna: 'Tegwyn Morgan of Hay-on-Wye started work 5th January 1889 as a labourer, late of Dowlais Works where he worked as an engine fitter. Left Dowlais without explanation after suffering a period of depression. Left Penydarren works July 1893, no notice given—Time flies, I didn't realize it was that long ago.'

Anna held her hand out. 'Please can I have that piece of paper?'

'Of course you can,' he said, handing it to her.

The first tangible piece of evidence she'd had in all the years she'd been searching and wondering. She grabbed the hand of Griffiths and shook it with much energy. 'Thank you, thank you very much.'

'Glad to have been of help,' smiled Griffiths. 'Good luck in your search. Be lucky.'

'Yes, all the luck in the world to you,' echoed Reg.

Anna hurried off, almost running, for she wanted to begin the next stage of her quest. Though where she was going next never entered her head.

Reg and Griffiths watched her speed away. 'Luck, she needs a miracle,' said Griffiths.'

'And a divine detective,' said Reg. 'I hope she's religious, cause only He can help her.'

Forty Two

Penydarren Ironworks, Cyfarthfa Ironworks, Plymouth Ironworks and a return to Dowlais with the hope her father may have possibly visited his hometown, but that was a chance in a million. She had learnt nothing about his whereabouts after her initial euphoria at Penydarren. She had concentrated on the local districts and because of this she had been able to call in to her home occasionally and assure Mrs Evans and the children she had not abandoned them. It became evident that the children took less notice of their mother each time she returned. The love and attention Mrs Evans bestowed upon them greatly outweighed the neglect of their mother. However, Anna didn't seem to notice the indifference of her little ones, for her thoughts soon concentrated on her next move. She needed to travel a wider area, which took her to places that required staying away for several days at time; days turned into weeks, weeks into months. She travelled around the relevant works in Neath, Ebbw Vale and even as far as Cardiff Docks. Often, when she was crestfallen, she doubted the action she was taking and asked herself what is the point of roaming around the country? She imagined her father to have crossed the border to England or even taken a ship to America. "He knew what he had to do," echoed in her head. The phrase the Penydarren men quoted of her father's words. There was something at the back of her mind which gave her concern, and that was the word Labourer. She had tried to forget the stigma of her father being the lowest class of worker, she imagined him finding a position in his original prestigious job and living prosperously somewhere. But slowly she was coming to terms with the probability she would never find him. However, she concluded whatever his station is in life, she wanted him desperately.

Somewhere along the line of enquiry a man she had asked for advice mentioned that people change their mode of jobs when there is nothing else around. "He could have taken up a job in another industry such as coal mining. There are many positions where workers are needed such as underground ostlers, haulers, face workers etc." he had said. This lifted Anna temporarily and gave her new hope to travel around the patches, drift mines and deep pits from Fochriw to Merthyr Vale. Coalmines and other industries were opening up all over the valleys, so many she could not keep up the quest. She asked at the local quarries of Morlais in Pant and the hillside near Pengarnddu but nobody could help her. Her search became spasmodic and depressing, her only emotional respite was in the bottle at night, making the mornings difficult to face. Her money was diminishing to a level of crisis after a long duration of searching. Expense such as meals in cafes and staying at different taverns and pubs had taken her purse down to the last few shillings. What good is a labourer to her? she asked herself. Anyway, if he's not to be found in the busiest place in Britain he's either travelled too far to find or he's dead, either way I'm chasing a ghost. Her enthusiasm waned, disillusionment turned to apathy and she finally gave up after her thirteen-month search.

Her last call had been in the white dust clouds of Vaynor Quarry where her spirit snapped and her heart hardened after another tiring journey from Neath to Hirwaun, from Penderyn to Vaynor. Her travels by coach, horse carriage and walking overland had brought a fruitless ending. When she emerged from the enormous rock-filled hole of rattling conveyor belts and the hammering of the crushers, she gasped and smacked her clothes and the dust billowed from them like bakers flower.

It was a sunny morning and she was winding her way through the country lanes of Vaynor, slimmer for her months of exercise. She travelled through Pontsarn and Ponsticill, her legs cramping up and her throat dry. Her tired mind blanked out the rustic surroundings she'd tramped through. She heard nothing of the rippling brook that went by, or the croaking magpies flitting from tree to tree, nor the bleating of a lonely sheep. The freshness of the morning grass could not be appreciated in her dusty nostrils. And when she went under the railway bridge she took little notice of the locomotive that thundered above her. As she rounded the bend a long ascending hill rose before her cutting along a hillside. To her left the embankment rose steeply covered in hazel trees where a freshwater spring emerged from somewhere in the undergrowth. The twinkling water rested in a small stone dam at the side of the road, then sank underneath and rushed down the right hand hill into the Taf Fechan River. Needing a rest and a drink she knelt at the "Ffynnon Dwyn," and dipped her lips into the cold water and drank voraciously. Lifting her head she cupped her hands in the spring several times and splashed her face. She sat there for some time thinking in a melancholy way. Thoughts of her children came to mind and a surge of emotion welled up for some love and true friends. She had not called in to see the children and Mrs Evans for eight months. She had left early in January when the New Year had given her inspiration and awakened her wanderlust after the anti-climax of the season's festivities. Now the hiraeth within was drawing her back and she wished she were home. She had thought of children when she was in search of her father, but it was a fleeting image; a picture of how well she had provided for them and how guiltless her conscience was after leaving them with the wonderful Mrs Evans and the ample expenses she had provided for. Now, however, her weariness was edging her thoughts to her comfortable home and her very own bed she could sink into. She could rely on Mary maintaining her house and keeping it clean and tidy so she could just walk in and relax. She'd find a job to pay her way and forget about her paternal hero. She imagined Mrs Evans telling her children that Mam was searching for their grandfather and would return soon with him, and they would all live in security and away from the filthy atmosphere of the industrial town. Tears came to her eyes as she realized it was not to be. It is time to return and be logical about life. I'm never going to find Dad, she concluded. And though her search had been in vain, the children would have their mother back.

As she was steeling herself for the long trek up to the village of Pant, she heard the clip clopping of a horse and the rumbling of cartwheels. Looking back, her heart lightened when a shire horse, pulling a long empty cart came around the corner. She stood at the side of the road and pleaded with her glassy eyes for a lift.

The farmer, pipe hanging from the side of his mouth and an old crinkled trilby on his greying head of hair, stopped. He said nothing but gestured with a side nod for Anna to climb up and sit at his side. She pulled herself on to the seat. They were silent for a while as they slowly rumbled up the uneven gradient, but the farmer could not help taking furtive glances at this female tramp. He could not go further saying nothing for it would be churlish to do so.

'Sorry about the bumps and bounces, no springs on this old cart.'

'I'm grateful for the ride. This long road would have done me in.'

'Pardon me saying so woman,' he said, his pipe in and out of his mouth each time he spoke, 'but you look as if you've had a hard night or two.'

Anna's eyes were looking to the top of the winding slope but she smiled a weak smile. 'More than a night or two, I've had a hard existence, and I find it difficult to come to terms with it.'

'Tell me more missus it'll make you feel better. It'll pass the time away till we get to my watering hole.'

'I'll just say I belong nowhere.'

'You must be making for somewhere.'

'I'm going to visit my children; to stay with them, to look after them, to love them—Ha!'

The farmer slapped the reigns. 'Come Nell, we'd better look sharp,' he said, but the horse kept to his steady pace. Then he gave Anna a strange look. 'What's wrong with looking after your children and loving them? That's what a good mother and Christian woman does, isn't it?'

'It won't work, that's why. I'm neither a good mother nor a Christian.'

'You're a confusing woman, one minute you're going to look after your children the next minute you've changed your mind. What does your husband say about all this?'

'He got killed in the steelworks,' she said, giving the fact without emotion.

He suddenly felt sorry for her. 'Oh you've had a bad time lately it seems. You'll gain your strength and make a fine mother.'

324

'Too late, I can't break the mould I was born in.'

'Give yourself a few weeks, woman, you'll feel better then.'

'A few weeks won't change my past. It rolls around in my head. A few weeks won't change my future. I know it before it happens.'

'Woman, you're in a bad way.'

'Did you mention a watering hole?'

'The Cad-Ivor, at the end of this road; I stop there for a couple of pints on my way to pick up some hay from Caeracca Farm, and on my way back when my cart is full. The finest pint in Dowlais and Pant is in the Cad Ivor.'

'I shall buy you a pint as payment for the ride.'

'You can join me missus, but I shall do the paying, you look to be penniless to me.'

'I've still got a few shillings, I'm not destitute.'

'What's your name anyway? I can't keep calling you missus.'

'My name is Anna, and I don't tell many people that.'

'Why is that?'

'Because I rather not. I'm telling you because you're a stranger, a man I shall never see again.'

'How do you know that? We may cross paths again.'

I'm a labourer, you're well off with acres of land and all the freedom and money you need.'

'No, no, I'm a lowly small-holder with a few cows and pigs, that's all,' his chest swelled as he tried to stifle a cough but failed, which resulted in a severe bout of barking. 'I haven't enough land to grow my own hay,' he eventually exclaimed.

'You should give that pipe a clean.'

'It`s too late.'

The farmer said no more and Anna appreciated the quietness. They reached the top of the hill and turned a bend where dust rose from the Morlais Quarry to the right. Around the bend the road sloped down passing a railway station on the left and then levelled out. The farmer pulled up outside the Cad-Ivor, straightened his aching back and slowly eased his stiff limbs down off the cart. He stood on the side of the road and stretched his slight frame as though he were about to do some physical exercise; arms in the air and feet apart, he groaned with delight as he extended his muscles and limbs. Looking at him, Anna guessed his age to be around fifty judging by his inarticulate body, though his ruddy long face had few lines and looked fresh. He gave his horse some water from a trough around the side of the pub, and then came to Anna to help her down. She accepted his hand, feeling her own body delicate and her legs weak.

'You're kind,' she said, as they both went in to the bar, where several people were already sitting down drinking.'

'What will you have Anna, a long drink or a short one?'

'I'll have the same as you. My thirst can't be quenched, though. That's my trouble. By the way, what's your name?'

'Donald,' he replied, giving her a questionable glance. 'Are you one for excessive drinking Anna?'

'It's my only true calling.'

'Ah, you must take everything in moderation.'

'So I've heard, but the more moderate I try the more extreme the world seems—the barman is waiting for your order Donald.'

He went to the bar and ordered two pints, then gave the barman a knowing wink. The barman pulled two pints and a double rum. Donald picked up the rum and drank it down. Then he went back to Anna with the two pints. They both drank half with one helping of gulping and swallowing.

'Oh that's better,' said Donald.

Anna closed her eyes. 'If there is a God, I thank Him for the man who had the imagination to think up this brew.'

'I'll drink to that,' said Donald as he raised his pint, Anna followed his example. 'Landlord, another two please,' called Donald. He turned to Anna. 'Join me in another one and then I shall leave you, but I suggest you leave with me—moderation, you see.'

'I shall leave with you, Donald. You can give me a lift down as far as the farm and I will make my own way down through Dowlais.'

'Well done,' said Donald holding his hand out so that he could take Anna's and shake it, and so she did.

Forty Three

Mrs Evans was changing Cerys's nappy and feeling a little tired. The two-year-old had proved to be a demanding child, for she frequently had bad nights crying and waking Mrs Evans. The crying frequently roused her husband who didn't take lightly to his rest being disturbed. The frustration was apparent on the good lady's face, so the visitor who had turned up for the third time in nine months took the baby from her.

'Here, let me do that I'm more experienced than you,' said Anna's sister-in-law as she relieved Mrs Evans of the chore.

'I've been doing it for the past two years Caroline, and I still can't stomach it. I feel a complete failure.'

'You are not a failure Mary, it's not the same with another's child so don't put yourself down. When and if Anna returns I'll have a few harsh words to say to her. You should have let her know how you feel when she came home last time.'

'I couldn't. She was so depressed and worn out I didn't like to tell her the difficulty I was having looking after the two of them. Daniel is no trouble. He was out of nappies when he was eighteen months, but this little darling…well. I feel she is not as healthy as she could be.'

'There's nothing wrong with her, just a little patience and she'll grow out of her problems. Anyway, I hope you don't mind me staying for as long as it takes this time. That neglectful sister-in-law of mine is going to have to come to terms with things.'

'You can stay as long as it takes Caroline, but I think Anna is not going to take your suggestion lightly.'

'She should welcome an adoption or even a foster mother taking care of Cerys. And it will be an advantage for the baby to have other older children to play with. Daniel is fine, don't get me wrong, but he does seem to be a little boisterous with the delicate Cerys.'

'He's a typical boy.'

'I suppose so. What does Mr Evans think about me taking Cerys home with me?'

'Quite frankly I think he'd appreciate it. His eyes are getting worse and the foreman has noticed he's not as good as he was. He was one of the best puddlers in the industry until a few months ago. It was then his guiding the molten pig iron got a bit difficult. He has neither the strength nor the eyesight for such a job anymore.'

'Won't they find him a place that's less demanding?'

'No, they don't take such a responsibility.'

'Oh dear, that hardly seems fair after losing his health on behalf of the steelworks.'

'That's how things are in the industry, I'm afraid. Anyway, what does Owen think of you taking on another child?'

Caroline placed Cerys in her cot and gave her a dummy; the child content in her dry nappy and her pacifier. 'I think he's secretly worried about the two children. After all, John was his older brother and he thought a lot of him. He feels he has a responsibility to the children, but I'm afraid he's not too complimentary when we talk about Ann. He thinks the children should be taken away from her, but he could not see them go into care, and he won't take on both.'

And so the women chatted comforting themselves in the knowledge that things will improve for all concerned soon.

Anna had her plans changed. She wanted to get home as soon as possible but the comfort and cordial surroundings of the Cad-Ivor was relaxing her and giving her a feeling of contentment. Besides, she thought, having done all that travelling and exhaustive searching surely she deserves some sort of reward, and what better way to do it than to enjoy the company of warm-hearted people and the modest of alcoholic drinks, real ale. She would not let Donald go unless he agreed to accept her offer of another beer, so he did. But when he had finished the pint, he stood up.

'Right Anna, I'm off, you can have a lift if you want, but you'll have to come now, and not a minute later.'

Anna looked up at him, 'Right Donald, I'll have a lift so far and then I'll make my way home.'

She stood up and was about to leave with him when a lofty man with a long grey beard came in through the door and made his way to the bar. He was unmistakable wearing his black suit and walking un-rushed and placid to the bar, as he always was when not preaching the gospel.

'Joshua! In a pub!—Donald, I will see you some other time. My friend and street evangelist has come in, a sight for sore eyes.'

Donald shrugged his bent shoulders and left. 'Goodbye Anna, and the best of luck,' he said, but Anna didn't hear him, she was already standing at Joshua's side.

'I haven't seen you here before, Ann.'

'I'm very surprised to see you standing at a bar.'

'I have my reasons. Well Ann, I hear you've been away looking for a relative.'

'Oh never mind that, I never realized you were a drinker, Joshua.'

'Can I buy you a drink, Ann?'

'Indeed not, I shall buy you one—barman,' she called excitedly.

The stout barman came to Anna looking her over as though she were a vagabond. He then turned to Joshua with a smile. 'It`s Nice to see you again Joshua. Same as usual?'

'Yes please Edgar and a drink for the lady.'

'The lady?'

'My friend Ann, here.'

He had a scornful glance at Anna, and then filled a glass of red wine for Joshua. He began to take down a pint glass from the shelf when Anna stopped him.

'Excuse me my good man, but I'll have the same as Joshua.' She turned to the tall preacher, 'And I insist on paying for the drinks.'

'As you wish Ann. Shall we sit at that table in the corner, my legs are weary from standing whilst spreading the word of the Lord.'

'Whatever you say is fine with me Joshua.'

They sat at the top end of the room where the light was not as strong, for the small windows of the pub were situated lower down the room.

'You appear to have had a long trek Ann.'

'Yes. I know I don't look as tidy as I should. If you feel embarrassed with me Joshua, I'll sit elsewhere.'

'Don't be silly.' Joshua put his hand in a cloth bag he was carrying and pulled out half a cob loaf and began to break it in two. He offered half to Anna.

'Will you join me Ann?'

Anna looked at him with understanding. 'Wine, bread, the breaking of; are you taking communion in a pub, Joshua?'

'The Lord said, " Whosoever should gather in my name, there will I be also."'

'And "Do this in remembrance of me." But in a pub, Joshua?'

'You can be with Jesus in a pub, a prison or an abyss, He will be present if you should sincerely call.'

'Would you be offended if I didn't join you?'

'I would be disappointed, the Almighty might be offended.'

'Then I shall unite with you,' she said, as she accepted the piece of bread.

Joshua lifted the bread up to head height. 'This is the body of our dear Lord I take it in remembrance of Him.' Then he bit a small piece off and looked at Anna who quickly did the same. He lifted his glass of wine, 'This is the blood of our Lord, I drink this in remembrance of Him.' Anna did the same. Then they both finished off the bread and sipped the wine quietly and slowly. Anna felt a load lift from her as though she was as pure as Joshua.

Though there was chatter and clinking of glasses in the room, and the smoke from pipes and cigarettes pervaded around, Anna had eyes only for Joshua.

'You stare at me as though I were a ghost, Ann.'

'There is something about you Joshua that intrigues and fascinates me,' she said.

'And what would that be?'

'I don't know. But whenever I'm in your company I feel at ease.'

'It gratifies me to learn so. Ann, I hope you won't be offended, and I know you've had a sad time lately, but don't you think it's time to cherish the little ones? Get cleaned up and put on fresh clothes and hold the children to your bosom. It will make you feel good and wanted.'

330

'You've learnt a lot about me since I've been away. Much gossip I dare say. However, the fact is I'm on my way home, but I haven't felt as relaxed as this for a long time, don't rush me away.'

'The local grapevine is very garrulous. Anyway, the children should always be priority, Ann. To neglect such a responsibility is very wrong. Remember what Jesus said, "Suffer the little children to come unto me."'

Anna suddenly felt sad, not because she'd been leaving her children with others, but she wondered did Joshua know about all of her offspring as well as Daniel and Cerys, and the fact she could desert her others so easily. Her eyes became distant. She lifted her glass without thinking and finished the wine.

'I wish I could be like you Joshua.'

'In what way would that be?'

'You don't participate in the company of others, but you're so sure of yourself, so solid and confident. You`re so steadfast in your faith I envy you.'

'Kneel and pray with me Ann and your troubled mind will clear.'

'No it won't. There are too many memories for me to have faith in love and justice.'

'Share those memories with me, maybe it will help.'

'No, they made me hard. I've had to think for myself. Many things in the Bible don't make sense. Some stories are like fairy tales. Tell me Joshua, do you believe you are superior to me?'

Joshua straightened his back and frowned at Anna, 'Of course not.'

'All other men do. They are convinced that women are inferior to men and that they haven't got the same rights.'

He suddenly understood and smiled kindly. 'In the eyes of God all human beings are equal, man and woman, unfortunately, the vanity of man gives them hard hearts and superior thoughts to shun the potential of the opposite sex. Didn't Christ protect and favour Mary Magdalene? Tell me Ann, do you believe there is a God?'

'Of course not, nor is there a Heaven. I've pointed out to people who have argued with me in the past; billions upon billions have passed over since time began, are they all in Heaven, and if so it must be very cramped.'

'There are many mansions Ann, Jesus promised that.'

Anna gave him an expression of despair. Joshua, Joshua, for goodness sake how big do you think Heaven is?'

'The universe is God's Heaven, and that's mighty big. But that's not the point Ann. The truth is you must have faith. If you can't understand God and His Kingdom, it doesn't follow you know best.'

'God is infinitely the greatest genius of all, it seems. He made the universe, the world and all that is in it. He made it all beautiful and perfect, but when He came to man He failed to make him perfect. He made me as I am, what can I do about it? I can't undo what God has created.'

'Then you do believe. God created you unblemished. It is the sins of man that has made you what you are.'

'I can't believe in these miracles of creation. It's just not logical.'

'If I lived a hundred years ago and somebody told me that one day I would be able to transmit my voice through wires to another city, I would think my intelligence was being ridiculed, but today it is an accepted progression. I would say it is one of God's wondrous powers. But my voice travels much further than the telephone; I transmit my thoughts to God in the form of prayer. So have faith and be content in the love of Jesus. Now, my dear, go see to your children.'

'As I said Joshua, I wish I could be like you. I've travelled most of my life through a world of bad luck and suffering. It has moulded me, you see? That's how I've been made. You talk of inventions, well, imagine me as an invention that has been made. If the machine can't operate as its inventor wants, who's at fault? You can't blame the machine it's only doing what it's capable of.'

'You're not a machine Ann, you have feelings and compassion, a brain to think and correct your mistakes. Those are the components of your body, soul mind. Use them for the power they hold.'

'I'm going to get another two glasses of wine, then I'm going home to my children, will you have one?'

'For you I will make an exception. Normally I just have the one, but today I shall take another. And then I shall walk a little way with you.'

When they had finished their wine they walked together through Pant, Joshua with loping strides, Anna quickening her step and content to be with someone who accepted her as an equal. Joshua stopped outside Pant Church momentarily and said to Anna,

'You see that lovely building? Those who worship there call it "The House of God." But what did Jesus have to say about such a vain statement?'

Anna quickly said.' "If Heaven is My Father's throne and Earth is His footstool, where on a footstool can you build Him a house?'

'Near enough Ann, that is an example of the vanity of man. They only raise God to temporal intelligence, and forget that God has created all. How vain we are to believe we can offer God something precious or new, He who has made all there is.'

They walked on until Joshua turned under the bridge that led into Caeracca, for he was on his way to Penywern. There, he would find a multitude of workers making their way home to which he could bless and say a kind word. As he passed under the bridge he turned and waved to her calling, 'Go to the little ones Ann, the little ones.' Anna, now light-headed from the drink and feeling better than she had been for some considerable time waved back vigorously. She then continued along Pant Road towards home.

Joshua had made her aware of the needs her children expected of her, and she was thinking how she was going to change her ways and be a good mother. She would not go out as often nor drink as much, but remain indoors and cosset and love them, as a good mother should. As she was approaching the Cardigan Arms in Victoria Street the soft breeze drew the smell of tobacco and drink out of the open door of the pub. To many people the staleness of the odour would be repulsive to them, but to Anna it brought pictures of cosiness and friendship and the lifting of the spirit. She stopped at the door and said to herself. 'Now Anna make this the last one and then head for home to the children.'

It was seven o'clock and Mrs Evans had just finished washing the children and dressing them in their nightclothes. She wasn't looking forward to the confrontation and was hoping Caroline would go back home to Owen when and if Anna should turn up.

She had been there for three days and the longer she stayed the more apprehensive Mrs Evans became. Caroline, however, was ardent in her intention to stay the night if necessary. She might even stay a week to face Anna and offer her the proposition she and Owen had agreed to. When she heard a knock at Mrs Evans's door she stiffened and looked at her host.

'This must be her, surely,' she said to Mrs Evans.

Mrs Evans stood up and braced herself. 'She normally walks straight in.' Mrs Evans went to the door and took a deep breath as she held the doorknob. Opening the door she was very surprised to see Owen standing there.

'Mrs Evans, is Caroline here, I've been knocking at Ann's door but can't get an answer.'

'Oh, Owen, we weren't expecting you, come in, come in, she's here.'

Inside Owen's eyes lit up to see the two children dressed in the nightclothes and looking like a couple of angels. He picked up Cerys and held her in his arms, then ruffled Daniel's fair hair.

'Hello love,' welcomed Caroline. 'I didn't expect you.'

He placed Cerys down at the side of Daniel. 'I thought I'd better come and see what's happening. Well, is she here?'

'Mrs Evans has given me the disgusting news that Ann hasn't been here for nearly ten months. I can't see her coming back at all.'

'Goodness me, hasn't the woman got any sense of responsibility. Well, I'm the next of kin after Ann, and as she is such an irresponsible mother and grossly neglectful, I believe that I am entitled to take them both to my home for protection.'

Mrs Evans stared at him. 'I don't wish to offend anyone,' she said, but I assure you they don't need protection from me.'

'No, no, Mrs Evans, you've been wonderful, but what if something happens to you? Who's going to look after them then? Back home at Carmarthen we have our family there. I have a married sister and an auntie and uncle who have grown up children.'

'Slow down now Owen, Mrs Evans is in agreement with us, she is finding it difficult looking after the two of them.'

'I should think she is. For all we know Ann may never come back. She was away for years when she first left John, years. The woman is impossible. No, I think we are within our rights to take them home with us. He picked up Cerys again and cradled her in his arms. 'Does Cerys want to come home with Uncle Owen and meet her cousins, and have lots of toys and lovely green fields to play in, yes, yes?'

Cerys nodded.

'Daniel?' he said looking at the boy.

Daniel looked at Mrs Evans. 'I want to stay with Bopa.'

They heard the front door opening. There was a shuffling in the passageway. Anna appeared at the living room door. She looked around in an alcoholic haze. Then her eyes focused on Owen sitting with Cerys, his arm around her. 'Ah my little darling, come to Mam,' she said and stumbled towards Owen.

'Stay where you are woman, you're obviously not fit to hold a dog in your arms let alone a fragile little girl. She moved towards Daniel, but he shrunk away.

'I want to go to bed Bopa,' he pleaded.

'I was about to put them to bed Ann, they're very tired. I'll just take them up and then I'll make a cup of tea for us all.'

Anna flopped down on the settee and remained there trying to comprehend the situation. 'What's going on here?' she slurred.

Mrs Evans ushered the two children out of the room and took them up the stairs.

Owen looked at Anna with contempt. 'We're taking the children into care,' he growled. If it wasn't for Mrs Evans they'd be in the workhouse by now.'

Anna suddenly sat up. 'The workhouse?' she screamed. You're not putting my children into the workhouse, damn you! Damn you!' She tried to get up but her legs were too weak to lift her and she slipped in the seat. She struggled to the sitting position again.

'Calm down Ann,` said Caroline. We're not putting them into the workhouse, we want to adopt Cerys. It's too much for Mrs Evans. She wrote to us and told us so.'

'You're a drunk and a wanderer, you have no right treating your children the way you do.'

'Owen!' snapped Caroline. Leave it for now.'

'My children are in good hands and well provided for I'll have you know. You ask Mrs Evans, they've never wanted for anything.'

'Only a decent mother, that's all.'

'You're cruel, that's what you are, cruel. If your lying brother had not deceived me years ago, I would have been shot of this place and married a man of sub...substan, ...substance,' she said and broke into a fit of weeping.

'What are you talking about you silly fool.'

'Owen if you don't shut up I'll be leaving you on your own. Now I suggest we continue this business tomorrow.'

'That's good idea I think,' said Mrs Evans coming through the door. 'Ann, come with me dear, I'll take you into your house and help you to bed.'

Anna looked up at Mrs Evans. 'I haven't many friends in this world, but I thank the Lord for having you Mary.'

The following morning Anna sat up in bed and held her head. It was early, seven o'clock, and she tried to retrace her steps through the previous day. She remembered having a lift on the farmer's cart, Cad-Ivor, then Joshua, calling into the Cardigan Arms but she couldn't remember coming home. She realized she was at home in her own bedroom. It was then she remembered the bad dream she had: Owen shouting at her, Caroline, the children, and herself crying. Mrs Evans...Mrs Evans, she has the children...it wasn't a dream. They're here, next door...taking the children away. She looked around and saw her grimy clothes draped over her bedroom chair. She quickly got out of bed and immediately held on to her thumping temple. Slowly donning her dressing gown she heard sounds from downstairs. With delicate steps she made her way down, wondering who, and how many were there. She was relieved to see Mrs Evans and the children in the living room with nobody else.

'Ah, Ann, I was about to come up and wake you,' said the good lady, curlers in her hair and an apron tied round her waist. 'I've made a little breakfast for you, just some toast. The children have already had breakfast in my house. I thought you might like to have them here when you got up.'

336

'Hello Daniel, hello my little darling Cerys,' she said with a gentle voice.

'Where've you been Mam?' asked Daniel.

'Oh don't ask, Daniel. I've had a terrible time, but I'm glad to be home with you now.'

'Did you bring a present home? You promised the last time you came.'

'Did I love? The first thing I'll do after breakfast is for us to go up the market and buy you both something from the toy stall.'

Daniel turned away disappointed and resumed throwing his ball to Cerys.'

'Would you like some toast, Ann.'

'I'll just have a cup of tea, thank you Mary.'

'Come into the kitchen, I want to have a little chat with you.'

Anna obeyed, though mystified, and sat on the stool in the kitchen sipping her tea. 'They're here aren't they?'

Mrs Evans, sitting in a tall chair nodded to her. 'Caroline and Owen, yes they are.'

'Did I hear right last night or was it a nightmare? They want to take my children away?'

'They want to adopt or foster Cerys. While you were away Bill had to have a couple of weeks off work and I couldn't cope. So they took little Cerys home with them for a time to give me a break.' Mrs Evans paused, feeling herself choking up from emotion. Clearing her throat, she continued. 'It seemed that Cerys was quite at home and happy to play with their children. When they brought Cerys back they were hoping you would be here. Owen was very upset he had to leave Cerys here without a mother. Anyway, I'm afraid I can't manage the two children and Bill. He's in work but can hardly do his duties. It's only a matter of time before they sack him.'

At this point Mrs Evans broke down and sobbed pitifully. Anna went to her and put her arm around her.

'I didn't realize. I'm so sorry Mary.'

Mary controlled herself, pulled a handkerchief from her apron and dried her eyes. 'I love the children as though they were my own, and I can manage Daniel all right, but Cerys needs more attention you see.'

'Yes they can be a handful. But I'm home now, so we can cope with them together can't we?'

'I wish I could Ann, but we've had to think things over seriously lately. Everything has happened to us over the last few months. If you hadn't come now I would have had to leave both children go with Caroline and Owen.'

'What has happened Mary? Tell me, please.'

'Bill doesn't want to be dismissed for incompetence so he's going to finish before he's sacked. He hasn't been too patient with me getting up at nights with Cerys, and has told me that I must not look after them anymore. At least not for long periods or having them stay overnight. 'We'll probably be on subsistence when our saving run out…I just can't concentrate on anything…'

'Don't worry yourself anymore Mary, I'll be able to manage,' said Anna, dolefully and holding her head. 'I'll find some way to cope, I'm sure.'

Mary stood up and put her hand on Anna's shoulder. 'I'm sorry Anna.'

'That's all right,' replied Anna staring into her cup.'

'I must go now. You don't mind, do you?'

'No, of course not,' she said quietly thinking.

'Oh, just one thing more, Caroline asked me to tell you they'll be calling on you around eleven o'clock to discuss things.'

'Yes, well, I'll have to think about the situation, won't I?'

'I'll only be next door if you want me Anna.'

'Thank you Mary, you don't mind if I don't see you to the door, do you?'

'Of course not, but remember, we're not cutting ourselves off completely.'

When Anna heard the thudding of the door closing on her, there was something final about it. She couldn't see Bill letting Mary get too friendly again. Heaviness came over her and she lapsed into a depression.

Forty Four

Over the next few weeks Caroline and Owen presented a persuasive case for their proposed adoption of Cerys. Between them they had a good balance of coercion and gentleness that eventually won Anna's consent. Owen was the tactless brute that highlighted all of Anna's shortcomings reminding her that she needed alcohol before she could face carrying out simple tasks like making a wholesome meal, or cleaning the house, that she was unable to go shopping unless Mrs Evans looked after the children, that she had become so estranged from her offspring little Cerys preferred the company of that good woman. Furthermore, her nights out carousing and making a fool of herself did little for the dignity of the family or the respect the children deserved. He dreaded the day when the children should grow to the age of reasoning and discover that their mother was a drunken layabout. She was a self-indulgent woman who cared about nobody except herself, that she was weak-willed and a hopeless case. He let it be known that John had been quite clear in his correspondence of all his deep worries concerning his wife's irresponsible ways.

Caroline made many interjections when her husband was making these cruel attacks, softly explaining to Anna that Cerys appeared to be a delicate child and needed much attention. That she realized Anna had had a bad start in life and needed to be understood, but the facts speak for themselves, she is unable to care for her two children until she "sorted herself out." That Cerys was an inhibited child who needed special care and nightly observation. That Cerys would have a wonderful chance to grow into a lady, educated and nurtured, brought out of herself by the company of her cousins. And finally, that Anna would have more time to look after Daniel, a boy who loved her and needed her.

Anna fought back by saying she is a changed woman now, though she said it unconvincingly, and that she is quite capable of looking after her children. But there were thoughts going through her mind of not having Mary at her beck and call that would make her a virtual prisoner in her own home. And would she have the patience to cope with Cerys waking her up every night. She knew in her heart that her social life, as she knew it, would not be possible without her friend Mary. She put on a brave front and categorically refused to let Cerys go, and denounced Owen a dictatorial tyrant, the exact opposite of his brother who had been a loving and caring husband. It was Caroline in a last desperate offer that convinced Anna to let Cerys go; Caroline suggested that they compromise and they foster Cerys for a year or two with the proviso that they make visits to Anna regularly to see how things go. It would give both parties time to assess the outcome of the move. Anna could see that the compromise was convenient and face-saving, so she agreed. The move was made hurriedly in case Anna should change her mind. And so, without further ado, Caroline packed Cerys's things immediately, supervised by Anna's watchful eye and bewildered brain. Suddenly, she was alone clutching Daniel tenderly.

Anna directed all her care and attention to her son the following months; she took him shopping and bought him presents. Made sure he was comfortable in his bed at night and cooked him wholesome meals. The bond between the two had grown and for a time Anna proved she could cope with life, but not without a few drinks after Daniel was asleep. She continued to be friendly with Mary, but asked her for no favours, she wanted to prove that she could be a good mother without the help of others.

Hannah got to hear of the fostering agreement and often tapped the window when passing. Sometimes there was a response when they were home other times a disappointing silence, though she never stopped. The twelve-year-old still had a soft spot for her mother, but never told Anna or her father. One day, on her way home from school she tapped the window. Anna had waited for her in hope that she would make an appearance. On seeing her, Anna gestured to her to come in. At the door Hannah was hesitant for a moment, not knowing who might be in the house, for she had seen so many strangers come and go lately. Her mother came to the door.

340

'Come on in for a few minutes Hannah. Daniel wants to see you and I want to have a word with you.'

Though Hannah had been in the house before and, unlike the last time when the atmosphere was cold and morbid after the funeral, she found the house lighter and warmer. This time she felt she could be at ease and she took in the character of her mother's home. It was much bigger than the one she was living in and brightly decorated. She stopped and looked down at the soft carpet she stood on.'

'Come on in, Hannah. Come in to the living room.'

She did so and found Daniel there with a toy pistol and wearing a cowboy hat. He turned around and pointed the gun at her shouting 'bang, bang, you're dead.'

'Now, now, Daniel, you can't shoot her, she's your sister.'

Hannah had never thought of herself as being Daniel's sister, even though he was her stepbrother.

'I've got to shoot somebody, I can't shoot you.'

'Put the gun away now, I've poured you a glass of lemonade—would you like a glass Hannah?'

'Yes please Mam.'

She hadn't been called Mam for a long time, and the sentiment brought warmth to her heart. She turned, almost embarrassed and went into the kitchen. She returned from the kitchen with two glasses of lemonade, gave one to Daniel and the other to Hannah. 'Sit down love don't stand on ceremony, I want you to feel you can call in anytime from now on. How are my other children faring Hannah? I never see them passing the window.'

'They're fine; Bronwen takes Carin and Emrys to school and brings them back, but they go across East Street. I tell them I'm going my friend's way home so I come around this way.'

'I see. They don't want to see their Mam, then?'

Hannah thought for a moment, she knew Bronwen always wanted to keep the peace with their father, and Carin had no thoughts one way or the other about seeing her mother; Emrys had almost forgotten about his mother after she had left when he was just four.

'I think Bronwen likes to please Dad.'

'I see.'

Hannah sat in a soft chair near the fireplace; though the fire was prepared it was not lit. She watched her mother move about unusually slow and a little cumbersome. For the first time in years she realized her mother looked much older and fuller in figure. Though just thirty-eight, her hips were prominent in the long black dress she wore, and her back was not as straight as she remembered. Realizing she was staring at her mother she turned her head to the ceiling and concentrated her attention on the glass fitting that housed the gas mantle. It was in the shape of an inverted tulip with gold lines sliding down its bulbous sides.

'That a nice gas fitting, Mam, I haven't seen one like that before.'

'Oh I've seen better in higher places in London.'

'You've haven't told me much about London.'

'London has got good memories and bad memories, but it's not London I want to talk about, Hannah. I'll be straight with you. Would you do me a big favour? Daniel is starting school next Monday and I've been promised a job washing dishes in a café. I've had to take any old job because my money is running out, but I'm sure I'll get something better when I have time to look around. Anyway, I can't accept the job because the hours cover the times Daniel has to be taken to school and brought home. If you could take him and bring him home with you I'd be able to take the job.'

Hannah thought about it for a minute wanting desperately to help her mother out, but also dreading the wrath of her father if he should get to know of it.

'I wouldn't be able to stay with him after school. Dad would know I was doing something if I was late getting home every day.'

'That's all right. Mrs Evans has agreed to stay with him for an hour until I get home. I'll be here in the morning, take him then so I can rush off, then bring him home after school.'

'I suppose that will be all right. I don't mind as long as Daniel will let me.'

'You don't mind do you Daniel?' urged Anna.

'I can go on my own. I don't need a big sister.'

'You can go on your own when you are a little older.'

'All right then,' he said, cheerfully finishing off his lemonade.'

'He won't mind being left with the teacher, will he?' asked Hannah.

'Oh no, I've already introduced him to her. I've been up the school and he's already taken to his teacher, haven't you Dan?'

'She's nice but she's fat.'

'You musn't say that, Dan, it's not nice.'

Hannah chuckled. 'I think you're talking about Miss Baily.'

'That's right, you know her Hannah?'

'She used to be my teacher for the first two years in the infants. She's all right when the parents are there, but stern and shouts a lot when they've gone.'

'Well, maybe that's a good thing. So you'll do that for me then?'

'I don't mind, but don't let Dad know.'

'There's no chance of that.'

'Which café are you going to work in?'

'The big one in Union Street.'

Hannah stood up. 'I'd better be going, Ruth will be wondering where I am.'

'Ah, it's Ruth who is doing his housework is it?'

'Sometimes. I don't know what time Dad'll home today. It's his shifts, you see.'

'Thank you Hannah, you're a lovely girl.'

Anna waited at the door until she was down the road. Hannah turned and waved generously.

Forty Five

Her humdrum existence of being a slavish labourer doing the lowest job in the catering industry was lasting too long. The expectation of the job being a stepping-stone to better employment had evaporated. Even though she had a good regular routine convenient for Daniel and herself, and Hannah was becoming more of a big sister than a stepsister, she knew she was in a rut. The dreary months wore on in the hard-working kitchen of the busy café. The days were getting harder and her back ached more and more from stooping over the huge sinks. The eight-hour day brought the same chores that had to be done, not in the kitchen, but in the lean-to wash-up area adjoining the kitchen where the stench of stale food came from the swill bins. The two rectangular stone, waist-high, washbasins fixed to the main wall of the building and supported by iron legs, were as big as bathtubs and filled with tepid water shining with grease from the late evening shift workers. Huge draining boards were regularly piled after lunch with saucepans big as buckets, some a quarter full of hardening potato, others with drying gluey peas. Left-over custard skin, sometimes half an inch thick came to her congealed in large pots, black frying pans, the size of dustbin lids, had burnt lard cemented on its inside and blackened spillage welded on the outside. Large wooden trays had remnants of concrete cake setting, while others were black with gravy. All this washing up came through from the kitchen and had to be cleaned and cleared before the afternoon customers arrived for their tea and cakes. Each afternoon walking home from her job she was drained of physical strength and in low spirits.

When she arrived home Mary would stop for only a few minutes asking her how her day went. However, the ashen face of Anna and the dejected tone of her low voice made the question unnecessary, and Anna came to reply with a shake of the head and a brief exclamation of 'I'm all done in, Mary.'

'You'll have to find another job Ann, love. You're no good to man or beast this way.'

'It's difficult finding a job to fit in with school times, Mary. I could get a job as barmaid down at the Puddlers Arms, but that would mean leaving Daniel on his own and coming home late at nights and that would be impossible.'

'I wish I could help you but Bill is adamant about me taking on such a responsibility again.'

'I realize that Mary, but I wish I could get out on a Saturday at times just to have a break from the house.'

'You could take Daniel out somewhere for the day.'

Anna looked sheepishly at Mary and shrugged her shoulders.

'I know, you'd like to go out for a drink and that would be an evening treat.'

'A bit of cheerful company and a drink is not asking much in life, is it? And I can't take Daniel into a pub.'

'What about an afternoon out in the country with Daniel?'

'It would be a change, I suppose, but hardly a substitute for a night out.'

'I've got to go now Ann, but I'll suggest an afternoon out one fine day up the country with Bill and invite you and Daniel along. That will be a break for you and Bill. Since he's finished work he's hardly been out. I'll work something out for you to have a private break when we're out.'

Anna looked up at Mary and wondered what she meant, but the lady was doing her best for her, she knew that. 'That's a wonderful idea Mary. Do you think Bill would agree to that?'

'I'll use my persuasive charms on him,' she joked. 'I'll tell him he hasn't taken me out since Noah left his ark.

'I'll look forward to it Mary.'

'I've got to go. See you tomorrow.'

As Anna closed the front door behind Mary she called up the stair. 'Daniel, I'm home.'

'I know Mam, I'm not deaf. I heard you talking.'

'Mary suggested we go out together one Saturday afternoon for a walk in the country.'

'I don't mind,' he shouted back. 'Can Hannah come too?'

346

Anna thought about it. 'I'll have to ask her.'

It was Saturday, Anna's day off. She squeezed herself into her white summer dress that was slowly beginning to fit her again, and donned a wide-brimmed hat. Mary had suggested to Bill they catch a train to the local beauty spot with Ann and Daniel, but he had turned it down and suggested she go with them. Hannah had told her father that she was entitled to have a day out with her friends after helping out with her siblings and household chores all week. Emlyn had agreed, for the youngster was a great asset to him and he could not deny her some time to herself. So the four met at Anna's house mid-morning and then made their way up through Dowlais under a blue July sky broken with white clouds. They had with them the necessary assortments of food and drink for a picnic. Anna carried a wicker basket with sandwiches, cakes and a tablecloth, all of which Mary had provided. Hannah carried lemonade and beakers in a raffia bag provided by Anna, whilst Mary held the hand of Daniel who gripped a football in his other hand.

At Dowlais Central Railway Station they caught the Pontsarn train along with a crowd of day-trippers. It was the first time Hannah and Daniel had experienced the roaring of the train as it went through the darkness of the mile-long tunnel. The screeching of the whistle heralded the emergence into daylight and the comfort of the tranquil run through the woods. Crossing the high viaduct that spanned the Taf Fechan River, they took in the panoramic view of the surrounding fields and farms that spread down the valley. Finally reaching the Pontsarn Halt, they alighted with a gross or more people, mostly of women and children, but a few husbands too.

The noisy excited crowd made their way up the dirt path to the main country road where the lone building of the Elizabethan-style Pontsarn Hotel stood. A couple of early drinkers sat outside on a bench and sipped furtively on their pints, for the hotel had opened early to satisfy the day-trippers. Already in the fields opposite the hotel were many people sitting around enjoying the leisure time. The newcomers mingled amongst them, finding their little patches of grassy ground, some on the top slope that overlooked that valley,

347

others in the shade of the trees. Anna and Mary relaxed in the coolness of an oak tree for a time while Hanna and Daniel ran off to play with the ball, mixing with children from different areas of the district. It wasn't long before Anna became restless, sitting up and looking around at nothing in particular, which didn't go unnoticed by Mary.

'It must be nice for you to relax and have a break from work, Ann. We're lucky to have such a nice day.'

'Yes, I've got today and tomorrow off, but the dreaded Monday to face.'

'Forget about Monday. Here, have a cup of lemonade,' said Mary pouring some into a beaker.'

Anna accepted the beaker then went into her handbag and brought out a small bottle of rum.

Mary's eyes widened, 'It's a bit early for that, isn't it Ann?'

'It's twelve fifteen, that's late enough,' she said, pouring some rum into her lemonade.

'I suppose it's alright taking it early once in a while.'

'Once in a while; I can't face that café scullery without a pick-me-up.'

'You drink at work?'

'Just a little one to start the day, it helps me, you know.'

'We'll have our lunch, shall we? I don't want the sandwiches drying up.'

'I don' mind, the children may not want to break away from their games.'

'Hannah is growing up in to an attractive girl, Anna. I do like her sandy hair.'

'Yes, she's a lovely girl, but her hair reminds me of her father.'

Mary looked around and waited until Hannah glanced her way. She gestured her to come over. Hannah grabbed Daniel and they both came running.

'What's the matter?' asked Daniel. 'We're not going already, are we?'

'No, no, I just thought you might like to have something to eat and drink.'

'That suits me,' said Hannah.'

348

Mary spread a cloth on the grass and set it with a selection of sandwiches: fish-paste, cucumber, and raspberry jam as well as cakes and apples. She poured the children some lemonade and told them to help themselves. This they did and the four were quiet enjoying the simple repast. The children were too engrossed in the food to notice Anna's drink a shade of brown, nor did they notice that her appetite was not as healthy as theirs. Daniel, however, facing the road that was some distance away, noticed a man on a horse stop outside the Pontsarn Hotel.

'Oh look at him, he's cowboy.'

They all looked, Mary and Hannah taking little notice, but there was an inquisitive expression on Anna's face. The man had a quick involuntary bout of coughing that sounded familiar to her.

'He's no cowboy Daniel, but I think I know who it is. He looks like that kind man I told you of, the one who gave me a lift on his cart last year. Yes he's got a trilby hat on and the same movements,' she added as she watched him dismount and tie his horse to the iron railing before disappearing into the hotel.

'Would you mind if I went and said hello to him Mary? I never did have a chance to thank him properly for his kindness.'

A shadow of a smile spread across Mary's face, but she knew she couldn't refuse Anna the opportunity to show her gratitude to a Good Samaritan, even if it was an auspicious moment and an opportunity to have a drink.

'No, of course not, the children will be fine with me. Take your time Ann, you need some relaxation.'

'Thank you, Mary, won't be long children,' she said as she walked off quickly.

Inside the hotel she was disappointed to see that Donald was talking to a man at the bar, and she wondered if he had arranged to meet him there. If so, she could not interrupt, it would not be prudent for a lady to accost two men in a pub. He was different from when she saw him last; he was smartly dressed in a light-grey plaid jacket and jodhpurs, a tan tie and primrose shirt. His face was still a little ruddy but looking healthier. He held his five-foot eight-inch figure straight and upright which gave him a proud and confident air. She looked around not wanting Donald to think she was staring at him. There were just two other women in the room as well as small groups of men chatting. Hanging in the sheaths of cigarette smoke up in the wooden beams were tankards of all description; some Toby jugs others earthenware glazed chocolate brown. There were small brass lamps and copper plates and trinket-like metal-ware. She turned back to the bar and made a quick decision and that was, to hell with conventional etiquette. She'd pretended she hadn't noticed Donald. She walked up to the bar and the barman, who was dressed somewhat like a butler, acknowledged her and smiled.

'Can I get you something, madam?'

'I'd like a glass of red wine please,' she said positively.

Something familiar must have sounded in Donald's mind for he instinctively turned and glanced at the woman at the bar. He turned away momentarily then glanced again.

'Anna isn't it?' Donald asked in a polite manner, his voice weak and husky.

'Yes, that's right, I wasn't sure if it was you Donald. How are you?'

'I'm feeling on top of the world today; I've had a pleasant ride in a wonderful sunny countryside. And you, how are you Anna?'

'I'm getting along, thank you.'

'What are you doing up here?'

I'm having a day out with my children, my young son saw you ride up and thought you were a cowboy, I was fairly certain it was you so I came over out of curiosity.'

'Ah, and I'm glad you did.' He turned to the man he had been talking to. 'Excuse me Ted I haven't seen this lady for quite some time.' The man nodded his assent as Donald made his way to Anna's side. 'It's nice to see you again Anna. How are things with you really?'

'I haven't interrupted you and your friend, have I?'

'No, no, he's just a man I say hello to and have a brief chat. You're keeping all right?.'

'I'm managing,' she said as the barman came with Anna's drink. She had her purse out ready to pay, but Donald brushed her hand to the side.

350

I'll get that Eddie, and make another one of those for Anna and a fresh pint and double rum for me. We'll have them at the table by the window. Come Anna, I could do with a soft chair and good company.'

They sat on the small leather-padded chairs and looked out at the people in the field opposite; children chasing one another, women laughing, a few men drinking and chatting under a tree. There were bicycles there too, resting against a stone wall, the owners squatting nearby drinking from soft-drinks from bottles and munching a packed-lunch meals.

'They picked a nice day for an outing,' said Donald.

'Yes. I wish I could be as enthusiastic as them and enjoy such trivialities.'

Donald turned his head away from the window and looked fixedly at her. 'Anna, I asked you how you were, but I see by your wan face you're not too well. But having said that, you are looking beautiful, you really are.'

'Anyone would look beautiful after seeing me tramping around the country.'

'You look quite serene in that dress.'

'That's enough flattery, Donald.'

'Sorry. Change of subject, what have you been doing for the last year?'

'I've been working very hard lately and sleep has been difficult at nights.'

'You've got a difficult job, or other worries?'

'Oh things pile up, but let us not talk about it.'

'You're still not a happy women, then? You've got to let the past go Anna. Look to the future.'

Anna smirked at him. 'I wonder how many people have said that to me over the years.'

'Why did you come over here to me? Did a twinge of light-heartedness come over you?'

'Who said I came over to see you? As I said it was curiosity…and an excuse for a drink.'

'Oh you've hurt my feeling now,' he said, nudging her elbow. 'I thought you had a soft spot for me.'

'I think you're a nice man Donald. I admit, I was grateful to my young son when he pointed you out, and if I make you glad to see me, then I take it as a compliment—cheers,' she said as she raised her glass of wine and drank it down.

He lifted his pint and reciprocated her toast.'

'How many children have you brought into the world?'

Anna gave him a mind-your-own-business look, and didn't answer but asked him the same question. 'How many children have you got?'

Donald stared into space for a time then turned to Anna. 'None, I wish I'd had an opportunity to have children. If there's one thing I'm sorry about it's not having children. I'm afraid I'm a confirmed bachelor, I've never known a woman that way.'

Anna looked surprised at him, for he was quite attractive.' You're the second benevolent man I've met in life who has turned out to be a bachelor. Don't you like women?'

'Goodness me Anna, you've got the wrong end of the stick my girl. I'm one of them old-fashioned bachelors who have never found the right woman.'

'Maybe it's not too late. You've still got your wits about you.'

'You think so?'

'I said so. It seems you've got everything else you need; smallholding, independence, probably well-off financially...'

'Financially I suppose I can't complain, but I sometimes feel at a loose-end now that I've sold my smallholding. It got too much for me, but now I'm at the other extreme, needing to find something interesting to do. You can only ride a horse for so long, you know.'

'You've sold your property?'

'It had a bad effect on my weak chest. Twenty-five years I worked at it; up in the morning milking the cows, feeding the pigs, tending my allotment. In my youth I wanted to be free from the world of authority. It was fine when I was young but it's too much for a man of my age.'

'Not knowing your age I couldn't judge one way or another.'

'Ah you're fishing Anna. I don't mind telling you I'm fifty-two. I won't ask your age.'

'I wouldn't tell you if you did.'

352

Donald laughed quietly which caused a slight cough. He pulled out his handkerchief and patted his mouth. 'And I don't blame you.'

'You've given up the pipe, I imagine. Have you seen a doctor lately?'

'Don't believe in them, and I haven't given up my pipe.'

'More fool you.'

Eddie came over with the fresh drinks Donald had ordered earlier. 'There you are Donald,

`One wine one pint and your rum—on the bill?'

'Thank you Eddie, the bill will be fine.'

'Just give me the nod when you're ready for another.'

Donald picked up his double rum and drank it in one gulp, relaxed back into the burgundy soft padding of the chair and gave Anna a warm smile. 'That's my medicine, I'll be fine now. I don't know what it is about you Anna, but I felt it when we first met.'

'Felt what?' she asked with a tone of suspicion.

'I'm at ease with you, as I was in the Cad-Ivor; I feel we have something in common.'

She sighed with relief thinking he might have had some furtive thoughts about her. 'I must admit I like you Donald, but at the moment the only thing we have in common is an attraction to alcohol. And I think it's doing you well because you're looking a lot healthier now that you're a man of leisure.'

'It must be the cooking Eddie's wife conjures up.'

'You come here every day for you food?'

'I live here; I'm the perpetual guest. It's tolerable in the summer, but a hotel room in the winter gets boring and claustrophobic.'

'It must be expensive.' she remarked. 'Sorry it's your choice, none of my business.'

'I can afford the cost, but it gets lonely in the dark nights. I've been wandering around the villages looking for cottage or a suitable place to buy, but then, I'd still be on my own.'

Anna's mind began to think of a way out for him, and the way she figured was lodging with someone. That someone could be me, she thought.

'Donald, I don't know if you've been to Dowlais a great deal, but there are places there that you can lodge and have company.'

'Oh no, I couldn't lodge with strangers. I'm an independent type who's very particular about the company I keep.'

'And what company do you mix with. Aristocracy?' she said with irony.

'No, no, of course not, but I have heard tales about the doss houses and the rough kind of people that frequent those streets.'

'I've heard that farmers are a mean lot, but I don't believe all I hear.'

'Point taken, but I'm sure you know what I meant.'

'I know of a nice lady who has a spare room and is looking for a lodger of your class.'

'What, a lady on her own?'

'She has a young child, but he's in school most of the day and no trouble.'

Donald was mildly shocked. 'You Anna?'

'Why not, I have a nice house and the spare room is furnished, even if I do say so myself. I have a lovely respectable couple living next door to me and my house is near the town centre.'

'You'd have me lodging in the same house as yourself and a child with no husband present?'

'If you're going to be puritanical forget it.'

'I was thinking of your good name, not of myself. For me it would be a dream come true.'

'Lots of widows take in lodgers to help their finances, and there are lots of widows in Dowlais. To be honest I need the income.'

Donald's eyes widened and a smile spread over his shiny country face. 'It' a dream of an idea, and I will pay a good rent to you.'

Anna offered her hand to shake and Donald accepted it enthusiastically. Then he looked up for the barman. 'Eddie, would you come over here for a minute please,'

Anna looked worried and wondered what Donald was up to.

Eddie came over, 'Two of the same?'

'Yes please Eddie. And I'm afraid I will have to give you notice of my leaving.'

Eddie appeared shocked. 'You're leaving? My wife will be redundant if you go.'

'I'm sure she'll have plenty to do and will look forward to less work. 'I'm going to lodge with Anna and her family in Dowlais.'

'What about Nellie?'

'Will you look after her for me? I'll see you all right.'

'She's been in my stable since you retired, I can't see her wanting to go anywhere else.'

'Thank you my friend. She's a faithful horse. Now we'll have those drinks.'

Forty Six

Donald settled in quickly and easily as though it was part of predestination he had expected. His nightly habit, after saying goodnight to Anna and going to his room, was to sit up in bed and have a good measure of rum and then slide under the blankets. As the weeks wore on he quickly made a friend of Daniel and even took him to school at times when Hannah was unable to attend through minor illness such as a heavy cold or flu. He adored the boy and was delighted to think that he could take the place of his father, though Daniel took everything in his stride having had Mary as his guardian for a lengthy time, and actually preferred the company of Hannah at school times. Anna explained to Donald that she had a little girl living with foster parents and had heard nothing from the parents since Cerys was taken away. She related the story of her late history and gained the sympathy of Donald. He offered to take Anna to see Cerys, but Anna declined saying it's too early, she did not feel she could take on the responsibility of the child until she is financially better off. Donald paid for his lodgings but it was not near enough for Anna to give up work.

However, Donald got into the role of preparing a meal for Anna when she finished work and settling down in the cosiness of her living room. Each evening they would enjoy a bottle of wine together, sometimes two, after Daniel had gone to bed. Furthermore Donald was prepared to allow Anna out a couple of evenings a week while he remained at home with the boy. He was of the opinion that Anna's laborious employment was such that she had to have a break from the house or lose her health both physically and mentally. After a few months of Anna being on her best behaviour and proving that she was a caring mother, hard-working, devoted to her son and coming home exhausted, it became obvious to Donald that her occupation was far too low for her station in life. Donald was an honourable man who was growing very fond of his landlady and beginning to feel quite like a family man. With those thoughts and the harrowing scene each time Anna came through the door after work, fatigued and pale, he had made up his mind on what he wanted out of life.

Having a drink one evening Donald asserted himself. It was nearing Christmas, the colourful decorations were draped around the walls and ceiling and a Christmas tree stood in the corner covered in small toys, trinkets and paper lanterns they had made. Daniel had been taken to bed reluctantly, dreaming of yuletide presents. Anna and Donald sat quietly in separate easy chairs near the glowing fire, snug and warm. Donald gazed at Anna with some trepidation, for what he was about to offer Anna may or may not be greeted with approval. The short time they had been lodger and landlady had taught him that Anna was indeed a woman of strong beliefs and opinions. But also that she appreciated his help and friendship. She could put him down or raise him up it all depended on the mood at the time. Nevertheless he had to speak his piece.

'Anna, would you mind if I gave some relevant opinions of our lives?'

She sunk into her leather-padded chair contentedly and sipped claret. 'Make whatever conversation you want Donald, but don't expect me to share your opinions. You should know by now I have a mind of my own.'

'If strangers should come into the house unexpected right now what conclusion would they arrive at seeing us sitting here drinking?'

'Knowing the small-minded chapelgoers around here they'd condemn us to hell.'

'No they would not. Being strangers they would automatically see us as man and wife.'

'Right, but when they found out we were not, they'd condemn us to an after-life of fire, brimstone and damnation.'

'And what would they say if I told them I was a lodger and you were a poor widow who worked your fingers to the bone washing dishes in a café?'

'What is all this coming to Donald, I'm trying to enjoy this wine.'

'They'd say why don't you marry the woman and make it legal, even though we are quite innocent of their suspicions.'

'I don't care what people think.'

'Well I do. I'm very fond of you Anna, no I'm more than fond of you, I want you for my wife Anna and I won't take no for answer.'

Anna shot up spilling a little of her drink. 'Are you serious, or has the wine gone to your senses?'

'Why shouldn't we be man and wife? Thinking logically and you being a logical woman, we are quite compatible; I'm in need of a lasting friendship and you're in need of financial security. So it seems a solution we both need. You find me repulsive of course, or grossly unattractive.'

Anna smiled at Donald's self-deprecation. 'You know I find our little arrangement very satisfactory, and you're a lovely man, but would being married turn things sour?'

'I don't see why it should.'

'You've only known me a relatively short time Donald. I'll be honest with you. There are certain areas of this town where people don't have a high opinion of me. Now I don't care what little minds conjure up, but I think enough of you not to have you hurt.'

'I'll be hurt if you turn me down. If you did accept me only one demand I'd make on you.'

'And that is?'

'I insist you give up that obnoxious job and be a respectable housewife.'

Anna's eyes glazed over at the prospect and she felt her heart well up. She knew that marriage would give her a new life again and be an independent woman. She looked at Donald with emotions rising up in her.

'Donald, have you thought about this deeply enough? Giving up work would mean I'd need more money.'

'It's been on my mind for weeks, money is no object. I'd be very generous as a husband.'

'If you're absolutely sure you want me Donald, I'll be your wife.'

His face lit up with a broad smile. 'I shall look after you and Daniel. We'll fight for the return of Cerys as well.'

'One thing at a time, I don't think Cerys would want to come back. Leave that for the future.'

'Whatever you say Anna, whatever you say.'

She finished her glass of wine with a distant thoughts running across her mind. 'The New Year, Donald, we'll wait a couple of months for you to be sure of your decision.'

'I know what I want, Anna, it's you must be sure. But 'I'll wait a couple of months.'

She clasped the bottle from the side-table and filled her glass, then topped up Donald's. Replacing the bottle on the table she offered her glass to Donald, he held his out and the glasses clinked with agreement.

'To future happiness,' he said.

'To a successful unity,' she replied.

Forty Seven

It was a great relief to Anna when she finished working at the café. It was not so much the exhausting fatigues that hurt her for she was aware that there were people of all classes who might work themselves into bad health. No, it was the stigma of being a skivvy, a dishwasher who had a poor position in life and little respect. When John was alive she had held her head high and proud, believing she was part of a level of a class of people that was looked up to. She could not believe a dishwasher had the right to be proud even though the morals of such a worker might be an exemplar of morality. Morality to Anna was having class distinction; the higher in society, the purer she felt. And now that Donald had made her his wife with all his worldly goods, which in his case was money in the bank, she felt secure. It was money Donald shared with Anna by giving her a generous monthly allowance for housekeeping and leisure activities, even little Daniel had weekly pocket money to spend and Hannah, on her visits, had her share too. However many times she declared she didn`t care what other people said about her, the fact was she wanted a position where other people could show her respect.

Anna's heart lifted higher and higher as time passed, for she was regaining her air of respectability and buying clothes that was deemed to be the latest fashion. The consummation of the marriage had lifted Donald's life to a new height, not just for the warmth of a woman but also for the dream he had believed would never come true. And later, when she told him she was with child, he was certain his life could not get better. He had his evenings out with friends he had made in the men-only Constitutional Club whilst Anna remained at home, and she in turn had her nights out with people she mixed with. At such times Donald carried out the child-minding duty and stayed at home. On Saturday nights they would go out together and catch a tram to Merthyr for an evening of entertainment, Mary next door would look after Daniel for it was just for a couple of hours. Donald would see to it that she was rewarded for her caring ways; it was a welcome recompense to Mary now that her debilitated husband was out of work.

Twelve months into the marriage Anna gave birth to a baby girl and named her Rachael. Daniel was a little nervous at first for he had a vague recollection of a baby girl who had been taken away. However, as time went by he soon got to like the newcomer and was amused by the antics of his sister. Anna gave the order to Donald that he should take his pipe and smoke it where it would not bother the baby, for he used to take deep pulls at it, breathe it in deeply and blow a cloud of acrid fumes through the room, doing his chest no good at all. The safety of his daughter was paramount and he gave up smoking, such was his love for the little girl. It was too late for his health, however, for his lungs were already in a bad way and worn, and his bouts of coughing were chronic during the nights and he sometimes remained in bed until noon.

Rachael grew into a beautiful five-year-old giving Donald great pleasure in seeing her look so pretty in the new dresses he bought for her. At first Hannah came to see the child often, nursed and fed her and entertained her dancing the Charleston competently, to the astonishment of her mother and Donald. The teenager was growing up and getting into the swing of modern music and mixing with others of both genders. It made her mother realize how time was passing so quickly. However, Hannah wanting to be with her friends more, and feeling a sense she was no longer needed, her visits became less frequent and she finally stopped calling on her mother and stepsiblings. Later she met a man three years her senior and fell in love. At first the relationship was looked upon with some scepticism. However the relevant families could see that seventeen-year-old Hannah and her young man were deeply in love and were allowed to wed.

One morning in June 1926, Anna went upstairs with a cup of tea and a biscuit (for Donald would not eat anything substantial) to call him and help him out of bed. He refused the beverage and biscuit and tried to get up, but his face turned a deathly paleness and he fell back on to the pillow gasping for breath. The gurgling in his throat shocked Anna. She stood over him holding his shoulders.

'Donald I'm going for the doctor whether you want him or not,' she said. 'This aversion you have for the medical world is ridiculous.'

'Anna, listen.'

'You won't change my mind.'

'I've never been able to,' he said, with a voice hardly above a whisper. 'But let me tell you what I'd like you to know and then you can do what you want.'

There's no time for talk.'

With intermittent words his breath would allow, his ghostly utterances gave her an account of his happiness during the short time he had known her.

'Anna, my dear Anna,' he said, weakly. 'In my younger days I didn't realize how lonely I was. Marrying you has made my life worthwhile. I know you didn't have the love for me as I had for you, but we've had a glorious time and understood each other's needs. I have made a will and left...' his breath was fading, his words coming in gentle gasps. 'I have shared what little money I have left between Rachael, Daniel and you, with amounts I feel is fair and just...' He said no more, but gave out three diminuendo breaths and passed away.

It was three weeks after the funeral when Anna began to relapse into her old ways of drinking too much and staying out late. Donald had left money to all three of them, but not enough for her lifestyle, Rachael was to have the bulk of it when she turned twenty-one. However, Rachael's share was eight hundred pounds and gaining interest, Daniel's though much less, should be given to him at the same age, and Anna inherited just 150 pounds. This made her bitter and she began to feel sorry for herself, which put her on the road to selfishness. Twelve-year-old Daniel would often take on the role of guardian and look after Rachael, but Anna knew that the reliable Mary would always be on hand if the children should need help. Hannah realized what was happening and would call in when she could to help her stepsiblings. But that did not stop the gossip and condemnation of Anna by her neighbours and those who knew her from past times, such as Emlyn and his family.

Daniel tolerated his boring existence and tiresome home life for a couple more years until he became disillusioned. He had left school, had no money and was unable to get a job because of the advancing recession getting deeper and deeper and the steelworks losing orders. Men lost their jobs and were living on subsistence. Areas of the works were closed down and demolished. The depression had a bad effect on Daniel. He was a healthy sturdy young lad who followed his father's build and characteristics and would not waste his time in a dying industry. He had determination on his young rugged face and would go out in the daytime walking the streets seeing gangs of flat-capped untidy men on street corners looking miserable with hands in their empty pockets and cursing the state of the times. The steelworks closing down had an adverse effect on other industries; very little coal was required from the collieries or stone from the quarries, which meant jobs from all quarters of these industries, were decreasing rapidly. Rachael was continually pleading with her mother to stay at home more often and stop drinking, but all her desperate entreaties fell on callous deaf ears. Daniel didn't want to leave her alone but he could see no hope for himself by remaining in Dowlais. He went next door and told Mary of his worries explaining he didn't know what to do. Mary told him to sit down and then she went into the kitchen and reached up for a round tin on a shelf. She took out a bundle of papers and thumbed through them until she found the address of Owen and Caroline.

'Do you remember me telling you about your younger sister who was adopted?'

'My uncle Owen you told me. I think I remember but I can't picture him. Why didn't he take me as well as Cerys?'

'He did offer, but you preferred to stay with your mother and me.'

Daniel thought about it but couldn't remember. 'I wonder what I'd be doing now if I had agreed to go,' he mused. 'I think I made a bad decision.'

'You were only four Daniel, and I was very proud when you said you'd prefer to stay.'

'Not my mother?'

364

'Well, she was inconvenienced at the time. Anyway, if you are intent on leaving Dowlais it's best you go to somebody who is family. Leave Rachael to me, I'll explain things to her and take her under my wing until she is old enough to take care of herself.'

'If it wasn't for Rachael I would have gone last year, but she pleaded for me to stay. I just couldn't leave her on her own.'

Mary caught his hand and pressed some money in it holding him firmly. 'Daniel, here are five pounds. It won't last you long so spend it wisely. Now make your way to your uncle Owen and aunty Caroline. I'm sure they will take you in and find some agricultural work for you.'

'I can't take your money Mary. You'll need it for yourself and Bill.'

'Take it I'm telling you, we'll manage all right. You can pay me back when possible.' She pulled the lad to his feet and turned him to the door. 'I want no arguments. Now go and pack whatever you can in a bag. Just write a note to say you are leaving to find a job elsewhere, but don't say where. Go on; make a new life for yourself in a healthy environment. The steelworks and coalmines of Dowlais are in bad shape.'

He gave her a hug. 'I'll go, but I'll come in to see you when I'm ready to say goodbye.'

'You will not. You'll say goodbye now. Write to me when you've settled.' She hugged him and kissed him on the cheek. 'Off you go now, and send Rachael into me before you begin your packing; I want to tell her of your leaving, so don't say a word, just go after she's come to me.'

Daniel went into the street. He turned, but Mary had closed the door behind him for she didn't want to him to see the tears roll down her cheeks.

Forty Eight

Anna was convinced that Rachael had been keeping secrets from her in a sibling conspiracy. In a foul temper she paced back and fore in the living room, screwing up the note in her hand and yelling at her daughter.

'You devious little brat,' she screamed. 'How could you do this to me?'

'I didn't know myself until you told me,' defended Rachael, whimpering, pain on her wan face. 'Daniel told me to go and see Auntie Mary. That's the last time I saw him.'

'You liar, you sly little liar, you must have known. He's been planning it for weeks, no doubt.'

'I didn't know…I didn't know…I'm just as shocked as you.'

'You must have known something. I know the two of you too well, my girl. I've heard you talking about me after I've had a few hard-earned drinks.' She grabbed Rachael by the shoulders and shook her violently. 'Why do you want to hurt me? You Judas! That's what you are. You'd crucify me if you could.'

Rachael broke away and collapsed on the settee crying hysterically and thumping the cushions. She began shrieking. 'I didn't know…I didn't know. I love Daniel…I hate you…I hate you…Oh God in Heaven…help me.'

So strident and dramatic was the scene it shocked Anna into silence. Rachael's plea for help suddenly convinced her she had wronged her daughter. Anna had never seen her in such a pitiful state before. She went to Rachael, breathless after the tirade, and knelt at her side.

'It's all right my love, I'm sorry. It was a big shock to me when I found his note.'

Rachael, glassy eyed and shaking from the trauma, turned her head and gave her mother a hard stare. The ten-year-old brushed her fair hair from her eyes and calmed herself.

'I didn't mean what I said…but…well I want you home more often Mam. I don't want to come home from school to an empty house I can't face it, now that Daniel not here.'

'You talk as though he's dead, girl. He'll be back. When he realizes how hard it is out there in the industrial wilderness he'll come bleating like a lost lamb, you'll see. Besides, the way you talk you'll have people thinking I'm never at home.'

'You're out more than you're in.'

'Oh, I see, you don't care if I'm in an empty house all day.'

'You can go out shopping in the daytime, can't you?' It's in the nights I'll be lonely.'

'I'll stay in with you, don't you worry… But I expect Mary will stay with you when I've got to go out.'

'You don't have to go out at nights.'

'Don't be stupid Rachael. I've got to have some leisure time. You like Mary, don't you?'

'I like to have a mother.'

'You're hurting me Rachael. I can't cope with your attitude. I was with foster parents at your age: chapel twice a day and three times on Sunday, forced to study the Bible by a dominant chauvinist, self-righteous bully of a man, day in day out for twelve tortuous years. I had to run errands and do my share of shopping. You should be grateful you have a mother at your side. You should be grateful you have a mother to look after; privileged you are, privileged my girl. I wish I was young and innocent again, just like you.'

Rachael had something to say but she didn't know if her spirit would give her the courage to utter the words. Her mother's head was bowed looking to the floor. She was dressed in a black silky blouse that had thin lacework embroidered on it and a black skirt to match. It was a colour that had long made Rachael feel nauseous. Her mother had bought nothing but black for the past five years. Rachael had brought the peculiar practice to her mother's attention over a year ago, but Anna had told her to mind her own business and that she felt good in black, and that it was the custom for widows to wear black for as long as they wanted. Rachael thoughts suddenly made her burst out.

'Pathetic!'

Anna jerked her head up. 'What? What's pathetic?'

'That's the word that's in favour today with the girls at school. The work situation is pathetic, Dowlais is pathetic and you're pathetic, and I don't blame Daniel for running off. Go out if you want, as often as you want. Mary is more of a mother than you, anyway.'

Anna shot to her feet. 'I don't believe you could say such a cruel thing.' She raised her hand and slapped Rachael across the face. The girl screamed and ran upstairs to her room.

She lay there sobbing for some time until the pain of the quarrel subsided. Going to the window she looked out sadly and thoughtfully. A couple of smoke stacks had been demolished and those remaining blew out no fumes. The mills and workshops had fallen silent and the stagnant ugliness of her surroundings spread an aura of depression. Even the arch made out of coal looked sad with some of its coal blocks missing and many others chipped and broken, and the sculptured dram had been dismantled for safety. Her thoughts turned to Daniel. She understood his reasons for escaping, but why didn't he take me with him, she thought. Yes, I should have packed a bag and gone. Then she turned away from the window and whispered to herself. 'Another few years Daniel and I'll be on your trail.'

Nothing was going right for Anna. The following day Hannah called briefly to let her mother know that Emrys had joined the Army. All she could say was: 'The silly boy, he's not sixteen yet. He must have lied about his age. What on earth is the matter with my children?'

But it was the shock of Rachael's censure that left a deep pain in Anna's heart. So much that she wanted to prove to her daughter that she could be in complete control of herself. As the months rolled on Rachael could see the change in her mother and the relationship between them improved. And though Anna took a night off now and again, and had her secret bottle or two hidden away, she had the strength and resolve to carry on for almost a year. As time progressed her nights out became more frequent for she felt the house was becoming a prison. Furthermore, the money Donald had left her ran out. It was essential that she find a job. She had begun her search months earlier when she realized the situation arising, and wanted a suitable occupation without success. She was looking for a position that Rachael would approve of and be proud of her mother. But Anna wasn't as smart in appearance or looks as she used to be. She did not impress her interviewers when she sought positions such as teacher's help or waitress in the better hotels in Dowlais and Merthyr. She lowered her expectations. Having had much experience in many a public house and believing her best chances of a job would be behind a bar serving drinks, she hoped to find such a job in a respectable establishment. In her mind was the image of Rachael, who was doing well with her lessons at Dowlais Central School and had been commended for her diligence, thus making her quite a lady in Anna's eyes. She could not face Rachael if a respectable job could not be found. Such a position had arisen in the Clarence Hotel near Rachael's school. It was a small hotel, but nevertheless its sign outside confirmed it was a hotel, even though it was more of a place for respectable lodgers who couldn't afford one of the smarter hotels. The barmaid had finished on ill health and the proprietor was looking for an experienced person to work behind the bar and fill in with the chores. Anna, being a past paying customer had got to know the owner, and went to see the man she knew as Patrick. At first Patrick eyed her up and down with a wry smile indicating that she wasn't the beauty she used to be, but he knew she could do the job. What's more he needed someone right away. He told her she would have to brush up her appearance, that he didn't mind a buxom barmaid behind the bar but one dressed in outdated black attire he could not accept. She agreed immediately and told him of the desperate situation she was in, that she had a young daughter at school and the money her husband had left her no longer existed. He sympathized with her and told her she would have to start that evening, as immediate assistance was required. She thanked him and hurried home. Entering the house she called out to her daughter.

'Rachael I'm home and I've got some good news.'

Rachael was stretched out on the settee reading a book. She had developed into a fragile young girl both physically and emotionally. She sat up and folded the book and placed it on the settee. 'What kind of news?' she asked, alarm in her voice.

'Don't give me that worried look. I've got a job in the Clarence Hotel.

Rachael stared at her speechless for a time, her delicate pale face full of accusation. The years of her mother's inconsistency and embarrassing conduct had made her nervous and sceptical about anything her mother did. Her mother's enthusiasm usually indicated she was indulging in something that profited her personally and gave Rachael something more to worry about. At school she overheard things concerning her mother's past, things that would be confirmed tenderly by Hannah when she visited.

'Oh Mam, what have you done? Serving behind a bar I expect, where the drinkers can leer and be crude to you.'

Anna sat down at her side. 'I shall be a waitress serving food and wearing a smart uniform at the evening meals. I shall only go behind the bar to take drinks to the clientele when required.'

Rachael was exasperated. 'I've seen them come and go when I come home from school. Some of them look quite rough to me.'

'Don't judge them all to be the same Rachael, we have no money, and this job is a respectable one. I'll be glad when you're twenty one and get your hands on the money you father put in trust for you.'

'So will I. I'll be able to afford to get away from Dowlais and live in a bigger and better town.'

'You don't seem to include me in those plans.'

'Mam, wherever you go it will be the same. You'll never change.'

'I've improved, haven't I?'

'I don't know have you? I'm in the senior girls' school now and I can remember the first day you took me to the infants, you had the smell of drink on you then, and you have now.'

I haven't bought a drink all day.'

'You have a way of telling the truth but not the whole truth. You've had a few bought for you, can you deny that?'

'You're too clever for your own good, my girl.' That's when Anna began to weep. 'I thought you'd be happy for me. I'm trying to do my best and be a good mother to you.'

'I know you've tried hard Mam, and I know you can't help it. But I can't stand being the joke of the school. They don't say it but they have that sly appearance about them.'

Anna became agitated. She wiped her tears away. 'Who's saying things about me? What are they saying?'

'I don't know. What I do know is that I'm afraid to make friends with anyone because I can't trust them to be true friends, they just patronize me. I'd hate it if they should feel sorry for me. Anyway, you take your job Mam and be happy', she said reconciling herself to the situation with a disinterested tone. 'Who am I to stop you when we are in such financial difficulties? 'I'm sorry if I didn't show enthusiasm.'

'We need the money badly love.'

'I know.' Rachael relented and sighed hopelessly. 'I'll hold my head up high and think, to hell with them all.'

Anna gave a pretentious gasp. 'Rachael, I've not heard you speak that word before.'

'You'll be surprised what new words you can pick up at school.'

'So you'll be proud of me working as a waitress in a hotel, will you?'

'I suppose so, at least it sounds good.'

'Good girl, good girl.'

The sun had set on a fine evening in August and Anna had been accepted after working the three months trial period and was now a regular behind the bar. She was feeling particularly pleased with herself, the past week had been a very pleasant at the hotel. The guests had been generous with their genial barmaid. They would offer her drinks, which she would refuse stating that the gaffer would not allow her to drink on duty. But she could accept the price of a drink and use it when she was off duty. The rule arose after she had got into an argument some weeks earlier with a "self-righteous" customer who verbally abused her for being a suffragette, she claimed. Anna had been accepting drinks on that night and lost control of her emotions. It was the customer who was in the wrong, but Patrick was aware she could have controlled herself had she not been drinking. Her well-earned reward, as she called the gratuities, should be honoured by using the money as it was intended, was her philosophy. So it was to be a good night out after a profitable week.

She had a couple of gins at the Canford Inn in Upper Union Street but found it quiet and boring, so she made her way down Horse Street, the dark terraced road that sloped down to the High Street. A couple of men came out of The Bute billiard hall and eyed her up with menace as though she shouldn't be walking there, but a cold look and a scowl on her face proved to be an adequate deterrent. She ordered a stout in the Forge and Hammer where there were no women and very few men. The industrial depression was having an adverse effect on the pubs, and many were closing down. Sitting alone in a corner brought the images back of Emlyn when he used to take her there. It used to be crowded and smoky and had a warm atmosphere. She asked the barman did he know Emlyn, but he was comparatively new there and couldn't help her. She left and avoided the Rolling Mill, for it still had bad memories for her. After waiting at the junction of High Street for a tram to pass she crossed the road and made her way along the narrow pavement down towards the Pelican. To her left was a stone wall that was five feet in height at the pavement but dropped twenty feet down the other side to the silent mills of the Goat Mill Road; another reminder of the devastation the town was experiencing. But across the road the Victoria cinema must have been showing a good film as a queue began to grow there. And further up on the opposite side were pubs, houses and shops. A shaft of light hit the pavement as The Kings Head doors burst open and a couple came out laughing and reeling on the pavement, evoking looks of disgust from pedestrians. Anna turned and smiled with amusement. There's a little life left in the old place, she thought. But where they get the money from I don`t know.

The black facade of The Pelican had always been intriguing to her but she never ventured through its doors. Walls, drainpipes, window frames, doors, were all dull black. The only bit of white was a fading pelican painted on a creaking, swinging board above the door. The frosted windows either side of the open door had "Bar" imprinted on the left window and "Lounge" on the right. Feeling in a daring mood she pushed the squeaking heavy panelled inner door and entered. Tobacco smoke gave the room a hazy atmosphere. A picture had recently been removed from the wall leaving a cream rectangular shape, but the rest of décor was veneered with nicotine. The mirror behind the bar had a brown film on it giving to those who looked into it the impression they were sun-tanned. The L-shaped room had an oak panelled bar with half a dozen regulars leaning on it. Some looked into their pints thoughtfully. One man puffed at his pipe looking through the haze that exuded from it, others turned and gave Anna a curious glance. There were another dozen raucous drinkers of mixed gender sitting around the room at wooden tables, smoking, laughing, shouting, and swearing. Anna turned to the bar straight into the face of the middle-aged barman staring at her. The thin-faced man, dark shaven and black glaring eyes didn't intimidate her. She did, as a gesture of defiance; screw up her face at the stained tea towel he wiped his hands in.

'I haven't got all night,' he said.

'You haven't got much at all in here except a motley crew.'

'Do you want a drink or don't you?'

'I'll have a half of brown stout.'

As he turned away, heaviness came into her heart. Here I am, she thought, middle-aged, among strangers and not one has an eye for me; I'm down among commoners and boozers in a stinking pub.

The barman banged her glass of stout on the counter.

She paid him, picked up her drink and walked around the bar. As she eyed up the chattering groups, a noisy gravel-voice sounded strongly over the rest, talking of a familiar subject:

'When I was working in the engine house I kept everybody on their feet, including the gaffers. They knew where they stood when I was around. Oh yes I was one of the highest earners in those days.' He went quiet as he lifted his pint and took a drink, and then began where he left off. 'My engines worked night and day and I kept them running with skill and maintenance...'

The engine house, the engine house, echoed in Anna's brain. She gingerly manoeuvred her way around the bar avoiding body contact and inspected the old gravel-voice. She stood at the table transfixed at the drinker before her. He was a big man but old with thick untidy grey hair almost covering his eyes, and a beard and moustache to match. His protruding, purple bulbous nose made him look like a big shaggy dog. Anna began shaking, it couldn't be him, he's disgusting and crude. He looks old enough, and if he turns out to be my father, I'll leave and forget he ever existed. He suddenly looked up and lowered his bushy eyebrows at Anna.

'Who are you looking at, woman?'

'I heard you talk about the engine house.'

'What of it?'

'I knew a man who worked there years ago, I wondered if you knew him.'

'I knew everyone who worked there from 1877 to 1925. I doubt if you were born then.'

She tested him. 'I was born in 1879 in a place called Hay, my mother came from Brecon.'

'So what?'

There was no shock or indication on the man's face. If he was her father he either forgot about his past or wasn't the man she had been looking for all those years.

'Did you know a man called Tegwyn Morgan?'

The man remained speechless for a time, but his eyes burned into Anna's face. 'Who's asking?' he demanded.

Anna drank half of her brown stout and let him wait for the answer. 'I don't intend to let the whole sordid pub know my business.'

'You lot, clear off and leave this corner of mine to me and the lady.'

He obviously had a fearful reputation for those who had been his audience quickly scuttled to the other end of the room.

'Sit down woman and tell me your story.'

Anna sat. 'Well, did you know Tegwyn Morgan?'

'Aye, I knew him. He was a thoroughbred in these parts just like me, not mongrels like this lot.' He stared around the room so that Anna knew who he was referring to. Pure Welsh runs through our blood just like old Tegwyn. '

'You're not him then?'

'If you knew him you'd know that I'm not him. What's your game, woman?'

Anna was relieved, and then snarled at the man. 'I'm his daughter. I don't know whether he's alive or dead. I never met him. He deserted me and my mother when I was born.'

'Good God, so that's why he took off without telling anyone.'

'Do you know if he's alive, or his whereabouts?'

'He was in a strange mood for weeks, and then he said to me one day, "I've done a terrible deed." And what deed is so terrible I asked him. "I'm ashamed to say," he said. But you see, both of us were only twenty-one at the time, and we had a keen eye for the ladies, and the ladies weren't shy of us, oh no, those were the times we loved. '

'Is he still alive?'

The man was living in the past just then and couldn't stop reminiscing. 'He could have made a factory manager could Tegwyn. Do you know he was a gaffer at the age of twenty? He was hardly out of his apprenticeship when they put him in charge of the fitting section. He was a management man. And then he disappeared.'

'Is he still alive, for God's sake?'

'Oh he's alive all right, but where he is nobody knows. Have you heard of the Scarlet Pimpernel? Well that's old Teg.'

'How do you know he's still alive?'

'Because he's not dead. Whenever an ex-steelworker dies everybody in the industry gets to know, whether he's here or on the moon.'

'Do you think he's still in Wales?'

He wouldn't go anywhere else. As I said, he's a thoroughbred just like me.'

Anna stood up. 'Thank you for your help,' she said and walked away

The man stroked his beard as he watched her make her way to the front door. 'Well, well, Tegwyn's daughter. She must be getting on herself.'

Outside Anna's mind was in turmoil. She had given up hope finding her father and she wondered was this just another trick of fate giving her false hopes. She looked up and down the road, a little further down was the White Lion, and further still, up the steps, stood the Dowlais Inn. The pubs she had frequented years before and asked questions. She decided to call in at the White Lion. There she had a few drinks, but the place was quiet except for a few men and a garrulous stout lady with rosy jowls and thick ruby lips who, uninvited, came and sat by Anna. The ample eye makeup she had plastered on and the long fingernails painted the same colour as her lipstick, amazed Anna. She assumed that Anna would like to hear her life story. The excess make up and stench of cheap perfume Anna found nauseating, and the words of the woman were heavy on her ears. But Anna could not ignore the most peculiar strong masculine voice the woman had and the lilt in her speech. She talked about herself and the times she worked the coalface in drift mines, digging away with pick and shovel, of a daughter she had living in London as a high society professional, of the times she could drink any man under the table, and on and on from one subject to another. At intervals she would take a gulp form her pint of ale and then begin her narrative again. Had Anna been more discerning and not preoccupied from her conversation in the Pelican, she would have realized it was a transvestite who had sat by her. When Anna did take notice of her and realized it was a man, she made an excuse to go and made her way to the Dowlais Inn.

As she neared the inn she could hear the singing of Calon Lan floating through the summer air. She walked into a crowded room just as the pianist came to the end of the song. It was a large room full of happy revellers, noisy, smoky and stuffy, almost fog-like in subdued lighting. She bought a gin and tonic plus a glass of stout and found a seat on a cushioned bench near where some people squeezed together making room for her.

The pianist began playing a quick rendition of Tip Toe Through The Tulips that gave the cue for an artist. Suddenly a big cheer erupted when a slim man, apparently in his thirties, dressed in evening suit, red bow tie, tails and a top hat, began tap-dancing in the middle of the room on a floor-boarded area. The crowd pushed themselves back to the walls making more room for him to swing his arms and let his tails fly. The applause was continuous thunder as the dancer twisted and turned, his staccato feet deftly keeping time to the keyboard. The man looked completely out of place. Anna had heard of him but never seen him perform. The drinkers were egging him on shouting his name. A woman yelled, 'Come on Johnny, on the table, jump you bugger, you can do it.' He spun like a top, his tails raising and flapping, his hands swinging, his tap-shoes clicking on the boards. His long face gave a permanent generous smile on his thin lips, his top hat firmly wedged on his head. He went on for a full ten minutes before he stopped, took a bow and gasped for breath. Then he held out his top hat and people threw coins into it. Just then a strange-looking stout woman waddled from the corner of the room and shouted for order in a masculine voice that had a pronounced female lilt. Anna twisted her head at the familiar tones. The transvestite had followed her down from the White Lion. One hand on his hip, and the other held out as though he expected someone kiss his wrist, he called for order.

'I think Johnny deserves more than a few coppers, darlings. Come on where is the silver.' he demanded. Johnny took another bow, held his hat out and received a few coppers more for his troubles. Then the female impressionist announced he was going to sing.

'Because of the miserly lack of musicians, I am impelled to be accompanied by the solitary pianist who, incidentally, is the best around here. I shall sing, On Mother Kelly's Doorstep.' A big cheer went up. 'And I want some order.' The place went into a hush. When he finished he took three unnecessary curtain calls.

Anna was feeling relaxed and began to enjoy the evening. Every half hour or so the dancer would appear followed by the transvestite until people lost interest and gave no money, so they left for another venue. Anna remained there until closing time and then made her way home. She took her time for her balance was not perfect and her vision was seeing more than was actually before her. An old man, who was obviously as drunk as Anna, came towards her on his way home and bid her goodnight.

'Goodnight to you all,' she slurred.

He stopped, puzzled. 'Am I not alone now?' he asked in an Irish accent.

'Well if you can't see your friends, you should see a doctor.'

378

'I've got no friends.'

'Ah, just like me, I've got no friends. She looked closer at him and realized he was alone. 'You are alone. Well I'll be a piddled puddler. I'm lonelier than you are, do you feel alone when you're in a crowd?'

The man scratched his baldhead and purposely amused her. 'Well let me see now. No, I've thought it all out, and when I'm with people I'm definitely not alone.'

'Ah, well I am. I can be a sheep in the middle of a flock, and I'm alone.` She leaned forward and stumbled into him 'Do you know what I mean?'

'I believe you, I believe you. Oh yes, I believe you and sympathize with you,' he said, gently pushing her away.

She studied him, unsteadily. 'You look old enough to be my father. Are you my father?'

'I'm not that old me little darling, to be sure I'm not.'

'Ah. You can't be, you've got the wrong dialect.'

'Thank God for that. If you don't mind now I'll be on my way. I hope you'll feel better in the morning. Goodnight now.' he said, and went on his way.'

When Anna arrived home, Rachael was in bed sleeping, but the noise her mother made manoeuvring around the furniture, bumping in to a table and then a chair soon awakened her.

'Where are you Rachael? She yelled. Are you in bed already and no welcome for your mother? No love, no company, just an empty house I can no longer call a home.'

Rachael had heard it all before, so she clapped her hands on her ears until her mother fell asleep on the living room chair.

Forty Nine

Rachael was determined to make a success of her life and move away from her mother. She was aware it would take a few more years of continued study and hard work. Her mother came and went, living an independent life from her daughter, leaving Rachael responsible for the domestic chores like cleaning and laundering that caused further arguments. Anna would take her turn when she thought it was absolutely necessary. Rachael did them in a trance and resigned herself to the situation catering for her own meals and trying to ignore some of the shameful states Anna sometimes came home in at nights. She felt she had to reprimand her mother at such times to show her disapproval, for if she appeared indifferent it might give her mother the impression that she was endorsing her lifestyle. However, she soon realized how futile it was to influence her mother on a new road and gave up on her. During these difficult years Mary's husband died leaving Mary no alternative but to move away to her relations in west Wales. It was an emotional blow to Rachael, for Mary was the only person in Rachael's world that she could rely on when help or a heart-to-heart talk was needed. Hannah's visits became less frequent, but told Rachael to call on her if she needed help. If anyone knew her mother better than Rachael it was Hannah. And so, Rachael bravely struggled along without friend or relation, for Anna was of the opinion that her daughter was at an age to look after herself. It crossed Rachael's mind that Daniel would one day get in touch with her and be united again, but he never did. As each year went by without news from him, Rachael came to the conclusion that he was being prevented from communicating with her. After all, his uncle and aunt were not hers, she being a stepsister.

In 1936 the Dowlais Steelworks closed except for the general castings foundry and the fitting shops. The town was left with a legacy of years downgrading the steelworks, which had a devastating effect on those who lost their jobs. Poverty spread and a great deal of the population was on subsistence. Fortunately for Rachael she earned her school qualifications that gave her a stepping-stone to her ambition, which was to become a nurse. She got a position as a trainee at the Merthyr General Hospital. The same year Edward VIII visited Dowlais to see for himself the devastation of the steelworks and the suffering of the people. "Something must be done," was the remark he made. However, there was no change in the place.

After serving six months the excitement she first experienced when she began training wore off. The work was hard and the responsibility severe. The novelty of being a nurse diminished and she had to knuckle down to hard work so that her ambition could be achieved. At times her new world seemed foreign to her, she would go home some evenings concerned whether she would make the grade. She had grown into an attractive girl but still delicate in features and slender in stature emphasised by the long white uniform: a cardinal blouse beneath a white bib and a broad skirt down to her ankles. When in work her long auburn hair was rolled up into a chignon to fit under her white cap. The demanding job she had chosen often vexed her, but her determination and diligence finally won through. She, along with her training group, proudly posed with the hospital medical staff on the steps of the hospital to have their photograph taken when she graduated.

It was then WWII broke out and Europe was embroiled in another disastrous war. News from the front was coming in of the battles and the thousands of casualties. Propaganda from both sides were favouring each other and Lord Ha Ha, the notorious Nazi sympathizer, broadcast over the radio that bombing of strategic British cities and towns would bring victory for Germany. However the British public took little heed of his threats and his ludicrous wild claims soon became incredulous and laughable and he proved to be a fool to the British and its allies.

Anna, however, had a war of her own as her lifeline job was put in jeopardy. It could only last as long as Patrick patronized her. Her personality and diminishing efficiency was not what he wanted behind his hotel bar. Anna became complacent and took things for granted. She had lapsed into her old habits of arguing with the customers on feminine equality and general matters concerning treatment of women. Because of the demands of war some light industry came to Dowlais and Patrick had improved the hotel to a higher standard, only accepting passing clientele such as business men or middle class people who wanted to hire the hotel's lounge out for private parties. Anna was no longer required and he had to let her go. This meant that Rachael was the breadwinner while Anna depended on what the Parish allowed her. The difficulties didn't help the feelings mother and daughter had for each other. The house became a burden to Anna for the rent was going up as each year passed. To add to her concerns she began to see how she had grown distant from her daughter. Rachael often ignored her when she came home after shopping or from her excursions into town. In her tipsy moments Anna expected a kind warm welcome from her daughter after shopping or 'looking for work' as she claimed. But Rachael was unforgiving. She could not forget the verbal abuse her mother expounded when coming home from her nights out. To avoid the situations, Rachael would be in bed at such times, but that didn't stop her mother shouting up the stairs and accusing her of neglecting her and showing no love. The house was big and didn't help matters; there was no closeness physically or emotionally. Anna decided a move to another house might help the financial situation as well as her relationship with Rachael. If she could find a smaller and cheaper abode, a complete break for her and Rachael might bring a more favourable situation. She had been told by an acquaintance of a house that was vacant further up Dowlais in Broad Street; it was a steep street that led to the bottom half of the Cwm. She had been told the rent for the house would be half of what Anna was paying for the High Street house. She thought it best if she should consult Rachael before making a decision. It was a habit of hers to go for her favourite tipple at a convenient pub a few doors up, The Sun, before facing Rachael.

Rachel was upstairs gazing through her bedroom window having a panoramic view of the financially and physically collapsed ironworks. There was devastation everywhere. Across the road stood the huge red-brick building that housed the blast engines, but that was the only building standing apart from Sir John Guest's abode, Dowlais House, inside the derelict coal arch. The rest of the vast area where once the biggest steel works in the world had stood, was acre upon acre of rubble; mounds of brick and stone, half walls of yellow brick not completely knocked down, old wagons, ponds of stagnant water, all surrounded by mountainous coal tips. No Bessemer converters, no chimneystacks, no coke works. She turned her eyes to the biggest monument of all, the man-made solidified lava tip, The Whitey, affectionately named by the locals. It had been the burning mountain Anna thought was on fire when first she came to Dowlais, but now it no longer breathed acrid clouds of poison. It had cooled into a mountain of rock. Its northern side grew steep and treacherous leading to a moon-like plateau. Its southern end blistered out in a huge bulbous protuberance looking over the village of Penyard. It was a dead mountain, the colour of a cadaver. Rachael remembered the stories her nursing colleagues used to tell of the deep crevices and cracks on the rough surface that descended down to hell, and the abysmal moans that rose from the crusty lips of the petrified skeletal mouths. From the deep throaty clefts came breathing and bleating whispers of those who died when creating the industrial monster. She turned away from the window for it was bringing on a depression.

'Rachael, are you up there. Have you had food, if so have you left any for me?' Come down girl, I want to have a talk with you.'

Rachael closed her eyes and prayed for patience. She reluctantly and slowly made her way down the stairs. Without a word she went into the living room and flopped in the armchair. Anna, who had reverted to her all black attire, slumped her heavy body in the chair opposite, her figure now grown corpulent, her grey hair rolled up in an untidy bun and her pale face becoming more lined and wrinkled with every year that passed.

'Rachael, I've been thinking, I can't see me ever having a job again. I don't think I'd be able to do any manual work...'

'Before you say anymore, mother, I've been thinking too. I've decided to go away and make a fresh start elsewhere. There is a vacancy in Brecon Hospital for a junior nurse. I wrote to the hospital last week and I have received an answer today. They have decided to give me an interview.'

'Don't be silly. Now listen to me. I know of a house in Broad Street—'

'Mother, are you listening? This place depresses me to the point of mental torture.'

'Broad Street is away from the deprivation of this area, a much nicer place to live, you'll like it, and it will be cheaper to live there.'

'Wherever I go in Dowlais it will be the same.'

Anna snapped. 'Rachael you must give it a try. For goodness sake girl, be reasonable.'

Rachael held herself steady. 'Mother, I am going away.'

Anna stood up and looked down on her daughter. 'You wouldn't be so cruel as to leave your old mother all alone. I can no longer afford to be without you. Good God, girl, would you put me in the Workhouse? I've told you of my life in the Workhouse as a child.'

Mother, it is 1942 they don't put people in Workhouses anymore.'

Anna sat down again. 'Well, special homes then, they call them Homes now days—1942? 1942 is when you're twenty-one…your inheritance is due. That's why you want to get away. You don't want to share it with me. You want to run away and leave me penniless.'

'I've already put some of it away in readiness for you when I leave; some of what my dad left me, I'll give one hundred pounds to you. If I could have my freedom I'd give it all to you.'

'You've already got the money? I didn't know that. Why didn't you tell me?'

'You're never in the right frame of mind to explain things of importance.'

'Rachael, I'm sixty-three years old, the money won't last long, what will I do when it`s gone? Would you want me to beg for my living?'

Rachael new she was already giving in to her mother. 'If you would only change your life style and act like a decent human being I could be proud to call you my mother…'

'You're not acting like a good daughter. You've become a stranger to me. I'm not a bad woman, but you don't make things easy for me. You avoid my company and hide up in that room of yours and lock the door; you won't answer me when I call up to you. You are an adult now Rachael, stronger and younger than me. I wish my mother could have lived as long as me, I would have been happy to look after her when I was your age... I don't know why they put us on this earth to suffer and be so sad.'

Rachael bowed her head in a hopeless gesture. 'I only ignore your calls when you come home in an unreasonable state at nights,' she said, her body shaking nervously.

'Oh that's just drink talking. I've got used to shouting the odds at the chauvinists in the town because I'm a suffragette and will fight for my rights till the day I die.'

'You're not a suffragette,' she said, weakly. 'You're not even a feminist, you're a selfish egotist.'

'I damn well am a suffragette and proud of it. When I lived in London we marched every week on some official building or other, sailed up the Thames and threw stones at the parliament buildings, chained myself to the rails of Buckingham Palace, was tortured in Holloway—'

'All right, all right,' screamed Rachael, shooting to her feet and pacing around the room holding her head in both hands. 'I'll move to your little house and fester in this dying town and they can bury us both in the same grave...would that make you happy, would it?' She ran upstairs and slammed the bedroom door behind her.

Anna shook her head, shocked at the tirade. 'That girl, that girl,' she murmured, I don't know what I'm going to do with her. She'll like it in Broad Street when she settles in. She doesn't realize we depend on her wages. It's not all her fault I know that. I'll have to take some of the blame and smarten myself up. That will please her.' Anna went to the stairs and listened at the bottom. She could hear Rachael whimpering. 'Rachael, Rachael,' she yelled. 'Tell me, girl, have you eaten yet?' there was silence for a few seconds, and then she appeared at the top of the stairs.

'You want me to make something for you?' she asked, brushing her cheeks with her sleeve.'

'I wish you would answer me when I ask a question. 'Have you had anything to eat since breakfast?'

'No.'

386

'Right, I'll make an omelette, we'll have half each.'

'I'm not hungry.'

'You're wasting away, Rachael. You'll have half and like it.'

'I don't want any so don't make some for me!' she shouted, and disappeared into her room.'

'The girl's insufferable. To hell with her, I'll have a glass of stout instead.'

Fifty

Rachael helped Anna to settle in and arrange the house as they both agreed, but it was with a heart that was not fully committed. She chose the bedroom that overlooked the street, for the houses had back-to-back small gardens and she feared the neighbours might think she was spying on them if she should sit in the window; such sensitiveness the girl had inflated in her nervous system. The front window gave her access to the few people who passed by, but there were not many of those for the street was not a shopping area. On one occasion when it was her day off and the road was quiet, she was sitting in the window, an expression of sadness on her ashen face, when she looked across the road. Inadvertently, her eyes focused on the upstairs window of the opposite house. Her heart suddenly thumped against her chest when an old woman in the window glared at her and with agitated forefinger tapped her nose several times indicating to Rachael that she was a snoop. Rachael quickly turned away and her pale face turned a shade paler. She felt ashamed and embarrassed that the woman should think of her in that way. What would people say if the old woman gossiped about her? She had only been there three months and suddenly she felt like a pariah. From then on her curtains remained closed, never to look out of them again. She said nothing to her mother about the incident for she knew her mother would challenge the neighbour and cause an embarrassing quarrel.

At work she nursed efficiently and conscientiously, her time keeping was superb. Her competence was first class and her quickness of wanting to finish her duties was spurred on by her anxiety to prove that she was a good nurse. Sometimes she would suffer a period of nervous tension and double check, at times treble check, everything concerning her duties. When her shift came to an end she would pack her things and make for home, leaving other nurses having a chat about their day's experiences, but giving them the impression she was too haughty and independent. She found it very difficult to make friends, and her loneliness turned into depressions. And though there was one colleague who was kind and understanding who tried several times to befriend her, Rachael's poor opinion of herself could not let anybody into her life. She had only one aspiration, and that was to free herself from her surroundings and find a brighter future elsewhere. She had forsaken her dream of going to Brecon Hospital; the guilt she had felt when her mother pleaded for her to stay was too much for her to bear. She had slim hopes that another opportunity would come along. Her diminishing hopes soon dispersed completely when the final blow to her fragile nervous system hit her hard. It was the dwindling of her inheritance and the continual demands from Anna always wanting money and living beyond her means. The money ran out more quickly than she expected and realized she would leave her mother destitute if she left. It meant her nursing wage would have to be used for all household expenses, including giving her mother drinking money, for as long as her mother lived with her she could not claim parish money. She was trapped for the duration of her mother's life. She brooded and fretted in profound introspection as each month drove her deeper and deeper into herself.

Anna rose late on a Wednesday morning to find the fire not lit and the room cold. The ashes in the fire grate had not been cleaned out and the table in the small kitchen still had remnants of her supper from the night before. She began to mumble to herself. A habit she had developed whenever she was alone. 'I suppose she expects me to light the fire and clear the table, wash the dishes. The girl has no thought of my old age at all. Gone off to her nice warm hospital…have her breakfast there no doubt while her poor mother suffers in this poky little house. I'll go up the café and have tea and toast.

She went to her handbag and pulled out her purse. Opening it she tut-tutted. 'Not enough in there for breakfast, maybe there'll be some money on the girl's bedside table.' Anna climbed the stairs gasping for breath on each step and opened Rachael's bedroom door. She stood there for a few minutes surprised to see Rachael sitting on her bed in her nightdress, her chin on her chest and her hair hanging over her face.

'It's not your day of, is it?'

390

There was no answer or movement from her daughter.

'Are you sleeping sitting up, girl? Answer me for goodness sake.'

Rachael made no movement.

'I need some money to go up the cafe for breakfast. Good God, Rachael you're getting worse.'

Anna moved to the bedside table and picked up some silver coins and pocketed them. She stood in front of Rachael, hands on hips, and shaking her head with disgust. She placed her hand under the girl's chin and lifted her head so that Rachael was looking at her. The ghostly, gaunt face that looked up at her shocked her into silence for several seconds. Her hand, supporting Rachael's chin, began to shake from fear. Her daughter's staring eyes were empty, as though there was no soul within her and completely void of expression. Her mouth was partially open, her thin lips dry, it was the saddest face Anna had ever seen.

'Rachael love, what is it? What's the matter?'

There was no response.

'Rachael, talk to Mam, please Rachael. Oh my God, Rachael, wake up'. Anna gently tapped Rachael's face with her open hand hoping that she could shock the girl into some kind of reaction, but there was not a blink of the eyes nor a twitch of a finger.

Anna laid Rachael down and tucked her in bed to keep warm. She then caught a bus down to the General Hospital and got in touch with Rachael's superiors. The matron was very sympathetic to Anna and promised to do everything she could to help. She explained to Anna that the staff had been worried in the past few weeks about Rachael for she had developed the habit of looking out of the hospital windows and remaining there for some time as though transfixed by the outside scene. The Matron said she would arrange a visit to Rachael with Doctor Jeffries within the hour to see her. And that Anna should go home immediately.

They took Rachael into hospital and kept her there for three weeks, but still Rachael gave little response. They moved her to a sanatorium for five months, but still no success. It was inevitable that the hospital authorities advised Anna to sign permission for Rachael to be admitted to a Psychiatric Hospital. Anna agreed, and

Rachael was moved to an asylum eighteen miles away. Twelve months later she had died. Anna was given no explanation.

Fifty One

Anna was claiming her entitlement from the Parish once more. Her money was spent mostly on her habit, and left little for sustenance. She lost all dignity in herself and would go around her estranged family asking for financial help. At first they took pity on her for the news of Rachael's death saddened them all. But Anna exploited the situation and soon her daughters lost patience with her. There was a suggestion that Anna was to blame for her youngest daughter's death, though nobody would own up to the accusation. It was then that Hannah felt her conscience could not cope with ignoring the situation and she took her mother in, even though she had five children of her own. Nevertheless, the good deed was done and Anna was comfortable for a time until she became restless. She demanded that she should have a couple of stouts every day, and she deserved to be treated like a lady, though she acted like a matriarch over everybody. The children became upset with her cantankerous ways and her continual orders that they should run down the nearest pub and buy her bottles of beer. She had grown into a heavy woman and difficult for Hannah to physically handle her for her bodily necessities. Hannah's husband was not a strong man nor was he helpful in the chores of the home. He had lost his job and his morale was low. Losing patience with his mother-in-law he told Hannah the old lady had to go. It was left to Hannah to find a place for her, and after many pleas and appointments with the authorities she eventually found a place for her mother in the village home for the aged. It was conveniently near Hannah's house and made it easy for her to visit her mother whenever it was convenient to the staff of the home.

At first Anna didn't get on with the rest of the elderly ladies, she was of the opinion they were too contented being shut up in a home where authority ruled, and she couldn't believe how subservient they were. But the truth was that the conditions were excellent and the food also. Nobody complained for there was little to complain about, and the large majority realized they were lucky to have such a home. It was not a big home, just accommodating sixteen women. It was more like a small hotel than a home for the aged. Those who were able could, if the weather was clement, take a stroll up the country road that was just a hundred yards away. The home had a sizable sitting room with soft easy chairs and a piano in the corner. On Wednesdays the local curate would come and carry out a short service. He brought along with him a pretty teenage girl who could play the piano, and after his brief sermon, hymns would be sung. It eventually softened Anna's heart and she joined in with the religious atmosphere, even though the songs had been taught to her during her unfavourable chapel days with her foster parents. But there was something unfathomable to her, for the hymns raised nostalgia lifting her spirits. Maybe it was the pictures she conjured up in her mind of her young days, or the time she was in service and wore a maid's uniform, maybe it was the fact that the past could not hurt her anymore, or perhaps she was feeling sorry for herself. Whatever gave her that soft warm feeling it brought tears to her eyes, tears she wiped away as quickly as they came, for she did not want to appear sentimental.

When the service was over, the women broke up into small groups and chatted amongst themselves causing quite a verbal volume in the sitting room. Anna sat alone waiting for the tea and biscuits that came round each time the service concluded. Anna, being close to the group that was talking to the curate, listened to them with some impatience. They were complimenting the curate on his short sermon and thanking the charitable young girl for coming along and playing the piano for them, and for giving them such joy. Suddenly she sat up with some annoyance. She heard one of the older ladies address the curate as father, and she gestured to the curate to come to her. He gave a broad smile on his oval young face and held his long black cassock up off his feet as he came to her.

'Hello, you're Anna I believe.'

'You believe right Vicar.'

'Ah, I'm not a vicar yet, I'm just a humble curate.'

'Not too humble to correct the wrong title that woman gave you.'

'What do you mean?'

'She called you, father. Didn't you remind her that Christ said, "…call no man father upon the earth for your Father is in heaven," did He not?'

'Really, is that right? I didn't realize that. Still, it does no harm, it gives me a warm feeling, you know.'

'Does no harm? Jesus gave you a command and you ignore it. What sort of example are you setting for those who want to do the right thing by Jesus? "Why call me Lord and do not the things which I say?" That's what Jesus said…Luke, I believe.'

'Oh dear, I'll have to mend my ways. Tell me are you sure? Where in the Bible is that recorded?'

'You don't know? A man of the cloth and you don't know? I left chapter and verse behind me long ago…Matthew…chapter 9, I don't remember the verse,' she snapped. 'Never could member the verse. I got into a lot of trouble not remembering the verse. It's obeying the word, is important, not remembering chapter and verse.'

'I shall look it up and repent.'

'You do that. You supposed to be guiding the wayward to Jesus, not illustrating your ignorance of the Testament. You called me Anna, didn't you?'

'I did, that is your name.'

'It is my Christian name, not just a name. And what might your name be?'

'My Christian name is James. James Trimble.'

'Then I shall call you James. You are not too proud to be called James, are you?'

'No, of course not, and I shall call you Anna by your Christian name because you are a Christian, is that what you mean?'

'Well, that remains to be seen.'

'What do mean now, Anna?'

Just then one of the staff, a pretty young woman who had been carrying a tray of teas and biscuits around, came to them and placed a cup of tea and a biscuit for them.

'That's yours there, James, no sugar, and that's yours Anna, sugar but no milk.'

'Thank you, Martha,' said the curate.

'Yes, thank you, Martha,' echoed Anna.

'I don't mind being called James, you see? Tell me, Anna, do you like it here? Everybody seems so happy here.'

'I didn't at first, but when I realized they were treating me like a lady, I became quite settled. They make my bed, cook my food and serve me as though I am someone special. Yes, I feel like a lady living here.'

The curate nibbled at his biscuit and sipped his tea occasionally glancing at Anna. He had heard a couple of stories about her from some of the other elderly guests, and found Anna quite interesting. Though the stories had been offered with some bias, he wanted to befriend her for he was of the opinion that she might be lonely.

'Do you go out for a walk now and again, Anna?'

'My body is too heavy for my delicate legs.'

'You could be wheeled in a push chair.'

'I wouldn't be seen dead in one. I can get about with my sticks in here and that's good enough for me. If I need anything in the outside world I have it brought in.'

'You have friends who visit you?'

'Family, my dear curate, family, I have a daughter who comes once a week and brings me my favourite tipple—you needn't look surprised, I have a little drink now and then.'

'My expression is one of approval, for I believe in everything in moderation.'

'I agree with you, many would not.'

'So you are up to date with the news of outside world, Anna.'

Anna stared fixedly at nothing in particular; she seemed to go into a fearful daytime dream and didn't respond to the curate.'

'Anna, are you feeling all right?'

She blinked her eyes and said, in a whisper. 'Hannah, my daughter came yesterday. My son left home and joined the army when he was fifteen, he died three days ago, just thirty one years of age. And now he's buried in a foreign land.'

James said little for a few seconds and then placed his hand on Anna's. 'I'm so sorry, Anna. You must be devastated.'

'Guilty would be more accurate. I couldn't hold him, I couldn't stop him going, I couldn't grab him and tell him I loved him. There is something inside of me that makes me distant from my

396

children…aloof. My children think I have no heart, but I suffer loneliness as well.'

'Of course you do. Everybody feels lonely at times. What was your son's name?'

'Emrys Rees, thirty one.'

'You must be very proud of him.'

'What am I saying? I don't want company. I'm happy as I am— what did you say you wanted?'

'I didn't, I just came to make my usual visit.'

'Well, you must want something.'

'You interest me. Tell me Anna, not wishing to be inquisitive but merely interested as a clergyman, what kind of life have you had?'

'You mean what kind of life have I led, don't you?'

'Had, led, experienced, I ask all the ladies here in turn. I like to think of myself as a disciple of the Lord and, therefore, responsible for bringing people to him.'

'Huh, many have tried and failed dismally. My life has been too hard to believe in such nonsense as Heaven and the afterlife. If God exists He would have had mercy on me. He would and given me a happier life; the basics of love from a mother and father for example. I had a mother for the first six years of my life. She died young having had no life at all.'

'That short statement has intrigued me, Anna. You must tell me more. But not now for I have another meeting in the men's' home. I wonder if you would be so kind as to give me a little more of your life each Wednesday I visit?'

'I would indeed. I would love to see your face when I tell you of the hard facts of life. Maybe I'll convert you to an atheist.

James gave a chuckle. 'Anna, I've been coming here for a couple of years and have heard many stories from the ladies, but I never lose my faith. I've bided my time to have a chat with you. I have heard you say such things to the others such as, "Good God woman!" and other blasphemies. It makes. me wonder who you are talking about, seeing as you don't believe.'

'Ah, just a figure of speech, but I shouldn't say it, "Take not His name in vain."'

'Ah, you have a special faith. We'll see next time I visit. Bye for now, and I shall look forward to next Wednesday.'

For the next few months Anna talked about her life in a slow and tired voice, sometimes resting and taking stock of the images running through her mind, her eyes glazed and distant. At times she would drift into a reverie, the volume of her voice diminishing until she fell asleep. James would rise slowly and leave her in peace but return the following Wednesday and remind her where she had left her story, she would then recollect and continue. From the beginning she had told the curate of her search for her father and of the rotten luck she had experienced throughout her life. James had listened intently and often politely contradicted what she'd said, but never argued with her. In a quiet corner they had occupied each week, Anna talked in a low voice and told him of her illegitimate birth, her getting married to John and then running away to London to be a suffragette; of the special friend Felicity she made and her suffering in Holloway. She told him about her maid's job, of her rape attack and dismissal, of her suicidal thoughts on Blackfriars Bridge, Of Timothy and her return and marriage to Emlyn and the children she gave him. She told of her reuniting with John and the children she had by him. She told of John's tragic death and the lies he revealed to her when dying. And later of her marriage to Donald and of his death, of Rachael's illness and demise, and lastly of her becoming an outcast and her family disowning her, all except Hannah, her first born, who still shows her love and understanding. On their last meeting, when Anna sat back and gasped a heavy sigh, she looked at peace with herself, and she fell asleep. James stood quietly and whispered, 'Sleep tight, Anna, I'll see you next week.'

Fifty Two

It was May 9th 1945 and the staff was putting up homemade decorations in the main sitting room, hurriedly constructed after the news broke. Paper lanterns, paper hoops linked together, cardboard placards with "Victory" boldly written on them. Anna watched with disinterest as the excitement and the hubbub the residents made became annoyingly persistent to her. She was thankful that the euphoria of yesterday had subsided and decorum was a little more normal than when the news came that the war had ended. Outside the church bell had tolled incessantly for hours. The cheering and screaming was deafening, and the war songs had erupted. Of course she was glad it was all over, but it was all too late for Emrys, they didn't even bring him home, buried in a war cemetery, she had murmured to herself. The images that crossed her mind was of the past six years that had resulted in the slaughter of millions of men, women and children sacrificed for a political cause that was not their doing. The destruction and carnage was beyond her understanding and left her depressed amid the celebrations. "When ye hear of wars be not afraid," she quoted the words of Jesus to herself. She sat back in her chair and huffed impatiently hoping the singing would subside, but every time a song ended the Matron would swing her arms like a conductor of an orchestra and start another. But then the door opened and the smiling James entered and stood there for some minutes enjoying the happy atmosphere. When the song ended he clapped his hands generously.

'Well done, ladies. I'm happy to hear you singing in such fine voice, I will expect as much enthusiasm and volume when next we have a service. I know it's Wednesday but the excitement of the occasion has altered the situation. I'm afraid I've temporarily lost my pianist to her boyfriend. The emotion of this historic period has gripped them and they have disappeared somewhere to join their young friends. However, that is no excuse for us to neglect our prayers to God. If we could suspend the activities for just a few minutes, I'd like you all to join me in a moment of thanksgiving. He tucked up his black cassock to his knees and knelt on the carpet. Everyone bowed their heads except Anna.

'Dear Lord, we humbly kneel and thank you for the peace you have brought to our people. We pray for all those who have lost their lives in defending our lands and ask forgiveness for the sins of our flesh, our weaknesses, and our vain expectations. We beseech you to guide us through the wilderness of life and deliver us to the purity of Heaven, through Jesus Christ our Lord. Amen.'

A chorus of Amen immediately ensued.

'Let us say together the words that Jesus taught us, our Father who art in heaven, hallowed be thy name...'

They all joined in except Anna, who remained quiet and still in her chair taking in the familiar words she had not repeated since the day she fled her foster parents. She felt a lump in her throat whether it was a feeling of sorrow or guilt she could not make up her mind. She wished that she could be like the people before her and carry out the robotic movement s and utterances. She would be free of conscience then. The responsibility would be on the shoulders of those she followed. But she couldn't, because she knew the responsibility lay with each individual and their consciences. And she knew the responsible of her actions lay with nobody except herself. She wished she could have found some leader or evangelist she could put her whole faith in and take away the onus from her, but the different weaknesses and the diverse opinions of the world never could convince her of any straight line to truth and happiness. She drifted into her thoughts and closed her eyes as the chatter of the women had taken over from the singing. James was making his rounds to the groups and eventually came to her side. He gently tapped her hand.

'Are you sleeping Anna, he whispered.'

She opened her eyes and slowly shook her head.

'No, I am not sleeping. I was pondering things over in my head trying to make sense of life.'

Maybe you are taking life too seriously.'

'Did Jesus take life too seriously?'

'Well...he did take time to relax and have food and wine with his disciples.'

400

Oh I've had plenty of food and wine. Did you know that the German people are Christians? The Italians, the Americans, the Russian Orthodox, the Greeks the Spanish and the British of course, they are all Christians yet they are all fighting and killing one another. Tell me James, if Christ had been living on earth during the past six years, do you think he'd be pleased with his so-called followers?'

'Anna, the world and its people are very complicated, we just have to do the best we can in such situations.'

'But the question is, are we doing the best we can, or are we opting out and hiding behind the leaders of our times? Jesus said, "No man can serve two masters, you cannot serve God and mammon." Have you read those passages?'

The curate thought for a while. 'Anna, you are entitled to your interpretation of the scriptures, but you cannot expect everyone to agree with you.'

'Oh dear James, you disappoint me. I could show you many things in the Bible that contradict the doctrine of the religious hierarchy of this world, but I know they have interpreted the Bible to their own convenient ways. I'll not trouble you again with my opinions.'

'Anna, I'll just leave you with my interpretation of your life if I may.'

Anna struggled to sit up straight in her chair so James helped her. She thanked him rather curtly, and then she looked him in the eye. 'Your opinion of my life will be much appreciated.'

'Well, I hope my words will not offend.'

'I've gone beyond being offended.'

'You have been kind enough to relate your experiences in life, and I don't blame you if you have bitter feelings from those experiences. But I am of the opinion that deep down you believe in God, and so you should.'

'You're very presumptuous, I'll give you that.'

'Then I am right, you do believe?'

'Somebody must have made us because I have always had a feeling in my heart that I have a Maker's number stamped inside me as have all inventions and creations, which proves that I am an individual and my life is my own to conduct in my own way.

Everybody wants to believe in the hereafter. And I admit of all the so-called greats in history I only have one hero, and that is Jesus. For only Jesus has made any sense of how mankind should conduct itself. A wonderful Lady told me that many years ago, and it has stuck in my heart and brain '

'I think it goes much further. I would say there is another reason, and that is God has looked after you throughout your life.'

'Nonsense!' I have told you of my ignominious birth, a birth I have never fully recovered from. Every step I've taken has met with disaster.'

'The conditions of your birth were not your fault. Neither was your poor mother's death. But you were taken in to care and had a good upbringing, perhaps better than you gave credit to. All right, he was a strict foster father, and I believe if you had remained with them you would have grown into a lady and be respected as such, and probably trained to be a teacher. But you didn't, you ran away for better things. That was your fault.'

'Was it my fault I couldn't cope? I learnt to hate him.'

'Nevertheless, when you learnt of your father's death you had nobody until John took you under his wing and married you even though you didn't love him.'

'It was as much for him as it was for me. He lied to me.'

'But again you ran away when you believed you deserved better, your fault again. But when you got into trouble in London that wonderful Lady you mention came to your rescue. You were dismissed from your job and were destitute.'

'That was not my fault.'

'I agree, but that young man reappeared and saved you from your own destruction.'

'He was a lovely man.'

'When you found John was no longer in Dowlais, Emlyn came along and he rescued you from further heartache, but were unable to tolerate his way of life.'

'John turned up, he was my real husband, I had no choice.'

'But he forgave you all and made a good home for you and treated you with compassion, even though you had children by Emlyn. Again disastrous fortune when John was killed.'

That's when he told me he had lied to me years ago.' Anna massaged her temple with her fingers and whispered, 'I couldn't cope with life. I belong to nobody.'

'You belong to God, Anna. Your trial and tribulations are not of your making. But the truth is that every time you got into trouble somebody came along and saved you. Do you think that those occurrences were merely coincidental? I would say not. When things got worse after John died, Donald came to you. Each time you were in trouble a Guardian Angel came to you and helped you through. And without that help you would not have survived. And that was the love of God. And Hannah, was it not the love of God that she gave to you and remained loyal to you? God Knows your needs before you ask, remember?'

Anna slumped back in her chair and gave a gasp of frustration. 'You are very wise for your age, James. And now you have come along to chastise me.'

'Not chastise, Anna. I am being practical. To survive this world we need to be pragmatic and accept those things we cannot change, God understands our world and Jesus will guide us through.'

'My first husband once said he'd rather live in a world full of church people than in a world of warmongers and power-mad dictators, well, I am of the same opinion, but I'm afraid I haven't the strength to follow Jesus.'

'It is faith you need, Jesus will give you strength. Enjoy your last years with the thoughts that Jesus has been at your side throughout life ushering you from your weaknesses.'

'I have mellowed over the years, I believe. I'm too tired to do anything except sit here. Had Donald not died my late years might have been different. Rachael would still be alive had Donald not passed away. Too late to make it up with my family, I have many grandchildren but most of them I do not know, nor have I seen their faces. I wanted independence and I was given it freely.'

'I like to think that I am your latest friend who has come to your aid, that is, after your daughter who took you in and brought you here.'

'Hannah, my first-born, and the one who is closest, yes she still visits.'

James clasped her hand then stood up. I must go now, Anna, I have a funeral on Friday and I have to go to the men's residential home where an eighty-eight year-old man has died. I know little of him at the moment except that he is called Joshua.'

Anna found the strength to suddenly sit up, with eyes wide open and mouth agape. She grabbed the curate's arm.

'Joshua, did you say?'

'That's right, do you know him?'

'Good grief, I thought he had died years ago. I had many a friendly discussion with Joshua.'

'Then you can tell me something about him.'

'I can tell you that he was a true Christian and looked upon himself as an apostle.'

'Did he indeed? You must have known him a long time.'

'Many years, but fleeting moments, I always felt he understood me. He was strict in his belief but sympathetic to me. In different ways we had common thoughts; "I dislike the religious clerics," he said. "They take their responsibility to Christ too lightly. To them Christianity is just a world-wide social club and not a vocation.'

James cleared his throat with some energy. 'Yes, well, on that note I think I'd better leave.'

'Oh, I think he'd like you, James.'

'That's nice to know. I dare say you would like to go to his funeral.'

'I must go to his funeral. Maybe Hannah will help me.'

'I'm sure she will—I must go. I'll see you before Friday. Bye Anna.'

Anna sat back and felt she had lost a friend again in Joshua, even though she thought he had died long ago, but she was glad she would be able to say goodbye to him. She gave a heavy sigh as tears rolled down her cheeks.

James turned around and came back to her. 'Are you all right, Anna?

She brushed her cheeks with her hands. 'Death is a terrible thing James a terrible thing.'

'No it's not Anna. I am sure Joshua would agree with me when I say that death is the passing of one phase of life to another in the evolution of the spirit.'

Anna stared at the curate. 'Do you believe that James?'

'I most certainly do. Does it matter how you suffer in this life when you are passing on into everlasting bliss?'

She slumped back in her chair again. 'Oh leave me be.'

Fifty Three

The cemetery was just a short distance away, and with the help of her walking stick and the support of Hannah's arm, they walked slowly in the heat of the sun to Joshua's grave, their black attire burning hot on their backs. Fifty yards inside the wrought iron gates the graveyard rose steeply to the left, it was a grassy hill scattered with leaning ancient memorial stones.

Fortunately for Anna, Joshua's grave was not far from the entrance and on flat ground. Two gravediggers stood at a respectable distance looking at the pile of earth they were about to replace in the hole they had dug, their shovels at their side. Hannah and her mother approached the spot in time to see the cortege, which consisted of the hearse, and one mourner car that had three sad-faced professional bearers in the back seat as well as the serious curate.

A staff member of the Gentlemen's Home whose duty it was at such occasions to attend and represent the home accompanied the driver of the hearse. There was no other person at the grave. Joshua had been away from his evangelical vocation a long time and was forgotten or outlived those he had befriended in life.

As the coffin was placed near the open grave, Anna and her daughter stood at the side of James whilst the three professional mourners, the driver and the staff member circled around it. Before the dedication began several people came through the gate to give respect to the deceased as a matter of local tradition, for they knew nothing of him or who he was. There was silence for a minute. But then James began.

'Our departed brother made a request some time ago to a fellow resident that his funeral service be kept simple. I will respect that desire. A good friend of his has told me that he was a true Christian who spread the word of the Gospels around the country and asked for nothing in return. Indeed, a man of such conviction and humbleness is surely in the bosom of Jesus—I am the resurrection and the life, saith the Lord: he that beleiveth in me, though he were dead, yet shall he live: and whosoever liveth and believeth in me shall never die—And so, we lay to rest the body of this evangelist known as Joshua, but the law must be recognized on such occasions, therefore let it be recorded that in this grave lies the body of Tegwyn Morgan who came from a village near Hay-on-Wye and settled...'

'What? What did you say?' Anna demanded, her body trembling and her voice hoarse, unable to get her breath.

'Anna, please,' said James. 'This is a solemn occasion.'

'Please, please James, repeat his name.'

'Tegwyn Morgan.'

Her knees weakening she begged. 'And from where?'

'He told a fellow resident he came from a small village near Hay-on-Wye. You appear quite pale, Anna. Perhaps you should sit down on that bench. Let us say the Lord's Prayer; Out Father who art in heaven...'

Hannah pulled at her mother's arm and escorted her to a nearby iron bench and sat her down.

'What is the matter, Mam?'

Anna didn't answer, in her mind she was going over the years and seeing her father before her. She used to talk to him and teased him. Ridiculed him but never knew him. Did he know who I was all those years ago? Had he known, surely he would have told me. He was the one man I never troubled with my search, never asked him if he knew of a man named Tegwyn Morgan. And I only told him my name was Ann, so close and yet unknown to us both, 'dear, dear, dear, dear.'

'Mam, are you all right?' snapped Hannah.

The tone of her daughter's voice brought her back to the present, by which time the coffin had been laid and the burial concluded.

'Take me back to the grave, Hannah. I want to say goodbye to Joshua.'

James came to her. 'How are you now Anna?'

'I'll survive. Help me to the grave please, James.'

'Would the lady like a lift to her home?' asked the driver of the mourner's car.

'Would you mam?'

'No, I'd like to stay awhile.'

'Joshua meant a great deal to you, Anna,' said James. 'It must be very traumatic for you.'

'More than I had ever known.'

James remained with Anna and Hannah for almost ten minutes looking into the grave as Anna kept staring at the brass nameplate on the coffin below.'

'Mam, I think we should leave now, the priest must have other things to do and the men are waiting to fill the grave in.'

'Come on Anna, I'll help you back to your residence. I just did not realize how much Joshua meant to you.'

They began making their way to the exit gate when Anna gave a great sigh. 'James, I have told you the story of my existence on this earth.'

'You have Anna, and a colourful but sad one it is.'

'One thing I didn't know and couldn't tell you because of my ignorance, up until a short while ago I was unaware that you were burying my father. Yes, you have laid my father to rest.`

Both James and Hannah came to a stop and held Anna tightly. They both looked at Anna with shock on their faces and tried to comprehend what she was saying. It was Hannah who spoke first.

'Joshua was my grandfather?' she gasped.

'I have been looking for him all my life, and found him dead.'

'You mean you had no idea?' asked James.

'Never further from my mind, take me back now please I want to lie down.'

All three in a semi trance walked on in silence. Hannah accompanied her mother to her bedroom and remained with her until she fell asleep as she did in times of stress. Then she made her way downstairs, James was still at the home giving the Matron the startling news. He called Hannah over.

'I've been telling Matron of our revelation, Hannah, and advised her to take everything in to consideration in case your mother should have aftershock.

'Thank you, I'll stay awhile, but I'll have to go and make the children some food. I'll come down for an hour or two this evening.'

'I'll keep a close eye on her, Hannah, and keep you in touch if you should need to know anything.'

'Thank you, Matron.' She turned to James, 'Thank you James, you've been a good friend to my mother since she came here.'

'That's all right. We'll be able to bring her through this. Don't you worry, Hannah. Your mother is an amazing woman.'

'Yes…well, you could say that.'

'Would you like a cup of tea, Hannah?' asked Matron

'That would be very nice, thank you.'

'Good bye, Hannah,' said James. 'I have other duties to perform I'm afraid. If you should need any help with your mother please let me know.'

'I will, and thank you once again.'

'I'll go and arrange a cup of tea for you,' said the Matron. 'Sit here for awhile

'Thank you Matron.'

As the years passed Anna mellowed and greatly appreciated the home to which Hannah had brought her. She witnessed the new residents that came and others who left through illness or death, and she appreciated the company and friendship of her fellow guests. The frequent visits from her daughter, the caring staff and the kindness of the clergy had given her the status of a lady she had always wanted to be. She lived until she reached the age of seventy-nine and passed away peacefully in her sleep in 1958.

Sometime before she died she had asked Hannah to promise that she would fulfil her last requests if it were possible. Hannah had sought the necessary permission from the official sources and assured her mother that her request would be fulfilled. And so it was, Anna was buried from the house of her daughter and was laid to rest in the same grave as Joshua.

Lightning Source UK Ltd.
Milton Keynes UK
UKOW041958170412

190923UK00001B/25/P